THE RISEN SERIES BOOK ONE

DAWNING

A ZOMBIE APOCALYPSE HORROR STORY

OUR NIGHTMARES
WALK AMONG US
AND WE ARE ALL
WIDE-AWAKE.

MARIE F CROW

Copyright

Dawning is a work of fiction. All names, characters, locations, and incidents are the products of the author's imagination or are used fictitiously. Any resemblance to actual events, locales, or persons, living or dead, is entirely coincidental.

Table of Contents

Note from the Author

It has been one year since the beginning of this journey. I am deeply honored by all of my fans who have embraced The Risen series. You have expressed to me your favorite characters and the connections you find with them. I feel this series is special in how it embraces the human element as well as the telling of classical horror.

As a "thank you" to all my fans, it is my pleasure to introduce The Risen Series: Dawning, Anniversary Edition. This book contains a variety of scenes and character depth not included in the original version.

- Marie F Crow

A world of fragile things, isn't that how they describe winter? It's a time when things slow down. When we isolate our- selves from the dark, seeking only the shelter of our families and the warmth they provide. A space of time when night comes sooner, and the dawns seems brighter. Months where our dreams are sparked with the yearnings for miracles and stories are shared of times gone by. Yes, that is how I remember winter.

I have a deep well of winters from which to drink. I hold memories of lighted trees and homes glimmering in the dark. I hold the smells of the holidays inside me. I can still hear melodies inspired to bring hope and goodwill, reminding us of the magic of miracles we choose to forget during the year. I remember the rush of children's joy as the first snowfall covers the world in a virginal haze. I remember laughter. I miss that sound the most.

Sound is a weapon now. It is something hidden and shrouded with fear and dread. There are no more lighted trees or glimmering dreams among us. Smells have become dank and smothered with loneliness. Our songs are now of silence and deaths. They inspire only regrets. It inspires the type of remorse lurking in the deep dark of your memories.

This is our winter now. This is our life. The nights are too dark. The dawn is too soon. Our nightmares walk among us and we are all wide-awake.

We all have our own scars. People we have had to kill. People we have lost. Stories and versions of how we first knew something went wrong. Now we are branded with our horrors and clinging to our ropes of hope. Those ropes are serving to bind us all together or serve as nooses around our necks. Social lines are a long distant luxury of a world few care to remember.

A comfort we can no longer indulge. The only line we have now is "them" or "us" and every day the line seems to shrink more for "us".

Perhaps it's just our hope that shrinks as if it is a worn out balloon wrinkled and discolored from being too full for too long. Every loss seems to let out more of the precious air we used to keep us afloat. We are sinking fast in this new world. I fear for not only our safety but also for our humanity. When one must kill the ones they love to survive, what does that leave of the soul? Where does that darkness go? Where does the heart house such sorrow and how does it continue to fight? How can hope even compete with such truths?

The dust-covered memorabilia of yesterdays has no value when supplies are in such short demand. It holds no comfort to give to hunger-cramped stomachs. They don't even make decent weapons against the flesh-eating monstrosities seeking to fill their mouths with our blood dripping deaths. Yet we still cling to the many "what ifs" as if some weight of self could be obtained from them. Perhaps we just would rather cling to what we have known versus facing the fears of unknown tomorrows. The last sparkling star of comfort before the dawn steals it away with either cruelty or death. I guess I have always had a hate for the dawn.

Chapter 1

"You should be going," Lawless says, with his coffee-colored eyes watching me.

He's right. I should be. Sitting here on the hood of my beat-up compact with his arms wrapped around me, it's the last thing I want to do.

The crude male laughter is hard-pressed to ruin my mood. Bikers fill the parking lot of Grit as Marxx and Rhett watch from the doorway of the bar. Another night. Another fight. Now the "warring" groups do the normal drunken "I love you mans" as the many beers cloud the reason the fight even started.

"Precious," Aimes says, rolling her eyes as she bounces the overly large sucker against her teeth. The noise is like a metronome, keeping time with the seconds until the dawn. "Why do men do that?" she asks, still watching the love fest.

"Eventually," Lawless says, dragging the word out for comic relief, "your fists start to get tired of hittn'."

"Aperentisly," Aimes smirks, returning his comedy flavor with her own mockery of pronunciation, "yo' face don't."

Lawless smirks, looking at me with amusement. "She's a funny one," he says.

"Says the one with the purdy bruise forming and a busted lip," I say.

A sharp whistle from the bar pulls our attention. The lights behind him in the doorway frame Rhett's looming outline. Being seen as only a solid black shape, it only adds more weight to the frightening reputation Aimes and I have given him.

"I guess Daddy wants all his boys back inside," Aimes says. She has a smirk that could scald even the strongest of egos. She is wearing it now.

"I dare you to go in and check," I whisper. The smirk fades some around the edges.

"Never have I been so happy to have a vagina," she says, and Lawless shakes his head amused with her blunt honesty.

"Says a lot about your past dates," Lawless says, before placing a good-bye kiss on my forehead and patting Aimes' leg as he passes her.

"Come on, think of something witty," I quietly taunt her, as we watch him walk away. The grinning skull of his motorcycle club's leather vest is further taunting her as well.

Her lips make a thousand different formations, but nothing comes out. Settling on a frown she says, "Maybe I'm just saving it for later."

"Riiighhtt." Smirking, I let her win this time.

"You ready to go home?" she asks me, searching in her pink purse for her keys.

Home. That's a funny word and I fight to keep the sadistic humor from my face. Is home where my family lives, where communication between myself and my parents are now nothing more than post-it notes left reminding me of things to do? Where my younger siblings. "The Hawthorn Angels" as I have dubbed them with sarcasm over their perfection, wait for me to wake them and start the normal morning routine, is that home? Is my home the place where I have become some tarnished stain with my dark brunette hair amid their sea of platinum perfection? God, I hope not.

Listening to the bikes roar to life around us, a part of me wonders if this is home. The gritty biker bar Grit formed around the local MC by the same name where I have been able to invent a new life. Casting aside the disappointment of Helena Hawthorn, I have been able to invent a new me, storing away the resentments I harbor for hours every night as a barkeeper. After punching a man who thought his tip was his hand, I earned the names Hells and I have kept it ever since. That's the joys of these men. You don't get to pick your nickname. You just get stuck with it. All- in-all, it's better than, "Hey, Barbie."

"O where o where has Helena gone?" Aimes sings beside me. "To the dark side." I wiggle my eyebrows, trying to steal some of the comedic flow she and Lawless so easily have. Watching her eyebrow arch, I know I have failed. "Ready to return to the land of the passive-aggressive? Oh yes please!"

Aimes almost snorts being caught off-guard with my honesty. "Which do you think of as home? Here or home-home?" I ask her.

"You mean this land of bikers, babes and bad humor?" she asks, gazing out at the collection of men stumbling around. "Kill me now." Her eyes skip over the scene as she says, "I mean sure, the 'rents fight but I'm kind of use to it. I think I would lose my shit if they actually got along. I swear one day one of them is going to just snap and shoot the other. How sad is that?"

"Head shots aren't the worst way to go."

Her face begins to glow as the smirk lopsidedly grows. With that look, I don't need to wait for where she is taking the conversation. "No. Just no. We are not making parent's deaths into a sex parody."

"If you answered without me asking, it pretty much confirms you were thinking it too."

"Just get off," I say to her, as I push her from the hood of my car with the normal combination of amusement and exasperation Aimes creates in those around her.

"That's what he said!" she shouts, as she heads to her car.

Opening my car door, I call back, "Hey Aimes, you getting your shots today?"

Her answer is the time-old charming one finger salute over her shoulder.

"By the way, it's face shots. Not head shots," I shout to her, as she climbs into her car.

Silly me for forgetting the lot full of drunken men who now stare at us both with unhidden delight.

"Starting tomorrow night for twenty bucks!" Aimes shouts out of her window, quickly pulling out of the lot and waving to me as she leaves me the lone female in the lot.

Not waiting for the men to start counting their cash, I too push the gas a little faster than I normally would exiting Grit's parking lot.

As the road stretches in front of me, autopilot kicks in from the many trips to-and-fro from here. It lets my mind wander back over the many years I have wasted locked in some battle with my family. Not that every battle scar is my parent's entire fault. I am just as guilty of throwing fuel to the fire. I made a game of pretty much picking and choosing the things which would upset them the most since the age of fifteen when they "let me" move into the loft of the garage. It's what led to Aimes and I first daring the other to sneak over into Grit. The whole "underage" thing never bothered them much- imagine that.

Spite. Envy. Hate. It's how this life started. Now it's our passive-aggressive lifestyle.

Reaching home, my keys make the metallic connection allowing me in through the back door. During the week it's my job   to wake "the Angels" and get them ready for school. You know, since you're up already, Helena, as it was put to me years ago when I started this routine. I will fight with Lilly over what she is going to wear. I will argue with Ashley over the exact amount of milk to put in her cereal. All of it will follow the fight with Conroy over the need for a coat. It's all mindless, robotic fun times here in the land of Hawthorn.

The smell of the house washes over me with its thick per- fume of crisp lemons and soft, subtle vanilla. These early hours always make me feel as a trespasser. Today I am violating a sacred shrine with my smoke-infused hair and overdone makeup. The swollen lips left from the moments of passion with Lawless don't help either.

It had been a brawl-infested night and we closed later than normal. That and the moments lingering in the parking lot and I am now running behind. The lost time leaves me without a chance for a morning shower before stepping into the perfect plastic bliss of this world. Now standing on the too white carpet, my feet sinking in the plush fibers removing all sounds of my ar- rival, I am required to start the day in what can only be thought of as "bar wear". Sighing to myself, I know the extra fit of drama this will cause from Ashley.

My black high-heeled boots softly click their way up the stairs past the rows of grinning moments of time. Various seasons blend, capturing memories of events. I never look at what could be considered a model's portfolio. I never pause to glance and reflect on the memories. There are none for me upon these walls. Twenty- three years later my green eyes and I still lack the strength to accept it.

I am lost in my souring mood when my body halts, leaving a few seconds for my brain to become aware. Something is different. Something is making my heart speed up and my brain slow down. I shiver as something I should be aware of caresses me.

There is a sound where there should be no sounds. The silent embrace of sleep should still surround us, keeping the house muted and hushed, but it's not. There are horrible wet sounds filling the air around me. It sounds as if someone is walking through watery puddles as they enjoy heavily splashing something thick in their wake. It's something that is misplaced and wrong, and yet shockingly real. Something my mind knows should not be here. Your mind knows when you should not be in certain places.

It sends hints with the hairs of your body or the skip of your heart. It sends them with the immobilization of limbs or reducing them to pure weakness. Unfortunately, we seldom ever heed our minds. We force through all the biological clues of danger in some misguided sense of immortality. We degrade ourselves with insults to inspire self-hatred of our cowardice. We do all we can to throw our lives away with the morbid curiosity of things and moments our minds know to leave alone, like I'm doing right now.

Every inch of my skin seems to beg me to turn around. My heart beats with a pattern of warnings as my legs continue to climb each step.

My palms glide along the railing as sweat gathers and yet I still inch forward with each slow step in pure misguiding rebellion to my senses.

My mother's hem is visible for a moment before it slips from view at the landing. The sharp peek–a-boo of her yellow night- gown contrasts with the surrounding white carpet around her.   I know this is wrong. My mind screams for me to realize this is wrong. Ye I cannot grasp the reasons for this to be dangerous. It's just my mother, or Carol, as I now call her and have for too many years to ever repair our bond. The only things that should be afraid of Carol are dust and weeds. She is the envy of her local club of sheltered women for her well-to-do life and time-defying looks. Yet here my body is recoiling with urges to run from just the smallest flash of her nightgown.

Unfortunately, it is not just the nightgown. It's the sounds. The sounds she too should be hearing. Sounds she should be calling for answers to and yet she is silent. Carol is never silent, and I think that is the most unsettling sensation.

"Carol?" My voice sounds overly large in the narrow hallway, as if it should hold an echo.

"Carol?" I call again when she doesn't answer.

Her enduring silence seems to amplify in ways silence should not have the ability to do. It takes a life of its own becoming more than just an action, but a thing waiting in the room with us. The indecisiveness of turning the corner has my mind racing with fear. I must either take this last step or turn and run with little to no explanation as to why. My mind knows something is very wrong, but my brain can find no real proof for it.

They lock in an internal debate as one encourages me forward while the other pleads with me to go back. The last step seems to cause a civil war of my thoughts. I have climbed the same step every day for years of my life. It should be no more of a thought process than of walking through a well lived in room at night.   It should be a motion memory of meaningless detail. Yet here it looms before me, causing a giant cliff of debate.

It is not until my eyes grow blurry with unshed tears that I begin to notice the details my mind has been fighting for me not to see. I finally see the discoloration of the carpet. I see the sprinkle-like patterns of red on the cream-colored walls. The landing itself slowly becomes a new place of sights from the one I have been standing so close to. Marking the moments of time as they pass, the downstairs clock's second hand sounds as loud as fired bullets in the white noise of my panic as wet slick sounds are blending into a stomach-clinching melody. My mind knew all along that the final clue was only one-step away and it wants no part of it, even as my legs climb the cliff.

At first, the scene before me makes no sense. Too much seems impossible. Too much seems wrong. My mind refuses to accept the information my eyes are sending it. It blurs the edges keeping the reality from focus. One would think adding red to white would make a pretty, soft pink. I always have. My boots touch the proof proving we are all wrong.

My mind focuses on the why of the new color, avoiding the cause of it. Red to white should make pink. It should not be this thick dark crimson shading encircling my baby sister, Lilly. What could she have spilled to make this much of a mess as it fans its damning proof around her still body?

Her blonde hair has become stained and clumped from the substance. The ivory flesh of her legs and arms are spotted with patterns of it making a mockery of her natural freckles. Even her tee shirt with its cartoon-dancing bears is heavy from the weight of it.

I watch Carol as her arms slide back and forth over Lilly as she tries to clean the mess. This is what my brain tells me she is doing. This is not what my mind is screaming. My mind is screaming this is wrong. Like a child watching a movie and asking for clue because they are too afraid to stare at the screen themselves, it's refusing to help me put the pieces together as it begs for me to take a closer look.

"Carol?" I hear my voice call out, but it sounds strained. Not the cocky self-assuring flirt I hear all night long. Even my voice knows what is going on and it too is unsure why I am still here, much less using it.

I can see Carol freeze in a fashion that sets my body tight with fear. My muscles tense as if expecting a blow, but my brain can't find the threat. Her yellow gown is soaked with a tint of red from where she has been kneeling and I can see the two-toned details as she stands in an unnaturally slow pace. Her shoulders lift as if being pulled from strings above and the rest of her slowly follows the force. Her arms are coated in the same red substance, giving them the appearance of slipping into long, delicate gloves. The shine catches the morning light from the windows, and if it were not for the pure panic the sight causes, it would be an almost beautiful effect. The second hand is back to shooting bullets as time slows before me.

Lilly is in full view now as my vision wraps around my mother's body. My mind makes one final attempt to block the horrors before me, but the edges are in focus now. There is no choice but to see the truth, and I do.

Lilly is lying on her back in the wide hallway. The many shades of crimson are almost a halo around her fallen body. Her blue eyes stare up, unblinking. She too wants to see anything but what is before us. One arm is outstretched, touching the wall and leaving a child-size red print, mimicking an art project from long ago. Its pattern is screaming fragile. Its smear is screaming broken.

The other arm is torn in irregular patterns of gore. Huge gaps of flesh melding with the perfection of ivory only a small child could possess. The red freckles dance in specks and smears oblivious to it all until the whole combination meets the sleeve of what was once a pastel blue shirt. The smiling bears upon her chest rebel in their scenic glee to the reality around them. All but one bear is able to escape the horror as his body has been torn in two, framing the ironic twist of revulsion. The missing bear's stomach highlights the same fact for Lilly.

What should be the soft velvet flesh of a five-year-old is torn open and jagged. It seeps the answer to the "why not pink" question I had as what can only be assumed as organs are shredded and missing. They spill their dark fluids out of her torn cavity. With reality finally upon me, my brain has no choice but to accept it and it releases the shield my senses were using to hide behind keeping me safe.

The smell collides into me, doubling me over in pure disgust. Sorrow and anger dance a duet upon my emotions blocking fear for a moment's peace. My brain finally screams, Lilly has been murdered, but my mind still clings to the refusal of answering the question of how.

So, I again ask the only person standing before me. My voice pleading with her for answers, "Carol?"

Her gown sticks to her legs, adding an extra dash of stomach dropping disgust at the sound of it sliding against her flesh. She turns still in that slow, unnatural fashion of shoulder leading movement. My brain whispers through my senses she is just in shock, as any mother would be. It attempts to calm my body that is tensing for an unseen fight as her face comes into view. The second hand has run out of ammo. There is only white noise as our eyes meet.

Her once a week salon-styled locks now appear to belong to an angst filled teen with their coloration patterns and not to the leading socialite of town. The tips are a blending effect of reds and crimsons. Her natural curl is now taut with their weight as they attempt to spiral up into her lighter hues. There are sparkles of colors that reflect the light resembling tiny stars adorning her, but my brain can no longer ignore the truth that my mind was attempting to shelter. What she is wearing is not sparkling stars. It is Lilly.

My mother's artificially sun-kissed face, always having been so perfectly made, is now a red smear of a clown styled design. Her pastel blue eyes have lost their light, leaving her with a sleep walking appearance, but there is no denial in the fact that she sees me. Her mouth emits sounds belonging to nightmares, dreamed in too dark rooms as her red-gloved arms begin to reach for me and yet my body, which was just doing everything it could to escape, can no longer move.

Carol's eyes twitch to something behind me, causing her vocal attempts in her grief to become louder.

"Mommy?"

It is a soft, gentle whisper at first that gains the strength of a full scream in one sudden inhale of breath. The scream is a blow to my spine, causing my chest to flex from the force of it. I feel my body move before my brain admits that it is. I turn to block the sight of Lilly from our siblings with my body.

Ashley is the source of the screams, using her voice almost as a weapon at such pitches. Her grief and fear causes my own to unfreeze and my knees buckle to hold her. I can hear my voice whispering words of empty comforting thoughts into her soft hair as if it belongs to another. The words are meaningless, and they go unheard over her screams. She is fighting to get past me to our mother. Someone I have forgotten completely amid my sister's distress.

Conroy in his blue pajamas of cowboys and horses stands frozen, staring at the scene before him. His eyes are darting from one point of interest to another. They have no set pattern as he tries to win his own war with his brain and mind. With Ashley's struggles I can't reach out to him but can only coax him forward with words and the repeating of his name. They all go unanswered.

Up until now, they have lived the perfect Hallmark fantasy. The biggest disappointment for Conroy in his seven years is the fact a horse could not fit in our backyard. My parents fixed that by renting a stable for him. I want to feel pity for him, really, I do, but I am tied up with other things at the moment. Like a ten- year-old in my hair.

Chapter 2

In moments of mind-numbing tragedy, it's easy to overlook reality. We cling to only what we want to see like a fractured mirror of the event. Our minds become too afraid of the smaller shards that could so easily cut us. We focus on the largest shards that hold the biggest images. Those images stand out the most. They are the boldest. We never see the small shards that are hiding and silently waiting for us to notice them. This is a pity. Often those shards do the most damage.

Conroy's eyes stop their dance of confusion and become wide- eyed with terror. I can see the effects as his body begins to tremble. His arm lifts, pointing an extended finger behind me. Even Ashley's body becomes stiff and ridged. The whole room seems to become electric with a new energy as both children react to some unseen shift of mood. My mind, still locked in its precious cocoon, begins to switch gears when my senses warn me some- thing is not right yet again.

My world had become so focused on Ashley's screams and her fighting that now, in the silent aftermath, even the soft whispering footsteps behind me seem as loud as thunder. Carol's steps are slow and steady, unlike my own pulse that is mounting in my throat. My whole being is telling me to not turn around.

In the short life span of time that has loomed before us, Carol has gone unnoticed by me. Ashley, who had just moments ago been ready to claw her way through me to reach her mother, has begun to mirror Carol's steps. The difference being that she is going back- wards towards Conroy. Conroy in return has figured out his sister's new path. She steps to the side to shield him behind her and I kneel watching it all unfold before me. I am a detached audience member of a well-choreographed show. Minus the mood inspiring music and the safety net that real life always seems to be lacking.

I feel the trembling of fingertips on my shoulder and my spine shivers from the touch. Carol's low moaning comes from above me with a never before heard tone from her. It snaps my eyes straight ahead and tenses my body. My eyes roll up the walls tilting my head backwards to keep my sight ahead of me until I am staring up into my mother's face. What I see paralyzes me with confusion of how such a beautiful woman could melt down to such pure animalistic hunger. When I feel her push against my body, it rocks me to the floor and the screaming starts anew. Except this time, the screams are my own and my pitch is just as high as Ashley's. I have never been in any form of altercation with my mother before. Our battles were always more of the passive-aggressive showdowns. Now as she collapses upon me with no heed to her own well-being, I am at a loss as how to combat this. I brace her neck with my forearm with chanting prayers of hope to keep her snarling face from mine. The stench and sounds coming from her throat add a new spice of panic to the attack. It kicks my lulled brain into action.

I can feel her body pinning mine with our struggles. Her hands try to grab some part of me, but her frenzied attacks are making her clumsy. They claw at my face and shoulders, but my curled legs keep enough space between our two torsos. Only her finger- tips rake to land their marks.

Slowly, I pull my legs up tight against me, fighting for every inch it provides between us. Every inch is safety as my body is fighting for survival. I fight for every inch until I am able to use the tight ball of my body as a counterweight, rolling us over and lifting myself away from my mother. She fights with the same urgency to keep me near her.

I drag my body backwards in some over-played-girl-victim-crawl to escape. Carol wastes no time crawling forwards after me. She is a pure hunter in motion and I finally realize I am her new prey. My chanting to God is growing louder by the heartbeat.

My back collides with the wall and yet I still make the motions of escape leaving me treading, reaching nowhere. The constant vibrations of my movements send the lowest framed memory crashing to the floor near me. I scream, afraid some new attack is upon me, but it's only a picture of my mother smiling and posed in a spring garden. It frames some mockery of the current events as my real mother is grasping at my jean-clad legs, snarling and crawling up me no matter how hard I kick at her.

I start to raise my hands to defend against her assault when the mental clarity of needing a weapon settles over me. My mind is finally switching gears from seeing this thing before me as Carol and now seeing it as my death. What I had refused to see only moments ago is now flashing before me and it is wrong. It is all so very impossibly wrong.

Carol was not grieving. She was not cleaning. She was killing. As I stare into those faded blue eyes glaring back at me, I know somewhere deep inside myself that this is no longer my mother. It's some kind of monster wearing her skin. The noises were never from shock but from a deep well of pure hunger and need. A need no sane person should have. A well none of us ever want to admit to owning much less from drinking.

Time seems to slow as I glance from the monster ahead of me, to my siblings beyond and Lilly beside me. My hands that I am holding out before me are shaded in red. I can feel my legs becoming cold as the blood from the carpet sneaks its way into the fabric of my jeans. It chills me with its truth. Spots of the blood dot my exposed stomach from my crawling escape and stain the tank top of my work shirt. The same exposed torso that I am fighting to keep safe is now covered in the damning evidence of what I was refusing to see before.

Sounds explode as I come back to myself. Screams, my own and my siblings, fill the air around us in a nonverbal punctuation of the situation. My eyes land on the smiling frame staring at me with its scenic beauty. The ironically twisted part of my self swears to hear the laughter captured in the picture as it watches the events unfold around us.

That imagined laughter strikes a cord of anger deep inside me. It's the anger over Lilly's death at her hands. It's the anger over being attacked. It's the anger over all the past smiles that were never for me and it fuels my desire to survive.

My hands grasp the picture before I even realize what I intend to do with it. With strength unknown to myself, I raise the fragile glass encased memory and bring it down upon Carol's head. New sounds fill the room as I lift and smash the frame, releasing all the fear and anger inside me with a scream each time.

Gore sticks to the broken metal and the glass in my hands. It coats the smiling face before slipping into the spider web design of broken glass I am causing with each slam until the room becomes still. I hold it high, holding my breath, waiting, but there is no movement from the thing before me. It's slumped over, half covering my legs and half draping onto the floor. Only the largest piece of glass still remains in the frame, leaving the precious memento vulnerable. It's as if Karma has reached out her hand in her own sick style making the two scenes match now.

I stare at the broken skull of my mother with neither remorse nor victory. The tiny glass shards entwine in the ruin of her blonde hair. They sparkle up at me like glitter in a red hue. These are the small shards. They get us every time.

Chapter 3

I kick Carol's body off of mine with a mixture of sick satisfaction and relief in my own recipe of survival. The sound of her dead body slowly sliding down the stairs brings a smile to my face as it gains speed from the weight of her limp body. The patterned sound of her head bouncing off the stairs as she falls almost brings a laugh. I am not sure if I need a smoke or a hug, but I do know there is time for neither. Something has gone horribly wrong in this house. We have to get out.

I use the wall to help me stand and for the first time I see myself in the glass reflections around me. Their beautiful stolen moments a stark contrast to my own image. My dark hair is wild and unkempt. Something I know would cause my mother angst if she were not dead on the floor below us. The flesh of my face is hardening from the splashed gore upon it. With the dark makeup from last night still going strong, my torn soaked jeans, newly decorated stomach and shirt I look like a bad B flick horror star.

I really wish there is a Director to scream "Cut!" right about now, but this is not a movie. There is no Director to coach me through whatever comes next. There is just Ashley and Conroy staring at me with their wide eyes as if I have some secret knowledge as what to do next and me, the mother-murdering-sister-slasher-savior. Try saying that three times fast with a straight face.

We exchange no words as I take their hands and lead them down the stairs. The normal morning routine is blown to hell and forgotten. There is no need to fight over getting dressed. Pajamas are just fine when your mother goes on a psychotic murdering spree. There is no need for breakfast. Whose stomach could hold down a meal at this moment anyway? The only thought process now is to get out. We need to get help. We need to find someone to make this seem okay in some small shape of a way, if that is even possible at this point.

We do not even pause to glance one last time at our mother's broken body. I think we have all accepted that it is not Carol. It will make it easier that way. It was not our mother that did these horrible acts just moments ago. It was not our mother that killed Lilly in some Dahmer-like fashion. It was not our mother who was possibly eating our baby sister for a light breakfast snack. It was not even our mother who attacked me in some unnatural killer rage. It was just a thing. It is a dead thing now. It cannot hurt us anymore. We believe all of this as we exit what we once thought of as a safe place. It is a pity how the world does not hold our beliefs as precious as we do.

We drive in silence for a long time. We are each locked in a prison of their own point-of-view. The surrounding landscape is silent in an almost inconsiderate way. Where is the panic-filled scenery that we are each feeling? Where is the screaming town with their mad, high speeding cars to escape? I will even settle for some form of gridlock traffic in a desperate evacuation attempt of the town. Someone, somewhere, should be running out to motion us to safety. There should be some acknowledgment around us of the horrors we just escaped. Some form of solidarity. There is nothing and leaves me with even more confusion as where to go. I just killed my mother. Do I run into the closest police station to confess?

The birds are still singing in some overly optimistic tune of theirs with cords and pitches that mock my frightened mood. The sun still shines in an all too vivid refusal of the past events and we drive forward to the one morning routine we still have to cling to in our own denial as noon starts to creep upon us. School.

"She was a zombie," Conroy's small voice startles me.

I over steer the car for a brief moment, and meet the rolling eyes of Ashley in the rear view mirror as the cost.

"Conroy, there is no such thing as zombies," I reply, matching the eye roll in the mirror.

"Think about it. She was eating Lilly. She was trying to eat you. That makes her a zombie. Hello, I've seen the movies!" he stresses his response.

"Conroy, there is no such thing as zombies!" Ashley and I shout together.

"Then what did happen?"

With our refusal for his logic, he is soft spoken and fearful of our answer. Who wants to admit their mother tried to kill them? I have no answers. I only know that the word zombie ranks right up there with sparkling vampires and teen heartthrob were- wolves with perfect abs. In my mind they are not real, lame and not real.

"Besides, did you hear her mutter the word brains even once? Everyone knows zombies go around saying brains over and over with some lame body limp walk. Duh!" Ashley informs him.

Yes, that is my sister Ashley. She is the keeper of all the perfect logic of the world.

I smile as they debate the beyond truth, well-known zombie facts that everyone should already know in the back seat. The small sliver of my responsible side knows I should stop them, but I won't. The sound of their child-pitched voices in their heated debate brings some small sense of normal back to the day and a smile to my face. It's something I have not really worn in a long time. After this morning, I cherish it now.

This is what our mornings are supposed to sound like. The birds singing in the trees around us as I drive faster than I should to make it on time. The hum of my small compact car as we travel down the two lane, small town roads. The horrible pop music they make me listen to, making me wonder how many people Taylor can break up with in one album. The kids spending the car ride debating some small fact that holds no real weight to the world, as they are now.

They argue as if some event of epic proportions depends on their side winning. I glance in the rear-view mirror to see the animated verbal tennis match causing me to smile wider. My mind drifts to mornings where Ashley would never agree with Conroy and Conroy would continue to counter Ashley's points until the whole thing dissolved into a giant "yuhuh/nuhuh" mess. That's when Lilly would join in, clapping her small hands and chanting along with both sides until I have to end it for pure sanity reasons. However, Lilly will not be joining in today.

My smile fades as my chest becomes tight with grief and reality sneaks up on me. I can see Lilly's broken frame on the floor where we left her, and I have to close my eyes against the image as I come back to the now. I can feel the sting of tears and I know if they start, I will not be able to stop them. Memories will flood and break the fragile dam holding back the weight of my heart.

I see my memories of her long ashen hair flowing behind her as she runs. She was always running. Always on the go. She was always laughing with her bell-like giggles. She was always gentle. Always loving to those around her with her soaked in perfect youth-filled innocence.

The new image of her twists the truths that I know of her. She was never so still. She was never so silent. She was never so broken. Yet here, in the back seat, remain two voices that are a reminder that I have no time for grief. They are depending on me to figure this out. Depending on me to find us safety. I breathe through the pain, rebuild the dam, and blink past the threatening tears.

I glance into the mirror once again and see they too are now silent as they fight to remain in control of their emotions. There will be time to grieve for our broken flower later. There are answers for "why" out there somewhere waiting to explain it all to us. There has to be. No matter what the sun and birds refuse to accept, there has to be.

Locked in the slow unraveling of my mind, I never saw or heard the truck racing towards us. The blaring horn jolts me, pulling on my heart and dropping my jaw as the truck careens towards the passenger side of my car. Pushing my car for all the engine is worth, I slam on the gas daring and praying at the same time for someone above to be watching. The truck never veers from our collision course. Its grill may as well have been open teeth should it strike us. It is a near miss as my car pushes through the inter- section as the truck slides through it, never stopping or the driver looking our way. One of those almost wrecks where both parties sit with disbelief as they examine their bodies and their pants.

"Douche!" Conroy shouts at the rapidly disappearing truck. "Way to drive, Helena," Ashley mutter as I recover from not only the heart attack of the almost wreck, but also the shock of hearing such a word from Conroy.

"Where did you learn that?" I stare at the reflection of him in the rearview mirror not fully able to detangle my fingers from the steering wheel yet to turn around.

"Aimes." Conroy shrug as if I should already know the answer. I kind of did.

"Way to pick a best friend, Helena," Ashley says with folded arms, and the perfect glare of a ten-year-old.

"Stop being a douche," Conroy tells her, and all I can do is roll my eyes.

"Let's do me a favor and stop saying that word, okay?" I ask, as I lean back into my seat ignoring the smile on Conroy's face before slowly easing back onto the road.

"Helena?" Conroy's small voice floats to me, and I can only wonder which combination of "douche" he is going to be using now.

"Hmmm?" Is all I dare trust my voice within my mix of grief and false confidence.

"Where is Dad?" he asks, as a somber feeling invades the car from reality crashing upon us all.

That is a good question. I glance back in the rearview mirror to let him know I still have no answers for him as another debate begins between them as to his whereabouts.

Where is Dad? That is a good question. Once again, where is the man we are to call Father when we need him? Or did we leave him behind as we left Lilly, broken and discarded for someone else to find?

Chapter 4

The school parking lot is at its normal capacity. The lot is filled with society's mixed ideas of the perfect family vehicles and an occasional mid-life crisis hiding in the rows of slanted white lines. At this hour, there is no crosswalk guard or teachers waiting to be sure our over-privileged darlings mingle well with one another. There are just the birds and the sun, like stalkers waiting to see what happens next with their most annoying fashion. I can feel the morning's events taking their toll on my under caffeinated thinking process. I'm fighting the urge to flash a middle finger with misguided self-indulgence and to explain to Conroy what douche-like really means.

My boots click too loudly against the school's colored tile floor designs. My dark colored outfit is a silent affront to this lurid pastel surrounding us. I often wonder who thinks to combine such horrible colors. Apart from each other, purple and teal are cheerful selections. When swirled together though they make an almost pathetically desperate attempt of pep. Adding too much pastel does not equal cheer. It makes a migraine. The pastel yellow walls are also someone's sick idea of children's décor. I hope that someone dies a brutal death to compensate for my many mornings of this idea of a welcoming committee. If I could bring them back to kill them again, that would be even better.

The school halls are silent and for once Ashley and Conroy are not rushing past me to avoid being seen with me as is their normal reaction to mornings where I am unable to shower and change before being graced with the chore of bus duty. Each has a secure grasp of a hand as they walk slightly behind me, allowing me to turn the corners first. Their eyes dart around as if some unseen horror is lurking there. Nice to know in their minds I am bait, or worse, their protection.

I hesitate at the double doors of the office. My "bar uniform" is enough to earn glares from the females inside, but add in the B horror movie makeover and I am sure the speculation will be super fun. The Hawthorn Angels are still in their pajamas and with none of their school materials, well that will just be the bright red cherry to my cupcake of failures they will love to eat up. Bitter? Who, me? Like arsenic. Should they ask about Lilly, my previous sins will crumble as I explain my newest crime.

There is no office staff today. The space is minus the glares. There are no gasps at my failures. No female-perfected-covered-whispering at the situation before them. The silence is almost anti-climatic to the verbal build up I was preparing myself to receive. Why is it we always have the best one-liners for times when they are not needed, but never for when they are?

"Mrs. Schinder is always here." Ashley's voice is filling with the same confusion that Conroy's face is wearing. "I mean, like, always here. I think she lives under the desk, for real. That's why we call her The Office Troll. You know, because a troll lives under a bridge?"

I glance over with one eyebrow of parental reprimand letting her know that I get it. At least I know I am not the only one not in the Schinder fan club, but troll is not as descriptive as I mentally have worded her.

I walk through the mini-cages of small offices looking for some- one as my new shadows keep their footing behind me. The security staff should have met us long ago with as much noise as my boots are making. This ignorance from a staff that almost tackled me for forgetting to stop by the main office on my way in one afternoon causes me to slow my step some. An over-privileged private school does not allow this sort of freedom on normal days. One thing I am sure of, it has not been a normal day.

Inspecting the many offices, the last one holds more questions than answers. Stopping the kids, I peer into the small space and try to make sense of what is there. The rest of the rooms are just empty, almost as if no one even showed up today. This one is in complete disarray. A purse left discarded and spilt, spilling its contents across the whole carpeted area. Lipsticks, coins, coupons and various other small items lay like shrapnel from a bomb. One pump in the hue of pink is left behind and it's stained with a dark- ness that almost punches my stomach with fearful recognition. A cell phone sits on the desk with a shattered screen and the same coloring along its modern art of a case. There is a chanting in my head with prayers and pleas for me to be wrong.

"Hey Ash, if there is a big deal event where does the school take everyone?" I force my voice to sound only curious, not worried. "First, I am not burnt remains of something to be thrown away.

It is Ash-LEY, thank you." She folds her arms, and I feel the over dramatic pout building. "Second, it would be the gym. It holds the most capacity in the school as anyone should know."

There is the perfect logic we have all come to adore.

"Fine. Would you please do us the honor of leading us to the gym, Ash-LEY?" I ask her.

"We can't go anywhere until we are signed in! It's the rules," she say and glares at my mocking of her sincere concerns over her name.

"Do you see anyone here to sign you in?" I as with a wide sweep of my hands to all the empty chairs and blank flashing computer screens doing my best to keep the office behind me hidden from their view.

She answers me with a pivot of a socked foot, flip of her blonde hair and a push of the heavy metal doors. Conroy gives me a thumbs-up and smirks at her disappointment of finally being proven wrong.

"Told you she is being a douche," he whispers with a cupped hand.

I'm not even going to try to correct him.

With a gracious bow, I hold the door open for him and we follow a dramatically pouting ten-year-old pretending not hear our muffled giggles through the overly peppy done hallways. I grow more curious with each empty classroom we pass in our progress to the gym. I scan for signs of some clues like the office, but so far nothing stands out to me. There are no signs of panic or disruptions in these rooms.

Small book bags line the classroom walls on color-coded hooks. Lunch boxes with their smiling cartoon faces stare at us with some secret joke they share between them as we pass. Lesson plans still outline a full day's activities on white boards in various shades of script. I glance out the windows to be sure I remember cars being here in this total lack of life that is surrounding us.

The school slowly takes on a monstrous costume with its empty desks and my boots clicking with their fight against the silence. By now, this far in, we should have passed someone. My Angels must have been running the same thought patterns. Their steps slow and become less deliberate with each room. Conroy often glances up at me in a silent exchange of mixed questions. I know their thoughts are filtering around this morning's events for the simple fact mine is too. All this time I have been expecting some giant, blaring billboards of acknowledgement of those events. Like tiny shards, maybe the biggest signs are the silent ones creeping up on us.

I can see the double purple steel doors of the gym waiting ahead of us. This is the same set of doors that Conroy must have passed through a thousand times, but now they cause him to hide behind me, peeking around my legs with wide blue eyes. I feel his fear vibrate up my body and place my hand on his back, pulling him closer, trying to calm him. His head rests against the back of my thigh as I call out to Ashley, still staring at the clown-inspired décor shades of the hallway.

"Hey, wait up a minute," I call out to her.

It is shocking to see the Princess of Arguments not only stop but also actually walk back towards me the few steps that have lingered between us this whole path. The out of character response leads

Conroy to cling tighter to me, reading his sister's actions as not obedient, but her own form of fears.

"Let me check it first," I say. I find myself impressed by my voice's certainty of my decision even as I am being met with two sets of wide eyes of disbelief.

"So, you just want us to wait here in the hallway alone?" There are those crossed arms of Ashley's again. "Did you think that through or just open your mouth and let the sounds rolls out like normal?" she asks me.

I admit it, I am having a few thoughts of volunteering her first through the door, but she is right. Leaving them alone when I am not sure what is exactly going on is perhaps not the best plan of mine to date. Besides, everyone knows the one standing in the back of the group gets to say hello to the monster first. I pull Conroy into the space between her and I and smile into her glaring blue eyes that are so reminding me of our mother's right now. "You two can wait inside this classroom. Just shut the door and wait for me," I say, shrugging as if it's no big deal to be left alone in an empty school in the middle of the day after your mother tries to eat you and after eating your baby sister.

I point to yet another pastel nightmare across from us. This one seems to be themed with Mary's Little Lamb. It does nothing to inspire courage with my decisions. Nor do the many painted black eyes staring out at us bring comfort to Conroy as he cocks one eyebrow up at me with the disbelief of his own.

I force a smile of encouragement and untangle him from my legs, passing the torch of comfort giving to our sister. Rolling her eyes, with the ability of a teen pro, she leads them both into the classroom and closes the door behind her. I motion with my hands on this side of the door's glass rectangle window to the two sets of eyes staring at me to turn the lock. I wait for the metallic click that signals that they are secure with Mary watching over them. The noise seems to echo loudly in this hallway. With no other delays I can find, I feel their eyes following me to the gym doors as we put my so well thought out plan into action. I hope those lambs in that room are the ones Mary kept as pets and not the ones led to slaughter because I am not sure on which side of the door which lambs are which at this moment

Chapter 5

I am grateful the narrow window only allows for a certain degree of a vantage point as I stand here before the double doors. I don't want them to see just how afraid I really am. The cold metal of the door handle drains me of all the false bravado I was presenting just moments ago for them as soon as my hand rests on it. My heart races from the silence that whispers from the other side. A gym potentially fully of elementary aged kids should not be this silent. I am sure there are many teachers, on many days, in many schools, which wish it to be possible. It just is not.

Humans are not silent creatures as a rule. We are quiet, but we are not silent. We shuffle. We breathe. We fidget. In some small degree, being alive means sound. This is why pure silence is the very core of fear. This is why we glance around subconsciously when we suddenly find ourselves alone in the thick of that silence. This is why our minds will seek to fill the void when silence tries to surround us with random thoughts and to-do lists yet to be done. So, what option does that leave waiting for me on the other side of these doors?

It feels as if the whole building just inhaled a deep breath, drawing in all the sounds and time itself as it waits. It is waiting to see what happens next. It and that damn sun with its ever-cheerful singing birds.

The disengaging noise of the door signaling the handle has done its job makes my stomach clench. Any hopes of going unnoticed are dissolving with each metallic scraping, taunting my attempt to slowly open the door. My body clenches as I hold the door frozen in less than half-swing.

No boogieman reaches through the crack to grab me. No sudden scream of horror-filled panic reaches my ears. Whatever monstrosity or mystery I had allowed myself to mentally invent is not unfolding before me as I had feared. I allow myself a small self-mockery and laugh in my relief.

Glancing over my shoulder to double check Mary's locked room, my smile fades. The monster is finally creeping out of the dark, but it is not with Mary. It is in front of me with boldness that only pure Evil can hold; one only true Fear can embrace.

The monster is flirting with my senses. It dares me with the truths of its twins. It is waiting to share with me the secret joke that I was only so curious about a few moments ago.

The smells hit me first. Smells that will forever haunt me now as smells often do. It surrounds me like phantom fingers caressing my face.

"Come look. You remember me," it seems to hiss in my mind's ear, and I do.

I hear my small escape of a whimper and I know now why the silence has been mocking us the whole time. I know why each unsaid word has been drawing us here in a sick twisted truth.

We are here now. We are right where everything has been waiting for us to find it and I do not know if I have the strength to look even as my head spins around in defiance of my fear. Morbid curiosity causes me to inch the door wide enough to see the room before me just as it encouraged me to climb the steps this morning. I will forever hate myself for doing both. The sight before me will stalk my dreams for years to come.

The sounds bring back every shiver of fear I have felt today. Every brightly colored memory of this morning stares back at me in a new form. I can feel the sweat forming over my body as I awaken to the vision before me. That same wet, slick sound that I had only just worked so hard hours ago to refuse is now all around me again. Kneeling bodies are working in tandem, mocking the motions of a single fragment of my memory wearing a yellow nightgown. The fear this time is being escalated by the facts before me from which I cannot escape. These are children and I know what they are doing. God help me, I know what they are doing, and I cannot look away.

I stare in horror at the sights before me even as I desperately desire to look away. Candy apple colored red streaks line the mas- cot-covered walls of the room. Their angled arches are marred with random downward rivers of flowing red patterns. It is such a contrast from all of the children's artwork I have passed in the hall and I lose myself for a moment staring in the disbelief of it as my stomach fights to lose what meager food still left inside it. The floor is a finger painting of red smears and mysterious pools of thicker fluids surrounded by random petite sized prints of shoes. There are thick pieces of red clumps with a slick gleaming shine in various spots. My brain tries to let me know what the objects are, but my mind slams that door shut with its refusal. Human limbs in different sizes with slack fingers extending for- ward, begging for help that never came, lay about like life-sized Lincoln Log toys. Each new discovery tugs at a cord to my stomach until I can taste every piece of content within it.

I can feel my legs giving out even as my breath begins to quick- en. Each intake of my breath is becoming shallower than the last. I want to scream out at the impossible illusions before me. I want to force myself to wake up from this visual torment. Even as I sit here, seeing it all before me, none if it makes any sense to me. Even though I just escaped it, I cannot grasp the actuality of it.

The most sacred of childhood places has become the source of macabre delights. Their tiny bodies fill the room with more ghoulish fright than my mind can contain from such defiled versions of innocence. My body slides to the floor, bracing against the door using it as a metallic shield of safety, but no weight of material can protect me the from the horrors that continue to visually unfold before me.

Small frames of bodies are scattering throughout the room. Some are standing in a frozen statue-like state. Some are slowly gliding across the rubber-covered floor in a slow action paced game of "Follow the Leader." They move dream-like over torn limbs and the shredded flesh strewn about. Their faces are always staring straight ahead with a complete void of emotions at the objects of disgust surrounding them. Their brightly colored clothing is soaked with various shades and patterns of deep crimson. Their tennis shoes are stained and tracking through the pools with complete oblivion to it. Swinging ponytails keep time with a metronome of dread from sparkling colored ribbons. Only the slight twitching of fingers or from a head separates them from being wind-up dolls of inhuman puppets.

There is no one over the age of eleven left in a life like state in the room, but the floor is a different story. It is littered with all ages upon it. No one was safe from the murderous mayhem that happened here. Nothing was kept sacred, as bodies lay torn and discarded about the room.

My brain tries desperately to rationalize it all as surely some hidden shoebox of mentally discarded facts will hold the key. Conroy's option from before is tapping me on the shoulder to be heard, but I just can't do it.

These are not rotting corpses shuffling before me. The room is filled with many children wearing blank faces that are normally adorned with smiles and laughter like the heavy perfume of youth. These are children with stains and slack faces. Children hunched over still bleeding bodies, feasting from them as if they were a Thanksgiving pudding. Children, with gore-encrusted hands, making irregular marks along walls that they aimlessly drag themselves past.

Children, who should be running and playing with a freedom that only childhood can inspire, shamble around each other. These petite packages of our town are now mindless murderers of their teachers and fellow classmates. The proof of their mindless cruelty and their brutal actions stare back at me from across the long room with their own blank stares. It is a sight to silence even the angels of heaven with the defining horror and sadness of it all. "Do you see?" the blank faces wordlessly whisper. "Do you understand yet?"

I do, behind hot tears of revulsion and fear, but I so do not want to.

Chapter 6

"Helena?" a small voice whispers from behind me.

I am too lost in my own layers of this private hell to comfort another from this sight. All I can spare from my own strength is a handheld up for her to grab. It is an anchor of support to lean upon while we both stare out into a dark void of hellish scenery. A forbidden territory of horror is spreading out before us. We are new explorers in this new untouched land and neither of us wishes to make any more discoveries beyond what is already gracing us with its presence.

She begins to whisper names of the fallen adults like a priest at a war memorial. Softly at first, then only to emotionally choke at each new name said. I follow her finger as she acknowledges each of them out of respect for their bravery and their lost lives but I really just wish she would let them be nameless victims, so they won't haunt us both later.

Some I recognize from the shreds of personal items left behind. I knew her finger first landed on Miss Lacey by the spill of raven curls draping around her torn face. The security guard, always a constant by the door, is the closest body to the door. The principal's ruined shell is in the center point of the destruction. The shading of colors around his body allows a clue to his death being the first of many. The rest of the order is anyone's guess as so many lay broken and misshapen about the room.

When her damning finger starts to fall upon the smaller victims is when I pull her down to me in a silent gesture of enough. What is left of their shapes will forever be burned into my mind. I do not need their names also. I have a feeling I have already stored enough memories just waiting to stare back at me in my dreams with their grinning, pointed smiles and their sharp teeth. I desire no additions.

"What is going on?" she asks me. Her voice is overflowing with the desperate need of understanding. I have none to offer her to slacken it.

"I wish I knew. I really do Ashley." The self-confidence is ripped from my voice as I stare into the gym. I have no understanding for what is before us or what it means for us.

"What do we do now? Obviously, we are not getting signed in," she says.

Yes, let us cling to the small irrelevant facts here. I guess the horrible bigger picture is so much less relevant that way in her mind.

I stare at her with a look of mixed confusion at such a concern and disbelief that she muttered it as her eyes continue to silently take roll call of those before us.

She says, "More so since The Office Troll is being made a snack out of by Charlotte. I always knew she ate meat. That whole week of vegan preaching about threw my patience out. Hypocrite."

I am at a loss in comprehending how she is mentally registering the facts around us. If she is really this misguided or if she is just using her ten-year-old sense of worth as a shield to help distance herself from what is around us. Does she really think her class- mates, on bad days, binge on office staff for comfort food, or is what is slowly surrounding us too much for her fragile shell of sheltered sanity? Did convincing herself of the short sightings of this girl help her excuse the girl's current actions? The answers come with the rapid blinking of her eyes, the shrug of her shoulders and her strong constant inhaling.

I have never seen Ashley cry over someone else before. Plenty of times I have watched her at her best of tear-filled rages over things, but never others. There was never a person born of earth that disliked the word "no" more than she did. Nor were there ever a set of parents who hated saying the word "no" more than ours. For that reason, I can't really blame her for the over-inflated sense of self.

All of the Hawthorn Angels were handled like fine porcelain china sets. Each is envied for their rare blend of beauty and they are coveted for their shining star-like futures. They were each being groomed for the spotlight to shine upon them as they were always promised. Now the only thing shining upon her face is the light of death and destruction. The only stars to this play are the fragmented bodies of her former classmates and the school's faculty. At twenty-three, I am at a loss for words for this situation myself. How do I expect a child to gauge the proper responses?

Stories that are only supposed to cause shivers of false fears are now demanding their due and they want their payments up close and personal. Today, they are wearing the costume of what is supposed to stay sacred. I glance one more time at the giant defilement of the thought.

I ease softly off the floor, helping Ashley to stand with me. Some deep unconscious memory of when humankind was prey holds our actions in sync. Every child is taught at a young age to never turn their backs on the monsters and that is evident now as we both ease backwards from the gym without a word passed between us. No one ever warns you of how the monsters can cheat though.

The horrible purple door refuses to close. Exchanging glances, we both stare at the gap between the metal frames, mentally willing it to fade even as it ignores us. Slowly, I reach out to coax the door closed by pulling gently on its handle. Every rustle of fabric seems to scream between the soundtracks of death playing in the gym. I clamp a small hand over my mouth for fear that even the sound of my breathing will attract their attention. The door does not move for us, but something else does.

Chapter 7

There comes a point in every horror movie where we begin to yell at the people on the screen before us. Sometimes it's to warn them of the impending doom that they do not see waiting for them. Sometimes it's to berate them for their choices to run up the stairs rather than out the door. Maybe it's because of the overuse of the choice to hide under the bed or in a windowless bathroom. Whatever the reason might be, everyone is guilty of it at some point in our movie-watching history. I wish someone were here yelling at me right now.

I know I have to get this door to close, but now knowing what is on the other side of it I am a lot less brave than I was when I was opening it. My actions are weak and fear motivated movements. If I use too much force, like a betrayal of trust, it will make the metal tattle-telling sound letting them know we are here. If I use too little force, like a schoolyard bully, the door will stand here mocking my efforts. Sometimes you really are damned if you do and damned if you don't. Right now, I am knee deep in damnation and it's creeping slowly higher.

Ashley is the first to notice the changes in the cherubs of death. I am focusing so hard on getting the door closed to hide us that I forget to keep an eye on them. Now their eyes are on us.

I cannot tell which cherub signaled the slow start of the stampede. For a heartbeat of time, we stand here both staring at each other, as if they are as shocked to discover us as we had been to discover them. Then all at once, they are moving. A single unit of death-minded dolls gaining speed and coordination with each determined step towards us. Their glazed eyes never once shift to look away.

"Run. Dear God, Ashley, run!" I scream at her, trying to keep my body as a shield between them and her with small backward steps, but she is not moving and we are losing ground. "Ash, go!" I scream again.

Conroy picks this moment to come out into the hallway to see why I am screaming at our sister further proving life's cruel aspect of programing children with their timing skills. With his screams upon seeing what is flowing towards us, I have no choice but to run past her. I reach out to grab her as I pass, but she flinches, shrugging away from me. I spin around reaching again, but I still miss.

My heart beats like a drum but the tempo does not match the speed around me. I scream her name and it comes out slowed as my vision narrows down to only the sights in front of me. Superheroes do not wear masks to protect their identity. They wear masks to protect their sanity. When the shit hits the fan, and it is your job to run into it, sometimes you do not want to see what is waiting to surround you when you do.

Ashley stands with her back to me as I lose my footing in my backwards spin to grab her. I feel the floor as my left knee slams against it, rocking my body with the impact, and I fight to stand back up. My boots are slick against the tiled floor and the few missed steps seem to cost me everything.

I never take my eyes away from her. She turns her head back to me, seeing me through the waves of the perfect golden shades of her framing hair. Her blue eyes pierce me, but not with fear. They are swimming in pools of sorrow.

The first few tears hang from her chin until others gather to give them the weight to escape her fragile face. They are fleeing from what is about to happen. I know she is not running. I know she has made her choice to not move. Now, I know which side of the door these lambs are on and I led them to the slaughter.

The area becomes deafening with the music box pitches of grunts and growls. Wave after wave of gore drenched dolls pour from the open door, causing there to be an almost jam of tiny bodies in such a narrow force-filled space. They push through it and walk over any who block their passage with an outstretching of arms and extending fingers. Yet, Ashley still does not move as I am sliding backwards on my hands and feet unable to grasp the contact my boots need to fully support my weight. Conroy grabs me, giving my panic-filled motions the solid force, I need to stand and we are both sprinting backwards screaming for Ashley to come with us.

A tug of war begins between Conroy and myself. I keep pulling him forward towards Ashley and he keeps pulling me backwards from her to him. I can see his mouth moving, but all of my senses are locking only on the oval around the little girl staring back at me over her shoulder with the silence of sadness.

In a child-like game, Conroy and I swat at each other's hands as I try to break away and he tries to keep me with him. He is desperately pulling at anything he can clutch onto with his small hands to keep me moving backwards with him. I know he is pleading with me with all of his voice and the weight of his body with each lunge, but it does not matter to me. I cannot hear him. I cannot feel his need. I only see her.

The little girl, who refused to eat her breakfast for the milk had made the cereal too "wet," is standing before me in her soft pink pajamas and white socked feet with monsters rushing to her. All external sounds have fallen away from me. I only hear my heart beating as I struggle against a seven-year-old and his fear-filled strength. I know my last visions of Ashley will forever be held in a secret chamber of my most private nightmares. The ones let loose only by the darkest of nights when all hope has faded away, leaving my soul vulnerable to their haunting.

Her eyes never leave mine. Even when the first tiny fingers latch onto her shoulders, she stays staring at me. Those sharp, sea-colored blue eyes hold no fear, no remorse and no blame. There is only the sharp sadness of acceptance inside of them on a tear-lined hidden face of youth who has given up.

I feel my scream of her name when they take her rather than hear it. It rips through my heart, not my mouth, as her blonde hair floats away from my sight. I continue to scream her name as they tear into her, pulling her down to the ground before covering her completely with their madness. She never reaches out to me for help. She never returns my screams. She is just gone. A pile of murdering, tainted and frenzied bodies, the same size as her own, replaces her in my sight.

I know later I will be thankful they overtook her in such a quick level of mayhem. Their cruelty saves me from having to watch what I know is happening below that withering mass of shapes. It saves me from having to keep a vision of her like the bodies in the gym.

Her broken body will not torment me like Lilly's will. She is not broken and left exposed as proof that nightmares now walk among us. She is just gone like a dream at dawn, and I am down to my last Angel.

Chapter 8

How long have I been standing here in my dazed state of disbelief, I don't know. I know my arms are sore from the strain of being pulled on repeatedly. I know sounds are slowly re- turning to me and the colors of the clown's prison seem to slowly become brighter as time regains its speed. I know that Conroy is pleading with his tear-streaked red face for us to move. I know the very things I have been trying to keep us from are now only a few feet away. I do not want to know what the sounds that drift up from their pile are or to what the colors contrasting with the pastels belong.

Awareness comes back to me as a limb returns from the loss of feeling. Pain and short, sharp stabs attack my chest and head. Panic begins to refill my urge to live as I slip from my sleep- walking state. One small step at a time, I am coaxed away from Ashley's gravesite until I gain enough speed and turn around, to run with the only Angel left in my care. As I spin, my eyes scan the sight one last time. Mary seems to glare back at me from her wall where she has kept her lambs safe until now. Their fleece is now as red as blood.

We run blindly down empty halls with only our grief giving us speed. Neither of us carry any conversation or plan any form of escape. We just keep moving with each twist and turn of the building like some demented never-ending hedge maze. Each hall is a brighter shade of pastel mockery to our pain than the last.

Colors start to overlap, and I know we are now lost in an exaggerated rectangle with Conroy only using the fact that he has to keep moving to shelter his soul from grieving. He is like an infant refusing sleep. If they stop moving, they have to give in to their body's needs. He is not ready to give in. He does not know how. Perhaps I am just over thinking the whole situation in my own refusal to my body and he is just completely lost to his panic.

"Conroy. Conroy, stop," I say.

I pull his body to me and I sink to the ground, cradling him. He seems to shrink into himself as he curls into my lap and I whisper soft sounds to him. I run my hands through his closely trimmed blonde hair, rocking him, as he uses my shoulder to hide from this horror-forming reality. His pajamas still hold the scent of the home we once shared in what seems a lifetime ago. His hair smells of flower-scented shampoo and it is a welcoming scent. It is a safe scent. It makes him seem that much more fragile and precious in my arms.

We both sink into emotional cocoons as we grieve the morning, completely forgetting what is a mere hallway away in our grief. Neither of us is speaking to the other. Small vocal sounds are all that is left of my vocabulary.

In my mind, I see Ashley fall over and over again in various rates of speeds before me. Her hair floats down behind her with its golden hues of beauty. I see Lilly lying still, soft, white and broken. Their eyes each look to me with anger and then panic, knowing I will let them die a million times as their deaths replay in my mind. Carol's picture smiles up at me even as her own red blood slowly swallows her frozen face.

A small room of my heart knows I have killed them. I have killed each one of them in my own way. It was either by my own hand or by my lack of actions. Hot tears burn my face as they soak Conroy's head like a baptismal of damnation. I cannot keep him safe, but I have to keep him safe. Ashley's replay starts again, and I lock the room of my heart.

It is such a soft sound that at first it goes unnoticed. The slight sliding of a shoe along the tiles. The soft whisper of clothing. It is the irregular pattern of a shadow projecting on the floor that makes me aware of it. I nudge Conroy to move, keeping my eyes on the growing shadow to the right of us.

He crawls backwards off my lap, keeping one hand locked in mine. His eyes are wide with trembling foreboding as he pulls me from the hall. He is as lost as I, but he is counting on me to get him out of this. He may want to take a note of those who also shared those same feelings only a few spans of time ago.

A small tennis shoe-clad foot comes into view as we peer out from our hiding spot in a doorway. Slender legs wearing a flower-patterned dress walk into view. She is no more than six with her dark blue flowered dress and its cropped jean jacket to fight against the first stirring of fall mornings. Her strawberry red ringlets are held in two pigtails by white bow-tied ribbons. Each step she takes causes them to sway on either side of her freckle-covered face. She is the very definition of youth's perfection and I hear myself exhale the breath I did not know I was holding before I remember what forms of perfection are lurking in these halls.

She lures Conroy into the same feelings and hopes of safety with her familiarity. He steps out from our doorway before I can stop him.

"Margaret?" he gently calls out to her.

Margaret freezes mid-step. Her little foot held but a moment above the ground as a deer freezes when sensing something has altered its surroundings. Conroy takes another step from me. Her foot lands softly back into its former placement with ringlets swaying. Conroy still slips further away.

"Conroy!" I hiss, still peering from the doorway.

He looks to me as she looks to us. He does not see what is staring at him. He does not see that same small tennis shoe turn towards us. Nor does he see the side of her that has been kept a secret from us. How lucky am I that I am the one to see it first?

Her right side is caked with gore, giving her the appearance of having been dipped down in a thick pool of a substance now dried and clinging to her. She is an almost perfect illusion of good versus evil side-by-side before me. Each side of her face is wearing the same hate filling hunger.

That same hunger spurs her on faster when she sees Conroy, but her right leg is dragging as it refuses to help in the journey towards us. It acts as a last-minute miracle of salvation, slowing her down. She makes no noise to alarm Conroy of the danger creeping towards him. She is a perfect killer in a child-wrapped package. I rush off the floor and lift his body into my arms, staring her down. I do not look back when I turn, running with my own precious child-wrapped package clinging tight to me.

My boots threaten to slide out from under me again and I know our combined weight was never meant for these spiked heels. Nor are my lungs made for all of this running from the many nights of working in a smoke-filled bar. I am the cliché horror movie chick in very inappropriate shoes running for my life. All I need now is a bright colored sweater, and a run through the woods, to make the whole sad scene complete. Maybe Conroy and I will plan a camping trip when this is all over.

I know I will not be able to keep this pace up and turn into the first set of open double metal doors I see. Rows of white tables sit in various formations in the constant purple and teal color combinations of the building. I know if we survive this neither of us will ever be able to stand pastels again. One seven-year-old emo coming right up!

Chapter 9

The room is still as I stand in its entrance clutching Conroy. A TV flashes static from its angled location in the high back corner. Empty trays sit perching on a shelf waiting to be of use. Two evenly spaced registers sit void of cashiers. I cannot see past the swinging doors of the kitchen and I have learned that silence does not always mean empty. I am debating the choices laid before me as the sound stirs down the hall behind us. Limping Margaret has finally caught up with us, and by the level of sounds, she is not alone. Nor is her new army happy with our escape.

I ease him to the floor holding a finger to my lips. Slowly, I close the metal doors and motion for him to walk ahead of me to the kitchen. There is no place to hide in this large room designed with that fact in mind. It is made for easy viewing by teachers from all angles. This room was designed to keep the twisted things we are running from safe and comfortable. For a moment, it feels as if we have run straight into a trap of their design. A room they have already spent hours of their short lives in wraps its arms around us in what I know to be our final meeting.

We pass through the kitchen's swinging doors as the cafeteria's doors mirror the act. I peer through the small round windows in our set of doors as the small bodies assemble in small groups. They seem to lose animation without our discovery to be found. Like wind-up dolls whose gears are losing tension with each movement, they slip back into a dream-like state and I allow myself to think we are safe.

They fall back into their unearthly game of "Follow The Leader" in small pockets of groups. Even in this new state, cliques form in common styles. I watch this all before me as if I am a documentary voice-over relaying the sights before me to Conroy huddled on the floor.

"What are they doing?" he whispers, in a voice that still holds his tender toddler years within it.

"Walking in circles," I say watching them move in impossibly slow formations. Each of their steps seem more exaggerated than the last.

"Why?" His curiosity overshadows his fear for a moment of genuine interest.

"Triangles are harder to do in a group formation," I offer.

I have no better answer to give him. The smirk he wears loosens the tension that has been surrounding us all day. Of all my siblings, Conroy has always been the closest to my own personality. It's something that has always irked our parents. My encouragement of it also held no amusement for them. Add in them catching him sitting on Lawless' black Harley and their minds blew over our antics.

The behavior before me makes me wonder if the children are truly mindless. To seek out the familiarity around each other there must be some form of working mind behind those blank stares. Is there some keeping of logic or is there only the basic behavior still stored? Did Margaret, now falling in with other girls of her stature, answer to her name or just the sound of Conroy calling out to her? Fifty small children wander before me each wearing their own version of crimson patterns and I am not brave enough to step out to find any answers from them.

As I stand here watching them, I wonder how can children cause such extreme feelings in those around them? By basic bi- ology, we are programmed to keep such treasures safe. We cherish each moment of milestones shared with them in photos and stories retold time and again. We will lay down our own lives to keep them safe. We will lay down the lives of those who do not. Those same sweet mouths that only moments ago kissed their parent's goodbye now seek to bite and consume. Small hands that once clasped together in friendships to gleefully play circle-spinning games now tear and destroy those around them in unison. Eyes that once danced with the joys of life now stare with muted awareness of only what lies directly ahead of them. Youth's softness that once gifted them with calming beauty now has turned her gift into a disarming weapon. That very illusion can cost us our lives. Until this point, we have been able to run, but the highlighted exit sign and its coveted path lies straight through them. They roam the room in misshapen circles. There is no safe passage between their miniature self-made carousels for us to sneak through. Ashes, ashes, we all fall down.

A sharp tone chimes its high-pitched signal three times throughout the building. Conroy is so startled in his already fragile state that he screams even as I drop to cover his mouth with my hands. Our eyes lock in the narrow space between us, sharing the panic over his response.

Easing upright, I keep my back to the door so our eyes can hold the emotions we are sharing. We are too afraid of the damage words can wield. Two porthole styled windows with their plastic-like glass urge me to peer through with a double dare style of knowledge. I have had enough dare for one day, so I choose the truth even if I have always preferred spin the bottle styled party games.

The door sways slightly as if from a pressure vacuum release. It is so slight at first, I wonder if my eyes are deceiving me. If it was not for the fact that Conroy is now standing also and staring at the door too, I might have been able to convince myself they have, but we both cannot have imagined it.

The door answers with a slightly wider swing, startling us both. A small hand wiggles its fingers into the gap caused by the movement, catching the door. We stare at the fingers with body-freezing dread. They hold the door open, drumming slightly as if pondering what to do next. Pink tipped nails shine with a natural gleam on those porcelain extensions and we both stare transfixed. The chime comes again, and all the hesitation has been resolved by the repeat of a scream behind me.

Conroy is still screaming when the door is shoved open with great force by a small five-year-old boy. Following close behind him is a parade of macabre visions.

For the first time I am glancing around the smaller room. Steel ovens gleam from one wall in their pristine stations. Many steel shelves cradle the various shapes and sizes of cooking pans throughout, creating a metallic peek-a-boo maze. Magnetic strips hold sharp and blunt cooking instruments securely against the walls. All encompassed within the same pastel shades as the rest of the building. It is what my eyes land on against the back wall that causes my heart to rejoice in our backwards retreat from the horde before us.

From ceiling to floor stand the doors to the staff's closet. It is shining at us like armor from knights of old. The handles were designed to be too tall for small hands to reach them. Magnetic pictures of smiling happy days gone by showcasing two women are scattered on the doors. Their smiles encourage my resolve.

Conroy will be safe in there while I distract the horrific animations before us, allowing him to reach the exit first. It makes perfect sense in my mind. I can even see the plan put into play before me like a movie with each glorious step to take. Too bad things are never as brilliant when released from the secure planning of our minds as they seem to be when in storage.

Chapter 10

The same boy who entered the room first is leading the monstrous army. He is keeping the same advancing speed to match ours as we retreat from them. It's making the rest of the youths fall in step behind him like soldiers. The perfect dance of predator and prey choreographed when the world was still more beast than beauty is playing out as they match our every step with their own.

I can feel Conroy's trembling body as he fights against his adrenaline's urge to run. I can see through the shelves the long train of death-clad children wrapping around the path. Their eyes follow my every move with the same interest as a predator's holds their prey. They are waiting on us to spark that needed animation for their frenzy and I do not know what is more chilling, the overpowering possibility of the monstrosity they are capable of or their calculated stares.

I tug on Conroy's hand to pull his attention away from the boy ahead of us. The boy's eyes follow up to me also. His hand twitches in an unspoken dare between us as his face still keeps its blank frame. He is watching. He is waiting. I know one motion from him, Dand the nightmare will begin for us. One wrong motion will result into a devastating crescendo effect of what I have already started.

Never removing my eyes from the new pair upon me, I motion with my head to the metal safety closet behind us. I am not so hopeful as to think that if we just stop, they will too. Inserting him into the closet will have to be a well-planed dance and with- out interruption to signal any change in the children. Conroy shakes his head with a frantic motion and the eyes swing back to him in unison. Their steps falter as a few presses against the ranks with quickening steps and my breath catches at the moment's confusion.

They are growing restless with the sight of us before them. I have thought until now that they were toying with us, but to them we are the ones refusing to play the game. Do they need our fear, our response of fight or flight to engage their motives? The amount of crimson coloring layered over their clothes shows hints at being well versed in their methods of attack. If it is not the lack of knowledge holding their actions at bay, then what is the missing ingredient? Are they so well fed already from their morning's mayhem that their crippling evil is discouraged from surfacing? Has it really been, all this time, a perverse game of "Follow the Leader"? Is this leader just not destructively motivated, or is he just more calculated, waiting for the perfect self-twist of footing to bring us down? My mind is filling with more questions than an over paid Hollywood elite interviewer holding a golden god in her grasp for an hour. The only difference between her and me is if she asks the wrong question the god will just storm out. If I make a wrong move, the devils before us will just storm me.

The closet is within our reach. The gleaming handles reflect the light with a warm glow, forming an almost beacon effect in the dark depths of our situation. Many nights Aimes and I have danced on the bar tables, planning our spins and twists to the time of the tempo vibrating from the live band, but never has the risk been so great before as this dance is now. At most, we may have slipped off the edge with a mistimed step, not been torn apart like a piñata by small hands seeking hidden sweets.

Stepping between the boy and my last Angel, I take the first dance step and it brings me closer to the boy than my body wants to be. My stomach recoils from the various scents rolling forward from the horde. Scents I have never been subjected to before, but something deep and primal within me knows them. My mind has become a mantra of calming chants to keep my adrenaline at bay. I know we should be running. I know the basic rule of all horror facts is never to hide. You get the hell out, but what do you do when hell is between you and the way out?

My hand grasps the handle and sending a silent prayer up to anything or anyone who might be listening, I firmly push down, releasing the latch. Conroy begins to struggle against my attempts to guide him inside. He fights and tries to slide away from the same arms he was grappling with to stay close to before. His agitated state excites the monsters before us. Glazed eyes begin to gain focus as his struggles start to become vocal. The small room starts to vibrate with the force of his repeated screaming of, "No! Not in there!"

The words echo off surfaces as he screams them rapidly, each time giving more animation and speed to the sea of creatures before us. I prepare to shove him into the space, timing the movement with the anticipation of myself having to run when he is safe. I never planned for what was going to happen next. How could I? Plans, like thoughts, often have the highest regrets. Once both of them are started, there is no turning back and we can never see where they will lead us until it is too late.

Something from inside the closet steals his body from me with such force I stumble with it. The door slams shut, sealing him inside, but it does not close upon the sounds of his screams. The small bodies before me begin to beat upon the door following their new nature. Arms reach high at unnatural lengths to reach the handles, ignoring any discomfort it must be causing them as shoulders begin to pop. Layer after layer of death-covered small bodies begin to beat and scratch the doors being encouraged by the screams beyond it. They have forgotten me for the moment, and I stare in confusion at what has just happened as I listen to him scream my name in a melody of his pain, fear and begging for my help. My body runs cold with the realization of what I have done, and I too begin to scream. The two women are not just on the door. The two women are inside, and they now have Conroy. Margaret, with her demonic tinted pigtails, is the first to turn to me. Her body language switches back to predator as she moves. Her head cocks slightly back to see up the length of me from her height and those eyes are now bright with eagerness. She separates from the herd a few dragging steps at a time, following me backwards, further away from her best friends forever.

I am no longer filled with fear as my ears are filling with his screams. I do not see this thing inching upon me as an innocent child anymore. The illusion is shattering with the growling from the depths of her throat and crimson half-mask she wears. Her small hands curl into claw-like formations and she reaches for me. We both no longer see the other as human, but we both now see ourselves as predators.

I have only so many options left to me now. My anger slips over any fear as easily as slipping into a warm coat. My anger is incited by the screams of my name from a little boy who is drowning in pain and pleading for me to save him; a little boy that they have taken from me for their own delights just as they took Ashley. I am desperate. I may not be their mother, but they are mine. They are mine to protect. They are mine to keep. They are mine, also, to so brutally fail.

The danger before me does not matter anymore. The only option left to me now is getting through these demonic dolls to reach him. Margaret just doesn't seem to understand she is the first in my path. The solid wall of the stoves behind me stops my steps short. I am not so brave as to turn my back to her. It forces me to quickly glance over my shoulders for any type of weapon, keeping her in my sight. I look to find anything I can use against her. I feel around to find some clue to our survival as time is running out for us both. I remember, rather than see, the magnetic strip over the stoves and begin to slap the wall for its location.

I know the moment my palm lands upon a solid handle of something dangerous as the eyes before me glance past me for the first time since turning around. Her face melts down to pure animal at my discovery. She drags herself at a faster pace towards me. Her sounds signal some unspoken event with her classmates. Pairs of arms retreat from their abuse on the door, falling limp and still at their sides. My eyes glance from the child behind me to the children beyond her and back. The finale is cued.

The knife slides off the strip with ease. The scraping sound it causes serves as its own battle cry, making their heads turn to- wards me with awareness of my actions. Margaret's lips pull back to expose small white teeth in a snarl that should be impossible for such a face to wear. I am conflicted with the fact that these are children before me and that my child is beyond them. I asphyxiate with the doubt and uncertainty of how to do the next horrible act. Despair washes over me and I know what I must do. These children must die so that my child may live.

The dam breaks inside me. I scream my first sob and bring down the knife upon pigtail-swaying Margaret as she reaches for me. The blade slides into her at the tender juncture of her neck and shoulder. It does not cause her to flinch in the least. She does not even stagger with the blow, but instead uses my closeness to latch onto my arm. Her head turns to sink those tiny white teeth into my exposed flesh, and I kick her, using the stove as my brace. Her small body falls upon the ground with her eyes never leaving me, her target. Dark blood pours from the wound at her neck and yet she still stands up angry and ready to try for my death again. I stare at the delicate white flowers discoloring from my attack on the blue dress when she comes for another round. There is no form of recognition on her face to the state of her body and the shoebox of misshapen clues is opening inside me with this final key-like fragment.

They are not real. Some freak form of animation is left, but they are not human anymore. Even as her tiny heart pumps itself out of her body, she feels no pain or panic over it. I stand crying from the clues presenting themselves to me and end the little form before me.

Her death is simple. She feels no panic. She holds no pleading cries. Just the simple fact of she is, and she was. My mind settles into a state of numbness as her classmates begin to run at me   in waves of their mayhem. I climb up upon the stoves to keep me safe from them rushing me as my Ashley was, and with no remorse, I take aim at each little body until there is no longer anything to aim at.

They finally lay still before me on the floor. They are a pile of holocaust-like imagery formed of small, delicate, still bodies. I can no longer tell if the blood they wear is theirs or another's as shades slowly blend upon them. I am certain any moment swift judgment will rain down from above upon me for such a sin.

The room is finally silent. The stoves no longer hold their pristine glaze. The once shining tiled floor is now a slippery mess of dark fluids. It takes me a moment to understand what is missing, to understand what I should still be hearing. This realization spurs me into action and coats me with desperation. I ease past the pile of corpses, fearing any movement or twitch, but every- thing lies horribly still around me.

"Conroy?" I call out in the silence.

What should only be a few steps before me turns into miles to reach the dented and marked door.

"Conroy?" I whisper against it, pleading for him to answer me. My hands are slick with the blood of those I have killed. They slide along the handle before making enough traction to allow me to open the door. There are ghosts waiting for me inside these doors. They cause a haunting that shall never be exorcised from my mind with any level of prayers or holy water. The ghosts whisper to me what is beyond the door before I fully open it with sounds and smells that seep out to greet me.

I have come to know them like well-hated friends. They spare me from the vision of torn blue cowboys trying to escape on horses spread before me by tearing hands and chewing mouths. I don't have to see the sightless blue eyes that will be staring beyond to a world I cannot see as Lilly's were. Like a coward, I slide down the door, refusing to open it any further.

My last fragile one is beyond my help now. He no longer screams for me or from pain. He is deep in sacrificed dreams and hopes. I let the door slip shut on my failure. I close the door on my final murder.

We told them monsters are not real. They are only in your minds. There is nothing to fear in the dark. There are no monsters in the closets. They are only in stories. They only live in books. They only seem real in the movies. They are fictional. They cannot hurt you.

Their final moments were realized by those lies. Monsters are now real and there is very much to fear from them. I have failed my Angels. One after another, I was there and could not save them. I tremble with the weight of that truth. Grief pours from me in silent screams as I rest against his tomb and listen to the hands beating against the other side of the door for my flesh, having already destroyed his.

Chapter 11

In mindless abandonment, I drive with no idea of what to do. I don't let my mind think of the things that have happened. The last thing I want is to be aware of what I have lost as the town is turning upside down all around me. The streets are becoming active with the madness missing from this morning.

Cars are piled upon each other as wrecks fill the streets from panicked people. The stranded people fight for the cars trying to wedge through the destruction as they pass by only causing more wrecks or worse. Many drivers, so afraid of what is happening, never stop when those stepping out in front of their cars try to stop them for help. I scream as I watch families mowed down or flung into the air by the cars in front of me only to see them land broken and dead beside my car.

Houses stand open with thoughtless escapes from their occupants as possessions become meaningless. I watch as the few who have barricaded themselves inside become victims of people looting. There is gunfire everywhere and I reactively swerve the car with each shot.

There are screams for help from various areas, but I never look. I never let off the gas because it is worse when the screams become just wordless octaves ringing through the air. Through it all, everywhere stands the calling card of Death, from the scents of his heavy perfume to his mind-numbing visuals. He is everywhere today, and every demon is wanting its pound of flesh with their tearing teeth or in dripping handfuls of those they steal it from. It's not a stroke of genius

I ended up at Grit. My autopilot with nowhere else to go drove me here. One by one, to the roaring of motors or the gentle hum of cars, we all made the connection that safe harbor might be here. If the dead are walking, then what better place than here where the Devil is believed to be, J.D.? With their black vests donned, even today with the many events that have unfolded, the men welcome each other, glad to see another brother is still alive.

Haunted eyes and warm embraces meet each new arrival as we all wear our clothes like badges of triumphs and defeats from the trip here. A few share their stories in whispers in the dark corners of the bar, but most just sit in private hells of their own making, with their eyes cascading from what they have lost. Conversations rise like the seas to a roar before being washed away over and again as the same questions float among all the tables. Why? What? How? It's what we are all asking.

Aimes and I have begun to do what we normally do when at work in our own attempt to block out the events the day has held for us. Shot after shot, beer after beer, we pour as the jukebox plays between the gaps of suffering shown around us. Aimes pink-streaked blonde hair bounces with our forced laughter. Her blue eyes used to shine with sexual innuendos everyone knew were false hopes to be had. All laughter has faded from her eyes and conversation is mumblings of disorientation.

Her outfit was just as damning as mine when she had arrived. Her hands tremble as she pours the drinks, giving hints to her unspoken words with punctuated clarity, and no one has the courage to press the matter. Nor did either of us ask the other in private when we showered and changed in our employee area about any details. Her body shook with silent sobs at the family pictures taped to her locker as she suffered in silence. I could fill in the blanks with enough imagined horrors on my own. I did not need her confirmations.

Now, as a majority of our bond-formed family is gathering around static screaming TVs and radios, we look to J.D. for answers. If this rag-tag of a bar-formed motorcycle club were to answer to a leader, it would be him.

His calm exterior is always holding back a force to fear. It can ignite in seconds and extinguish just as fast. His eyes hold the depths of someone always watching and weighing, not only your actions, but also your words. His stillness is not of nonchalance, but of preparedness. His smile can melt your heart or freeze your blood when he fixes it upon you.

For most of us, he has become the father that life has neglected to give us, with his strength that allows him to not only control, but also to comfort such a diverse collection of souls. We form our self-value around his approval. He feeds us our daily bread of encouragements and our wine of confidence. Among all of us, no one is this truer for than our Lawless.

He and J.D. sit huddling together at a table, trying to appear calm in their whispering debate. With false smiles lingering in their conversation, they are attempting to reassure those watching that everything is okay.

J.D. is doing a better job than Lawless. Lawless' eyes are darting too quickly from table-to-table around them. The muscles of his honey-tinted arms are twitching with every sudden sound as he plays with the flame of his metal-encased lighter. The two of them are as confused and lost as the rest of us, but the only difference is they will not admit it, male pride at its best.

Lawless' deep brown eyes keep mine for short seconds of time. My heart drops with each connection at the depths of their sorrow staring at me. It is heart breaking to see Lawless so broken. His boyish grin and normal one-liners sync well with his normal laid-back attitude. There is nothing he will not do for those he cares, and if the dare is big enough, for those he knows.

He flirts with Danger as if she is a favorite lover. He knows just where her breaking point is but encourages her anew each day with ease. The sound of his Harley makes women melt from miles away just knowing who is rushing towards them on that blacked- out machine of his. I have watched married socialites primp at the roar and mock pose as he rode past them. At most, they only earned a smile or wink from him for their efforts. Life is a game for him, and they played well together until today. Today life has broken the rules, all of the rules.

He runs his hands along the path of his dark, close-cropped mohawk as he stares up at the ceiling before sliding from their shared table. Whatever J.D. has said to him has rattled him. He comes in our direction, and even with the events around us, I feel the familiar stirrings within me as he slides over the bar counter with the strength of his arms to support him.

Falling into those arms to the sounds of whistles around us, I wordlessly seek his comfort. We are the favorite joke of the club. Even today's horrors could not change that fact.

Today though, his defined arms are trembling as they hold me close. His hands rest on the back of my body, pulling me in tighter than normal. As I melt into the heat of his body surrounding me, I know his mind is not with me. I am taking reassurance from him, but he is taking strength from me. Whatever chore J.D. has asked him to do his mind is already running through it.

"You done?" J.D.'s strong voice shakes us back to the world we so want to escape from together.

I feel, more than see, Lawless pull himself together, slipping away from me slowly and reluctantly. The light from his eyes dims and his smile melts to blank serenity. He wraps both hands around my head and places a lingering kiss on my forehead before following J.D. out of the bar. Aimes and I both stand watching the two men who have become our universe slip out wordlessly.

We both have learned in our early days not to ask questions. No matter how loudly those very questions may echo in our minds. When I hear my voice doing just that, I am not sure who is shocked more by it.

"Where are you going?" I ask, and my annoyance is not even the least bit masked.

"Disney World," J.D. answers, slowly with a mixed smile of amusement and reprimand. "So, why don't you and Alice there keep the dwarfs happy while we are away?"

The door swings shut behind them, but not before Lawless gives me a wink so full of false hope my soul hurts for him.

"If I am Alice, who the hell are you?" Aimes turns to me with her mock anger expressed on her face.

"Since the dwarf mention, I guess I'm Snow White." I shrug, filling another glass with ice.

"I can see it. He is not the most creative, but I can see it." She smiles her signature smile. "I suppose we should just be happy he didn't ask us to give them all free rides with the theme park analogy he was trying to rock there."

We both wrinkle our nose at the thought, causing a roar of disappointment among those sitting at the bar and the flow of joking begins. The world may very well be ending, but still the familiar male thought is constant. Under the mounted replica of the club's grinning skull, we continue our games of flirting and pouring. Life goes on because it has to. What other choice do we honestly have?

Chapter 12

"You sure this is the way to go? It feels wrong. Just, wrong," Lawless asks.

His dark jean-clad legs are holding his motorcycle in place as he lights the end of a cigarette. The glow burns bright from the first rush of inhalation. His black tee shirt clings to the many contours of his arms and wide shoulders under the club's signature leather vest. The grinning skull upon its back is a little more fitting than normal today. Staring across the lot from behind dark sunglasses, he scans the area watching the shapes move around them. "Dunno man. These are our people," he says to the older man beside him.

J.D.'s hand grasps the back of Lawless' neck, bringing his focus roughly around to him. "Says who? How many of those in there do you really know? Huh? Gimme their names and we will save them all. Blaze of glory. The whole deal." His voice echoes with the heavy acid of sarcasm. "Look around you, son. You see any of them big saviors heading in our direction? You hear any of those loud sirens screaming towards us? They have all left, son. None of those big brave saviors left around here now. No, we are on our own. It's just you and me to see this through. Whatever the hell is happening, we are on our own here. I am not letting a room full of weak-willed excuses drag us down." J.D. leans in close so that they are almost eye-to-eye with each other and says, "We take care of those that care about us. You know that. The rest, well fuck 'em. I never wanted to save the world and I ain't about to now. You let me know when those balls of yours drop so we can do this. Those pound puppy eyes of yours only work on your skirts and this ain't no time for skirts."

J.D. lets Lawless go with a small shove before leaning back to his own motorcycle. Its chrome glares under the sun's rays, mocking any need to hide from the world. He waits with a relaxed stance, finishing his own cigarette as if the other man has all the time in the world to come to a conclusion about the road they are going to take. There is no going back for J.D. It is just a matter of when they start down the path ahead.

J.D. knows Lawless will do as he asks. He has become his right-hand replacing Rhett. It happened not out of need, but out of the respect Lawless has earned.

Lawless knows the depth of J.D. like no other ever will. They have become so well-tuned to the other that a simple shift of his face or a roll of the shoulder can give answers as well as any vocal conversation.

J.D.'s desires in life are simple. Keep the ones you love safe. Destroy the rest. With Lawless at his side, and the MC backing his actions, those desires have become that much easier to obtain. It is one of those very desires they are going to conquer now. The knowledge brings a grin of anticipation to J.D.'s face as he looks to one of the few trusted men beside him.

Lawless nods as he starts his Harley, more out of male frustration from being called out than the belief in their actions. He is still nodding as he takes one last glance at Grit before following

J.D. out with his own echoing engine roar. His machine is lean and low profile, allowing him to easily catch and out distance his father of necessity.

Their destination is one of future preservation for the club, and personal satisfaction for J.D. J.D. always knew there would be a day for his style of reckoning for a well-known man in town. He has waited, biding his time, looking for the perfect day to strike out. Now the world has given him a golden invitation with calligraphy script telling him just how to do it and he wastes no time putting his R.S.V.P. to the invitation.

It is not what they are about to do that is causing Lawless to pause. He has known this day was coming and prepared for the course they are about to take long ago. It is just another wound for his soul to heal and scar over. He has lost count of the number of scars he now wears for J.D. It's the price for his friendship, his trust and his love. Every piper has his payment.

The mere thought of having to leave those Lawless cares for the most in the world behind unprotected is holding him hostage. Getting lost in a world of their female laughter and perfume gives him a reason to push harder each day for their smiles. Without them, his world would rip apart at the seams, leaving only the void he feels when he is truly alone. Only when he is lost in a world of their own making can he find peace with everything he has done to please the man they all depend on. Even with the warning he slipped to Rhett and Marxx about J.D.'s plan, there is so much that could still go wrong.

His mind is still racing through the possible reenactments of what may happen when they pull into the parking lot of the shop. The next chapter looms before him, unflinching and waiting. It is as judging as the steel blue eyes watching him. They are both waiting for his fall out.

"You know the plan?" J.D. asks, staring at the younger man. "Yeah," Lawless says with his eyes safe behind the dark tint of his sunglasses.

"You know what happens if you fuck this up?" J.D. asks, looking around the car-cluttered parking lot.

"Yeah," Lawless says, as he dismounts and adjusts his black leather gloves. He stares at his hands wondering whom they really belong to anymore.

Leaning in close to Lawless as J.D. passes him, he whisperingly hisses, "So, what aren't you going to do?"

Lawless stays silent as the man passes him. J.D. is not really looking for an answer. He is just making the point stick that the damage this will cause with its ripple effect if not done just right. Lawless is already well aware of the damage they have already done just by leaving the bar. He just wonders if J.D. does.

The bell makes a sharp tinkling sound with their entrance into the shop. Lawless, never removing his deep tinted glasses, steps in front of the man he has trusted his care to for so many years now. He places one foot following the other as his mind falls blank knowing what he is about to do. The only thought process to him now is a silent prayer of forgiveness repeating itself.

"Man, we are closed. I know you think you need a gun, but there are not enough guns to help you handle your shit in here. Not many have the balls to shoot their own families and neighbors anyway. Try the church. That's what we all need now to get us out of this," calls out a man from inside the gun shop.

A lanky man wearing his normal flannel plaid shirt steps out from behind a stock room door. A moment passes before the man recognizes the men standing before him with their silent acknowledgment. A simple moment which costs him everything as two bright flashes spark before the pain tears through him, spraying the broken bones of his skull and thick matter of his brains against the wall behind him in a wash of red. Lawless stares at the drops as they become streaks as he prays his silent prayer of forgiveness.

They say the Devil laughs when he collects his debt. They speak of how he will tempt you and seduce you into taking the fall. They warn you that he will wait forever, watching and waiting for you. Laughter is now filling every inch of the store and it is the song that sings the shop owner's farewell.

"Let's clean this up," J.D. says, as his laughter dies. "Can't let the girls see this mess. Hells is jumpy enough as it is."

Lawless nods as the body of the shop owner slides down the wall as he dies. The streaks of blood follow him down, outlining the body. To Lawless they seem to be asking, "See what you have done now?"

"Hey, pound puppy, get over here," J.D. barks with the hesitation from Lawless. "I want to get this place locked down before anyone tries to sneak in here when we head back. These guns are going to be what keeps our asses safe in these coming days."

With his tongue gliding along his teeth, Lawless swallows his guilt into a pit as both men start hiding their sins.

Chapter 13

The sounds of J.D.'s and Lawless' motorcycles leaving the bar sent a wave of shocking disbelief through the room. The depleting sounds had most standing as if they could watch them leave through the thick walls. It sent some deeper into their ex- cited conversations. Most of all, it just sent them looking to us or Rhett and Marxx for answers.

With false determination to remove unseen spots, Aimes cleans the glass in her hand. "I hear Florida is nice this time of year," she says, avoiding their gaze. I can hear the disappointment in her voice.

Her emotions open the door for others' emotions, also. Emotions from those who have come here for help are now left stranded without answers. Their confusion pours out like a flood around us.

Some begin debating their next move, wondering if J.D. and Lawless are coming back or if they are taking the coward's way out by leaving so many behind. Some begin to argue with such an insult presented, as anger is always an easier emotion for men to admit to than the fears they may be feeling. The women sitting around the area begin blending further in with the walls around them as voices rise and finally the tension breaks. It crashes over the crowd in angry words and threatening innuendo-filling sentences.

The results cause some to slink out with fears for their own safety while others just leave, soaking in self-absorbing worry about what is to become of them. Marxx and Rhett take up their normal mantel of enforcers, removing the most hate-filled patrons with glee. They strip the deserters of their vests in the process with just as much enjoyment. Daddy might not be home, but his rules are still violently felt. No loyalty. No vest. No protection.

When the waves finally calm, it is just a handful of us left amid the debris from the storm. Rhett, with his smiling enjoyment of the fight, stands guard over the back door with his lip bleeding from a lucky shot someone landed. Marxx stands with his silent glare at the front, daring any to attempt to come back a little worse for wear, but just as violent.

Chapel sits in a back booth where he has been watching the whole event while sipping on his frosted mug. He is never bothered by the drama or bothers to help stop it. He sat watching it all and now sits waiting for whatever is next with the same lack of interest.

Aimes and I stand behind the large oak bar playing rock, paper, and scissors to figure out who gets to clean up what, with our own lack of care. With what the day has already given us, what is a bar fight? Regardless of how each of us is feeling about what has just happened, we never would've wished upon them what is about to happen.

Bridget's screaming brings us running to the large tinted windows as other feminine screams slowly join in her chorus. The monsters have found us, and they are surrounding the parking lot with shuffled steps and grunts of their vocal sounds. Glazed eyes begin picking their targets with eagerness, splitting groups into smaller numbers as they spread out towards their new victims.

The loud noises from the many roaring Harleys' engines are acting like a dinner bell to their ears. Lines of shambling bodies form down the streets heading to the bar like a horrific Halloween parade. Long arms reach out, pulling people from their motorcycles, or the motorcycles down all together, as person-after-person falls to the walking nightmare versions of our town folk.

"What the hell are they?" Aimes whispers, staring out the tinted windows as they amass around the bar.

Chapel's lifeless voice from behind us at his booth offers the first answer given to us all day. He says, "Their flesh will rot while they are still standing on their feet. Their eyes will rot in their sockets. Their tongues will rot in their mouths. On that day, they will be terrified, stricken by the Lord with great panic. Each man will seize the hand of another, and they will attack each other."

"Did he just quote scripture?" Rhett's forehead creases with his question. He shakes his head in amusement as his twisted sense of self continues watching the window. "Is that what you think Chap? Last time I checked, when God wants us gone, he just washes it clean. Kind of like a final judgment deal. Not a survival of the fittest."

Aimes looks to me and says, "New twist to any kind of Hunger Games spin-off?"

My eyes slowly roll to her with blank shock from her words. "Really?" I ask.

"Too harsh?" she asks, shrugging as she stares back to the murders occurring in front of us.

All around us it is the same as it has been all morning. Never-ending terrors even the darkest of plots never would dare to imagine surrounding us, eating from our humanity to feed their survival. I am still not sure which is worse. Is it when the screaming starts or when it ends when our panic should start?

Both have their own signals for the events that are unfolding in crimson-soaked colors. Is it what they are that makes it so horrid?

Is it their style of attacks that make my blood run cold? Is it knowing what they do to those they attack that makes my heart quiver with fear? Perhaps it is the truth of it all combined into one horrific package wrapped with a bright, shiny, blood-dripping bow.

"They are the Risen," says Chapel, drawing a long sip from his beer, "and it is what we will all become. One by one, until there is no one left but the Devil himself to walk this earth."

No one has the voice to argue with him as we watch those who were sitting among us only moments ago being devoured. Aimes and I huddle together under the window, covering our ears from the remaining fading screams. Their screams will reach us no matter how deep of a sleep we shall ever again be blessed to reach.

"What the hell happened here?"

The deep voice startles everyone in the room. It causes Rhett and Marxx to reactively reach for their holsters as they spin to face the back of the room.

J.D. does his normal chuckle at their reaction as he makes his way to us over the broken tables and the remains of the many crushed glasses with Lawless following behind him. The two men who started all of this with such a simple act stand so calmly beside us at the window and we are at a loss for words.

J.D. does not seem surprised to see that we are all that is left of the once filled room. He is eyeing the destruction with the annoyance of missing a good show upon his face. I can feel Lawless' guilt seeping from him like a wound as he is watching the all   too real horror show framed by the window. Each fading scream becoming another notch of failure he will wear forever upon his soul.

"You left!" Aimes screams. "How could you do that? You left and they all freaked out. Went total white trash talk show at being left behind. The only thing missing was a "who's your daddy" moment to complete it."

Her screams cause the Risen to pause. Slow searching movements bring their focus to where we stand but the bar's dark tinted glass used to keep prying eyes away protects us from discovery. Some stare transfixed, as if seeing their reflections for the first time. They stare confused at what is being shown back to them, cocking their heads left and right trying to figure out what it is they are seeing. Others return to their previous victims with disinterest at what they cannot chase.

"We had precautions in place for you and Snowy there," J.D. says, answering her without removing his eyes from the carnage. "By the way, Blondie, who is your daddy?"

Marxx and Rhett shuffle some, trying to hide their amusement and stay out of focus from Aimes' firing line.

Marxx glares down at us while talking to J.D. with his deep gravel-filled voice, warning Aimes to not push the topic anymore. We both cringe under the heat of it.

"When you two pulled out for your joy ride, not too many were happy to hear you go. On the way out they ran into what Chapel here calls the Risen," Marxx says, as he looks toward the window "Risen, huh?" J.D. shrugs, staying silent for a moment as if weighing the word. "It works for me. Not as if those things out their care one way or another what we call them. Just as long as we feed them. How many did Chapel's Risen get?"

"A good bit, but don't worry. Chapel says we will see them again soon. It's all very cheerful like," Marxx says, leaving the window and its visions of death. He is the first to break the train wreck trance that is holding us captive.

"Yeah, like dripping snow cones or melting cotton candy on your tongue. You know, when it gets real stiff like right before going soft and flesh-like," Rhett says, and Aimes and I both grimace with the comparisons.

"Anyone have a plan to get us out of here or do we all just sit till Chap's reverse Rapture kills us all?" Marxx asks, ignoring the man. "Yeah, we got a plan," J.D. says, still watching the feasting forms outside.

If he feels any remorse for those who have fallen, he will never admit it. Those of us left in the room read him in ways where vocabulary is not needed. We understand his mood swings.

Watching him softens some of the anger we are feeling about his departure.

"We had to," J.D. almost whispers it as his cold, slate eyes roam the carnage before him. "We can't make our way anywhere with so many of us. Look at those things. They are all over town. Walking. Stumbling. Watching. Hell, some are half missing pieces, but they keep coming. One after another, they just keep on coming." He turns to stare at us saying, "We had to thin the herd. Take only what we can protect. Only those who can protect each other. I knew as soon as we left most of these cowards would file out like rats on a boat without us here to hand feed them. What if that would have happened when we are out there? When we are depending on them? We had to. The silent ones are just wolves in sheep's clothing. They will kill you just as fast should the mindless herd suggest it. So just stop with the bullshit glares and get up," he says to Aimes and I. "We ain't sitting here all day to be food for Chap's idea of a second coming."

Aimes and I cringe under the misplaced anger. We wait until he steps away from us before we even begin thinking about getting up ourselves. Like fearful children, we wait until Daddy is out of reach, and only then, do we help each other to our feet. We keep our backs to the window so we may keep another very real threat in our sight.

J.D.'s stride is filling with rage with each step as he makes his way to the bar, not looking to see who is following his lead. The crunching glass beneath his boots as he walks wordlessly tells us his opinion about the situation.

"If I hear one more word about your religious ranting Chap, I'll feed you to your Risen myself. Then we can all see on which side of your Maker you sit," J.D. says to Chapel who just takes another sip of his beer as he watches us.

Chapel shrugs, staring down into that beer and says, "Seems fair."

J.D.'s tells us his plan and it's simple. Simple as in a suicide attempt is simple with its many plot-caving holes. His logic is guns and lots of them. Somehow, the end of the world has turned into a boy's playground as each man in the room slides a slow smile onto his face at this revelation. Where does one find all these guns for them to play with? Well, that is the cherry.

He is sitting upon a stool as we all stand around him, like the good little children we are waiting for a story. Children left alone amid shards of broken glass and splintered tables. Maybe this is why none of his wives ever suggested kids with him. Daddy doesn't quite grasp the concept of safety first.

He has been divorced now from wife number four for a few years, depending on which side you speak to, the exact number of years change, as does the exact reason why. Neither detail matters much to me enough to really explore it. We all have our own scars and to explore others' invites them to explore yours. No thanks. Right now, he is taking full advantage of his scars. His last wife left him for another well-known hell raiser in an either very ironic twist or an impressive act of self-hatred. The new husband, Lee, is the owner of the most well stocked gun store in town. Lee could often be found boasting this in his normal drunken state here at the bar and wearing a flannel shirt every day. He would brag there is not a model or make made he does not have either on the shelf or in his very locked safe. I guess J.D. is about to call that bluff.

He is wearing a proud smirk as he tells us his plans. They leave me torn between annoyance and amusement with him. The smirk on his face tips it to amusement. What can I say? I am a sucker for a good smile and a biker. Sue me.

The fact that our genius's plan is to try to break into a place better armed than the police station, owned by someone with less self-control than one, makes me pause to wonder when exactly I thought J.D. to be smart. Aimes must be having the same thoughts with her half-cocked eyebrow at me over the flow of male conversation around us. Sometimes it really is depressing to be the only girls in a crew full of men.

"You want us to break in and steal these items?" Chapel asks, and his voice still holds its empty echo of numbness.

"The world has gone to shit. I don't think the rules apply any-more," Rhett mutters.

"Then we really have fallen," Chapel whispers to his beer, in its never-ending mug he seems to have.

"You worry about our souls and how about I worry about our flesh, eh Chap? We will see which one turns out to be more important," J.D. calls out, never acknowledging the other man with so much as a glance in his direction.

"OK, moral code aside," I offer, trying to diffuse the building situation, "how are we going to even get close to that place? Lee had a "shoot first" point of view before all of this. I can only imagine how welcoming he is going to be now."

"He won't be a problem." The voice J.D. uses has a finality about it that makes us all look away.

I look to Lawless to see his reaction, but he refuses to meet my eyes. Aimes squeezes my hand in a silent communication to let it drop. She is right. If I have learned anything today, it is there are many worse things than what J.D. may or may not have done to Lee. Worse is to think of what Lawless may have done to help him. Who knows, by the time this all plays out, I might be envious of Lee and whatever the truth of him might be.

"…and after the guns?" Aimes asks in a whisper. She is still holding my hand and I am haunted with the images of smaller hands that also needed my strength hours ago.

"My hunting cabin," J.D. says, making his voice gentle for her. "I always keep it fully stocked for when you girls annoy the shit out of me, and I have to go shoot something." He lets a slow, teasing smile sneak onto his face, and we are not sure if he means it as a joke or a warning. We are not asking. Smile and nod, baby. Smile and nod.

"We should be good there for a long haul." J.D. slides off the stool, wrapping an arm around us both. "You are my girls, right?" he asks.

This is J.D.'s normal way of asking us if we are on his side. We always nod and smile like mute bobble-heads on a car's dash. We are almost a complete sell-out to how easily we are geared to please him, but there is something comforting right now in the pure strength of his presence with so much not making sense around us. We both respond to him on a very girl level. I hate myself for it.

"Then there is nothing to worry about. We won't let nothing happen to our girls," he says, patting both our butts with his sentence.

I wish the others' eyes were as reassuring as his. They only glance at us and then around at suddenly very interesting objects in the room. Only he and Lawless have the courage to keep our gaze, and we make a note of it as we look to each other with our own shared gaze.

Aimes and I gather the remaining supplies we can find from the bar, including the all-important stock of her lip-gloss, ranging in every shade of pink made, to store in bags in my car. We both change into the more sensible spare shoes we have stored in our lockers. That is if sensible is cowboy-style boots with their deep brown leather and stitched scenery. Apparently, neither of us ever thought to pack for the end of the world unless it is to involve lip-gloss loving Marlboro men. Pity, it does not.

"You boys ready?" J.D. asks, with the pump of his shotgun daring them to answer incorrectly. "Let's get this over with," he says.

Marxx inhales, pushing the door of the bar open silently as J.D. pulls a table to the large windows. Lawless and Rhett are braced against the last window along the wall as Aimes and I huddle with the heavy bags behind Chapel. How do you escape a carnivorous lunch hour? Noise; lots of noise.

I can hear J.D.'s laughter as he climbs on top of the wooden table after taking a deep inhale from his cigarette and braces the shotgun against his body. The window explodes from his first shot, shattering the glass as he shoots through. The glass serves as shrapnel-like projectiles, shredding the first group sitting near it like razor wire slipping through their bodies. As Aimes screams, J.D. just laughs louder, lost in his pure elation of the moment.

Marxx kneels to take aim at the ones standing to head towards the bar. Kneeling as he is, he is hidden as J.D. takes full stage in a play based on his insanity. With his fist wrapped in a towel from the bar, Lawless breaks the glass of the window in front of us. The glass falls like rain from the window frame, shattering like droplets as it hits the ground around us, and we follow him through the newly made exit amid J.D.'s shotgun blasts.

Risen explode around us with each of J.D.'s loud laughs. Their dark fluids from their ruined bodies brutally showering the ground as Aimes and I wedge ourselves between Lawless and Rhett. The pavement is slick and if it weren't for the strong arms of Chapel, I would have fallen several times into the disemboweled bodies ripening under the sun's rays.

The outhouse smell of death is everywhere. It hangs around the bodies the Risen have destroyed and it lingers from the Risen Rhett and Lawless dispatch as we escape to our vehicles. J.D. emerges from his broken window frame still targeting the Risen with his shotgun blasts. They are crowding around us now and he shows no interest in a fast escape. Marxx easily catches up to him and I watch from my car window as Marxx struggles to stay with the older man.

J.D. should run. The path has been cleared and their Harleys are waiting, but he doesn't. He strolls casually through the carnage as he reloads. He stops to flick the ash from his cigarette as he surveys the situation and racks the pump of his shotgun.

Marxx is out of rounds, gripping his knife, he stands ready to defend J.D. as a female Risen reaches for his back. J.D. beams one of his amused smiles at Marxx, and fires the shotgun over his shoulder directly into the woman's face. Her face is obliterated into a red rain of flesh and blood as her head explodes. He never flinches from the outburst or the recoil, keeping his smile straight as he cocks an eyebrow as if Marxx is the one with issues.

"What's the hold up?" Rhett shouts as even his nerves are being tested by their delay.

"Just a ball check, Rhett," J.D. calls back, stepping around Marxx with a male chuckle. Tucking the shotgun between the handlebars and the wide wind deflector of his large motorcycle, he mounts it and looks back at Marxx who is still fidgeting with his ride. "You waiting for a prom date, Marxx? Get that thing going."

Marxx' engine roars to life and I hear Rhett ask J.D. as Lawless and Marxx exit the lot, "Can I wait for a prom date?"

"That's some sick shit," J.D. says with a smirk, revving the engine of his Harley before leaving Rhett laughing behind him.

We follow behind the men on their Harleys of various shades of black and personal styles like their own versions of warhorses in my small compact. Sunglass covered eyes glance nervously around at every corner as their engines' noise roars down the street. What they had always before considered as their calling card is now a death sentence and I refuse to look at their jury slipping up on all sides of us. Instead, I focus on Lawless' back like a lighthouse in a storm showing me the way to safety as we are weaving around various panic-caused wrecks clogging the roads around town.

My compact scrapes through intersections filled with such aftermaths that leave me wondering if there is any safety left in the world. I know if there is, he will find it for us as I glance to the back seat in the mirror and stare at the imagine of bleeding blonde children that once held the same faith in me.

"You know, it just came to me that I really wish we had voted on Chap's Arch Angel instead of that grinning skull they all wanted," Aimes says.

She is sinking low in the seat beside me with her boot-clad leg braced against the dash and refusing to look out any windows. I can smell the deafening sweet smell of her gum with its extending bubble matching the pink streaks of her hair. She is a sensual combination of woman and child, which men find so seducing and endearing. They yearn for her attention and are ready to defend her hurt moods with the same hot eagerness. All of this she uses like a well-stacked hand of cards to play at her discretion to either handle them or encourage them. Today, she seems to be handling nothing.

Amelia is the name I called her when we were children. She has been my friend for as far back as I hold memories. Many years we have spent in her room talking about subjects all parents dread to discuss with their kids. Each year bringing more depth to them as we grew until nothing was sacred. Now as she sits here, trying to hide from the world, it is such a contrast to her normal mischievous self. Watching her deflating slowly before me, the weight of the day sinks into my bones.

"When did we get a vote?" I ask her, my voice sinking with my depression.

"By vote, you mean share our opinion for them all to ignore and then blame us for not speaking up when it all goes to shit?" She sighs as she says, "God, he's right."

"Who?" I know I will regret asking her before the question is out of my mouth.

"My dad. He's been saying how I sound just like my mom." And with that, the car fills with silence for the rest of the trip.

You do not pick at other's scars. No ma'am.

Chapter 14

Apparently, we are not the only ones who thought of Lee's place when neighbors began making breakfast out of each other. Wreckage surrounds the shop until it grows too thick for Aimes and I to make it through. We are forced to leave the car and walk the rest of the way to the store. It does not coax the warm fuzzies at all.

We carefully walk through the debris in the parking area of ransacked cars and hasty departures. Each time we pass a broken body, we fear any sudden movement from it. The sounds of the buzzing flies are already heavy in the air with the many dead who sit staring out windshields or windows as we pass. Their dead eyes are wide, and it feels as if they are watching us as we try to sneak pass them. Our once small, sleepy town is now stomach-churning, and fear tipped.

My lighthouse is waiting for us as we slip past him through the doors with the tinkling of a bell above us. The smell of him makes my palms itch with the need to touch him. My dam's walls creak with the weight of it even as I refuse to accept it. He caresses my lower back when he passes us, acknowledging the need we are both withholding from the world. We do not look at one another as he passes. We are both too afraid to let the other see that ache and I let him join the guys in their childhood joys of guns as a bubble-gum scented breath whispers in my ear, "Kinda hot."

"Like a wake," I mutter back.

"Well good thing most of us are already in black then, huh?" Aimes asks with a pop of her gum, as we enter the main area of the gun shop.

J.D. is pulling one duffel bag after another from the store's racks while shouting orders. He instructs the men of what to grab and which bag to place it in. He might as well have been a football quarterback for all the meaning the various numbers hold for me. To me, it is just row after row of handheld metal shapes with a few versions of larger sizes mixing in for good measure. I know enough from having a baby brother and watching TV which are considered shotguns, rifles, and pistols, but specifics are beyond me.

I sit on top of a glass display case as my only female partner-in-crime makes patches of fog on the glass beside me with her scent- ed breath. We watch as gun after gun is checked and packed with its coordinating ammo with feigned interest. I am sure if they found a pink one her attention would perk. Hell, mine might perk. Each man is picking up certain styles of guns and placing them into duffels of correct sizes. Lawless and Marxx are selecting metal tubes of various lengths and matching them to partnering guns with holsters of many sizes and material. They stash kits of cleaning tools in their other bag from the various areas of the long rectangular room. I watch as they all work wordlessly together, gathering up what has been appointed to each with a silent, mutual agreement.

They are so aware of each other's movements and assignments; they never need to make eye contact or even see the other person slipping around them to avoid any blockage of paths. Like worker bees in a hive, they each go about their assigned tasks with no thought of it or need to think about it. The only difference is there is no Queen to answer here. They have a King; a King who communicates without words, but with nods and his eye contact to keep his little hive in order and on their tasks.

For a momentary flash, I see Conroy running with this wood-grained imitation rifle chasing Lilly around the cases. The men are oblivious to the two of them filling the room with child- pitched laughter as they run between and around them. I close my eyes against the sight, breathing deep to exhale their ghosts from my mind when her voice pulls me back.

"Ready for a fun question?" Aimes asks me. The glass near her is smudged with hearts and smiling faces as she looks to me. This is why we would never survive a crime scene.

"I do so love your fun questions," I say with exaggerated interest, still watching the men in private amazement.

She flips me a middle finger and blows a kiss to me, asking, "Where do they think all those bags are going to go?"

She has a point. My compact is already full of the bags from the bar and now our bees have a growing pile before us.

"Want to go car shopping?" I ask her with a smile.

"Looting and grand theft auto? It must be Tuesday!" she says with glee, bringing the room's attention to us.

J.D. smirks at the sound of her voice between checking a shot- gun for shells. He calls out to us as we retreat from the room, asking, "And just where do you two think you are off to?"

We both call out without thought in our normal one-minded fashion, "Disney World!" as our laughter takes us.

It feels good to laugh again as we find our response more amusing than it truly is. Stress is a many-sided coin. Right now, it is shiny and bright but before we know it, it will return to its normal dark-sided self. It will rob us of the humor we find now, replacing it with whatever mood swing it wants to share with us. Our Disney is depressing, and our laughter dies upon our lips as soon as we exit into the bright light of the sun. In black-clad Bibles hell is described as a tormenting place of heat, but all I feel is winter's chill as it sneaks upon us with the change of the seasons. Cars race by in high speed escapes while past wreckage lingers from other's attempts to do the same. Store windows are broken and spill forth their items onto the surrounding sidewalks where it is hard to tell mannequins from human remains with their blank eyes and frozen forms so equally posed. Papers are whipping through the air with each passing car, creating a snow globe effect all around us. I only pray that no one shakes our town any harder today.

We tiptoe from car-to-car, peering into each like a toxic dare. Some are a blessing while others are damning with the horrors they hold. The further we slip into the shopping areas, the more we are damned with their sights.

Still, we make good use of our shopping trip as we gather various supplies in Aimes' ever present bag. I will never again mock her idea of purse sizes as we fill this one with what is left of the looted pharmacy, café and general stores of the square. Let the boys have their guns. We have the three C's -- coffee, chocolate and condoms. According to Aimes, these are the main staples for any apocalyptic conflict.

We creep from each store, constantly afraid of what could be waiting for us when we leave them. Each well-formed exit allows us to be braver and relaxes the tension between us. Our comedy seeks to replace the depression that has been following us all morning. It floats around us like bubbles at a child's party, flying higher and higher and perfect with its rainbow shades in the sun's light. Pity it is just as fragile when it comes to a crashing halt.

The streets are as still as the moments after a murder. Even the birds have escaped, robbing us of their songs while another sound fills in the void they leave. They always come with a soft whisper. They use just the faintest of caresses to tickle your senses. They want you to stumble upon them. They want to creep up on you just when you are feeling that the danger is depleting around you. Always, just when you start to trust the sun again, the Risen find you.

There will always be sounds we know to fear from birth. Sounds that can cause you to bolt awake from a sound sleep or the types of sounds that can cause you to pause in your normal day-to-day with dread. In all of my stored recordings of sounds, there has never been another that I fear as much as I fear the one surrounding us now. The thick watery sound we know to associate with a new horror is stalking us again.

I do not know if she heard the noise too or if she is just reacting to my frozen form, but her body mirrors mine as we sink behind the car from our latest attempt at shopping. Peering under the car, I see the many bent forms of Risen crowding over their latest meal. Hands pull and shred the flesh making the body twitch with movements as they dig to reach hidden sweet meats within its deep cavities. Each one of the sickening sounds draws a shudder from us both in a cocktail of fear and repulsion in a glass salt-rimmed with our tears as we watch a man being devoured right in front of us.

We kneel here watching more and more gather upon one another, reaching past to secure handfuls of what was, only moments ago, just another person trying to survive this hell. If our timing had been different, would our places have been exchanged?

Our eyes are holding an in-depth conversation as Aimes and I motion with nods with an attempt for a silent plan to form. The width of our eyes showing our agreement or refusal to the ideas we are silently sharing. It will only be a matter of time before they fully destroy the body, leaving them hungry and ready for more. I do not want to become another tragedy within a tragedy-filled day. We have managed to slip almost a block away from Lee's gun store and our security. We are too far away now for my lighthouse to show us a way to safety. Upon realizing this, their sounds seem to begin to grow by decibels in matched pace with our fears at being alone.

"Please tell me you have a plan!" Her excited whisper is more of a hiss with all of our silent planning falling to ruins.

I place my finger to my lips, glancing around for some clue out of here. I am finding myself wishing for once, I could be the follower. I am not sure how in this comical twist I keep stepping into the shoes of the leader. I, with all my fears and failures, am picked yet again to save the day. It is only noon and I have a longer list of defeats than victories. I wonder which one of our three C's is going to save us now.

As if reading my mind, Aimes hisses again, "I do not have a condom in this bag to cover just how screwed we are!"

Something calls to me from across the street. Maybe it's the sun, filtering through the clouds and casting a light upon her. Maybe there really is a God and he finally deciding to throw me a crumb. Could it even be the Devil, with his hidden plot line, not ready for me to take the final fall yet? Whomever, whatever, whichever it may be, I am not about to ignore the help and send a silent "thank you" to whomever is either helping or extending my life.

She is huge and intimidating for someone so used to a compact and yet at the same time welcoming, with her large retro truck- styled safety. Her windows are rolled down like a silent whispering invitation among so many doors of escape shutting before us. She does not give the Risen an inch as their gore-dripping bodies push against her. Like some beast of old, their smudges are only adding to her rugged beauty.

She is clothed in chrome grills and full-length running steps. Amongst her black body, they shine with blatant attitude that would give any of the men's motorcycles an identity crisis. She is my own warhorse with her large, southern style tires, allowing her to ride over any obstacle placed in front of her. This beast may not start with a C, but suddenly I am feeling much more apocalypse ready.

"How fast can you run?" I whisper, as I try to gauge the distance between the large truck and us.

"We are surrounded by flesh-eating monsters. Your question does not give me a lot of hope in your plan," she whispers. Maybe she has been paying attention to my scorecard after all.

"I'm going to distract them. I want you to make it to the truck over there. Swing it around and pick me up. I will jump in the bed." I try to ignore the voice that reminds me how well my last distraction plan went as our vocal volley begins.

"Have you lost your mind?"

"I have been wondering that all day."

"What if it's a stick?"

I stare at her in mute disbelief before saying, "Wait for me to get their attention and then run."

"So, we are not even going to have the stick discussion." "We are so not even going to have the stick discussion." "I hate you," she tells my back with false emotion.

"It's a long list," I return. It's easier than risking a goodbye. "With the current town population, probably isn't," she offers, also not wanting to say the dreaded goodbye.

I glance back at my best friend with a smile and another prayer to whoever is listening this will not be the last time we see one another.

Chapter 15

I run, kneeling to keep the cover of the cars between the feasting Risen and myself. I want to be sure I have enough space be- tween us before I play the role of a suicidal jack-in-the-box. Aimes is a hunching ball of stealth waiting for me as she situates the purse and her position. My mind fights against what I am about to do, causing several false starts before Aimes mouths a word reserved normally for men's frail egos. It's so easy to judge when you are not the bait, but I smile at her just the same. I signal back my opinion of her insult with one simple finger. We exchange one last smile and I nod, shutting off my mind's rebelling screams.

Time is ticking and we don't have any to spare for kitty cats under any name.

At first, they pay no attention to me. The Risen are so engrossed in their current victim and, in total female fashion, I find myself feeling insulted for a moment before using their slow wits to better place myself further from Aimes. I counter her angle with hopes to form a wedge in their path, allowing her to hide from view when she makes her move. It all feels very strategic in my mind and it fills me with hope. I know my soul cannot take another loss. My sanity cannot store any more failures, and my heart, it gave up this morning.

"Hey! Hey, over here!" I shout and wave my arms, in a total cliché formation of attention seeking.

I am almost ashamed at the lack of my originality, but a cliché is a cliché for a reason. They work and I really need something to work right now.

Slowly their heads turn to me, locking their eyes with mine. Their bodies rise in my direction with their slow, unnatural style. Their growls and snarls make my knees grow weak under so much focused hatred. A few stay hunched over, mouths working the dripping meat in their hands, but their eyes watch me as they weigh the possibilities of a new meal versus the mouthful they currently have.

I bang on the abandoned cars next to me, making as much noise as possible against their metal frames. Each loud sound is drawing away their humanity as their faces melt into an animal-like hunger.

Lips pull back, showing snarls of discolored teeth. Limp go- re-torn fingers hook into claw-like talons as anger takes them. They are itching to feel how my flesh will shred to feed them. They want to know how my blood will drip between their fingers as they feed from me. Glazed eyes fill with hatred and intentions of destruction as I draw their attention.

My mind begins to flash images of their previous victims and the potential harm there is as they head towards me. It is like a mental reality check of my actions, snuffing some of my bravado. The dead man's face is slack from his death, casting an almost sad quality to it. Even now, he appears to lament and doubt my plan. He seems to already be mourning for me and he is not the only one doubting it at this moment with hell's escapees stalking towards me.

I know I cannot run yet, but they are not moving fast enough for my plan to form. They stalk me with their eyes. Their bodies are waiting to spring forward with the hunt. Even as the first few gather close around me, I must stand my ground. I know with them this spread out I will not be able to keep their attention and allow Aimes to slip behind them. They move in clumps of different degrees and motivation, making my plan falter before me with their refusal to cooperate. Panic dances inside me as I watch them while trying to decide what to do.

I know the few left occupied will not notice her, but if one of the others standing should alert them to her presence, they will overrun her before my eyes. I have already seen it proven once. One haunting is enough. I have failed too many today. I can't fail another.

I stand, keeping my ground, even as my mind is screaming at me. Even as my knees begin to grow weak from the adrenaline rush screaming at me, I stand my ground. Even as my heart beats so fast it feels like it is trying to break free and run away from this itself, I stand here screaming and courting Death. I flirt with him as well as any well-dressed courtesan ever has, all in hopes he will not be tempted to take another from me today. My flesh for her flesh. My death for her death. I stand before him offering myself to him all in hopes to save another.

I can smell them now as they begin to enclose me. They wear rot and death as if it is a brand of cologne. Waves of their scents roll towards me, crashing upon my already fragile senses. My screams come more out of a release as fear mounts me. They know it. They seem to smile at me as their animation reaches its start. What they had once started as slow calculated steps, now gathers speed at such closeness to my flesh and scent of my fear. It is my own style of perfume to them and they lust after it.

I begin to inch backwards, still waiting for them to gather more tightly around me, but Aimes gets the point. She begins to inch around the car's hidden comfort zone while keeping her eyes on me. I can see her own fears growing as she begins to mentally plan the path before her. We glance one more time at each other and it feels like a goodbye. I turn to run, dragging hell with me and hopefully salvation for her.

I use the parked cars like an obstacle course, swaying and blending around them. Some of them follow my every turn. Some continue to run straight around the cars. Separated like this, I can see them begin to spread out around me. Instead of being a stalking shadow, they have now become a surging plague threatening to overflow this small one-way street.

Their sounds bounce off the buildings, echoing terror through me. It spurs me faster in pure panic. I fight to keep my wits about me, but every reflection in the stores' windows strips me of all logic. I realize too late they do not have the restraints like I do. They do not feel their bodies crashing into the cars with such force that they rock the vehicles with their frantic movements.

They can push their bodies faster than normal. Their muscles do not cramp or their lungs ache with the abuse of oxygen levels. Mine do and, beyond all my efforts, I am slowing down. My mind screams to run faster, but my legs are slowing down.

With the clarity that I cannot outrun them the first hot tears of acceptance blur my vision. The reflections keep showing me how fast the gap is closing between us with each passing storefront window in a strobe light effect. I can feel them now even before they actually touch me. Their shadows are reaching my senses first. The first fingertips brush against my back, trying to grab me. I scream with each feather-like sensation of Death's greetings. The panic of my mind steers me to cross the street in an attempt to regain some illusion of hope. My heart begins to accept my death and I begin to lose the strength to keep going.

I struggle against each store's locked door I am running past. Sounds of frustration with each discovery of disappointment mingle with my sobs. The windows shatter any hope of escape with the scene reflected behind me. I watch, almost detached, as the first one reaches me. I have run out of Grace and am falling into their hands.

A male grabs a handful of my hair, pulling my head back. It exposes my neck in an arch of pale ivory with the force, and I fall to my knees with sacrificial acceptance. My plan was to keep them from reaching Aimes. It was never to survive myself. I offered Death myself for her and he is here now to collect the bargain.

I feel the sidewalk connect with my knees. The pain flashes white-hot through my legs even as I slip further down upon my hands. His hands desperately fight to pull me backwards against the fall, forcing them to lose their grip against gravity's strength. I struggle forward, finishing gravity's encouragement with the ripping of my hair. Freeing myself from his grasp, I fall into the brutal arms of the other's.

Hands clutch my legs, my feet and my shirt as they pull against my escape with their hunger-driven desperation. I can feel myself losing ground as they pull me backwards down the sidewalk. My nails and my fingers are shredding against the rough pavement   I am clawing along to gain any inch I can. I fight for every inch that I lose, feeling them dragging me backwards to them. Teeth grind upon the fabric of my jeans, making me scream from the pain as my legs bruise under their assaults.

They fall upon me one-by-one. Their weight is pressing down any attempts of my escape. An escape I have accepted will not happen when a child's face, covered in a blonde shroud, stares back at me from my mind's eye. She is watching me fall under my own imprisonment of death with her cold blue eyes. I was not brave enough to wonder what Ashley's last moments were. I keep the knowledge of the details of her death wrapped in tissue-thin paper so easily ripped with too much handling.

Now as my body is wracked with the pain of their attack, I know. I know the terror from which I did not save her. The paper is ripping and spilling all around me as they tug and bruise me with their many hands and teeth. They are fighting and seeking to discover any access to my death when the first shot fires.

One moment, I am looking over my shoulder at what I know will be the first real bite, sealing my fate because when the others smell the blood pouring from the wound it will become a frenzy to further tear me open. His teeth are exposed from behind his shredded lips. His hands press down to firmly secure me in place with his weight upon my shoulders. Like a gag from a rapist, the anticipation of my death locks my throat from the screams swelling within my mind.

I see no flashbacks of cherished memories before me. No white, comforting light of which to ease my pain illuminates now. There are just the teeth of a dead man seeking my throat, while his dinner mates seek their own tender spaces of flesh to dine on. There are just his hands upon me with crushing reality, squeezing my collar- bone in his excitement for a new meal. Just my heart racing with the truth of what is about to happen and I'm watching it all.

His head suddenly rocks sideways with a jerking force so ruthless the left side of his head explodes, coating the pavement behind him with his blood and thicker fragments. He falls limp upon me, covering my upper back as the screams finally free themselves at the sensation. My Angel walks away. She leaves me alone again to face this world now that she must wait for me to join her.

Risen after Risen jerk around me, before falling limp in a helter-skelter pattern amid my screams. I feel strong arms lift me, holding me tight against a warm body and my screams still pour from me behind my closed eyes. Each scream growing rawer until I am nothing but soundless motions.

I can hear my name coming from what seems somewhere far away. Someone is holding my upper body in a rocking motion as hands search my legs and waist. For a moment, my mind tells me that I am under attack again. I want to struggle. I want to fight off these new attackers, but my body refuses to obey. My mind begins to slip under a dark blanket of safety it creates for me. My senses close down to avoid what I am sure will be the first flesh-tearing sensations at any moment. My limbs begin to fall limp, too heavy to support themselves as comforting darkness overtakes me. The Risen are chanting my name with this new attack upon me and in the last conscious moment that I hold on to, I wonder how that can be.

Chapter 16

With one daring sense at a time I wake. My sanity is slowly testing the safety of it. I can feel myself resting on soft fabrics wafting musty smells around me. They wrap me in the warmth created from my own heat. My legs are tender with any movements and throb even with stillness, but otherwise, I feel none of the white-hot searing pain I thought my death would incur.

The confusion encourages me to slowly open my eyes against the bright sunlight. It filters in through the plaid country-style curtains over the small bedroom's windows. I can hear birds singing their many wordless melodies in a clash of who is the loudest somewhere close. The walls are covered in faded white bead board. It climbs the length of the walls, as the only décor upon them, and touches a stenciled border of ivy. Cliché is the flavor of the day.

The hardwood floor is cold with the lack of a summer's sun to warm it. My legs scream in protest at moving, but the cool floor feels soothing beneath my bruised feet. The small daybed is made with a simple sheet set, and other than a small dresser, it is the only furniture in the room. I have no memory of this room. Nor of how I came to be here, sleeping in just my tee shirt and a matching shade of panties. Neither of which I was wearing when the trip started. This worries me more than where I might be.

My legs are various shades of red and purple. My own natural coloring has hardly any space to show through with the many bruises of irregular shapes upon them. Bruises you know will linger for a good amount of time before the sickly yellows and greens start to show through. My shoulders are too tender to move. It allows for only small movements of my neck as I glance around the room. Even those rip gasps of pain from my throat.

My fingertips are raw with thick, meaty scabs covering them. My nails show shattering at the tips from torn, jagged edges left by the cement. Each injury flashes before me like a movie premier showing their starring roles and I am repeatedly a victim again back on the sidewalk. My breath shakes from the memories that engulf me and I am becoming as scab covered as my fingertips with each new ordeal I survive.

The soft hum of male voices drifts from the other side of the room's wall. It drags me from my private hell with my curiosity upon hearing their sounds. The gap in the curtains shows a large wooden porch nestling in a clearing of tall trees. Sunlight is casting through the many shades of fall leaves and the trees' bare branches, causing shadows to dance among the wooden planks with soft breezes. I part the curtains further to gather a better idea of my predicament and I see a sight that brings calm to my soul.

My lighthouse is balancing upon the wooden railing, gazing out into the surrounding forest in front of my window. He is lost in his own memories as his eyes stare at nothing and everything at the same time. He is lost between regrets and wishes. He is without his identifying leather vest, and for once, I can see him as we were before. When we were just a boy and a girl, testing the thin ice of life, praying for it to hold our weight as we prayed to always hold each other's hand.

I remember how afraid I was at the thought of being on his blacked-out motorcycle the first time, and how it made him smile his shy grin. I remember how the first ride turned from the feeling of fear to a feeling of freedom as it roared under us, eating up the highway before us. The smell of the skin of his neck as I rode pressed up against him. The way he would randomly throttle the bike faster just to feel me grab him tighter. The sounds of his male laughter floating back to me in the wind with each of my squeals. I remember our ling of fear to a feeling of freedom as it roared under us, eating up the highway before us. The smell of the skin of his neck as I rode pressed up against him. The way he would randomly throttle the bike faster just to feel me grab him tighter. The sounds of his male laughter floating back to me in the wind with each of my squeals. I remember our late-night chats. We would lean upon my car after I closed the bar on the nights, we were both seeking reasons to avoid heading home. We had become each other's blankets of comfort. The soft fabric of it served to soften the edges of life's hard lessons. We wrapped ourselves in it so tight that we have become the others main source for comfort in this life. Its seams were sewn from the many shared laughs, the heart-felt moments and our stolen glances. The fabric has been wearing thin as of late. The seams are shredding as the threads unravel. I would give anything to have that warm blanket wrapped around me now.

Pulling on my pair of folded jeans on the floor, the fabric feels like sandpaper upon my tender flesh. Gripping anything sends pinpoint of pains through my fingers. At this moment, I am very happy for slip-on boots. I am not happy with their new marks. They seem to be as battered as my flesh, with deep gouges through the leather mimicking my many bruises. The toes are scuffed beyond repair from my desperate sliding along the rough pavement from trying to escape. I am so engrossed in the damage to my boots, and the disappointment it causes, I do not notice the person coming into the room. His deep cologne of leather and stale cigarettes announces him for me.

J.D. rests against the white wooden doorframe, watching me with his soul-seeking eyes. Neither of us says a word to the other for a few moments in mutual silence. His eyes are taking me in as he waits for any female minefields, he fears he will have to navigate. I wait for his anger to whip through the room at my actions in the form of his own male minefield. When nothing explodes between us, a smile slips upon his face, tugging mine out to play.

"Shame about the boots," J.D. says, in the closest thing to a playful voice he has. "Always love a girl in a good pair of boots." He drags the words out, adding extra heat to them.

"Well, seeing as how they are still in one piece, I guess they are still "good" boots," I reply, ignoring his attempt to annoy me. I turn my legs side-to-side to gain a better vantage point of the damage. "I'm sure Aimes will just call them broken in."

"That she will. That she will. What would she call that little stunt you pulled back there?" he asks, watching me now instead of the boots. He is tipping his toes into the water of the real reason he started this conversation.

"Suicidal gifted," I say, smiling my best "look, I'm just a harm- less girl" smile with hopes to save myself from what I feel forming with his question.

He chuckles with a deep laughing vibration. "That would be a good summary. I would call it a massive fuck up. What were you thinking?" The playful tones melt away as his voice lowers to a pitch warning of his disapproval.

"That I had to save Aimes. Other than that, the truck would have been nice to have," I reply with a shrug, meeting his gaze.

I hold no attempt to earn approval from him. I did nothing seeking any rewards, but just the safety of my friend. Therefore, his opinion of the event is meaningless to me. I would do it all again. I may just run sooner next time.

He not only stores the words I offer, but also the body language I hold. J.D. never wastes words. He tells you what he needs you to know only in the moment, leaving you to fill in the rest of the conversation yourself. What you fill in, is up to you. What you do with the filler is what he will be watching. It is a tightrope type of relationship with him and the truth is your only balancing tool of safety.

He lets his silence fill the room with its own weight, waiting to see if I will cave before him. Waiting to see if I will beg for his mercy and understanding to regain any lost good graces with him. He is testing the strength of my resolve for what I have done as a doctor would test one for shock after such an event. Whatever he finds suits him and he nods before giving me his smile again. "Next time you want to go all Zombie Barbie on me, give a guy a heads up. If it wasn't for your banging on those cars, we never would have even looked for you two. It would be a shame to lose your sweet ass. We may just need those balls of steel you are hiding somewhere. Though next time, you might want to pick an automatic if you want Blondie to drive it," he says, waiting for what he has hinted at to settle in.

When I roll my eyes realizing where the plan went wrong, he starts to laugh.

His deep laughter follows him into the dark hallway beyond the room. He moves without a sound, which always amazes me for such a large man. Not even the well-worn wooden floors moan under his steps. They do not want to attract his attention any more than the living do. The darkness absorbs his form as if he is a missing piece of it. It welcomes him home.

I have always thought of him as the Boogeyman. Until now, he was the most mind-wracking fear I have ever met with his icy- cold exterior and the limitless levels of his ruthless destruction. The fact he is now on the "good guy" side of the world shows just how far up the evil shit creek we are and I do not have a paddle strong enough to fight against the current rushing towards me with each hour that slips away.

I make my way slowly through the same hallway with small shuffling steps. I use the wall as a guide being not as comfort- able in the darkness as the one who went ahead of me. My legs are almost a dead weight of pains and aches. It reminds me of Margaret with her swaying pigtails as another memory crashes through me, almost doubling me over. I had come close to having more in common with her today than just my mobility.

The whole place is decorated in a retro country theme with bead board paneling in the various shades of white clichés. The wooden floor creaks under my feet even with the few well-worn runners spaced throughout in some attempt of a color scheme. Windows are covered in various plaids and have been bleached to pastels from years of sunlight. Seeing those shades, I cringe without a conscious effort.

The furniture is sparse. Even to say "bare necessity" would not be an exaggeration of the rooms. It's the same with any personal touches that may give a clue to the owner of this place. There are no mementos. There are no framed faces or events in well-placed spots. There is nothing here to associate J.D. with this place at all, much less any of his personality reflected upon it. No Harley décor or half naked women in ridiculous, uncomfortable poses plastered along the long walls. For a male hunting cabin, it looks more like an old woman's knitting retreat.

There appears to be four bedrooms in which bags have been placed. A wooden ladder bolted to a wall leads up to an open loft style bedroom. I can see the duffels from Lee's gun shop stacked against one of the walls. Various smaller guns are lying out along the loft's edge. I can't help but wonder if that is their idea of a final desperation set up or just boys being boys with their toys. It brings me no comfort to see them already either this prepared or this on edge.

"Hey, Zombie Barbie is up!" Rhett calls out, as I pass the door- way of what opens to a small kitchen and dining room.

"I think I preferred Snow White," I mutter to him, returning his mock smile.

"Trust me when I tell you, Zombie Barbie is way better than the other things they were naming you," Aimes says, coming to stand before me from where they had been sitting playing a random card game.

Aimes and I smile at each other before it all melts into silent tear-filled embraces. We cling to one another in a silent affirmation of our friendship, the survival of today and the freedom of being a girl that allows us to do this.

"I'm so sorry," she whispers over and over again.

I hold her, knowing deep inside she is not just apologizing to me but to herself in her imagined sense of failure. I know because I have done the same thing myself when I am surrounded by true pastels, fallen Angels and the perfumes of deaths that feel like a lifetime ago. I know because I have enough of my own failures to apologize over. I hold her and let us both be okay with them amid a slow whistle from Rhett as his mind takes him to a different type of show; boys will be boys.

Chapter 17

Dinner consisted of canned goods and meats in various colors and shapes I had never seen in any supermarket. At the time, I was so hungry I did not think much of it. Now as I do, my stomach does a warning roll to stop.

The conversation around me ebbs and flows with various mood swings. Each time it flows to a serious note a new tide is inserted to change its course. No one has the strength yet to talk about the day, even as long glances are being cast my way when the swings go south. We are all curious about the shadowed looks the conversations place upon each of our faces, but no one wants to share first. Who would? "Hey, I stabbed a room full of kids today. How was your morning?" is not the most encouraging of starters. Chapel decides to do it anyway. His own soul is bursting with the need of it. I wonder if all religious men are so immune to other's efforts of avoidance of soul bearing or if ours is just super talented at ignoring it.

"I lost them all," he whispers, once again staring at his beer.

His statement brings the room to a hush. Everyone at the table does their best to find something amazing on the walls around us. Everyone, that is, but J.D. He leans back in the chair as it moans in protest, giving Chapel the full weight of his blank stare. If Chapel is going to be strong enough to take the in the protest, giving Chapel the full weight of his blank stare. If Chapel is going to be strong enough to take the journey, then J.D. is going to be strong enough to travel it silently with him. It's like a duet and I think they are both insane for dancing it.

Lawless discovers how interesting the engraved art is on his lighter. Rhett makes an amazing find under his thumbnail and seemingly worried about what it might be, he begins to stare at it with concerning confusion. Marxx is overcome with a sudden urge to wash his plate, and Rhett's plate, and even Lawless' plate if it will take him away from not only the table, but also any involvement in the conversation. Even our lighthearted pixie begins to treat the leftover vegetables on her plate as if they are a scientific discovery of wonders.

I, myself, am curious. Will his be as bad as mine? Will I find some redemption for my sins in his story? Will this finally open the door for all of our ghosts who have been haunting us through- out the day to storm through or are we still too fragile to open the door at all, much less speak of what haunts us in our minds? Chapel starts with a whisper, still seeking comfort from his beer. "It started with the little ones. They complained of feeling bad last night, but other than a small fever they were fine. We sent them to bed. We checked on them a few times before we went to bed ourselves. They were fine, a little warm, but fine. My wife woke earlier than normal. Trina was so sick. Her fever just kept climbing, but she kept refusing to go to the hospital. We would have had to wake the kids and all. You know, a mother's logic being what it is. I left to get her a cool rag. She was right there in the bedroom. I could not have been gone for more than a few minutes. I came back and she was gone. Her body still burning hot, but she was gone." With his eyes shifting side-to-side, he's not seeing us right now. He is reliving his own projections of memories behind those eyes. "I was so confused. Who do you call behind those eyes? "I was so confused. Who do you call and?

I admit to letting your wife die while you were getting her a rag? A simple rag? I just shut off; you know. Tucked the blankets in around her trying to make her more comfortable like I guess," he says shrugging, "and then I just left her. I don't know. I just left her. God forgive me, I just left her and went to sit with the kids." His voice never cracks as the first tear escapes, forging the path down his lined face.

"…and the kids?" I ask, earning a glare from J.D.

Chapel inhales slowly before starting again. "Their little bodies were all contorted in their beds. The sheets were tangled around them something forceful. It's their eyes though, all glazed over, looking right at you that tells you they are gone. I don't remember walking into the room, but I must've. I must've because I remember touching them. Their little bodies were soaked and so stiff. Like soft plastic but still warm. I always thought the dead were supposed to be cold, you know. They were warm. Not as warm as Trina but still… warm," he says. He keeps whispering the word "warm" like a taboo word in church. It's as if the word should hold some damning qualities the rest of us haven't noticed yet. "I just shut their door and sat there in the hallway. I don't remember how long. I don't remember how I got the pistol, either. My wife is dead. My kids are dead. I just wanted to join them. I didn't want to be alone. There I was in the hallway with all our pictures looking at me and I could not imagine being without them. All of those damn pictures. I was just about to pull the trigger when I heard it. It was like something fell in the kids' room. I remember just sitting there. Just listening, when I heard it again. It was the damn door. Something was hitting it. Hitting it hard."

It seems no one is breathing now as we watch Chapel. We know what is coming next. We have seen it. Now we get to hear it.

His hands begin to clench into tight fists before releasing to only repeat the process as he fights for control. He seems to hunch over with his grief as he talks, his shoulders falling inward. He seems to be shrinking as I watch him.

For the first time, I see Chapel broken and brittle before us. I look to J.D. for his reaction and those powerful eyes still set in a blank face hold mine. Like me, he is waiting for the revelations to begin. It makes me wonder what sins of his own he is measuring Chapel's up against.

Chapel's beer is no longer enough comfort. His eyes bore into the wooden table, burning with his grief as he says, "I remember seeing that damn doorknob move. Just a little. It rotated so slow I thought I must have been imagining it until the damn thing did it again. I just sat there, gun still to my head, just sitting there like a damn daydream when the door started to shake. The damn fingers. Their damn fingers were under the door pulling on it. Shaking it. I just sat there, sitting through it all. God forgive me, I just sat there as they tore open their damn fingers pulling so hard against the wood of the door. I called out. Told them stop it. Kay, Ken, you stop it, I said, and they did. They just froze there, but then they started back up again rattling the damn door. They never said a word no matter what I called out. I remember the door opening finally when the knob gave way to their rattling. I think I was almost relieved; you know. The noise stopped but the door just sat there. It doesn't move. It doesn't close. It just sits there and me a grown man too afraid to go look. I am their father and I am too afraid to go look. They were gone. I checked. No heartbeat. Nothing. Gone. Yet here are their damn fingers under the door still. Just sitting. Those tiny little fingers bleeding and torn just sitting there."

I notice how he never says dead. Is the word too final or just impossible to believe? The dead do not put their fingers under the door to escape from a room. To begin with, the dead do not try to even escape a room. At least they didn't until today. Today the dead have a completely new bag of tricks.

"I called out again," Chapel says, still staring at the table as if he is the only person in the room. "Hell, if I know why, but I did. Those fingers slid up the doorframe, never stopping. They just slid right around and there they were. Standing there. Staring right at me like they were as confused to see me, as I was to see them. You know, for a moment, I was so happy to see them there. My kids, you know. My kids. Something just wasn't right, though. Their eyes. It was something about the eyes. Like fisheyes. Dead fisheyes when they cloud over like that. That's what it was like. What they are all like. Why is it always the eyes?" he asks the room, finally looking up to see us as if we hold any answers for him.

He pauses to clear his emotion-clogged throat. Aimes slides him her glass of water, still amazed by her plate. No matter how hard they have been pretending to not be here, at this moment, they are. Each of them is lost in the moment as they ingest every word he says. Only J.D. and I have the strength to be here openly. We both sit, listening to Chapel confess every moment of the memory like a sick version of truth-or-dare between us.

When Chapel starts again, I wish I had called dare instead of asking for more of the truth. "I called out to Kay, my little girl, my sweet girl. It was almost funny really the way their heads cocked slowly at the same time. We used to own a little mutt dog that would do that same thing when it heard something. That cock, you know. It never attacked me though. They did. I swear they did. Came right at me. Still all calm-like and just walked right up to me like they needed a hug or something, but then they attacked me. Those little hands that I have held a thousand times just started to pull on me. They kept trying to bite me. My kids. Fighting me. I didn't want to do it. God forgive me, I didn't want to do it. Those fish-like eyes staring at me from the faces that used to belong to my kids. God forgive me, but I did it. I shot them. One bullet each, I shot them right there in the hallway. In the hallway surrounded by all those damn pictures."

"...and the wife?" J.D. asks, his voice showing no reflections to the story told.

"Didn't take any chances," Chapel says on the matter, as his body begins to shake.

"Till death do you part," J.D. says, as he downs whatever amber liquid was left in his glass, "then to death again."

"It was my old man." Lawless never looks up from his lighter, completely unmoved, when he speaks. If you didn't know his voice, you would never have guessed it was him who spoke.

"He wasn't feeling well. Took him to the doctor just the day before. Viral they said. Gave him some shots, some new vaccine, too. Supposed to help save your life. Make you live longer or something. Irony huh?" he asks, with his words clipping short. His sentences are providing no more than the basic needs of his ideas. That warm voice I have grown so used to is now dull and flat, tired and defeated. "So, all is good. It's just a normal day. I go to get him up and he's just standing there with his back to me. I thought it was just going to be another one of those days when the Alzheimer's really gets a hold of him. I'll go in. Put him back in bed. Turn his T.V. on and wait. He'll wake up. Bitch at me for being in his room and want to know why his breakfast is late. No big deal. I don't even think about it. I put my hand on his shoulder to help him back into bed when he lunges at me," he says, and shrugs before continuing to inspect his lighter. "I'm used to it. He gets combative sometimes. No big deal. I push him off me and normally that's it. This time he came back again. Harder."

Each "no big deal" was accented with a short shrug of his shoulders. The engraving is becoming more interesting now as he brings the lighter up close to his face to examine it when he pauses. He never takes his deep brown eyes off the lighter. It's such a small object for him to use as a shield before such a large monster sneaking up on us.

Something on my face must have shown my concern for him and again it places the full weight of J.D.'s eyes on me. His finger silently taps the glass's rim in his hand with our eyes locked. I know what he is not saying to me. One word from me and Lawless will lose the fragile thread of bravery in the room. I will rob him of his need to release these confessions. I say nothing. Like a priest in a wooden booth, I say nothing to break the spell.

"Chap's right about the eyes. Never thought of fish, but yeah, it works," Lawless says, rubbing his thumb over the igniter. "He kept coming at me. Wouldn't answer to his name. Just kept coming. I hit him. Right in the face. He bounced right back up. His nose was all messed up, but it never even slowed him down. So, I hit him again. I thought of my mom. All those times he hit her. I thought of all the times he hit me." He shrugs, flipping the lighter to spark its flame before shutting it again. "He isn't going to be hitting anyone, anymore."

"I thought my parents were fighting," our pink tinted pixie says as the sharing continues like a round table of revelations. "They did that. A lot. Mom would say something to get him really sparked and it would go back-and-forth until she hit below the belt. Verbally. They never actually hit each other. Mom's words did more damage anyway than any blow she could ever land. She was a peach like that. Dad would storm out and come back hours later always smelling of smoke and that same perfume which always caused him to smile when Mom noticed it. Mom never had a come back to that smile." She smirks at the memory before catching herself. "Anyway, there they were, Dad on top of her, holding her down and choking her. I thought this was it. After all these years, it has finally come to it. I was screaming for him to get off her and he kept telling me to go back to my room. Go upstairs Amelia. Just like when I was a kid and they would start in on each other. Go upstairs, Amelia."

Though I had just had the exact same dinner as she, I could not recognize the vegetative substance on her plate. As she uses it to paint a green abstract of art style patterns, her eyes never focus. Not the way the eyes of everyone around her are now focusing. We stare at the small woman among us with unrestrained sorrow. When Evil dances with a male, it's more bearable than when it chooses such a partner as she.

Aimes tilts her head, staring at whatever masterpiece she sees in her mind before starting again. She says, "She was making these strange sounds and really fighting. She just couldn't reach him no matter how much she struggled. He was just sitting there choking her as if it was the same as reading the Sunday paper. No emotions in him at all. I went and got the little gun Mom kept in her nightstand. I was just going to threaten him, like they show on those shows and the man always backs down. He wouldn't though. Just kept telling me, "It's not what it looks like. Go to your room," over and over. I kept screaming for him to stop and he kept screaming at me to go. I don't know how it happened. It just went off. It was so fast I didn't even understand what had happened at first. He was yelling and then he was down. But it was okay because I was just protecting Mom, so it was okay. Till she started eating him."

Aimes stands from the table, taking her new modern art piece to the sink making Marxx wince with her proximity. Losing her own emotional battle, she still reaches out to comfort Marxx before turning to leave the room. Our gentle pink pixie is broken and retreating.

"He was never hurting Mom. I shot the wrong one," she says, as she leaves the room and there is not a sound following her exit.

Chapter 18

The days at the cabin are mind numbingly uneventful. Up late, Aimes and I giggle under sheet-made forts to cover our flashlight's beam. Some nights our laughter will invigorate the cabin, bringing life back to its many cobwebbed corners. Those nights a telling stomp will come from the loft above us as J.D., like an annoyed father, signals for us to go to sleep. Our giggles turn into full laughter with his annoyance, resulting in our names being shouted by him as he once again becomes the father figure we have made him.

Other nights, Lawless will sneak into our room and we will all snuggle in a dog pile sort of way amid mocking innuendos. It's then when I am wrapped under the night's seclusion and surrounded by the safety of our little world, I am able to find the ghost of the girl I used to know.

We have fallen into a routine here, creating private jokes as we invent a new normal for us. Laughter is free flowing, healing the wounds of our minds. Lawless and I have begun creating stolen moments, searching for comfort in desire-inspired embraces under the full moon and its many stars.

There are no more sessions of the round table at dinner. There are times when the conversation lapses and those who have confessed their sins look to those of us still holding on to ours. We keep neutral faces as if oblivious to what they are looking for in us.

Then there are nights when I swear, I can hear Lilly's laughter. Her small feet dance across the wooden floors of the hallway in a swirl of white hemmed lace nightgown and her blonde hair. Her tiny hands clapping along to a song only she can hear in her joy- filled moment. I watch her and my heart refills with the hope I have lost. She notices me standing there in my silent worship of her and smiles at me with her shining blue eyes.

The room fills with the perfume of her baby shampoo and soap causing me to lose myself in the innocence of her as if she were still with me. She never says a word to me, but her laughter fills conversations with my soul and I forget how to breathe for a moment. I can feel her fragile hand in my own as peace with all that has happened begins to wash over me. I want to stay like this forever, but even as I drown in the joy of it, I know something is wrong.

It starts so slowly. A small spreading of color against her all white floor-length gown begins to take a life of its own. It coats her before dripping to the floor with a heavy sound. Her smile never falters as her gown becomes soaked with the crimson stain. It never falters as her body crumples before me like a porcelain puppet with its strings brutally cut. It never falters as her baby blue eyes lose the light which once so brightly shined in them and it still never falters as I wake screaming, still thinking I am clutching her fragile hand in my own.

Some nights I scream her name. Other nights I just wordlessly scream as the waves wash over me. Every night I stare at my own hand, a hand so empty now.

Aimes is always there to talk me down. Lawless comes in some nights to hold me until I can sleep again. My tears become a lake of regrets upon his shirt as he shelters me in the strength of his arms. I become a small child and I pray every night he will keep the monsters away while the sound of his heartbeat sings me to sleep. To their credit, they never ask what I see when my eyes close. They never question my demons. We just wait until the dawn comes to chase them away.

"Who do you think this place really belongs to?" Aimes asks, from behind the wide-styled sunglasses she swears is the rave of fashion. If bugs are now fashionable, then I guess so.

We are both wrapped in various moth-eaten quilts, trying to build a barrier against the battling weather as we walk through the wooded paths before us. The sun provides the warmth of the last days of fall, but the wind holds winter's vanguard with its chilling touch.

"You mean you don't believe he kept this placed stashed in his pocket the whole time?" Lawless asks, swaying easily under low hanging branches of the trees before us with his normal ease and grace.

He is leading our little trio through the fall-kissed forest surrounding the cabin we now call home. He turns to us with the same mock disbelief we would hold for J.D. before returning to the path. Our feminine laughter floats through the crisp air over the rustle of thick fall leaves under foot, causing him to smile at us.

"You don't like his hunting cabin located in woods seemingly bare of any wildlife?" I ask.

"Maybe her sunglasses scared them all away?" Lawless asks, looking to me with a wink. "I'm sure we can find another bunny foo-foo for dinner if you want, Aimes."

I giggle remembering the ordeal of having to finally inform her of what our meals were consisting of. The fish she was okay with, but once she realized Rhett was serving her rabbit, it was a meltdown of impressive feats making Rhett giggle like a little boy with his teasing. When she began to release the rabbits from Rhett's traps, he was no longer amused.

"Douches, both of you," she says pointing to us both and my memory skips back to a morning long ago before she starts again. "I just mean it's not exactly J.D., a little old lady J.D., maybe, but not our J.D. I mean, come on; he is sleeping under a pastel painting of a barn. Pastel, people! Of a barn!"

We laugh over her punctuation.

"He must have forgotten to grab his pin ups on our way out of town. I guess you think you own the color pink now? Or, is it the barns you want ownership over?" Lawless teases her, tossing a handful of leaves in her direction.

Their ember hues float among her sharp contrast of white blonde and pink streaks, framing her in fall's beauty. She returns her own handful, but he is too fast for her as the trees shield him from her attack. I watch the sun roll over his natural golden skin tone and dark close-cropped hairstyle. His lips hold a soft colored hue of seduction with his teasing smile. He weaves in and out of the trees, taunting her with jests of a girl's aim and strength with his faces to match the insults. He encourages her playful wrath with ease. Her mocking insults match his taunts until they are both using more laughter than words while the forest sky be- comes a ballet of fall's beauty with their mock combat.

I watch it all, selfishly holding my tongue as I refuse to join them. Their joy only reaches my surface and I am envious of their abandonment in it. I am not sure when the numbness crept into my heart and truthfully, it's not even the coldness that scares me the most. What worries me the most is, what if I can never find "me" again?

I am lost in self-absorption when the first pinecone sails past me with a soft whistle. I look to see Aimes covering her face behind folded hands, holding her laughter at bay. Lawless is posed to throw the next cone at me with an exaggerated arch. I cannot stop the smile that slips over my face at his wiggling eyebrows and playful warning smile.

I take a few steps back, pointing at him with the same mock warning as he tells me, "Better run, Hells."

I do.

My feet crash through the branch-bare forest. I can hear two other sets falling in fast behind me as we rush through the paths with the thrill of our game chasing our every step. Her laughter coaxes my own to come play with girl-styled squeals. We slip and slide over the many leaves piled thick along the trail.

I feel Lawless before I see him run past me. He pulls up short, spinning around to corner me and catches me in a giant bear hug. Kicking my feet, I am weightless in the air as we spin. The world tilts past me, lost in a smear of oranges and reds. His strong arms support me and hold me close to his body as we spin. He heals my wounds with this time-stopping memory and our laughter, but time always has to start again. It does for us with a scream.

Her scream is ear shattering. The spinning stops so suddenly we both have to stagger as our equilibrium attempts to catch up. Lawless pulls me instinctively closer to him as his eyes scan for the danger making Aimes scream. Her eyes are cast on something we cannot see from our vantage point. Whatever it is it makes her walk in a sideways pattern to us, too afraid to turn her back on it. Lawless pulls me behind him, kissing my forehead as I pass before he walks to meet Aimes. Each stride pulls the strings of his mood swing from him until his face melts down to one of blank preparation to meet whatever is beyond the trees. He never missteps, leaning down to take the gun from the top of his boot under his loose-fitting jeans in one fluid well-rehearsed motion. The click of the safety reaches my ears with a finalization of the reality of what is about to happen. He reaches her, swinging the gun around in an almost choreographed single dance movement when they pass each other. He never flinches at facing down whatever she is seeing before them.

With Lawless as her shield, she finally gains the courage to turn and run. I reach out to her, but her eyes change from relief to panic as another scream escapes her very pink lips. She is reaching for me, pulling me to her and guiding my steps further sideways to the cabin's path. I don't want to look. I want to stay in my ignorance, but as he begins to squeeze the trigger filling the very forest, which was just our playground with echo after echo, I do.

We had allowed ourselves just one unguarded moment of happiness. We had been lured to an apathetic attitude about our safety with the amount of uneventful days having passed. The days began encasing us with a refusal of admittance to the events happening around us. They allowed us to be untouched by the horrors showing on the small screen of the den with growing details. We were a cocoon of our own making. We were safe, secure and turning into something beautiful with our new little family. Now surrounding us are the consequences of that in the forms of shambling shapes and glazed eyes that are rimmed with hate. Risen of various persona have filled our playground. They trample through our imaginary swings and pretend slides invented to stir childhood glee. They bring us childhood fears as the wind brings us their inhuman eagerness to come play. Some amble to- wards us looking like torn remnants of what they were in life. The missing flesh or limb telling the horror stories of their deaths.

Some bare no marks, and other than their glazed eyes, one would almost think they were still human. If you didn't notice their graceless steps or their ignorance of any harm occurring to them. If you don't see their many layers of stained and torn clothing or hear the sounds coming from somewhere deep inside them being inspired by the sight of us, they look like sleepwalkers. No matter which group you see first, there is no confusion of either group's ambitions.

His gun follows his eyes with a synchronized motion as he slowly walks back to us with one firmly placed step after another. He squeezes the trigger and Risen twitch, falling as he is picking his next target. He is trying to keep the edges from spilling around us while randomly aiming for the center cone of the ones nearest to us. His mouth moves with each squeeze in a silent whisper.

Lawless is counting backwards, keeping track of exactly what is left in the clip. He is keeping track of how long until we need to panic. The more that fall, the more that seem to materialize between trees in a horrific game of "hide and seek." I don't know how many he has killed. I only know it seems to be hopeless, and when I hear him say for us to move, I know it actually is.

Aimes and I run together as our forest takes on a new, darker feeling. The leaves underfoot only hours ago feeling of Fall's glory, now crack like brittle bones. Branches we weaved through before, now claw at our hair and faces, trying to slow us down for their new friends to find us. The wind that brought winter's greetings, now steals the breath from us with its bitterness. Even our once playful Lawless, now randomly stopping to send an echo through the trees, encourages us to move faster and faster until the cabin appears before us. Its occupants spill out toward us with rushed movements hearing our arrival.

They had begun prepping for our arrival when the first echoes reached them. Chapel and J.D. are pulling the last of their motor- cycles around to the back door when we burst through the tree line. My warhorse is lined up with the length of the side windows and its chrome grill gleams like bared teeth to what is coming rapidly behind us. The steps are removed from the porch, leaving a shoulder high gap of space to overcome. Rhett and Marxx are kneeling with outstretched hands, encouraging us to jump.

I slow to allow them to pull Aimes up first. My boots slip on the carpet of leaves under me with my sudden reversal of speed. Lawless steadies me, helping me with jumping into their waiting hands, before he lifts his own body up and onto the porch.

J.D. bars the door after we spill into the small main room. The men take formation, peering through aged curtains and chambering ammo in various dark barrels. Their metallic clicks and the sounds of their sliding barrels somber the room quickly. Chapel stands by the back door. He is keeping watch over what may become our only exit while keeping an eye on our room too for guidance from the oning ammo in various dark barrels. Their metallic clicks and the sounds of their sliding barrels somber the room quickly. Chapel stands by the back door. He is keeping watch over what may become our only exit while keeping an eye on our room too for guidance from the one-man hell has made for these situations.

"We should go. We should just go now!" Chapel shouts from his spot.

"Now just hold on, son. Hold on," J.D. says in his calm voice. "Keep your panties on. We are just gonna' sit tight and see exactly what is out there before we go running off anywhere."

"How many are there?" Rhett asks with a sly grin, finally enjoying the thought of action while chambering the various black handguns placed among the windows.

"A few," Lawless answers, reloading his empty clip as he fights to fill his lungs with air from our run.

Aimes makes a baffled noise with Lawless' response from our spot on the rug where we lay fighting to reclaim our stolen breaths.

Lawless smirks, inserting his clip and chambering his gun. "A couple more than a few," he says and shrugs, smiling at us.

J.D. lets out a sharp whistle, tilting his head towards the front windows to let us know the Risen have arrived. He motions for Aimes and I to turn the lights off in the cabin. Night is creeping its cloak over the area, allowing the perfect backdrop for Evil to make its way to our paradise while we were waiting.

Aimes and I creep through the cabin turning off lights and pulling curtains tight with a deluded sense of covering our movements with such thin material. They never ask us to glance out the windows or to keep watch. Sometimes it is good to be a girl. The first shot is from a high-powered rifle and it seems to rock the cabin with its force. The shadows begin to shift at once with a silent mutual agreement to head in the direction of the noise.

Aimes and I also share a mutual agreement, heading to the side of the cabin where my warhorse is waiting.

There, in what has served us as our room, we find the many bags piled high by the window waiting for us. As the shots begin to ring out in closer patterns, we begin to gently toss the bags into the long bed of the truck. The after-market lining allows us to slide the bags in. We keep our minds busy avoiding the truth of the monsters lurking in every shadow around us. We should have been paying better attention. Like a rabbit walking into one of Rhett's traps, we are about to become someone's idea of dinner.

Chapter 19

Truth does not like to be ignored. She will wait until you think you are safe before creeping up on you with a jagged blade. A blade so sharp, it will slide into your flesh without being noticed at first. The jagged edge will do so much damage, the scar will forever linger to always haunt you with the memory.

Truth takes no prisoners. She has no interest in your longevity. She only wants acknowledgement in the moment to satisfy her bitter needs. Then she will wait while you grow lax, needing reminding yet again of her blade's potent poison.

Our truth comes slipping around the corner in the dark. It is watching, waiting for Aimes to be the most extended from the window, allowing her to be the most vulnerable for his attack. We are on the last of the bags when he decides to strike.

Her white blonde hair shines brightly in the night air as she leans under the opened window, reaching for the next bag I am about to pass to her. I watch with a scream locked on my tongue as she jerks backwards into the darkness beyond the plaid-framed window. Her eyes grow wide with the sudden movement forced upon her. When she turns to see the cause, we both become acquainted with the level of horror these monsters are capable of holding.

The truck is sitting so close to the cabin it leaves only enough space to spare my warhorse its paint. By the warm safe rays of the sun, this made perfect sense. Now with the darkness of night and its cold sightless moon upon us, there is no sense to be had. The male once had dark brown eyes, almost black, but now they are the color of dried mud. The left side of his face is sheered down to the bones from the rough wood of the cabin. Wet gore drips from the raw wound splattering the dark thickness upon his body. His chest is torn and tattered. It exposes layers of glistening tissue like wet meat shining under the silver rays of the moon. He was so eager for her he had forced his body into the thin space between the truck and wooden planks of the cabin's exterior. Since neither side of his captors was willing to give space for his body, the wood took its vengeance on his soft, rotting flesh as the truck kept him pinned against the wall. Standing before us, he is holding on to Aimes with the only arm he is able to raise while his body is weeping its fluid upon the ground.

I cover her mouth with my hand as her lungs fill with air when she sees what is pulling her down. If she screams it will cause the shift of shadows to head our way, possibly blocking our escape. Most likely, it will also cause our deaths once they begin to climb into the window. Her hot breath screams into my hand as she watches the Risen try to tear at her flesh. She continues to frantically tug against his hold. She gains no freedom, but the constant movement causes him to miss his chance to bite into her flesh as his body is wedged too tightly in place to gain any vantage point for the attack.

My hand fumbles with the sheath of my hunting knife. The latch is catching under my fingers, but it is refusing to unclasp. I focus my coordination on keeping Aimes from harm, adding weight to her tug-of-war and I can't fully find the grasp to open the magnetic snap as it defiantly ignores me.

I need to remove my hand from her mouth, and I pray she will instinctively understand the importance for her silence. I need my body separated from her so I can firmly undo the metal snap mocking me in my time of need. As the man's attacks become more desperate, the thought of her coming to harm outweighs the risk of her screaming, even if it does mean my death if she should bring them all down upon us.

I take the risk, and as luck would have it, she does not scream. She continues to fight maniacally against the dripping nightmare holding her. I am able to undo the closure, and firmly grasp the handle of the large gleaming blade while my memories ride my sanity with their pointed teeth and swaying pigtails.

I lean around her to wedge my body against the wooden window, mimicking the mutilated man's predicament. The first splinters bite into my flesh in a warning of what could be if I am not careful. The blade slides into his damp temple with ease. I push until my hand connects with the raw film of his flesh as red pigtails flash before my eyes, but it's not enough. It's not enough for me at all.

The blade slides out with a wet sucking sound, sending shivers of satisfaction through me. Slamming the blade into him again, I let my aching soul find release. Repeatedly I smash my fist against this head as the blade finds its mark again and again. His dark blood sprays against my wrist and arm and not until his body fully goes limp do, I stop. He does not fall so much as melt back- wards against the bed of the truck. His mud-colored eyes still stare at us as his blood seeps to cover them.

We retreat into the room, falling upon its threadbare rug. The sound of our labored breathing fills the darkness around us. My sideburns and I can feel the wetness on my palm thickening as it chills before sliding down and coating my fingers. I swear his eyes are still staring at us, motionless and judging.

How does one really know when the dead can no longer see you? I roll over onto my stomach to completely avoid the mental debate I feel beginning in an attempt to avoid dealing with what I just did. I look over at Aimes, watching her trying to weigh her response.

"Did he bite you?" I ask, as the silence grows too thick.

"No. I don't know how he didn't, but no," she says, with her eyes seeing only the ceiling above her.

"Well, we can dangle you out the window again and let them try harder if you want." A "precious pink" tinted fingernail is raised toward me as her response.

"Can I quote you on that?" I ask her with a smirk, and we laugh. We laugh because we don't want to cry. We laugh because we don't have the energy to fully break down. We laugh because we have to. Sometimes, you just have to.

"You girls taking a nap? Want me to get you some pillows? Rub your feet?" J.D.'s voice is sharp and soft.

His voice holds more power when it's soft like now and we both startle as if he shouted. I sit up, watching his eyes slide over me before following a path to the window. Aimes' arm is coated with her own war paint. She stares at it now with shock as if seeing it for the first time. The large man kneels down beside her small frame to check her over with a blank, passive face. He smears the area with his thumb looking for any wounds. There are only many tender points causing her to wince, which will surely bruise should we live to see morning, under his examination.

He nods, satisfying his concerns with his findings, and still wordlessly, he walks to the window to stare at the corpse against the truck with its muddy eyes for a few moments. Grasping the handles of the last bag, he throws it into the bed, aiming at the dead male's desecrated body. He manages to break the neck with a brutal snap from the force of his anger and the heavy bag. Now those eyes stare at the heavens and I wonder if it is as curious where God is lately, or if those thoughts are left for only us to endure.

"Get ready. When we bring the bikes around, you two exit this window and get in that truck of yours," he says, as he exits from the room. Once again, I am happy I am on this side of the line of J.D.'s world. "Oh, and Barbie, I wouldn't trust the driving to our girl here. We're kind of in a hurry and don't have the time to track your asses down again." His chuckle carries him into the deep darkness of the hallway where creatures such as he is the most comfortable.

I glare at her and she gives me her bashful shrug at the memory while the lights in the front of the cabin are coming on. The tele- vision begins to blare random noise as they carry it to the front windows. They are trying to create the biggest distraction they can, coaxing the Risen to the front of the cabin from where the noise and light stream. It finally sets in for us we are truly abandoning the only safe place we have had for weeks, our private haven in a world gone to hell.

Like teens in a prolonged sleepover, we glance around the room we are now leaving with remorse. What was once just an attempt to bend the rules of our small town by forming their little bar- based club has now become a new family for those of us under this rusting tin roof. We had tricked ourselves into the hope of this being our new future as we held hopes of it becoming our new home. Truth so hates to be ignored and now the monsters we had let slip away have returned for us.

We lay here in silence, listening to the various sounds inside the cabin as they prepare for our grand exit. We are trying our best to ignore the many sounds from outside the cabin as our imaginations are forming images to match. We hold the bravado of small children at night wondering what the thing in the closet must look like no matter how many times our parents tell us we are perfectly safe. Every child left by now knows no one may ever be perfectly safe again. We just don't know why the monsters made it out of so many closets at once.

I grow restless waiting for the men. We should already be in the truck when they come around. It makes no sense to me to be risking our exposure over their loud engine noises as we crawl around in the dark. The truck would make a better path for them to follow behind than allowing them to ride through the center of whatever is out there waiting for us.

If they are hoping the noise will pull the Risen away from the roads, it may not be the best idea. I still remember the way the demonic dolls watched Conroy and me. The way they waited for us. They are not mindless husks, but pure predators behind those eyes that think, watch and wait.

"I don't know what you are thinking of, but no," Aimes says, watching my forehead crease.

"I am thinking we need to be in the truck before they come for us so we do not end up playing pass the pixie again," I say, and we launch into our rapid way of answering the other.

"I hear it's a totally overrated game." "Certainly not a crowd pleaser."

"You are going to make us do this, aren't you?"

"Nope, you can sit here and wait." I stand as my side protests the stretching and say, "I am tired of the kid gloves."

"You know if I sit here now and wait you pretty much just called me a wimp?"

"I was thinking chicken, but if wimp makes you feel better…" "No, being thought of as food, yet again, brings me the best

sense of comfort ever," she sarcastically says.

"I think you are more of a snack. A whole meal is a lot of pressure for that small body of yours."

"Well, we can't all be a four-course like you."

She dodges the pillow I throw at her with an exaggeration of the accomplishment.

"Come on, Bok Bok," I say to her, as she makes playful chicken noises as she follows behind me to the window, and I pray Truth has had her fill with us for just a few moments.

The worst part about sticking your head around something is the fact you are about to stick your head around something. Your mind's eye sees a thousand dangers just waiting for you. Each one of the dangers pictured for you is worse than the one before it. They are hunching over waiting with whispers barely containing their glee for you to do something stupid. Like for you to stick your head out for them.

For a moment, I debate about putting Aimes' head out first if it would stop the noises. My thoughts must have shown in my eyes as her sounds are reduced to covered giggles as stress and fear make her nervous.

The night is oil black. The trees, even with their leafless arms, seem to cover the area in thick shadows. My eyes strain for any movements that would signal danger around us, but they see nothing. Now, to only find the courage to climb out past the broken body sitting beside me. It all sounds so easy in my head, but my own body refuses to make the first move. It always sounds so easy in my head.

"Do you need a push?" she whispers behind me, and I jump, hitting my head on the raised window.

We knew it was going to happen to one of us. A raised window waiting with two frazzled girls? The Fates were stacked against us from the start. Lucky me. I glare at her again and she mouths the word, "sorry". Unfortunately, her giggles do not convey the best of sincerity for the matter.

The window of the cabin is only half the size of most modern bedroom windows. My upper body fills most of the space as I slide out using the truck for extra leverage to pull against. The further out my torso slides past the Risen, the more images begin to play in my head of his sudden reanimation. Surely, he has al- ready used his one free horror style pass of coming back to life. It would just be cruel if they were to have a pass for each form of "life." Whatever Gods are still watching over us could not be that perverse. His glazed eyes do not encourage me to dare them. The exit from the cabin was much more graceful in my mind than the actual belly flop into the bed it results in, bringing more giggles from behind me. Like a beast, the truck does not budge as I help Aimes through the same small window. Her eyes are staring at her near-death experience resting so close to us as she passes it, making her limp and clumsy. I would pay money to see the body twitch right now. I never claimed to be a nice person.

The truck door opens without so much as a sound, exposing the wide bench seat. Her keys gleam in the ignition, sending a silent hint letting us know that even she is ready to be done with this place. The first headlight sweeps around the back of the cabin as Aimes and I slide into this new metal safety net of mine.

Roar after roar of engines fires the yard to life. My heart begins to accelerate, not knowing what is ahead of us in the night's thick darkness. I begin to shake with the fear of not knowing if our escape will really be our salvation, or our tragedy, or if I just need to keep my panties on like J.D. suggested to Chapel.

My warhorse starts with the same deep roar, daring the bikes to outdo her. J.D. motions for me to take the lead of the charge into the dark wooded path after the duffels from Lee's are dumped into the bed with the bags from our room. I guess even the Boogeyman some- times is afraid to be the first to step into the dark. The thought sneaks a smile onto my face even in the middle of these circumstances.

J.D. is not as fear resilient as I had always thought him to be. The man I thought was steel-lined is now unable to meet my stare with the private knowledge we have shared between us. Our rock has just as many ghosts as we do who walk with him daily. Has his blood-painted past finally caught up to him? With Death as our new consort, does he finally fear the payment due?

His grimace shows how angry he is at letting his walls slip before me. His eyes dare me to question our new understanding of one another, but I do not need to ask him anything. I have already seen the truth.

The very thing he is now afraid to do, I have already done before. I have faced these hell-tainted demons already on my own more times than my sanity will admit. I have already found myself in harm's way to save the ones I love. I have run with hell at my heels and I am about to do it again. He no longer holds the power over me I have so easily given him all these years. I tell him so with my smile as I rev the truck into our exit with my own dare to him.

Only once we hit what is left of the tire-rutted road do I look behind me. Our paradise is crawling with dark masses and shapes. They have used each other as a ladder to climb upon the tall porch. Hands slam against the windows, silhouetted by the many glaring lights beyond them. The ancient glass is already be- ginning to give against their assaults with spider webs of circles. I wonder if they will ignore the sharp edges of the glass, they must slide through to gain entrance, or will their hunger-forced animation desist once they find the place empty of human life. Will our perfume of flesh linger for them long after our exit? What does the Devil do when one once again cheats him of his prize?

The woods are filled with their waiting eyes before us. They stand motionless until alerted to our passing. Their eyes always find us moments before their bodies awake, resulting in a spine-chilling feeling of their stares. Their gaze is catching the light from my headlights in reflections that project an eerie glow. I push the truck to speeds unsafe for such a winding dirt road at the sight of so many of them staring at us. Their stained clothing, and decaying forms, brings the night alive with their spectral images.

The large tires bounce over, what I pray to be, ruts in the well- worn path below us, but I don't look to see. The steering wheel fights to jerk free from my grip to further capitalize upon the known risks I am taking.

My job is to clear the path for our family behind us. My panic sets in under the pressure of holding the risk of losing all of them to the monsters who have already taken one family from me. I am achingly exhausted from the many failures I already hold guarded behind my high walls. I have no more mortar to build the bricks any higher shall I fail tonight.

They ride, almost huddling close together, avoiding any unneeded space. Their level of skill and ease with their motorcycles shows as I press them hard to keep up over the rutted and slick, leaf-covered path. Only Rhett has a sense of enjoyment with all of this.

He calls out to the hidden death threats the forest is trying to keep veiled, allowing them to sneak up on us. I can almost see a smile on those lips as his "come what may" thrill-seeking side is finally finding a world in which to thrive. I cannot hear the words he is yelling at the desperate attempts the Risen take to reach them, but whatever he is shouting, it brings pure death-daring male smiles to those around him.

That is to all of them except Chapel. He is stone-faced in our hell-themed amusement park roller coaster of an escape.

J.D. is using his blinkers to tell me which way to follow the path as I try to keep my eyes on him and the path before us. His headlights tell me when to speed up with a flash. We have no signal for slowing down, not that I would.

Luckily for us, by the time the Risen have awoken to us we are zooming past in a leaf-covered cloud. Even at such speeds, this ride of terror seems to take forever. My arms are starting to ache from fighting the truck's natural responses and I can only imagine what the motorcycles are doing to their riders' bodies. Instinctively, I glance to the rearview mirror and count the men behind me with a prayer on my lips.

"There! There!" Aimes screams, pointing ahead on the path.

Glorious pavement shines like a holy river of salvation ahead to our right, and on cue, I see the blinker flash in the darkness.   I force the truck harder at the sight of our freedom. Her engine roars into the night like a beast announcing its victory and her call is returned behind me in an answering chorus.

I don't know if I am happier to see the pavement, or to feel it when the large tires grip and propel us forward. I begin to ease off the gas for the first time since the trip began, allowing them to come around me. J.D. flies around us, giving a nod before leaning his bike into the space in front of us. Lawless comes from the other side, giving a smirk and one-by-one they file past until the leader is now the follower.

"Hey, want me to drive?" Aimes asks, breaking the tension and it is my turn to give her a single finger answer.

"Can I quote you on that?" she asks, repeating me from earlier and her joyous laughter fills the truck as I settle into what I am sure will be a long drive.

Chapter 20

"Home sweet home," Aimes says, as she claims a spot in the back of the abandoned Welcome Center. Her voice carries the exhaustion the rest of us are feeling.

The glass doors had been nailed shut with various scraps of plywood. Litter floated along the night's breeze in the parking lot where empty cars stood parked, and abandoned with no signs of their owners around. Once again, life is a snapshot of time. It was these clues that made J.D. assume it would be safe for us to crash here. Even though he made Aimes and I stand in the shelter of the shadows of my truck while the men soundlessly secured the room. We have driven for what mentally feels like hours. My numb legs judge it to be days. Rhett's crude joke as he had dismounted his Harley let me know the men are feeling the same way by their laughter.

The building is an open floor plan, making it well suited to allow for the ease of human traffic once gathering within these walls. The layout leaves plenty of space for the bikes to be brought in along the wall that once boasted the many reasons to stay in this town with glossy postcards and brochures. Their head- lights watch us like sentinels of darker times with the blacked- out frames aligned in riding formation. My truck covered in dust from the dirt road blends with the other deserted cars forever left between the diagonal white lines.

The only other room connected to this one is what once served as an office for the staff. It's secluded behind the service desk where smiling attendants once stood to greet people, and answer questions about directions or nearby attractions. The only door is the one we came through, making it easy to spot anyone, or anything, trying to come in. Watching us sleep is most likely the only thing anyone on guard will do tonight. It's not an altogether unwelcoming thought.

Lawless has haphazardly reaffixed the wood we took down to gain our access, attempting to hide any clues to any changes we have made. The butane lanterns cast only the faintest of glows and provide just enough light to ease the earlier visions from our minds. They form an almost night-light effect for grownups.

"Sleep sweet sleep," Rhett returns with Aimes' chant, and it is decided Marxx will take the first watch.

The soft sounds of rustling fabrics float through the space as we prepare to rest our aching bodies and overstressed minds. Sleeping bags are unfolded and zippers slide along metallic teeth giving the illusion of security when the fabric shell closes around the occupant inside. I prefer to leave mine undone, minus the small amount needed to keep it held together. My blade, with its disobedient sheath, slips under my pillow for security. With how life is churning, it's becoming more soothing than any teddy bear I have ever owned.

I am grateful for my body's fatigue in hopes it will win over my mind's need for the nightly terror-filled blue eyes and golden hair it shows me. As my eyes begin the losing battle of staying open, I watch J.D., Marxx and Lawless sit upon the bolted couches huddled in discussion with Rhett already snoring in his sleeping bag. Chapel sits in a far corner, holding his head as he prepares to battle his nightly demons of sleep. Lawless holds my gaze with his warm, brown eyes helping me cave to my body's demands. I cannot help but to think how familiar this all feels as I drift off to sleep.

My body tenses as my senses awaken before my brain does, signaling some unseen danger near me. Reflexively, I reach under my pillow even before my eyes open, grasping for the blade to swing at what my body screams is behind me. A strong hand covers mine and a familiar voice settles my racing heart.

"Shhhhh," he whispers, coaxing me back to sleep while his strong arms wrap around me, pulling me close to him.

I am drowning in the scent of his skin and I welcome the decent. My body betrays me by molding into his frame, enjoying his heat and the comfort he offers me. We adjust in our perfected sleeping position, giving each other as much as we take.

I was wrong about the blade being the best teddy bear to date. Lawless holding me close has claimed that title as his body melts to mine, luring us both into the seduction of sleep.

I wake to the sound of muffled voices and male bodies peering out between the plywood boards. Aimes motions for me to stay silent as she crawls to me while I fight to drag myself from sleep. Something bad is happening on the other side of those boards.

Something that is making even J.D. anxious, as his fist clenches and releases with the knowledge of it. I can see Lawless' jaw muscles clench as his eyes move, following the hidden action.

Chapel breaks first. He turns from the scene, taking himself to the couches to bury his head in his hands. Aimes and I watch all their reactions until my curiosity gets the better of me. I will once again wish I had better control of that. How many lives does a cat have after all?

The Welcome Center was designed with all your traveling needs in mind, just as the overly cheerful billboard reads. Apparently, they too did not foresee just how fast our needs would be changing with their giant, smiling family advertisement.

Other than the building we are hiding in now, there is also a small convenience store/restaurant combination and another building holding restrooms across the shared parking lot. Once the rich green landscape, now fall-covered, wrapped around the place for weary drivers to walk along and children to burn off pent-up energy to their family's road weary relief.

Aimes and I had run along these spaces last night, screaming with glee as Rhett chased us along the paths. We chased fireflies, sparkling like stars in the attempts to remove the images burned into our minds before being brave enough to try to sleep. Outside of the once well-lit restrooms stand various vending machines that still after all these weeks hold a wide variety of salty, satisfying cravings.

Rhett and Lawless had happily discovered these, returning them to a cheerful state and their mood was contagious. After such a long night, it had felt good to be surrounded by male laughter and their rough jokes again. As a group, we had decided last night we would wait until daylight to explore the other building for any more hidden treasures. No one wanted to break the spell we were under allowing us this rare gift of peace. Now it seems others had the same idea, but peace was not their gift.

A blue minivan is slowly becoming overrun with Risen as they rock the vehicle with their strength and sheer number, treating it as a mere child's toy. Randomly an arm will extend from the driver's side window to stab at a body, but even as it falls another takes its space. A smaller clump of Risen have huddled over some- thing a few spaces away from the van. The red slickness pooling around it catches the sun's light. The way they kneel, the hidden horrors of my mind know all too well what has happened and what they are doing. Suddenly, I have completely forgotten my morning hunger as my empty stomach clenches.

Small movements from inside the store's windows thankfully steal my attention from the massacre. A man randomly comes into view from the other side of the windows. His wide eyes are panic, and pain rimmed as he watches the parking lot. Sometimes a woman, whose red hair is hard to miss even from this distance, will share the same look as she joins him in the space between the walls before ducking from view. Their story unfolds as we watch from our vantage point.

This group had come to find their own supplies, lured by the hopes of survival from which we all cling. They had left the driver in the van as a look out while the other three had gone inside. Something went wrong with their exit plan though. Now one lies dead, blocking the path to freedom for the other two. It's a twist of bitter agony to lose someone you care for and the loss being the very thing keeping you from escaping the same fate. They are now stuck in a prison of their own making. Their wardens are holding a death sentence for them.

The van is now a layer plus deep in Risen. The arm no longer risks exposure with the pointless attempts of preservation. There seems to be some communication between the two sets as both the male and the female appear in the window wearing the same frantic fear from something, we are unable to see from our room. The van inches forward with jerking motions and the revving of its engine, trying to push through the rotting mob around it. It is slow progress until the driver grows either braver or more desperate, pushing a path using the pure force of the van's hood to nudge his way out. Some of the Risen fall under the tires' path becoming a red ruin as the wave follows the moving target out onto the highway. The van, with its Pied Piper appearance, rushes from the Welcome Center parking lot with tires screaming from the escape.

"He left them?" Aimes whispers, being subconsciously fearful of alerting the remaining Risen feasting upon the fallen friend of those across from us.

"What did you want him to do? They are behind walls and he was a carrot on a stick. He probably just went for help," Rhett observes with a shrug.

This whole time he has been snacking on whatever vendor goodies we have stashed while watching the scene outside as if it was no more than birds and squirrels fighting for trees in the spring. Sometimes his ability to detach from the world's horrors worries me. Other times I am just grateful someone here is strong enough to mentally accept it all.

Something Rhett has said has caught J.D.'s distracted attention. His cold eyes slowly come to rest on Rhett, causing the other man to look affected with their weight. Once again, the men share some private code of eye contact and it stirs them to action. Both Rhett, J.D. and Chapel begin checking their ammo with determination of discovery as Marxx and Lawless pull long dark barrels from the duffels with haste.

"Are we going to go save them?" Aimes asks with a child-like hope.

"No, Sweetheart. That's not the plan," Marxx gravel voice answers gently. His voice holds the same kid gloves tone that Aimes invokes in the men around us.

"So then, what is all this?" she asks him weakly as she and I watch their actions.

"Protection," he answers her, never being brave enough to meet her eyes.

Now I understand. The ones trapped hold the thought of help with prayer. We are holding the thought of help with preparation. The first scream shatters the feigned calm we are all draping across our minds. Marxx and Lawless make no movement to ac- knowledge the sound. Only their cringe with each rising decibel shows they are aware of anything other than their chore at hand. Chapel and I rush back to the door being the only ones willing to watch through the plywood peek-a-boo at what is about to happen across the lot. J.D and Rhett turn their backs to become deeply absorbed in a discussion over the best plans to defend against the invisible attackers and Aimes sinks deeper into her bag as she pulls it over her head to block the screams. I wonder which of their refusals to look is from hardness or weakness.

The Risen have become disinterested in the body they have left exposed and violated under the sun. If not for the basic form of it, it would be hard to say it had been human at some point. They have left nothing to mark any clues of the person's once upon a time humanity. It's now nothing more than so much red meat and broken bones, laid bare for all to see with no shame or afterthought.

The Risen slam their crimson-coated limbs against the protective glass of the storefront. The smiling vinyl faces who were once put there to encourage your patronage and dollars spent are slowly becoming gore-covered with each moment passing. There are no smiling faces beyond the glass though. Only wide eyes and open mouths shouting orders or pleas for suggestions. With their lack of enthusiasm, I am guessing there is not much of either to be had as the glass starts the first pebble-like effect under the trauma of so much force.

"They are gonna get in," Chapel whispers with a realization of what we are about to watch.

"Not our problem," J.D. says in an attempt to remove any confusion over our part in what we are watching unfold.

He expects us to all sit in here. That is his decision, his call. We can either watch or not, in that he holds no judgment, but we are not to help them.

"You can't seriously mean that?" Chapel's voice is still razor thin. It barely cuts the tension of the room with its reservations for asking a question to which we all already know the truth.

"Look," J.D. says, "I would enjoy being your idea of some decent guy, but the truth is, I'm not. Not ever gonna be good enough for you, or even all those like you. All I am is a man. Just smoke and mirrors for whatever I need to do to get us through each day. Today, today we stay in here with our own. Now, take that pretty little golden trinket of death off your neck allowing you to so easily place yourself above the rest of the world and man up or shut up. I don't care which one, but I don't have time to babysit your fragile sense of right or wrong today."

J.D. has walked straight to the other man to stare him down while explaining his point of view on the matter at hand. The room fills with frozen forms as we watch the two men in their silent duel of wills. Chapel breaks the stare first under the heated anger of J.D.'s gaze before returning to keep watch. With that simple disconnect, the room begins to fill again with oblivious activities as we all try to avoid the same fate. Daddy is on a rampage. That is, all but me. My mind wanders back to our escape yesterday and the fear I saw in J.D.'s eyes. I wonder how much of this decision is truly about keeping with our own. Is this now an attempt to prove that he can, in fact, keep us safe or is it just another attempt to cover his own failures with the power he holds over our small group? He feels my gaze upon him and turns slowly to face me.

"Something you want to add here, Barbie?" J.D. asks me, in a blatant dare to voice the thoughts he can read upon my face.

"No. I am sure you have your reasons for making us sit in here. Do you want us to just cover our ears when the screaming really starts or sing a round of "Kumbaya"?" My voice is a neutral friendly tone as I ask my questions. My words are not.

He closes the space between us with three steps of anger at my rebuttal. You do not talk back to the monsters. You bow your head and refuse to meet their eyes for the fear they will cause you. He now knows I no longer fear him, stripping him of his hold over me.

We stand a breath between us as he stares at me finally, really seeing what is behind my eyes. I have tasted death and J.D. does not hold the same metallic taste in my mouth with his presence anymore. His eyes roam my face trying to read my thoughts, looking for any clue it may give him. I keep my face blank, waiting for his next move.

The room grows thick with their anticipation of our standoff. The men are torn between their biological DNA to protect me, a girl, and knowing the fact any harm coming to me will be from the man they each obey without question. They fidget with their mental debates of what they should do.

Marxx holds a hand on Lawless' arm, preparing for what will happen depending on the path J.D. decides to take. Aimes stands watching the whole room. She is taking mental notes, storing them in her own chamber of secrets for later use.

J.D. leans in so close I can feel the heat from his body that hovers over mine. I can feel his hot breath at my ear when he whispers to me, "You best keep those ideas of yours in check, Helena. I'll mourn at your grave, but I will bury you just the same."

I feel my heart skip at his calmness, letting me know he is holding no bluff between us. My stomach drops as he places a soft kiss upon my temple right above the ear, he was whispering in.

"Why don't you start a round of "Kumbaya"? Been a spell since you blessed us with that soft voice of yours in something other than screams," he says with a taunting tone as he turns from me. To the room, it is a teasing jest. To J.D. and me, it is a further illustration upon his whispered promise, and something clicks in the eyes of Chapel as he watches J.D. leave my side.

Chapter 21

We return to our roles as we prepare for any possible danger from an outside group. We know what the Risen hold for us. They have one thought process to them. People are a different volume of threats. Risen may kill us. People will destroy us.

Chapel and I watch as the red-haired woman begins to roll empty racks in front of the doors across the parking lot. We both know the flimsy metal on those thin wheels will do nothing to brace the glass doors as the Risen begin their entrance into the building. We also both know sometimes it's better to try any- thing versus just sitting and waiting for Death to come. Any minute stalled could give one last chance of hope for just one more moment of life. Something most of us took for granted before this all started.

Each pitch of her scream causes another memory to dance through my mind. A past life feeling of horrors is swirling together with her tempo of dread. The memories dance faster and faster in my mind, flowing from one scene to another when I stood by and watched my Angels die as I am watching this woman stare at her death now.

I was unable to stop it then. I was not prepared for the world to tilt the way it did, tossing us all around with the action of it. I was not prepared for Evil to jump forth from what we only knew as pages of books or shows on our televisions. Yet, it has. Evil is once again in front of me, preparing for another round and this time I will not just watch.

Chapel stands beside me, still watching it all unfold. His mouth moves in what I imagine to be silent prayers. If it's for our souls or theirs is the only question lingering between us. His gun hangs lose at his side. Its holster is unfastened, and its metal clasp is winking at me. His head turns to me slowly with his mouth still silently echoing the prayers in his head. I lower my eyes slowly to his chest, taking his eyes with mine. We stand there, his mouth still moving silently as we stare at one another in our private moment of time.

He nods and adjusts his torso, unblocking me from the gun with its flirtatious clasp. His eyes never leave mine as I wrap my hand around it, lifting it and fulfilling its taunts with an almost seduction-like satisfaction. The cold metal is heavy in my hand, taking me by surprise with its weight. The world sinks down to just the face in front of me with his silent prayers. As I realize what I have set into motion, I hope those prayers are for me.

I hear him remove the wooden barrier we have been hiding behind. I hear the shouts rain down upon us, colored with their confusion and anger. I feel his hand on my shoulder squeezing me with encouragement, and yet his grasp coats me with anger at his weakness. The anger fuels my determination and I slide through our glass door with the sun watching me yet again. This time it has no heat. There is only coldness around me as if Death has already taken a seat to watch the show.

The first pull of the trigger snaps my hand back with the recoil, missing the target of the woman's body in front of me. My shot lands further up in the pile, staggering the wrong one with the blow. His shoulder is forced forward nudging the body in front of him with a domino effect of accidental merit. They both freeze in the Risen's form of awareness when something has changed around them. One by one, they all take on the sudden lack of movement. It's more frightening to watch than their attacks because I know their focus is about to become me. My heart gains speed with every extended second, they mutely stand there.

Shoulder by shoulder they turn to stare at me as they wait for their bodies to move in the new direction. Glazed eyes become alive again as I come into view for them, animating their limp bodies with renewed hate and hunger. The torn and rotting mass before me moves as one with their new hunt. Sounds of their stalking stir my own body with renewal and I lift the gun again. My aim goes wide, hitting only shoulders, chests and the glass behind them. It only staggers the ones I do hit as their bodies react to the puncturing, but their minds never acknowledge the wounds. They cannot feel what is already dead. Only their brains are still alive in some inhuman fashion and that's the target I must find.

I exhale as the gap between us shrinks with each of my misses. They are in no hurry to reach me. What is left of their minds somehow has figured out I am holding something threatening to them. Watching them, I am once again reminded these are not the ones who were made to fill nightmares on wide-screen movies. No, these are walking nightmares of their own making.

They are plotting the best path to me, separating into small groups to take me down. They divide before me, giving me more targets to worry about as each group assumes a different speed towards me. To focus on only one side will be my undoing from the other side. They drag my attention to each section with their sounds only for another group to start their own distractions, causing my shots to go wide in my panic. They are attempting to mentally tear me apart, reducing my threat to them before they can tear into my flesh.

They stalk towards me, waiting until the gap is small enough to rush me in their perfected killing style. I have seen them hunt before and I force the images to stay buried as Lilly's laughter floats down the halls of my mind. My hands twitch with the feather soft memory of her gentle fingers. I inhale the scent of her baby shampoo and calm washes over me in a welcoming, numbing fashion. This time as I take aim, I can feel the slow draw of the metal trigger. The recoil has no jolting scorn. The target crumbles finally, fully broken upon the ground.

With each crumbling form I walk forward to meet them, filled with a new determination. The gap slowly folds around me, causing them to finally rush forward, removing all hunting skills with their fierce intentions. I answer each teeth-bared snarl with a shot from Chapel's gun and their heads snap back, bowing them backwards.

I can see the store now through the clearing I am slowly forming as I drop one body after another. The doors are open and the two from before are now joined with another male. They stand watching with mixed waves of emotions upon their faces. Crimson gore slinks its way down the smiling vinyl faces around the open doors. It frames them with a carnivorous mouth of fore- shadowing should I fall.

I stand my ground, aiming at each of the Risen before me. The perfume of my humanity fills them with a new lust-filled frenzy. Their vocal excitement escalates their hunger, driving each of them deeper into desperation to reach me with their flesh-torn limbs and skeletal fingers. I stand against an army of rotting demons and I wonder if my army is still watching. Is J.D. watching me with hopes of having his threat carried out for him? Will he still mourn?

Chapel's clip snaps empty and I still fire twice more before I come to realize what the sound means. I reach for my knife and find the holster missing from my side. My mind flashes a picture of it still under the pillow I was resting on just a few moments ago safe in Lawless' arms. How has the morning gone so wrong so fast?

There are still five Risen left before me. They are frozen in the way only the dead could hold such poses. Their minds are searching to find the change in the situation once again. Only their eyes move as they mentally assess me. The one closest to me seems to grin as he reaches the conclusion of how vulnerable I am before the others do. It causes his dull eyes to slowly brighten with the dawning of it.

I am transfixed by the changes melting over him before me. The calmness, which filled me moments ago with determination, evaporates watching him. Like a child with a water gun, I continue to dry fire Chapel's gun in his direction. Each of the empty clicks is spreading his wide grin into a snarl.

I know there is movement behind me, not from my own aware-ness of it, but because of his eyes. They were once trained on me, but now they are watching something else. They dull again making his face slack as his brain once again seeks to figure out what is happening behind me.

Risen think and react, but it makes them slow. It's the only exposing weakness I have discovered, as they stand confused for a few pauses in time trying to interpret their prey. With their minds so engaged in the situation, their bodies seem unable to move. Just their eyes are watching, gathering and plotting a new way to kill you.

His eyes follow something coming up behind me along the ground. With the rate of his eyes, I know it is coming fast and   I instinctively look. The sun reflects off the metal blade sliding towards me. The metal is hissing along the sidewalk with its progress towards me like a snake warning those around it of the danger. My knife is coming home.

Over my shoulder, I see Aimes standing outside our Center   as hands wrestle Lawless back inside. He is fighting to be free   of them and pleading with me to come back to him. Kneeling to grasp my old teddy bear, I smile into those pleading brown eyes of my current one. Our eyes lock, draining him of his purpose. He knows I must see this through. My stubbornness, the very thing he once loved about me, is now coming between us. I only hope he can forgive me. Aimes screams my name, bringing me back to myself. I realize too late the mistake I have made. I have turned my back on Death and the pause is over.

Pulling my body in tight, I wait with some mentally stored basic knowledge of self-defense. His hands grab me, forcing me still for his attack and I wait even as screams come from all around me. I watch our shadows slowly merge into one as he lowers his mouth to my flesh and I still wait as my heartbeat fills my ears with its pattern. I hear his snarl so close to my face the scent of his breath expels all air from my lungs and still I wait despite my body joining in with the screams around me.

Lilly's laughter encompasses me again. It helps to block out the world around me as I focus on the sound. Time slows down, dragging the rate of his attack with it. The stench of his rotting breath is heavier. The sounds at my ear, even the caress of the wind slows as I finally begin my own hunt.

My left arm swings up, locked at the elbow to take the shock of the attack. It blocks his reach for my neck as it collides with his face, tilting it sideways. My right arm follows the gravity of the attack, coming down on his tilted face. The blade slides with snapping sounds into the space between his temple and eye, pulling me around with the force of his fall. I stare at the man crumpled next to me before removing the blade with a wet, sucking sound. Her baby soft laughter dances around me and I wonder, for my own pause in time, if I am finally losing my mind. A part of me truly hopes so because I still have four more to go.

I give no time for my body to reconsider my course of actions. If I stop to think about what I am marching up to, I will lose all confidence in myself with my brutal truths. The blade drips black crimson drops with every step I take like my personal drummer for this battle.

The female Risen before me has been turned longer than the male. Her face has melted down to cling to her sharp cheekbones. The skin around her eyes is yellowed and almost bruised-like in coloring. Her lips are chapped and torn, shredding the tender flesh around them. Her hair is cut short and matted, making it limp and clinging to her face. It further emphasizes the decay of her features.

Her arms reach for me, seeking a target for her never-ending hunger. It has become the only purpose left to her. I slide in between those deceptively weak arms of hers, keeping her body away from me with my own. I thrust the blade into her face forcing it to its hilt. Bracing against her fall, I let her slide off the blade with gravity's help. Her death coats the blade with more crimson material for the drummer to use. Three more.

The next to reach me was once a female teen or young twenty-something. She is dressed in a tragic emo-style. It now mocks her walking death with its black fishnets and skull decorated dress. Her long blonde hair is a sharp contrast to the image she tried so hard to portray in life. Even with the added bright colors, now a stark contrast to the faded fabrics of her dress, she still never really was able to grasp the concept.

The flesh of her left shoulder is shredded and torn, exposing bone and wetter objects for the flies to sample. The injury makes it slower than the right arm and I use that side as my opening.

I never pause in my step, but reach up with such false bravery and skill to plant the blade in my right hand into her temple. Her slower, damaged arm allows me to go untouched even as she falls before me, leaving only two more.

The blade is slick now and slides around in my hand. The grip was never meant to be this coated in so many layers of blood and thicker matter as it is now. My palm becomes cold with the wet- ness that tries to wrap itself around it. The knowledge creeps into my mind of what I am doing, and it is covering my heart in so much more stone. The drummer has picked up his tempo with the amount of splattering I leave in my wake, a crescendo to an almost demonic-like dance.

As I brace for the last two, they jerk backwards with a loud echo and violent destruction. It vibrates the area around me, and I startle at their motions. I mimic them as I freeze in my path, trying to figure out what has taken place. When I feel my body spin around with a powerful force, I brace for a new attack.

Brown eyes swimming in anger stare down into mine as his hand clutches my shoulder and the other holsters his weapon. He steadies me from the effects of his spin. Even with the anger flowing from his body, my own melts into his with all my bravado gone. The blade falls to the ground with the finale of my battle song as my arms wrap around Lawless, pulling him close to me. He hides me in my weakness with his arms around me. His hand presses my head to his shoulder and the other pulls my back toward his chest. His head rests on the top of mine and I am thankful to not be able to read his face right now. He allows me to huddle there absorbing his strength and stability, listening to the rush of his heart telling of his fears. I stare at the honey-hued skin of his arms, marveling at their strength and yet how gently he holds me to him as if I really am as fragile as I feel right now. "You came for me," I whisper into his chest. My voice giving away more of my weakness than I am ready to admit.

His silence makes me hold my breath. He is so still before me with only the sounds of his heart talking to me. I wonder for a moment if the price I must pay for my disobediences will cost my soul too much.

"I will always come for you, Helena," he finally answers me. His voice is just as weak as mine as he says, "I just don't know if you are living to die or dying to live anymore. All I know is you are killing me with it." I feel his voice echo through his chest.

It vibrates something deep in my core with its flatness. His high wall of protection it comes from strips me of my walls. I feel my first tear falling for my payment. Our golden tilt-a-whirl of a romance is spinning away from me and I feel him slipping from me while I stand here desperately clinging to us.

He drops his arms from around me, side-stepping from me. He never looks at me but keeps his eyes straight ahead when the sound of our group reaches us. I am left cold and alone with- out him to hold me. My mortar begins to crack. My world is crumbling.

Chapter 22

The two groups stand with an imaginary line drawn between us. We apprehensively exchange greetings as we each verbally test the other out. J.D. does not bother to hide his annoyance and distrust with any small talk. Lawless does our talking with a forced cheer to help soothe J.D.'s remarks. His voice holds his normal charm, but it does not relate his body language.

As friendly as he is being, he is not letting it be confused as an invitation. He is blocking Aimes and I with his body from those before us. Rhett stands to his left with his hands resting on his belt buckle in total ease with the situation. One look into his eyes will show you a different story.

Rhett is memorizing every feature of the group ahead of us. Every movement they make he is submitting to analysis. He is watching their mannerisms, hoping they will alarm him of danger before the danger has time to form. J.D. may draw your death out, but Rhett will just kill you and then go about his day as he had planned before you inconvenienced him. I am not sure which one of them scares me anymore, or for that matter if they even scare me at all.

The one male we had not noticed in the store until now is named Simon. The tall African American male acts as their voice to the questions Lawless asks them. He offers no more of a welcome than he is receiving. He stares between Rhett and Lawless to capture my gaze, ignoring any attempts to gain his attention from Rhett or Lawless. It sets our men at greater discord and I can feel the tension surrounding us.

"That was some stunt you pulled," Simon says to me, ignoring the building agitation he is causing. "Name is Simon." He reaches through them to extend his hand to me.

Rhett's eyes go the cold color we have learned to avoid. Lawless tilts his head from side-to-side slowly as if he is working out a sore muscle group in his neck. The male posturing builds with Simon's boldness.

"It wasn't a stunt. I couldn't stand by and just watch is all." I take his hand in my own with the normal sign of greeting, hoping to ease down the men in front of me and say, "Helena, and this is Aimes." I gesture to the blonde pixie beside me who is beaming with amusement at the situation. Her sense of humor may be a bit twisted.

"And the two men you just sealed your fate with are Rhett and Lawless," Aimes says, as she motions to the men in front of us who are no longer trying to hide their annoyance at the disrespect shown to them. "J.D. back here wanted you dead from go, so you may want to slow your roll on the death wishes." She wears her sweetest smile. It even reaches her eyes with its charm. Honestly. Simon smirks, taking it all in as his stare roams over each male figure. He is not bothering to hide his dare to call him on what he is doing. I know from years with Lawless the tilt of his head is the first sign of his anger. The second clue is his tongue dancing along his back molars before sliding along his front teeth behind clamped lips. The sniffing from him is his final build up. It signals Marxx to join his right side with his own gestures of annoyance.

It has now become a bomb waiting to explode and the detonator is one wrong word or look from Simon who seems to enjoy pushing their buttons as much as Aimes does.

The other male steps in between the standoff with an open arm smile. He is careful not to break the imaginary line the men have placed between them.

"Let's all just breathe here. I mean, it was a pretty amazing thing to watch from this side here. One little girl against that whole mess? Seven men and only the girl had the courage to step out. That is crazy!" he says with amused embarrassment.

Guess who just spoke the wrong word? Go on, guess. I'll wait. "What are you trying to say?" J.D.'s calm voice holds more anger than a shout, letting the question hang in the air. It rolls outward sneaking up in a warning of caution. Once J.D. gives the signal, this will all go south fast and Rhett smiles with the knowledge of it.

"No, no I am not calling anyone anything. I was just explaining Simon's amusement is all," his voice trails off, as J.D. steps up to fill the gap between Rhett and Lawless, pushing Aimes and I further back. "I'm Ross," he says, extending his hand to J.D. as an apology.

J.D. pretends to not notice it, still staring at the man. Rhett tries to hide his chuckle with an exaggerated cough. He fails.

Ross' shaggy light brown hair is showing the stress of the day with the many runs of his hands through it. Pale teal eyes seek some hint of closure from me as the men face him. Simon is still smirking into the face of Marxx as Ross inches this closer to peril. "This is Leslie," Ross says, motioning to the redhead beside him undiscouraged by the insult.

She is as annoyed as I am with their male egos. She gives a simple nod and a wide fake smile to further prove it. I think I may like her.

"Well now that we are all fine friends here, where are you folks holding up at?" J.D. smiles, but it has no warmth to it.

"And why the hell would we tell you that?" Simon smiles his own empty smile back at him.

"Well as I see it, your friend there left you for dead. My girl saved your asses. I see it as you owe us. Unless you just want to camp out here till someone from your camp remembers where they left you." J.D. shrugs. "Doesn't bother me one way or another."

J.D. makes some small gesture that sets the men to action. Whatever it was, the rest of us missed it. By the time we react, Lawless, Rhett and Marxx are pushing their way through into the building. Simon follows with a small skipping motion to catch up to them. Ross glances at Aimes, Chapel and me for some clue, but we have none to offer him.

J.D. places his hands in his front pockets and rocks on his heels with male delight. "Like I said, you owe us."

Ross' and Leslie's faces fill with the look of disbelief as the sounds of destruction drift out of the store. Destruction brought on by my attempted efforts to save them. Everything happening to this group now is my fault. I brought them into our world without their permission. Now they are being forced to accept the actions of a man who holds only one truth to be true. His.

With annoyance, I walk towards the open doors only to have J.D. grab me, setting those nerve wracking eyes on me.

"I think you've had just about enough fun for one day, Sweetheart," he says.

His voice holds so much anger it is almost a whisper, reminding me of his earlier warnings. We stare at each other over this new divide forming between us. Our foundation slowly cracks under its weight.

"Nothing much left in there," Marxx says, breaking through our standoff. "Looks like whoever boarded the place up went through it pretty well."

"Pretty much just basic shit." Lawless joins the discussion, exiting the store with a relaxed walk. His eyes dart from me to J.D. who still is holding on to my arm. They hover to Aimes quickly for some insight before returning to us as he says, "A few jugs of water, basic camping gear, plenty of tourist crap."

"Any food?" J.D. asks.

"No," Marxx answers with his seemingly limited vocabulary. "Well, at least none left on the shelves," Lawless adds, leaving the unspoken words open to interpretation and J.D. interprets. "Rip it apart," J.D. says, with his voice calm and face blank, still holding me in place.

Lawless pivots, patting Marxx on the chest signaling him to follow when J.D. pulls the next scheme from his dark depths.

"No. Not you two," J.D. says, turning to the man behind me, "you."

Chapel exhales, running a hand slowly over the lower half of his face. To refuse this, would mark him forever in their books. It will make him slip from their trust, which was deadly before this new world. Now it will be devastating.

J.D. knows this is on the boundary of Chapel's comfort zone. This is his punishment for helping me and his punishment for being too weak to stop me. J.D. knows the man has been in an internal war with his ideas of morality since the world tilted.

Someone who once held life so precious in the encasement of his family is now standing alone in the darkness, seeking any light to guide him home. He wears his ghosts like a shroud of many weights. He has become nothing more than a melancholy phantom of his former self. Now Chapel is being told to wade deeper into the darkness of what is left of his humanity.

Lawless and Marxx watch the scene, wearing their masks of disinterest to cover their thoughts. J.D. keeps his eyes locked on his target, wearing thin the shield of shelter from which Chapel uses to hide. Too long of a delay is just as damning as a no. The clock is running.

"There really is no need for all this." Ross steps forward to ease down the tension. I have figured out his role in their group already. Leslie's eyes roll to confirm it. "She did save us. I am sure, we can all work something out here that would best suit everyone."

As J.D.'s grip tightens on my arm, I make a mental note to thank Ross for that little reminder again. The man may as well be handing J.D. a shovel.

"She must have one hell of a Guardian Angel," Ross says, with a chuckle.

"I lost all my Angels a long time ago." I jerk free of J.D.'s grasp as eyes turn to me with secret knowledge. Their anger simmers some at the implications of my words. "Where is Rhett?" I ask, refusing to submit to their stares.

"Testing out his new knife," Lawless answers me as his mask slips around the edges with the tremble of his voice.

I refuse to give in to it. I refuse to allow his pity to pour out my own pain. "On what?" I ask.

"Whatever gets in his way," Marxx's deep gravel voice leaves more questions than answers, stirring panic finally within Ross. We find Simon and Rhett in a classic, old west scenario. All that was missing is the well-known whistle of a sound effect for the situation, which Aimes provides for us at our arrival unable to help herself. Rhett's back is to us, blocking Simon from their already packed supply run in anticipation of our leader's next move. I don't know if it their standoff is about the supplies or not, but it does allow J.D. to once again check Chapel's resolve.

"Go." J.D. motions with a head nod, letting the man know he has not forgotten his test.

Marxx and Lawless mirror Chapels steps, blocking Ross and Leslie with their own movements from the bags and our man. Their hands fold together in front of their bodies, or tuck into pockets in their false relaxed stance while watching the other two for any resistance.

"Wait, let's just all step back here and think about this." Ross plays his role well.

What others may see as weakness is his strength. He doesn't have to know our men well to see what is about to happen. It's obvious.

Simon will never allow Chapel to reach those bags peacefully and Rhett will never allow Simon to reach Chapel. Once the fighting starts, Ross knows how his group will fare. His role is to make sure it doesn't happen, no matter the cost to his pride, the most precious thing to a man. That is what makes Ross stronger than any of those before us.

"Let me just talk to them for a moment. I am sure we can all work something out that makes us all happy. Okay?" Ross asks, not waiting for an answer.

He walks forward with palms upright with hopes of safe pas- sage between Marxx and Lawless. Neither man moves to spare him any room; making him well aware of how fast this could still go upside down with the shoulder jabs they place upon him as he passes.

Rhett melts backwards to us. He never turns his back on Simon as Ross passes him. Rhett's actions let us know which male he believes to be the biggest threat with one final insult to Ross and Simon smiles with the acknowledgement. Leslie walks around Aimes and myself using us as a shield between her and J.D. To her credit, she never glances back to be sure if they moved toward her. Her shoulders twitch when Marxx shuffles his feet for a grin, but she doesn't look back. We are separating into our own groups again with another imaginary line drawn.

"We ain't leaving without those bags," J.D. tells us, once we are collected around him.

The words cause the men to do some type of preparations allowing Simon to see our course is not altering. Rhett nods, rolling his shoulders one-by-one. Marxx flexes his arms, crossing them in front of him before pulling them back. Lawless just waits. Still in his false relaxed stance, he stands waiting and watching. At most, he does his telltale sharp breath inhales, but otherwise he is relaxed and waiting for the words to start the fight.

I grow tired of it all. I am tired of the fighting to live. I am tired of the fighting within and now the fighting with others. I am just tired of the fighting.

Every day is a new struggle, or an illusion of security and I just can't help but wonder how much longer we will last. How will we last, not only in this new world, but also with one another? Already our bonds are cracking under the strain of it.

Friendships are faltering, as one must choose what to obey and what to question. Every day we are being tested under some new paranoia of J.D.'s with his constant threats upon us. My skin is growing thin with it all. My nerves are fraying, and perhaps Lawless is right about me as I find myself picking another fight just for the release.

"What do you think is exactly in those bags that will make all this worth it?" I ask and my voice sounds bored where my heart is hammering in anger.

"She has a point," Aimes adds her voice, fresh with her annoyance. "So, you go all rumble fest, get the bags, high-five testosterone each other, then what?"

Four sets of eyes are upon us now. Only Rhett keeps his eyes forward on the other group, but he is very aware. Chapel's eyes shine in solidarity with us while the others rest upon us, judging us.

"We make this place secure. We settle in here." J.D.'s voice is once again serpent sharp. His eyes are a blank pool of emptiness holding plenty of meaning. Aimes is tiptoeing a line she has never danced before.

"A rest stop? By the interstate? Where plenty of others will be desperately driving by?" Aimes' voice lowers to a hissing whisper with her frustrations. "What part of that says "good thinking J.D." to you? No one will ever find us here!"

J.D. looks at me as if I am to blame for her newfound backbone. I can't stop the smile I feel spreading across my face as the pixie finally shows her claws. Sharp, sarcastic claws.

"Look at them. That Simon is the only one with any amount of balls and this is the crew they depend on to send out to scavenge. Obviously, they are somewhere safe. Safe, as in not the side of the road with a plywood fence for protection and three well-trained attack monkeys," she says, even as Rhett makes a wounded noise at her directional comment.

"Instead of doing this dick measuring contest, we should convince them that they need us, J.D. We don't need a whole new group, but a nice addition or two can make life a lot easier," I hiss. Something about my words makes Lawless do another of his anger testing sharp inhales as Chapel watches it all, silently trying to warn me with his soft colored eyes. Chapel isn't the only one who notices the discomfort though.

J.D. sneers in our direction with some twisted amusement saying, "I don't think your boy there likes the idea of adding any new bodies to this crew of ours. You in need of some new snuggle buddies, Barbie?"

His blow is meant to hurt. He knows now my own fears, and like a sharp blade he slices me with them. I stare into Lawless' searching eyes and for once, I say nothing. I pray it says everything.

"This crew needs the help," Chapel's voice tests the waters gently with its volume. "We will run out of ammo soon. Only a matter of time until we are overrun again, if we are not discovered first. This is not a sound place to set up. So, we either go place-to-place, hoping one of them will stick or we see what they have and try that out. No one is saying we have to stay. A decent meal, a good night's sleep and then we can decide what to do." He shrugs, his voice growing stronger as the other males listen to his words with sincere interest.

I never realized before how little they rely on Chapel or his opinions or how very shy he feels around them. When did this divide grow, separating us all into our own little worlds as we fight to live in this world together?

Rhett, Marxx and Lawless all look to J.D. for his support, or refusal of the plan. Aimes and I exchange looks over their behavior and wait as the gears turn in J.D.'s head. If there was something to drum those new claws of hers on, she would be.

J.D.'s mind is engaging in a civil war and it is easy to read on his face as he battles between the desires to keep us separate from all others, and yet the undisputed need for more protection. There is an exchange of facial expressions between him and Lawless and only they seem to understand it as Rhett and Marxx watch their silent codes.

Lawless tilts his head and shrugs, giving approval with the understanding he will do whatever the other man wants. Marxx and Rhett nod, backing the silent plan. Aimes makes a raspberry-like noise with her mouth as she rolls her eyes over their mute actions. "Well alright. Let's go plan us a sleepover, kiddies," J.D. says, with feigned excitement.

"Great, I want the top bunk," Aimes says, matching his false enjoyment.

"You can top me anytime you want," Lawless teases her, play- fully shoving her forward.

Chapel and I trail behind them as they navigate through the wreckage of the store to the group ahead of us. Simon watches our progress with a guarded expression, signaling for the others to notice. Ross' thousand-watt smile is instantly on and beaming in our direction. His face is a direct opposite of his other two friends, making it stand out even more. It's nice to feel welcomed. "So, Cupcakes, seems we have us an impasse here. As far as impasses go, we seem to be on the winning side." J.D. smiles that good ol' boy smile and it can be taken in a thousand different ways.

Simon is not taking it well. "Is that so? Just how do you come to that conclusion?" he asks with sincere disgust for J.D.

I don't mean to smirk. It just happens. I also didn't mean for Marxx to see it.

"Well seems to me, you're the only real man here for your team. Hell, my girl here has more balls than your boy. Where do you think this will really land if we decide to play ball?" J.D. asks, still wearing his country boy charm.

It's not really a compliment J.D. has given me. It's a bus with a large horn. It just ran me over and is now slipping into reverse for good measure.

Simon's eyes lock with mine spreading a masculine, fantasy-filling smile as he says, "That she does."

Ross' smile only falters a little before returning to its blinding state.

"I'm also thinking you may be the only real tough guy for your whole set-up. Must be hard having to take care of everything all by your little lonesome there. Setting it all up for just one little troop like us to take it all apart. You being left behind like this after all you have done for them; that can't sit well with you now,"

J.D. draws out each word, letting it sink and soak in any paper cuts of a wound Simon may have. "I'm just thinking it might be nice for you to have some back up is all. A little support in all your efforts. Maybe even the chance to have some men around just to escape all this lack of spine you seem to be surrounded with." J.D. smiles as his mind games start to build.

"That could be helpful in a few ways." An exaggerated south- ern drawl flirts into the conversation, snapping Aimes and my heads around.

We had both been making faces at the other as we listened to J.D., We have seen this show before. It doesn't get any easier to swallow no matter how many times he does it.

Leslie is smiling her own style of blinding charm and she aims it at Lawless in his waiting stance. He returns the smile, letting his eyes glide over her with pure male interest that sets my heart back a beat or two. J.D.'s eyes bounce from him to me and back to Leslie before a different smile creeps along his lips.

"Oh hell, no she didn't," Aimes whispers in my ear, with as much shock at the woman's boldness as with Lawless' reaction. "Someone must've totally just missed the zombie death machine a few moments ago. Between Simon and chick-in-need-of-dick, there are some serious death wishes in their camp is all I'm saying," she says in an attempted whisper, letting it carry loud enough to those around us.

"There are some serious death wishes in our camp," Lawless answers back to her.

His eyes are still gliding over Leslie's body. He keeps his back to us, shutting me out one-step further as our previous conversation floats in my mind. J.D. smiles at me, watching another slice land on my bruised ego.

Chapel's hands rest on my shoulders with a gently squeezing massage, trying to lower the tension building. Silence may be golden, but it's one bitch of a thing to obtain.

"I so hate it when the kiddos fight," Rhett says. He mimics a small pouty lip as Aimes flashes her favorite one finger salute at him. "Wounded. Really," he says, as a smile dances in his eyes, baiting her for a response.

"Not yet, but give me five good minutes," she promises, tilting her head as she smiles. She radiates sweetness with her "who me?" posture.

"Any time, Sweetheart. I'd be more than happy to play with you." Rhett's posture hints at things not so sweet, but just as playful.

"You two done?" J.D. cuts through their banter with a winter's edge in his voice.

Rhett's smile fades in a shrug as he returns to his watchful gaze of those before us.

Simon has stood silently watching the make-up of our circle in the short play we just performed before him. Our conflicts and bindings rolling by in our oblivion to whomever may be watching. Whatever he saw in our exchanges has relaxed his stance some, even as Ross continues to smile and Leslie encourages Lawless with her own smirk.

"Let's talk," Simon says, motioning for J.D. to step away with him.

The two groups merge as the alphas step away to play. Rhett keeps his distance from the two men but refuses to leave too much space between himself and J.D. He pretends to find the tourist items on their rotating shelf suddenly very intriguing. Lawless allows Leslie to slip up beside him, starting a whispered flirting conversation filled with smiles and her soft butterfly touches to his chest. Marxx joins our little circle unsure of whom to protect or block anymore with disgust for Lawless displayed across his face.

"You should totally shank her. Right in that skank face of hers," Aimes, the picture of warmth and friendship, mutters.

"She's just testing you. Leave it be." Chapel's gentle massage is ramping into forced rotations on my shoulders with his nerves or either his nervousness about mine.

"He knows where he belongs," Marxx' gravelly deep voice tries to reassure us with the disgust at the show before us.

"Yeah, but does his dick?" Aimes asks, bringing a small laugh from us all at her blunt honesty.

"Dick is a tricky thing," Marxx replies, looking at our pixie with her catty comment bringing a smile to his lips.

"I can't shank her anyway. I dropped my blade outside." Even as I say it, I am already mentally picturing the satisfaction it would bring me.

"You could always just take my gun again," Chapel nonchalantly comments, bringing our laughter louder this time and it reaches those around us.

Lawless half-glances over his shoulder with his mask of indifference fully secure again hearing our laughter. His shift of body language is a cold shower to Leslie and her attempts at flirting. Anger fills her eyes in a blatant dare with me, causing my own body language to answer hers. Chapel is no longer even bothering with the pretense of a massage, but simply holding me to him. For whose benefit, I am not sure.

"Yeah, dicks are tricky things," Aimes says, staring at Lawless without bothering to censor her emotions. She is ever the best friend.

J.D. and Simon come to some hidden mutual agreement. Both struggles to allow the other to place commands and suggestions. It only serves to confuse the rest of us in our rooted loyalties as the bags are loaded into my truck while Chapel keeps watch over us.

Leslie is Lawless' new shadow. She follows him closely, never letting an excuse to glance my way slip past her. Aimes constantly whispers into my ear with each battle line drawn like a devil on my shoulder. She whispers with each lingering touch Leslie places on the body I have thought of as mine for so long. She hisses it with each of his refusals of acknowledgement for me in his flirting with her. I think about Chapel's gun with each smile Leslie is flashing my way.

Simon, Ross, Aimes and I squeeze into the length of my truck's cabin. The closeness of the situation sets Aimes and I at unease, or perhaps it's just Ross' smile. It seems to grow when he is nervous, showing more teeth than it had before.

Simon has become a locked chamber of emotions. His only speech is instructions of where to go. I wonder if he is second-guessing all of this now that it is becoming real. The deep growl of the engines behind us telling there is no turning back now. Not for Simon, and not for me as I steal one more glance at arms resting where mine used to.

As their motorcycles follow us out, I stare at the surrounding area swept in the last of fall's beauty upon the ground. It turns the hillside into a colorful scene as the leaves' reds blend with the oranges to fade into gentle yellows. It resembles the flickering flames of warm fires. Even as the air bites with cold fingers, the ground holds the illusion of warmth all around us.

It's amusing how we think of fire as comforting as we crave its light to burn the darkness away and making us feel secure from the night's dark secrets. The crackling flames are used to fill our bodies with desire as its heat warms us on cold nights. We never see the possibilities of the destruction the fire can hold until it's too late.

Until one spark escapes, stealing all we hold dear in a blazing defiance for our well-being, we never really consider how risky craving something can be. I watch as Leslie rides behind Lawless, grasping his waist tight and I pray the new fire we are each seeking will be gentle with us.

Chapter 23

We drive in awkward silence due to the close proximity of the cab. Even the beaming Ross seems stilled as each mile draws us closer to either a new victory or a new tragedy for both of our sides. Simon is taking us through back roads and winding countryside paths with clipped directions and added avoidance to our conversations. With no one to watch the show, the man that was so eager to flirt just moments ago is now more of a pouting partner than a fondling flirt.

We pass Risen on these back roads in their statuette states. They slowly awaken hearing the noise of our arrival. Rhett doesn't pass up the chance to toy with them in his twisted ideas of fun. He begins an obstacle course, swerving around and through them with reckless enjoyment. It does nothing to encourage peace with Simon as we watch the show in the mirrors of the truck.

"Are all of you crazy?" Simon asks.

He is finally forced to smile when Rhett cuts a corner a little too closely, almost becoming the toy himself. It would bring me a certain amount of joy to watch him drop his motorcycle now. Every man needs a little ego check.

"No. Just Rhett. Hells is just an extra special touch of "Hey y'all, watch this"," Aimes answers with offhanded flair. "Where are we going anyway?"

"You'll know soon enough," Simon says. His voice still holds that edge of warning and doubt.

"You know for future references; I prefer my surprises to be the sparkly type wrapped in gold. Not so much a mysterious location with possible rotting people wandering around as an extra special welcoming committee," she says, exaggerating the last part with false enthusiasm.

"I'll keep that in mind." His flirtatious smile is back as he keeps his attention straight ahead on the road, searching for something. "There is a turn up here. It is pretty easy to miss if you're not looking for it," he tells me.

I am not looking for it. I am still watching Rhett as an excuse to stare in the direction behind me. I am using it to watch Lawless and his new rider. I don't want anyone to know how they are destroying me as I watch them. I use Rhett's antics to cover the fact my heart is beating with each slide of her hands over Lawless' chest. That my stomach is clinching as her hands sneak to caress his inner thighs and how I am growing physically ill with his smile.

"We should have buried Shaw," Simon's voice drags my eyes forward.

"Who?" I ask, not out of interest, but more for the excuse to distract me from the mirrors.

"The one they killed. We should have buried her." His voice is coated with regrets. I have a sense they are stacked deeper than just the one body we have left behind. He says, "She was Leslie's friend. We shouldn't have just left her there like that."

"Yeah, she looks real torn up over it. I can hear her sobs from here." Aimes is watching the same show in the door's mirror as she replies.

"We all deal with stuff differently," Ross offers. I can feel his smile without even having to look at him. It's a dazzling white shade of a forming migraine.

"Well, her path of healing must lie through her vagina," she offers back, winning a new red ribbon from me.

Even Simon has to smile as her observation floors Ross into silence. It takes a moment to get used to the shock factor of my friend. Her lack of filter is what I have always loved about her. She does not play any games or hold any schemes. She is just her- self with no apologies for it. I am hoping she and Ross are stuck together more often just to watch the smile choke from his face, because if he keeps his smile up, I will most certainly choke him myself.

Simon is right. The turn is a sharp, hidden secret and I have missed it. I slam on the brakes, scattering the riders behind me with my sudden stop. Reverse is a wonderful thing and I slam the truck into the gear, making her engine roar with the force   of my backtracking. Her lights cast a red glow upon Lawless as I take up every inch of space between us before slamming on the brakes again. He never flinches in my dare, but Leslie's scream is satisfying enough for me.

"Holy shit, Hells!" Aimes says, from the force of my actions. Her face is one of pure pride.

"Hey y'all, watch this," Simon mutters, still bracing against the dash.

Ross says nothing but just stares at me. If slinging the truck around will remove his smile, I may learn a new way to drive.

"This turn here?" I ask innocently, ignoring them with my eyes still staring at the man behind my truck in the mirror.

Lawless' eyes are safe from me behind the tinted glasses he is wearing. His face is blank even with Leslie animatedly talking   in his ear with exaggerated hand motions. Rhett and Marxx both start clapping from the show as J.D. laughs, staring down at his fallen motorcycle with amusement over my brashness.

"Yeah, this turn here," Simon answers, and I can feel his eyes on me. Men are so afraid of our feminine mood swings.

My warhorse navigates the turn with ease after Chapel helps

J.D. lift the fallen Harley. They follow us into the sharp curve as we turn onto a narrow access road leading us through a tall, un- kempt grass field. Deep ruts are visible from the many attempts to keep large service vehicles on such a narrow strip of asphalt. Even with their large size, the tires jar riding over so many deep potholes, forcing me to keep my attention on my driving.

I no longer feel the need to watch what is going on behind me. I think I have made my opinion of his actions very clear. I do hit the brakes a little too hard here and there along the path just to watch them brace behind me. It's the little things in life.

Simon reaches over and taps a pattern with the horn. The smart asses behind us play a game of "Simon Says" with the same melody. I don't need to glance to see which two it was. Aimes and I exchange questioning glances at his sudden need for musical skills.

"Slow down or you'll be running over my crew this time," Simon tells me, as a giant barbed wire fence comes into view.

"What the hell is this?" Aimes asks, taken aback by the first sight of our new home. "Are we at a prison?"

"Close," Simon answers her, wearing a mischievous smirk upon his face and Ross just smiles.

The gate does not swing open to allow us through but slides to the side. A man stands at the entrance with a high-powered rifle slung across his back. His green eyes, so close to my shade, are watching us drive towards him. His clothes give hints at the well-toned shape of his body even from this distance. He waits with a shy stare as I roll my window down for him to talk with us. For a moment, I forget how to speak.

"Dolph, did Ramero make it back?" Simon asks of the man. "Yeah, a few hours ago. Was wondering when you'd show up,"

Dolph answers in a soft-spoken southern drawl. He never turns his body fully to us. He leans sideways into the conversation, keeping the men behind us in his sight. The view of his well- toned arm keeps me entertained more than their conversation. "What's all this?" he asks.

"We made some new friends," Ross answers with his smile. Dolph leans in closer, resting the same arm I have been memorizing the shape of on the truck's door to see the man. His face is showing his disappointment with the answer or perhaps just with Ross all together. "Guess this was your idea?" he asks Ross with annoyance.

Ross just smiles still, ignoring the question. Ross doesn't seem to have a very big fan club.

"Family reunions, so much fun," Aimes says to me, hinting at being ignored by their conversation.

Dolph holds her in his sight, trying to figure out if she is serious or toying with him. The emotions flash across his face before releasing her without any comment as he pulls back from the window. Aimes is making no new fan club members today either. "Lock the gate up and meet us up at the school. I will fill you in," Simon tells him.

Dolph answers with a short head nod and a step back, allowing us to pass. Leslie and he exchange greetings in glares as Lawless drives by him. He doesn't seem too thrilled with discovering her either. Maybe he is just not the cheerful type.

Chapel is the last one through when Dolph slides the gate shut behind him. There is a finalization with watching the gate shut. For better or worse, we are now a part of their world and they a part of ours.

"Should we wait for him?" I ask. I am still watching Dolph, and Simon doesn't try to hide his amusement. "It just seems rude to leave him like this," I say, trying to hide my discomfort of being so transparent with my thoughts under the guise of kindness. Sometimes it works. I see with Simon's grin this is not one of those times.

"No, it's best to let him walk back to the school. He needs some time to adjust. I can only imagine how your crew and Dolph are going to get along," Simon tells me with the same amusement upon his face.

"He seems pretty harmless." Aimes allows the statement to hang, forming more of a question.

"Yeah, you silent ones always do," Simon says, as he catches my eyes in the rear-view mirror with sincere honesty.

I can't help it. I look at Ross with obvious disbelief at that assumption. Feeling my eyes upon him, he does not smile at me but Aimes does. She is having the same thoughts as I am about the "silent ones" being dangerous.

We are used to our blusterous crew with their foul language, short tempers and male jokes. That to us is dangerous. Not the quiet man at the gate with his shy stares and short framed sentences or Ross with his instant smile and crowd pleasing needs nor me for that matter with all of my baggage stacking up around me. At this rate, I can go on a world tour and still have plenty of clothes packed for the return trip.

"Wait, did you say school?" Aimes asks and I was wondering how long until she picked up that clue.

"Yup," Ross's smile has rejoined us, "a high school."

"We really are in a prison!" She melts down onto the seat as a sigh escapes with the realization of where we are finally settling over her. I love my Aimes.

High wire fencing surrounds the perimeter of the school. I hope the barbed wire wrapped around the top is an afterthought of our new world and not part of what they once considered necessary for a school day. The school itself is a giant brick building of gothic intent. The slate coloring is a depressing grey against a darker roof matching the asphalt drive. Rows of narrow windows etched in the same dark coloring prove what a monster this place once was with its looming three stories. From our entrance, the building appears to be a giant rectangle of connecting halls wrap- ping around itself. Standing against an overcast sky, there are no welcoming feelings expressed from what I am seeing.

Simon instructs us to pull through an archway that has been opened for us with our approach. The inner courtyard is completely protected by the high thick walls of the building keeping the heart of the building secure. Many archways provide entrances to each internal section with various heights of steps to each. It casts an illusion of different depths to contrast against the dreary, grey coloring. People are scattered about with their silent stares watching our approach. Their distrust mounting as each loud engine pulls in behind me. Their cold demeanor is matching that of the building they call home.

"Cheerful. Think they know any campfire songs?" Aimes asks, sinking down on the bench with the weight of the stares.

The courtyard itself is a main slab of dark concrete attached to the building with just as darkly colored paths leading to the many stairways. A dry, brown lawn circles the concrete in an attempt to provide scenery with its many benches. Aimes is right. This is not like any high school I have ever seen. These kids were truly in a prison. The people who live here now seem no friendlier than prisoners themselves.

Simon instructs me to park over to the side of the concrete where it has been designated for such a purpose. Many cars, in many sizes are parked in rows along the one wall. I spot among them the blue minivan from the Welcome Center. It still wears the markings of its encounter as either proof of its survival, or its shame depending on which side of the event you sat.

A woman is running toward my truck with tears upon her face, and for a moment I pause in uncertainty over what to do until Simon steps from behind me to catch her as she falls into his arms. She clings to him with desperate strength from a deep relief of finding him and the fear she held of never seeing him again. They speak in soft tones to one another, ignoring the world around them.

"When he came back without you…," her voice cracks under the strain of having to finish the thought.

"I will always come back. Always," Simon tells her, holding her head between his hands so she is forced to see into his eyes. He needs her to see the depth of sincerity the words hold. His thumbs glide in a comforting pattern along her face to help ease her fears. He holds her to his body as they both still seek the reassurance of one another. I am watching them providing the proof to their hearts they are both still alive. Today did not take the one pos- session they would not survive to lose. I can't help but to wonder how much of his dedication to this woman the reason for him is siding with J.D. Here J.D. has been thinking his mind game al- lowed us passage, but it very well may be that Simon has used us. "Where is Kira?" He finally finds his voice, regaining his composure.

"She is resting. When you didn't come back with Ramero, she didn't take it well," she says. I listen to the bits and clues of their conversation she is giving me.

"I'm sorry." Simon closes his eyes as pain streaks across his face and I wonder who Kira could be to cause such emotions. "I'm so sorry," he says again.

"You're here now. That's all that matters," she answers softly, trying to ease his pain. "I guess we have you to thank for that?" She turns to me with her face still damp from their emotions. "Shelia," she says, extending her hand to me.

Shelia's skin is richer in color than Simon's. Her eyes hold the beautiful depths of color only their race can obtain. Those eyes are red rimmed from expressing the sorrows she thought had come to call her heart home. Her hand trembles slightly from her frayed nerves with the morning's events. I can only imagine what the fear must feel like to watch the one you love to leave you knowing he may not come back and then to watch those fears come to life. I hope I never have to.

"Helena," I answer, taking her hand. I grasp it firmly, letting her know the sorrow I feel for her. "Not so much my doing."

"Yeah, she only chopped her way through a whole caboodle of dead peeps to reach your man here when he got left behind by his own. No big deal," Aimes adds an ended point to her words with a sharp pop of her very pink gum. She has perched herself on the edge of my warhorse's bed, swinging her legs adding to her abundance of charm. "How is Romeo anyway?"

"Ramero," Shelia corrects her. "He isn't doing well either." "Yeah, guilt is a bitch like that." Aimes smiles her "look how cute I am" smile, popping another pink bubble.

Shelia has no answer to another award-winning observation from Aimes. She does not offer one. Instead, she eyes the men behind us with curiosity and caution. Unconsciously, she steps back into the safety of Simon, watching those behind us.

"Are they with you, too?" she asks.

Aimes pivots her upper body to glance at the group of men huddling together over the black frames of the motorcycles. Leslie is still perched on the back of Lawless' like a Queen holding court. Her comments make the men laugh and they return her flirting with their smiles. J.D. has been watching us with Simon. His smile is forced and not amused by what he is seeing around him. I guess redheads are not his style?

Now as we look in their direction, he runs his fingers down Leslie's arm, trying to prove to us how easily we can be replaced. Aimes calls the bluff by blowing a kiss to J.D. and it lands its mark better than Cupid could with his sense of irony. J.D. frowns with a moment of regret upon his face, his fingers pausing on Leslie's arm as if they are touching something offensive before returning to rest at his side. The men around him with their silent attunement to him notice the shift in his mood. Their eyes all at once come to rest on us watching them.

Rhett waves an exaggerated wave with just as comical a smile in our direction. Aimes returns it with a wave that would make parade queens proud. The kisses he sends her would make one swoon. Even Shelia laughs at the sight of such a larger than life man fooling around with our pixie.

I notice Dolph as he enters the courtyard entrance behind the gathered group. Adjusting the rifle onto his back, he squints against the afternoon sun flirting in and out of the clouds teasing us with its warmth. The sun's rays catch the many tints of his hair from a dark red brown to its hidden golden hues. His long stride tells of his ease in any situation as his eyes continue to glance down before coming back to rest on our new groups.

His short head nods are becoming his trademark. He signals Simon with one when their eyes meet. Dolph pauses halfway to us, making Simon step away and cover the gap left to speak with him. His face doesn't hide his suspicion of us and J.D.'s group does not help his assumptions. They are starting their own stare off with him, as they grow silent. Simon had hinted at this on the way here. Now the tension is simmering like summer's heat in the space between our groups.

"Boys…" Aimes begins, before I can clear my throat to stop her from speaking whatever her little fun-sized mind is going to spill forth next.

"Shelia, why don't you take them and get them set up?" Simon asks of her, eyeing the tension brewing. To us he says, "Make sure your boys follow you out, okay?"

Simon does not need to place any more meaning into his words. He knows he cannot control both sides should egos erupt. He is counting on us to help him diffuse what could be a volatile situation with so much male pride on the line.

As far as first impressions go, the men are blowing it. The other residents are now clustered into small fragments of groups watching it all. If social media was still available, I can only imagine the many updates this groups would hold from their many highs and lows of this morning.

"Aye aye, Capt'n," Aimes says, before whistling for the rest of our once happy family. "Here Attack Monkeys. Come on, Attack Monkeys," she yells across the divide, using the term of endearment from earlier.

It successfully breaks the male angst with her antics. Dolph even has to cock one eyebrow in her direction with her title for the men. His body relaxes some with the humor.

Chapel breaks rank first and makes his way to us. He is as tired as I am of the constant posturing but unable to escape it as easily as I can. Rhett and Lawless begin imitating the animal call of their new nicknames, jumping over the Harleys in their path to follow Chapel over to us. J.D. and Marxx stare at Dolph, sending a private male message to the other man before following the group. Leslie sits alone and stranded on the back of the bike without her newly formed male court around her. They leave her without a second thought, causing her mouth to hang in the air with her shock. It also sends a private message to those watching. Leslie is on her own, as far as they are concerned.

"Oooo, shanked," Aimes whispers to me, over the now abandoned woman as she jumps down from the edge of the tall truck. I smile, watching Lawless return to me and arch an eyebrow at the redhead who is glaring at his back. I smile, but a part of me knows, he is not returning to me at all.

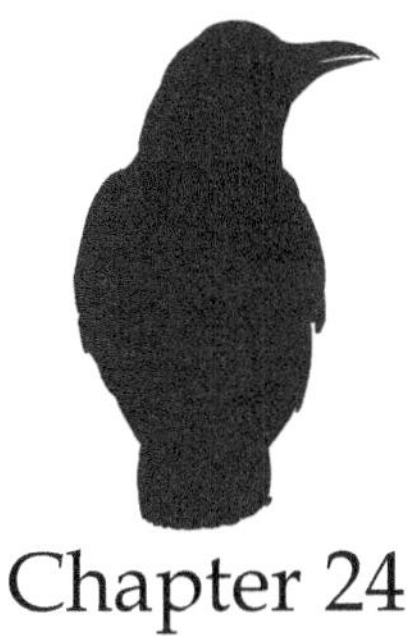

Chapter 24

We follow Shelia into one of the many tall arches from the courtyard. Lawless and Rhett are still enjoying their calls to each other until a firm look from J.D. reduces them to silence. Like naughty boys, they still under his gaze. I find them now more humorous than their zoo rendition and I let my smile tell J.D. so. He smirks at me, forgetting our earlier conversations for the moment. It eases the fluttering in my stomach threatening to grow into so much more with the knowledge I am about to enter another school. Last time it didn't go so well, not for me and not for those in my care.

The interior of the high school is the same color scheme as the outside. It's grey, dark and wonderfully depressing. No happy mascots of false cheer here to stare down at me with the secret knowledge of my sins. Shades fade from white to a silver-grey with a strategic process that refuses to form any real patterns, but simple shading along the walls and tiled floors. The tall windows are embedded with a crisscross wiring of security. The sun filters through, allowing just enough light to fill the hallways.

"Depressing," Aimes whispers in my ear.

She doesn't want to upset Shelia with her opinion. She is holding hope this could be a new start for us as one behind us is determined otherwise. J.D.'s scowl is meant to offend, and he is just waiting for someone to call him on it.

"It's fitting," is my answer to her. I am unwilling to admit how happy I am for the lack of pastels.

The stairwell is behind heavy steel doors. It requires Shelia to lean into them with the full weight of her small body to have them open for her. She smiles at us with a shy touch of embarrassment over the fact.

Chapel reaches over her, holding them open for us with a simple return of her smile. His six-foot frame easily supports the weight of them and allows her to slip under his arms. I bet he was always picked first to play "London Bridges" in school.

"Thank you. Simon says I will be happy they are so heavy should we need the safety of them, but I can't help but wonder about it every time I have to come up and down these steps," Shelia says. Her dark natural skin tone hints at a shade of pink standing so close to Chapel.

Each one of the men bounces the weight off their palms as they follow us through, judging the logic of her words themselves. Rhett chooses a different test.

Rhett swings the door back onto Marxx with the full strength of his arms. He and Lawless skip ahead a few steps to distance themselves from the man who caught the weight of the steel door mostly with his face. Their laughter taunts Marxx as he does his own half run to catch up to them, intending to repay them for their humor. J.D.'s simple slide of his shoe with his turn to look at them is enough to stall all three of them in their actions. Their laughter dies, leaving only Marxx' glare to mark the event.

"What naughty little boys we have," Aimes muses with annoyance.

"So, how did that weight feel? Your face thankful?" J.D. asks Marxx, with a dangerous smile.

When there is no answer and the coughing used to disguise hidden laughter is finally through, he turns back to Shelia as if nothing happened. He silently stares at her to continue with the tour with nothing more than his eyes to let her know he is waiting.

"We set up the living quarters on the top floor. It makes everyone feels safer I guess." Shelia leads on, but not before glancing one last time at J.D. before turning her back to lead us further. She seems to be having second thoughts about that safety concept now with J.D. on this side of those heavy doors.

"Just what exactly is the top?" Aimes asks.

"The third floor," Shelia responds. Her smile isn't meant to mock Aimes, but it does.

"Totally rethinking my shoes. How about you, Hells?" Aimes raises her eyebrow to ask if I can make it.

This is where I would normally point out my She-Ra status, but I hate to brag.

"Nah, Barbie here is just fine. Hers are all broken in. Right, Girly?" J.D.'s voice snakes its way up my spine with its pitch. He is gaining a gold star today with the skill of his hidden threats.

I don't answer him. I let my eyes meet his with my silent answer. I let him know I understand where he is heading with his hints and what exactly he is aiming to remind me of before we are subjected to more public stares. A thousand replies form on my lips, each with their own dosage of poison to be ingested when Chapel's hand gently touches my lower back, taking the sting from J.D.'s look.

"Don't give him the win," Chapel whispers in my ear, using his own long shoulder length hair to cover his lips.

It must have provided a different appearance of what he did by the sharp male inhale from behind us. Maybe it was what Chapel had meant for it to look like in an attempt to cover his dare of overstepping J.D.'s lead. In his mind, J.D. holds grudges longer than Lawless. Thinking of how quickly Leslie was able to slither her way in, I am not so sure about his logic.

I let Chapel's hand guide me further up the steps to where Shelia is waiting with Aimes. Amusement dances in my friend's eyes, confirming exactly what Chapel's actions just looked like to those around us. Neither Chapel nor I try to deny or suggest otherwise. We allow them to come to their own conclusions and I smile up into his warm eyes, letting him lead me. Another imaginary line is drawn.

The third level landing is alive with layers of sounds slipping from beneath its heavy doors. Conversations of different pitches mingle with sounds of footsteps and even the pitter-patter of running. Laughter fills in the many pauses caused by lapses of words. There are sounds of children playing and I feel my mouth go dry with their laughter. Her laughter from my memories mingles with theirs, making my chest tighten with the sound of her voice.

I am afraid of those doors as much as I am rejoicing in them. Feeling my nervousness radiate through me, Chapel's thumb begins a slow, small circle on my lower back. There is irony in the fact the man they have deemed our weakest link is now my strongest rock. He will be the first man through these double doors while the rest stand back, having grown very silent behind us.

Shelia smiles at me over her shoulder. She assumes my reaction is due to anxiousness to see what lies ahead. She does not under- stand our scar rule, so I just smile back. I am still smiling as she opens the doors and watches my face for the joy she must feel with their set-up. The pride she must feel over being able to hold on to something when the sky seems to be falling down around everyone else. I smile, thinking of the cabin and how we felt back then. I understand her joy.

The hallway is a long, hollow rectangle keeping the placement of the courtyard in the middle. The many classrooms repeating along each side have been converted into small apartments for those who now live here.

The stairwell opens into a large sitting area with benches and many brightly colored toys are spread around in the space with an attempt to encourage mingling with the many families milling around. Conversations slowly fade away as people begin to take notice of us watching them. The hissing of whispers replaces the laughter we had heard as speculations are forming over who we are and the possible reasons for our arrival.

"Yo," Aimes says, with a little wave, trying to break the awkwardness of it all. She fails. The whispering only continues louder than before making her reply, "Tough crowd."

"It has been a bit since we have added anyone," Shelia offers sheepishly. "They will come around. It has been a rough morning with the possibility of Simon being gone. I am sure he will hold a meet-and-greet later after you have had time to settle in." Shelia has genuine care for our predicament.

"Well, color me excited!" Aimes' false excitement causes us all to smile.

"Don't worry, we don't bite," Shelia says, encouraged by the smiles.

Playing the perfect hostess, Shelia starts to walk again down one of the long hallways. She smiles and makes small talk with the random people standing around as we make our way down the hall. They may hold conversation with her, but they are silently staring at us.

"Really?" Rhett asks, also encouraged by the conversation. "Because we do." His smile reaches his whole face.

Shelia, with all of her love for Simon, still blushes with his innuendo. It only further invites him, allowing him to lean into her in a joking manner. A part of me knows Rhett is not a flirt by nature. He will tease you. He will play along in any word game of your choice, but never one to first openly flirt with strangers. It took years before the man would even acknowledge Aimes and myself with more than a brief word or a stare. Now, he is drop- ping smiles on a woman he met just moments ago. A woman he knows belongs to another.

One glance at J.D. and my suspicions are confirmed. His grin is one of approval, not enjoyment of Rhett's actions. Shelia doesn't know it yet, but she is now part of their game. A game I am sure is aimed at Simon for his disrespects to them earlier. An eye for an eye is the only game J.D. knows.

Aimes and I share a look of understanding over their new plot. We both silently agree we will only let it play out so far. Our reaching this decision to stand in the middle of their plotting shows how far our group is rebuilding around a new rulebook. The days of us both smiling and nodding, along with being "his girls" at Grit, have flipped as simply as one would change the many months of a calendar. Not wanting to risk him ruining what could be a home for us, we no longer wish to be the pin-ups for him to visually enjoy.

"Soooo, where are we heading?" Aimes slides between Shelia and Rhett with a complete innocence of her demeanor.

She takes the space between them completely, giving Shelia pause at the meaning of it. Aimes smiles at her, trying to put her nervousness at rest. I think the woman is just prone to nervous- ness. Wait until she sees the real Rhett.

"We have some spare rooms up toward the end. I don't know how you want to divide it up." Shelia leaves off with her con- fusion over who goes where with whom. I don't think we even know that little fact at this point.

Conversation lapses the rest of the way to our new rooms with the question hanging in the air around us. Only Shelia's glances, trying to figure out our many details holds any form of a language exchange. We are all blank faces, making it a one-sided conversation for her. Those are never fun.

"Well, here we are. The desks have all been removed and small cots put in their places. The rooms right now have three each. I am sure we can find more if needed," she says fidgeting with her hair. She does not try to hide her nerves anymore. At this point, we aren't exactly shocked to see them.

"Don't worry, Darlin'. We can do the math and figure it all out," Rhett offers as he smiles again.

Rhett rubs her shoulders letting the smile breach her defenses. It works. She smiles before correcting herself, glancing at Aimes to express her apology for her actions. Aimes is not playing along anymore and Shelia walks away unsure of what to do to appease her.

"Darling? Really?" Aimes waits until Shelia is out of earshot to call Rhett's bluff.

"What? I can't be friendly?" Rhett has brought down the watt- age of his smile back to his genuine mischievous look. "Maybe I like a little milk chocolate," he says with a shrug.

"Oh, just stop. I'm gonna be sick." Aimes covers her mouth and with her best acting skills pretends to be ill. "Just the thought   of you being all romantic is super creepy. Like bloody valentine creepy. And a shoulder rub? Really? If you put it on any thicker, you're going to have fake more than your smile."

"Not a virgin. I've learned how to fake it, Sweetheart," Rhett says. He cocks one eyebrow to match his smirk.

"Yeah, but I wasn't talking about you remembering their names." Aimes lets her words hit home. It more than projects her idea of his sex life.

"Maybe I've never found a girl worth going a second round with or one to make me want to remember her name afterwards," he says, shrugging at her with the false feelings of loneliness making his statement that much more comical with his exaggerated sad eyes.

"Very romantic, Rhett, very romantic. Let's rush off to buy roses." Her eye roll is anything but false but still as comical.

"Naw, that's Law's deal," Rhett says. His words make everyone inhale a breath with his hidden insult.

"Who is going where, and guess who my vote doesn't lie with?" I ask, being tired of the word games.

"The girls will go in one room leaving Marxx, Rhett, Lawless and me in this one. One of us four will keep switching off to keep watch," J.D. answers me, watching as the meaning sinks in.

Chapel does not even flinch with the insult but stays blank. It's my turn now to come to his rescue. I am not sure how well of a rock I will make, but I am going to try.

"Have I ever told you, Chap, how I can't sleep unless I have something to hold?" I let my body slide against his when I walk past him into our 'soon to be shared' room. My voice lowers to something of a purr. His eyes follow my movement with a heat I have never seen him hold before.

"No. You haven't." Chapel's voice is thick. It fills the hallway with his male hopes and needs.

"Oh, it's true. She is quite the screamer at night." Aimes drops her voice to match his pitch, letting her words carry a double meaning to peak the needs of those watching us. "We just love big, strong arms around us to keep us safe and sound."

"I like to snuggle," Marxx says. His deep gravel seems out of sort with his random outburst.

Trying to picture Marxx snuggling brings a smile to my face just as he had planned.

"I guess you'll have to take that up with J.D. He made the room choices." I take Chapel's hand and pull him into our room behind me as I whisper to Marxx, "Maybe he likes to snuggle, too."

"We can always find you boys Leslie. She seems to enjoy more than just cuddling in her cot."

I hear J.D. say to my back. With that, J.D. throws the final gauntlet to my bluff. I close our door before he has his proof of his new wound upon me.

"I know how much that cost you," Chapel whispers on my neck, holding me as I lean against the closed door. His large body is covering my own as he bends down to comfort me. "He is losing you and he knows it. He only knows how to keep them in check with fear and pain. You don't fear him anymore, leaving him only one weapon left. He will turn you and Lawless against one another if you let him. He can't let Lawless go. You need to be preparing for that." He places a soft kiss on the top of my head before turning from me.

"Dolph is kinda cute," Aimes offers, as her own eyes are showing the pain, I am feeling over Chapel's truths.

Seeing her sharing my same fears and heartache allows my first tear to fall. We hug one another with the freedom being a girl allows us, supporting each other in this new chapter of our lives. Our pages are now plot-less with no direction or clues as to where they will lead us. We have both done what is normally a death sentence. We have crossed J.D., calling his actions into question and he has made it known our little group is in his sights. We now live in the dangerous crosshair of his attention.

"We still have to go out there to get our bags," I mutter into her shoulder.

"I'll get them." Chapel stands from his cot where he has been watching the two of us. "Just stay in here until I come back. He won't do anything with the others still around. Marxx won't let him, but I wouldn't push it."

He kisses the top of Aimes' head as he exits, trying to calm the fears coursing through her like a river. The door closes behind us with the soft reality of being alone.

"Do you think it will get that bad?" Aimes asks the air around us, more than she is asking me.

"No. I don't. He would never admit to being out done by a girl and any actions he takes would do just that." I hug her, lending her my strength. "We will just keep on with these word games. He will try to hit us where it hurts. He will use the guys against us if we show him any weakness to it. Our best plan is to just avoid him until he comes around and he will once his male ego is appeased."

"…and what is it going to take to appease him?" Her fear forces her to ask the one question she fears the answer from the most.

"Me. It's my pain he wants. My weaknesses. You have to let him have it. Don't jump in. Don't run interference. He and I need to play this out," I tell her.

"…and Lawless? What are we going to do about him? How can he do this?" Her voice rises with her pain and confusion over his actions.

The man we have given our hearts and trust to is turning so cruelly away from us. It leaves us both raw from it for different reasons. I have no answers to comfort her, as I am as lost in this river's current as is, she. I am no longer trying to swim against its strength. I just want to keep my head above the water.

Chapel finds us still exploring these thoughts with his return. Aimes' tears gliding along her face causes him to pause in the grief of seeing her this way. He tries to give us some silent communication, but we fail to grasp it in time and Lawless walks in behind him holding our bags in his hands.

Seeing us both in the midst of our emotions, Lawless goes cold and we separate. He never slows from the sight before him but simply follows Chapel to where the bags have been placed, dropping the ones he is carrying with the others. He exits with the same blank face and aversion to us, causing Aimes to slam the door behind him with her frustrations.

"So much for not getting involved?" I ask her, waiting for the doorframe to settle from the vibrations.

"You said that was for J.D. This is a whole different ass." She crosses her arms, further proving her feelings by saying, "The dick."

I shrug, giving in to her judgment of the situation. Chapel tries to cover his laughter at her female outburst but ends up giving in to it. Hearing him laugh with such openness is contagious. Slowly we are each laughing, letting it release the emotions building inside us.

"I feel like I could sleep for days," I say, with a yawn to further prove it.

I test the cot with the weight of my body, slowly sinking into the firmness. It doesn't give much under me, but my body at finding rest does not complain. Aimes pulls the other two cots close to mine making a good size bed out of them. Chapel fidgets, watching us with the realization we may not have been completely bluffing with our invitations from earlier. It's plain upon his face he is confused over if he should be excited or worried.

"Easy, big boy. We will keep our little claws to ourselves." Aimes enjoys his discomfort, which makes him ripe for her playful teasing. "No rest for the wicked," she says, tossing the sleeping bags to me to help spread out across our makeshift bed.

We arrange the bags, so each is contained in their own space but allowing us to reach out for comfort if we need it in the middle of the night. Of course, all of this Chapel watches from across the room, making as much space between us as possible. Perhaps he is rethinking the bluffs he also placed earlier. Is he still so eager to dare Lawless?

Aimes and I begin our normal nighttime routine of aimless chatter. Subjects float from what we would kill to have right now, to what we would have done if we had known the world was going to go to hell. Sometimes we even randomly compare whom we would have done had we known what was going to happen.

Her selections are always humorous and so out of our reach. Unless well-known actors think to themselves, Hey, I would like to date a barmaid from a small town before my face is eaten, I think she is out of luck. We do all of this while we change into our sweats and tee shirts for the night.

Aimes smirks at Chapel's reaction to us undressing before him with a mixture of male curiosity, and shyness. I have never seen someone arch so much to remove their socks. The woman may have missed her true calling in life.

"Bathroom?" I ask, smacking her forehead telling her to stop it. "You are going to give him a stroke," I mouth, wordlessly to her.

She teasingly whispers back to me, "Maybe I'll help him with the stroking."

I roll my eyes at her less than hidden innuendo.

"Sure. I could freshen up before Chap here keeps me warm all night," Aimes returns my exasperated look with a smile. "Do you know where they are?"

"I imagine they will be the well-lit rooms adjacent to the hall," I tell her.

"You're so smart with them big words and that fancy book learnings' of yours."

"I can't help it. You just make me look so dem' edu'm'cated."
"Touch of rude. Dash of unnecessary," she says with a false glare.

Our laughter carries us through the door. It covers how nervous we are to finally be stepping so close to J.D. We did not expect however for Chapel to come stand over us or for his glares to keep us safe as we pass their doorway. He gives their room a look of caution. Standing in the space between it, he dares them with his presence until we are far enough away to be safe from any stray remarks. Even then, he leaves our door open to further prove the weight of his dare for them to stir any trouble.

Chapel has finally found his light to guide him home. In this void he has been living in, he finally sees a spark of hope at being needed again. A man who has already lost one family is now claiming ownership of another. He is taking back his place in this world and he is starting with Aimes and I.

We have begun the healing process for his bleeding heart, proving to him love can still be felt in this new design of a world. He has seen the bond Aimes and I still share even with all the horror we have witnessed and endured. Through all the pain we have drank of, we still believe in each other and he wants that.

He wants to feel that warmth of human touch again. He needs to feel the bond of trust again deep in his core to ease his self-doubts and the many monsters who stalk him in the dark corners of his mind. The man they have dismissed as being weak now stands alone, leaning against our doorway with his version of their re- laxed stance. He is watching and aware of his surroundings as well as any of them have been in the past. He is not just drawing another line. He is demanding it to be seen.

J.D. takes the bait. He comes to lean on their doorway, staring Chapel down across the divide placed between them. Steel-colored eyes are watching every movement, cataloging any weaknesses before him. J.D. hopes to break Chapel with his presence, as he has always been able to do before. He wants to make the taller man bend to his will again with the pure fear of him.

"Yo," Chapel calls across to him, in a mimic of Aimes' exact word only moments ago.

The word is so simple but says more than the one syllable ever could hold. Chapel is declaring on whose side he now sits and to further prove it, he reaches down into his shirt, pulling out a gold chain attached to a small golden cross. His "trinket of death" and the sign of his faith that keeps J.D. so on edge with the fact of it. Chapel smiles to J.D. as the chain falls into place next to his heart. Chapel has lost everything only to find everything again in our laughter and our tears. He is no longer afraid of J.D. or what this new life may hold. Chapel has come home. With disgust upon his face, J.D. turns, returning to the room he shares with the others, slamming the door behind him hard enough to give Aimes a run for her drama title. What naughty little boys we have.

Chapter 25

The first stirrings of confusion nudge me from a warm, deep sleep. The sun is too bright. The arm around me is too heavy.

The scent is too sharp. I feel my heart race with the confusion, until the events of last night catch up to my sleepy mind.

Aimes and I had returned to find Chapel filled with mirth over something he would not share with us. It made the once shy shadow of a man become playful with Aimes, returning her jests as fast as she could serve them. Their verbal tennis match filled the time we had left until our bodies grew lazy with sleep. We had fallen asleep to our laughter as we made hand puppets on the flat tiles of the ceiling above us. We were lost in the joys of our bonds when sleep found us.

The heavy arm slung across my waist must belong to Chapel as he sought innocent reassurances in the pitch darkness of the night. The male scent surrounding me is the strong soap lingering on his skin. I roll into his heat to stare at the man, who up until now, has been a stranger to me.

He rests on his back, softly snoring the way men do when reaching their deep stages of sleep. One arm is resting on me and his other is tucked under Aimes' head as she sleeps on his chest. She has cuddled up close to his side, seeking her own reassurance in her sleep. His shoulder length hair mingles with her shades of blonde, weaving the many shades between them. I lie here watching them dream in their peaceful sleep when the door opens, invading our private moment.

Chapel startles instantly with the noise, pushing me down and pulling Aimes closer in an attempt to protect us from the danger his sleep-filled mind is imagining. Shelia is at the door looking in the room without trying to see what is before her with her averted eyes. She wears her embarrassment the way a woman wears a well-fitted gown. It covers every inch of her, making us aware of her for reasons that stir curiosity within us.

"Breakfast is in an hour. We only serve meals at set times to help keep track of our pantry and to conserve energy. I didn't want you to miss it," she explains, as she withdraws from the room, never meeting our curious eyes.

Sharing a look of confusion between us, the three of us watch her leave. Her awkwardness is easily forgotten though when our stomachs remind us of the meals we skipped yesterday as drama enfolded our family.

We choose our separate corners of the room to dress, as conversation is freckled with our laughter encouraged by the new ease found between us. Chapel waking up beside someone seems to have cured him of his nervous fidgeting.

The tall man now in our life is not a replacement for Lawless. I watch him with his back turned to us and I crave the amber coloring of another man. Chapel's laughter does not stir me the way Lawless' does. Nor does his smile, as warm as it is, comfort the depths of my soul the way another's does.

Our comedy is one of shy testing, not full of hidden meanings only years of shared moments can bring. I am wondering if I have the strength to let another become so close to me. Can I trust again, to such a degree, or shall I always keep people at the surface where their loss cannot cut me so deep with haunted memories and damning dreams?

"Everything seems much more depressing before coffee," Aimes whispers in my ear, putting an arm around my shoulders. She could feel the weight of my thoughts from where she was standing across the room.

"Then I need a lot of coffee." I smile at her, my constant counselor and navigator through life.

"I can make that happen." She smiles, placing her face close to mine with her bright smile and says, "Just promise me you'll brush your teeth afterwards."

She dodges my shove, skipping away with her laughter following her and Chapel out the door. He pauses, holding on to the doorframe. He is waiting for me to join them with a look of concern for leaving me behind.

"I'll catch up," I say, sitting to slip on my boots.

I smile to let him know I am fine, and I will be right behind them to ease his fears. His face wears a moment of doubt, but he is forced to leave me when Aimes' constant chanting of his name in different pitches starts from further up the hall. I hate morning people.

When I exit our room, I find Lawless is waiting for me. He is leaning against the opposite wall with his head down. He lifts his head when he hears me, giving me a small flash of his smile. He can still make my heart skip with one look and my body betrays me, stirring with his presence despite the amount of anger I hold for him over yesterday.

"Morning," I keep my voice neutral.

I meant for the word to be more forceful than the soft whisper that escaped me. My mind is chanting to keep walking, forcing one step in front of the other to make it past him. It screams at my eyes to not betray this façade of calm I am wearing as I go past.

"Wait," he calls to me softly, but I don't.

I continue down the hall to the bouncing pink streaks just a few saving steps away and the other man who kept us safe when Lawless chose his side last night. I walk to the two who stood beside me when J.D. sliced into me with his veiled threats and dark eyes. I walk to the two who had the courage to be with me in my weakness and not judge me for it. He does not call for me again and I don't look back. I keep my head forward, listening to his steps following mine down the hall.

Breakfast is composed of a lot of nervous eye contact and pancakes, but not a lot of conversation. Out of habit, or unsure of where to go, our little dysfunctional family found one another   at a table to one side of the school's cafeteria. Sitting around us are small pockets of groups engaging in their morning routines surrounded by their normal morning faces. Our faces are drawn and blank. We watch those around us who are lost in their small worlds with private envy of their joy.

Shelia sits with Simon and a small girl at a far table in a family picture of bliss. Their love for one another is evident in their gentle touches and the shy smiles they share. His tenderness is only proving his flirting yesterday was all for show and pure irritation spurred by male ego. Dolph and another man sit with them, enjoying the chance to be included in such an atmosphere. Their smiles are genuine at the jests shared with their group. The little girl shows every person at the table attention. It only reaffirms their group's closeness with her trust for them.

"Cute, huh?" Aimes asks. She has been watching the same table, but her mood sours quickly. "You know what is not cute?" I follow the motion of her head to see Leslie slinking her way to our table. The tension doubles with each pair of eyes that notice her. Most of the table has the decency to look away from where Lawless and I sit beside each other even with our strained relationship. Most being all but J.D., but he was never known for holding any level of decency. He watches, an amused smile upon his lips and Chapel's words from last night come back to me.

The bitterness rising inside me wants to pout and lash out like a toddler when Leslie's arms encircle Lawless' broad shoulders. Sharp barbs float over my tongue as her fingers seduce the muscles of his stomach under his grey cotton shirt. The soap opera has been set and everyone is waiting for my fall-out.

They have underestimated me. I learned this passive-aggressive game a long time ago from the best. A smile is the deadliest of poisons to those trying to upset you and that is what I feed to her. "Sorry to hear about Shaw. Simon was telling us how close you two were," I offer, as if we are all the best of friends.

She pauses at the sound of my voice. She is unsure which way the wind is blowing, and I smile even wider.

"If you want, we can take you back there to bury her. I mean, if my best friend ever were to become zombie chow, I would totally do everything I could to make sure she was put to rest properly." Aimes comments, chewing her breakfast nonchalantly, feigning serious concerns for Leslie's well-being. "Wouldn't you, Hells?" she asks me.

"I would. I just don't know how I could ever live with myself if I didn't," I answer Aimes, with an over exaggerated sense of duty. "What about you, Lawly? If your best friend forever were to become suddenly, I don't know, destroyed or left behind, would you do everything you could to make it right or just walk away forgetting about your loyalties and feelings for them?" Aimes asks. She cocks her head at him, making her eyes larger than normal with her sincere interest of the matter.

Rhett chokes on the bite he is chewing, trying to recover from her words. He looks to Lawless sitting across from him with the still confused Leslie draping herself across his shoulders. Rhett arches an eyebrow waiting for an answer. He is not going to help his friend in this matter. Like all men, Rhett laces his tennis shoes at the first hint of female drama. Perhaps this is the real reason for his dating habits and not the guise he hinted at yesterday. Wimp.

I am noticing Lawless for the first time since he has sat down. As her fingers trace circles across his chest and stomach, his body is ridged. His hands sit clenched on the table, despite her soft whisperings in his ear. I can see his lips pressed in a tight line of discomfort, not the male smile he was wearing yesterday with her flirting. He turns his head to look at Aimes and I and what I see in those eyes speaks more than any sharp reply he could form. Lawless is not playing the game. He is a pawn in it as much as we are.

What he may have said, or Aimes might have tried to do to soothe the hurt in his brown eyes, we were saved from when Simon joined our table.

"Les, why don't you see if Paula needs help in the kitchen?" Simon asks the woman who is making a shawl of herself across Lawless' shoulders.

He may have phrased it as a question, but it was anything but one. She lets her fingers slide slowly up Lawless' chest, drawing out the "goodbye" just to place another dare to me before leaving. "You really need to start keeping your knife around more, Hells. You just never know when you may need to stab some- thing," Aimes says and her words flow in time with Leslie passing behind her. "Still wearing your piece, Chappy?"

"No. I figured it would be safer not to with Hells around," Chapel answers in what he meant to be a teasing jest over yesterday's theft.

"When a man can't keep up with his own piece, then yeah, it's safer if he doesn't wear one," Lawless replies to that jest first, proving his anger from my actions is still evident.

Simon's laughter turns all of our heads to him. "Wait," he says, "let me see if I have this correct. You stole this man's gun. You stepped out, on your own, without your group's agreement; to save a bunch of people you have never met before; who had no clue you were there; risking your own life against a bunch of those things. Should I go warn Les now or later about who she is picking a fight with?"

"Later," Aimes says. "You forgot the best part though. Going all chop-suey on the Risen with the blade that yours truly slipped her." She makes a grand motion of pointing to herself as declaring it.

"Risen, huh?" Dolph's southern drawl joins the conversation, questioning Aimes' title for the new brand of danger that stalks us all now. His rifle is gone, but the bulge of his shirt hints at other weapons.

"That's what Chappy has dubbed them. It kinda stuck for us," she says, shrugging. "What have you been calling them?"

"We haven't." His answer leaves no room for further conversation on the topic.

Aimes just widens her eyes at me. "Well, okay," she mouths in my direction, from the shock of his response.

"When you guys are ready, I'll take you for a tour of the place," Simon offers. He is still wearing his smirk. He is finding many things amusing this morning.

"Ready!" Aimes and I shout at the same time in our typical fashion. We are both looking for any freedom from this stalemate of our making.

Simon looks to J.D. for consent. He is trying to rebuild the bridge so badly damaged with yesterday's posturing from both sides. Dolph watches it all, his eyes swaying from his leader to ours with interest. He is taking notes of every shift of the conversation. It's obvious his trust is not something he is ready to hand over just yet. Like a virgin at prom, he will make us work for it.

J.D. holds Simon's gaze, making him wait for his answer before nodding his consent. J.D. has been silent for most of the morning, his eyes taking watch of every motion his children have made. I wonder what information he has stored from watching us. What weapon is he assembling in his mind for our next round and what ammunition have I loaded for him to use in his shiny new weapon?

Unfortunately, there is nothing I can do about it right now. I know he is waiting, just as I am, for our games to begin. The only difference being he is anticipating it. I am preparing for it. He is plotting it. I am planning for it. Like a bride on her wedding night,

I am terrified by what I know is about to come, and yet knowing it will soon be upon me, it is thrilling.

"Are you showing us or escorting us?" J.D. stares at Dolph, who is taking a position behind our group with deliberate steps. "I guess that all depends on you now, don't it?" Dolph's south- ern drawl holds no subterfuge at the meaning of his question.

Dolph is waiting for one wrong move to be made. He is waiting for us to give him one reason to prove to Simon how unsafe we are. He does not stare down J.D. with hidden threats. He does not mix any verbiage in a vocal debate. Dolph has plainly laid his hand on the table. The only dare before us is will J.D. call it, or fold.

Chapter 26

Our tour starts on the first floor, as logic would entail. The bottom floor holds what one would assume to find in any high school. The halls are divided by the front office space, a gym with coordinating boys' and girls' locker rooms, a large library and the cafeteria we have just left is situated towards the back. It provides a nice view of the courtyard while eating.

At this hour with people starting to go about their day, most of the rooms are filling with life.

The second floor contains various sized classrooms. Now they are being used as storage for items needed to run such a large compound. A few rooms have been set aside and these have been designated to store the many weapons they have collected behind locked doors to keep prying eyes and itching hands away.

There is no one on the second floor other than us. It is eerily quiet compared to the noise we have left behind once the heavy doors were closed. The men talk shop about various aspects of keeping the place running. They talk about the small details such as security and precautions taken, the number of people located within and the many roles they play. The same names are mentioned time and again and the same names are omitted. J.D.'s eyes tell me he is taking note of it all.

Dolph and Richard seem to be the main security and providers. Shelia is the housemother, making sure everything runs smoothly as far as comfort and demands are made. A woman named Paula is the cook and nurse for the place. It sounds as if Simon just tries his best to keep everything going. I notice how neither Ross nor Leslie is mentioned in the list of important details. I guess great teeth and being easy is not real helpful for vital necessities.

"How do you still have electricity?" Marxx is the first to test Simon's openness with his question.

"The school has backup generators. We keep them fueled and they keep most things up and running. The vending machines, once their coolant was disconnected, take less energy to run than a hallway full of lights. Cold showers work as well as hot despite what the women say. Candles are for more than just ambiance. We have had to learn to be less dependent on some things though. Mostly, it's just about learning how to rethink our lives. Do stuff when the sun is up. Sleep when it isn't. We haven't had many issues," Simon says, shrugging with the simplicity of it.

"A lot of mouths to feed," Rhett states, fishing for more information.

"Hasn't been too horrible either. Dolph and Richard do a lot of the hunting. There is a good-sized garden to one side of the building we were using before the weather turned. The rest Paula has learned to be very creative with what we can find. Serving set meals, a day has helped a lot." Simon makes it all sound so easy while Dolph offers nothing to help pass the tour. He follows behind us like one of the many shadows we cast.

We come to another set of looming, locked doors. Plaques are lined up announcing different names as winning different recognitions for the once heavily used school. I wonder where all those children are now?

"What's in there?" Aimes is growing bored with the male chatter around us and looks to find anything to amuse her.

"Music room." Dolph steps past her, rattling the keys to unlock it.

"You keep the music room locked? Simon sings that badly?" She smiles, finally finding her a source of fun.

"More rooms locked, the less we have to keep track of people.

But yeah," Dolph answers her, "he sings that badly."

It might be the first time I have heard more than two words from him, much less an attempt at humor.

"Sorry dude, no "Love Shack" solos for you." Aimes turns to Simon with false sad eyes. "And here I was so counting on you for the tin roof part."

Simon smiles at being the subject of her humor as Dolph pushes open the large doors. The room and its hidden delights are show- cased by the sunlight streaming through the windows. Many chairs sit in a half circle facing a white board. It still holds the next selection to be rehearsed. Music stands are tilted, waiting for their sheet music. The whole room seems frozen in time.

Like kids again, we run around beating out tempos on drums and playing childhood tunes from forced memories on the many instruments lying around. Horrible renditions of "Row, Row, Row Your Boat" and "Twinkle, Twinkle Little Star" in various pitches fill the room. The only one among us with any real musical talent is Lawless and he is not among the ones mercilessly destroying classic songs.

He leans against the wall with J.D., Simon and Dolph as they watch us reliving our childhood memories. He still holds himself in his separation from us with an unspoken duty to J.D. Where, as before, he would have been enjoying these moments with us, now he only watches with his blank face and cold demeanor.

Chapel is the one who finds the old red acoustic guitar hidden behind the many stacks of plastic chairs, but it is Aimes who smiles with the discovery. She smiles at me and I know where her logic is taking us. My stomach becomes a pit of dread. It seems to be bottomless as I fall into it.

"Hey, Lawly, come see if it is still in tune," she calls across the room to him.

Only his lips move in a short frown before he recollects his blank face.

Lawless waits, still leaning against the wall with all of us watching for his answer. Slowly he peels himself off the wall as if gravity holds him hostage. Each step is deliberate as he makes his way over, winding around the rows of chairs and stands between us. We make brief eye contact when he passes me. He is testing the water between us. He also knows where this path Aimes has placed us on is heading. He is just as joy-filled with it as I am.

Many nights the three of us have spent under the stars with Lawless strumming songs around warmth-giving fires. Some songs he and I would sing duets on, with our voices perfectly matched. Sometimes he would sing to us, his voice holding rich emotion with the words he sang. Occasionally, I would even be brave enough to sing a solo, earning a smile from him when our eyes would catch as he watched me. I know this is Aimes' attempt to reunite our trio with our past memories. She also saw the pain in his eyes this morning with her words. This is her peace offering. Like a penny a child throws into a fountain, this is her hopeful wish.

"It's not too horrible." Lawless is adjusting the many pegs as his fingers slide along the strings, making them sing.

He is strumming several short tunes from those past nights. It lets Aimes and I know he understands what she is doing and what she is wanting from him. He may be brave enough to send this private smoke signal to us, but his eyes never leave the guitar while he is doing it.

"What was that song you used to sing for us, Hells? The one in that different language?" J.D. calls to us. He is not blind to the small healing we are attempting.

"Ave Maria," Lawless answers for me. He takes some of the heat J.D. sent for me.

"Right, "Ave Maria." Isn't that one of those religious songs, Chap?" J.D. is drawing all of his targets into one bucket. When he finds a barrel, I may start to panic.

"Yeah," Chapel gives him one solid word, understanding the game has started.

"Well, what ya' waiting on, Law? Play for her so she can pray for all us sinners," J.D. says.

He has put his game into play, and I have to give it to the man for his cunning mind. If Lawless plays the song, he is siding with mine in our prayers for them. If he does not play, he may rejoin J.D.'s group of sinners. The word play is so simple if one were not familiar with J.D, one would miss the threat. We are very familiar with him and we have missed nothing. Now we all wait for the next move to be made. A move no one can help Lawless make.

Lawless stands still while he pretends to be tuning the guitar in his hands as his mind races to pick a choice or find a way to appease us both. Rhett and Marxx are struggling to go blank with the realization of what line has been drawn. Each of them is rushing through their own ideas of how to help their friend with this new battle. Their conflict is plain upon their faces but once again, it is Chapel who steps into the fire.

"I know this one," Chapel offers, holding his hand out for Lawless to hand him the guitar.

Chapel is providing him a way out. A chance for Lawless to let another man bear the burden of J.D.'s anger rather than take sides. The two men stare at each other for a moment before Lawless hands the instrument over. Disappointment covers Chapel's face with the other man's choice and Lawless has a hard time meeting those bitter eyes.

"You ready?" Chapel asks me, stepping around Lawless with a rude dismissal of him.

Chapel places himself between J.D.'s gaze and myself, letting not only Lawless, but also all of them know he is the one keeping me safe. I nod, hoping my voice holds as I stare at the back of the man in whose hands, I used to place my heart as I wait for the chords to play. The melody floats in the air with the beauty only an acoustic guitar can hold. With the same ease of memory as a sinner praying the Lord's Prayer on Sunday, the lyrics begin to pour from my mouth. I find they have the same amount of sincerity, but sometimes, God tosses us a lifeline.

The sound of running feet puts every man on high alert. The drama was thick between our group, yet when danger is rushing towards us, all lines are blurred as our family comes together again. Chapel places the instrument on the chair beside him while moving to huddle Aimes and I behind him. Rhett and Lawless take a stance on either side of J.D. and Marxx has placed himself in the extreme left side, slightly behind us all. Whatever is heading toward us, our men have the room completely covered.

Dolph has watched their silent formation and something about his smirk is not amusing. He follows Simon with a backwards walk to check the hallway as the feet reach us. Without turning his back to the stone-faced room, he glances to see who has caused such a shift of mood. J.D. smiles while he makes a mental note of Dolph's reaction to them. He casts a wink to Rhett who returns his broad grin.

"You have to come quickly," a woman says between panting breaths. "They are outside the fence."

"They who?" Simon asks her.

The look of fear on the woman's face stirs our men to action. They are already checking clips and unfastening the leather bindings of their blades. They don't need her answer. We haven't had the luck of being hidden behind stone walls since this all started. "The things, they are outside the fence," she says, and finally

Simon's mind clicks the pieces together.

"Why don't you just let me and mine handle this," J.D. offers with his good ol' boy charm. His sneer doesn't match his tone. "We wouldn't want any of your pretty folks getting hurt now, would we?"

"He just called you ugly," Aimes mockingly whispers to Chapel. Chapel casts her a very parental reprimand of a look over his shoulder. His grin almost kills the depth of it though. Almost. Marxx' look makes up for what Chapel's lacks and Aimes pre-tends her nails are suddenly very interesting. "We can handle it," Dolph says.

"Like how you handled almost letting Simon die yesterday?" Lawless asks.

"I wasn't there." Dolph steps into the space of Lawless, putting the two of them too close for Rhett's comfort.

Lawless never flinches. He takes the final step left between he and Dolph, accepting the man's threat and dare. "Was that going to be your excuse for Shelia or just to yourself?"

I can hear the tension between the two of them. It's like static on phone lines in the summer heat. Their tension bounces to every male in the room. If either Dolph or Lawless so much as twitch, the room will erupt.

"So, the plan is to what, fight each other and let Risen just stroll on in?" Aimes asks, still peering at her nails from behind Chapel's back. "Let's just send Hells out. She does a better job than any of you anyway."

"Chapel isn't wearing his gun," I meekly say with so many male eyes on me with Aimes' comment.

Simon pulls Dolph from Lawless. Stepping in between the two males he says, "Pinky is right. We don't have time for whatever this is. We will go upstairs, settle everyone down, get Richard and then go see what is going on outside."

J.D. pushes his way past Simon and the still simmering Dolph. His face is contorted with disgust with the two men. As the men follow him out, Aimes and I are swept along with their exit. Marxx won't let us stay behind. He wedges himself behind Chapel and forces us to walk with them.

When Aimes tries to lock her feet, Marxx whispers into the space between her and I, "I will pick you up and carry you out of here like the spoiled child you are imitating."

Aimes doesn't call his bluff. His bone-deep voice inspires no bravery in her normally sharp tongue.

"Where the hell are you going?" Dolph shouts with our mass exit.

"To do what you're too scared to do," J.D. calls back before Lawless can open his mouth. "You go on upstairs and put some pretty panties on. We will have this shit all cleaned up before you can find your matching bra."

Rhett spins to walk backwards do he can see the damage his words will cause. He says, "Unless that is what Richard is really for, Dolph. Does Richie tell you how pretty you are when you are scared?"

Lawless laughs a little too loudly, adding the extra twist of the verbal knife. Marxx doesn't join in with their exchange. He is too busy keeping his hand on the shoulder of Aimes. Every time her jaw moves, he clamps his hand tighter to keep her silent. What Marxx isn't prepared for is Chapel's reaction to what he is doing. Chapel reaches around her, sliding his arm between her and Marxx and pulls her to the space in front of him. Locking his arms around her, Chapel never looks at Marxx and Marxx doesn't question the man. It leaves me now between the two of them and their private male battle. Too much testosterone can make a girl's head spin. If I only had pea soup to fully complete how I feel. "Do we have an actual plan?" I ask, once we are all in the stairwell.

"Since when do you give a shit about plans, Barbie?" J.D. asks.

His voice holds the threat of anger if I answer wrong or at all. "Great, so we all agree? I'm just going to go again alone?" I ask

him, not smart enough to shut up.

J.D. stops so suddenly, Rhett and Lawless almost trip over him.

J.D. takes the steps between he and I two at a time and I know my face is showing my fear as he climbs towards me. Chapel pushes Aimes to one side and places himself directly in J.D.'s oncoming path. The two men stare at each other. Their eyes are exchanging words their mouths don't and whatever J.D. sees in Chapel's is enough to not push the matter in such a tight area.

"You best do your damn job this time," J.D. threatens to the face of Chapel. "If she gets out, I'm taking it out on your ass."

Marxx leans on the wall behind Aimes, and with his presence so close to her, it is enough to keep her mouth shut. Even with

J.D. so close, I still have to admit it's a neat trick Marxx has learned. J.D. mistakenly takes my smile as a threat to him and before Chapel or I can react, he has a handful of my hair, pulling me close to his face.

"If I want you, no one can save you, Barbie," he whispers into the thin space between he and I. "Not Chapel. Not Lawless. No one. You best remember that."

He lets me go with the same force he had grabbed me with and it's Marxx who catches me. J.D. narrows his eyes slightly when he sees who holds me. He hadn't counted on Marxx. His name was not on the list. With the glare Marxx is sending him, maybe it should have been.

"Let's get this over with," J.D. says, turning his back to Marxx. "I feel the need to kill something."

His threat hangs in the air, but it's losing some of its heat for me with the two men standing so close beside me. Small blessing Aimes has chosen to stay silent. The looks she casts Lawless is sharper than anything her mouth may have formed. When the noise of Simon and Dolph entering the stairwell comes from above us, we are all moving again towards whatever had upset the woman.

Chapel turns to Aimes and I once our group reaches their motorcycles parked in the courtyard. "You're not really going to stay inside, are you?" he whispers his questions as the rest of the men are exchanging ammo from their saddlebags to better suit the other's gun.

"Not a chance," Aimes answers for me.

Chapel stares at me. I can see his mind working on how to best handle me. My choices will not only land me on the short end of J.D., but also him. The wheels on the bus go round and round as I throw us under them.

"You sure about this?" Chapel asks me. He is giving me one last chance to save us both.

It's Aimes who comes to our rescue.

"How do you guys plan to carry all that?" she asks the men who are stuffing their pockets like children trying to store candy.

The looks they exchange speak the fact they hadn't really thought it out. They are just going on normal impulses.

"Give it here," Aimes walks to the truck, pulling an empty spare duffel from inside the cabin. She walks to each of the men, holding the bag open as they deposit their spare rounds or clips. When she comes to J.D., they both stare at each other. He cups her chin with his spare hand while letting his many clips litter the ground around her with a smile.

"You're gonna' be screwed when you unload your first round," she says to him and adding a smile, she goes in for the kill, "and from what your exes say, it won't take you too long."

Pulling the handles of the bag over her shoulder, she pivots, leaving J.D. to clean his mess himself. She holds the bag open for Chapel to store his before zipping the bag closed. She smiles to us as we listen to the chuckling J.D. picking up the mess he made.

You never know with him how he will take a slap to his face. Sometimes your nerve will amuse him. Other times he will make you pay in some twist of irony best suited to his amusement. Aimes was lucky this time or he is just more forgiving with her than he is with me.

"I guess you and I are on ammo duty?" I ask her when the men start walking through the courtyard doors.

"You get to go out and play. Chapel gets to keep his teeth. I get to not sit on the sidelines," she says. "Seems all a win to me."

"Depending on what is waiting for us, that is," I reply as we leave the safety of the high school.

"Can't be any worse than the cabin or the Welcome Center," she offers.

"You know happens when you dare life, right?" "You do something stupid?"

"Asks the one who keeps picking fights with J.D."

"I was wondering if you were going to bring that up." She smirks at me.

We follow behind the men without a word the rest of the way. The men aren't chatty either. Their eyes roam the space beyond the gate, looking for any sign as to what had the woman upset. It doesn't take us long to find it.

A group of Risen has somehow found the metal links keeping them on the other side of the school. They had reset to either resting or thinking before we came upon them. Hearing us, their eyes slowly sway to our direction while their bodies hold still and frozen from their previous actions. I've seen it before. It still unnerves me to see how they can all move at once, focusing on us with their eyes locked on our every move.

They come alive. Their voices join in growls and almost screams from somewhere deep in their throats. They shake the fence with their hands as if they are the prisoners and not us who are locked on this side of the gate. The same hatred for us upon their face is mirrored on J.D.'s for them.

"You can drop the duffle, Blondie. We ain't gonna be needing it," J.D. says, flat and hollow.

This is not the fight he was itching for, but it is all there is. He's going to make it personal.

J.D. reaches, not for the large hunting style of a knife he wears attached to his belt, but the small knife he keeps in his pocket. Rhett puts the action to logic and the tips of his lips curl into a smirk the Devil would envy.

All their guns are quickly tucked away in waistbands or bootstraps, being replaced by their small collection of handheld blades. Right on cue from J.D., they follow the man to the fence. The Risen grow excited thinking food is within their reach. The men grow excited thinking a release for their anger is within reach.

J.D. reaches the fence first, standing face-to-face with the creature standing across from him with nothing more than the thin metal fence between them. What is left of the woman is sneering, growling as she presses her face directly to the fence. As I watch their standoff, even with all J.D. has done, my stomach still lurch- es with the risk he is taking.

"You're one ugly bitch," J.D. says to her as if he is shocked to see it.

"Waiting for a prom date?" Rhett asks J.D., shoving the thin blade of his knife into the eye socket of the male across from him.

J.D. smiles at Rhett, and not to be outdone, he too shoves his knife through the woman's waiting face. "You keeping count, Barbie?" he shouts to me as she falls.

"Of the stupid things you do? Check," I reply.

I hear him chuckle as he forces his blade into another snarling face. The men follow suit, stabbing and violently turning the fight into a hand-to-hand brawl. Their anger takes over their common sense, encouraging them to reach through the thin links to grab fistfuls of hair to steady the heads of Risen before their blades slice and mutilate. The force of their fighting arches the rotting blood, splashing it high on their arms or covering their fists with it. The men are not just taking care of the threat. They are destroying it with savagery and male anger; something J.D. knows how to stroke within them.

Even our gentle Chapel is vicious with the ones he can reach. He is smashing his fist against their skulls, burying his knife as far as he can shove it. His eyes are as glazed as the Risen's he is attacking. Whatever he is seeing, he is feeding his grief with the utter destruction of what is in front of him. Aimes and I cringe with each sound the men are making until we have to turn away from the scene.

When the rattling of the fence stills, we look back to see them panting and covered in dark streaks of blood no longer holding any crimson to it. It's black and it drips from their hands and arms like a river of oil. Lawless laughs first, letting the tension escape from him. Rhett catches next, joining the younger man's release. Slowly they all start to laugh as they either pat one an- other or lean against the fence dripping the same river. I look to Aimes and she just rolls her eyes, shaking her head.

"You know," J.D. says. between his ragged breathing, "if they had started to climb, we might have been in deep there."

I look up to the barbed wire circling the top links and wonder, is that possible? If they can learn to open doors, what chance does a metal fence really have?

"Feel better?" Simon's voice startles me, and I jump.

The man who must be Richard places his hands on my shoulders to settle my nerves. Rolling his thumbs over them, he whispers to me, "You're pretty."

I laugh, remembering the insult Rhett had handed Dolph.

Apparently, Richard has been informed of it as well.

Lawless and Rhett do not take well to my laughter. Lawless' tightens his hands into fists, sending the river into unsteady drips from the action. Rhett's eyes watch the man behind me as if some- one has taken his favorite toy away and he's plotting how to take it back. Chapel shakes his head and I'm starting to feel sorry for the man.

"You boys come out to clean up the mess?" J.D. asks. "Told you we would have it taken care of for you. You didn't have to rush out here." J.D. is cleaning the dark matter from his blade on the leg of his jeans. "But since you are here, why don't you remove your hands from my girl there before I let my boy remove them for you?"

J.D. doesn't look up with half-masked demand. He acts like Richard is not enough trouble to fully give him any attention. Instead he focuses on making sure his pocketknife is free from gore before snapping it shut, but I catch the small glance he casts towards Rhett and Law. Aimes does as well.

"…but she is wearing my matching bra," Richard says, and it is all Aimes and I can do to stop the rush of male bodies toward us.

Chapter 27

After Simon helped us separate the many bruised egos, Aimes and I followed Shelia around like lost children for the rest of

the afternoon. She has spent her time checking in on the many families that dwell inside this makeshift apartment building and we have the chance to meet many of the residents within these walls. We are learning that high school is high school. The games seem to have never ended with their politeness cloaking their whispers when they close the doors behind us.

Even with all of their stares and whispering, which I blame on Aimes' hair, it is nice to be with Shelia. It's easy to see how genuine she is as I watch her care for these people. She keeps track of every person's needs as well as the supplies needed to take care of them. Everything from medicine to toys, she makes a tally of what to present to Simon. Their system is almost flawless as the ruling couple. She is their gentle Queen and he is their brave King. Together, they are keeping their little kingdom safe from the monsters that lurk outside.

The three of us have spent a great deal of time bonding over the details of what could be our new life and slowly the shock factor of Aimes' wit is reducing to slight blushing and laughter for Shelia. She tells us about how most of these people are from the original group who set up here at the school. A few are from fragments of other groups who they have come across as time has gone by. Together, they have all formed this new little community. Even by today's standards, it's not an altogether easy life here.

Gardens are planted and tended by various people. Some are given the task to keep the school clean and secure. Others help with the running of the day-to-day needs. In essence, everyone has a job to do. She tells us that Simon believes this way everyone takes pride and care to keep it running smoothly. He wants to keep everyone busy and not lamenting away the days in fear or panic. That I can definitely understand.

When I ask about the little girl, I saw this morning, she tells me her name is Kira and the one Simon asked about yesterday when we first arrived. She is their three-year-old daughter. They were on the verge of divorce before everything changed. I guess who left the socks on the floor is no longer the button pusher it used to be. Hurrah for your neighbors going cannibal to save your marriage, I suppose. I am not sure Hallmark ever thought of that card.

"So, what's next?" I ask her, after every converted apartment has been visited and the long list of their concerns have been written down to be passed to Simon for review. Some of their concerns make Shelia a saint for even bothering to write them down, much less to actually present them as if they hold any real meaning with everything else far more pressing going on.

"We check in with Paula and Ross downstairs. Paula will be able to tell me which of the medicines Simon needs to keep a watch for and Ross will know where to get them," Shelia answers, with her normal warm smile. Once again, it's all so simple.

"I don't get it. Why will Ross know where to get stuff?" Aimes wears her doubt. It puts a frown on her face.

"He was a taxi driver. Taking people to different locations was his job. It allows for a lot of stored knowledge of the town," Shelia responds, leading us down the stairway.

His smile makes more sense now.

"What was Dolph?" Aimes smirks at the woman with the purpose of her question.

"Dolph and Richard came from what was left of another group. I don't know a lot about them. They don't share much." Shelia laughs at Aimes' obvious question. She teasingly asks her, "Should Rhett be jealous?"

Aimes and I both pause with the indication of her question. Hearing our steps no longer following her down the metal stairs, she also stops as we stare at her with our confusion.

"I'm sorry. I just thought you two were together, but this morning you were in bed with Chapel. I know it's none of my business. Forget I made the joke," Shelia says, with her hands motioning her apology as her face shows the nervousness of possibly upset- ting us.

We can't help it. Both of us begin laughing at the thought of us with either of the men she has listed. Everything is becoming crystal clear about her reaction this morning at our door. Sweet Shelia, with her one love Simon, thinks we are sluts. You know the world has gone to hell when you find it funny when someone questions your sexual lifestyle.

Shelia is lost in her confusion. She is not sure if she should join in with our laughter or run for reinforcements. "So, you are not with them?" She pauses, holding out the last word in a soft whisper afraid they might overhear our refusals of the facts.

"No, no, and ick, no!" Aimes is waving her arms to fend off the mental pictures the question is causing for her.

"We have been together for so long, as friends, I guess the lines blur for us. It's like a giant group of your older brother's best friends. You can flirt without harm. Everyone knows it's all in good fun," I add, trying to help her understand, to help her work through her panic. "No one is really with anyone." Those words sting more than I want them to.

We watch the gears turn in her head as she tries to put the pieces together. "I guess that's why Leslie was in that one's bed this morning then," she speaks more to herself than to us.

I feel the floor fall out from under me with her words still floating in the air with the echo of the hallway. She turns around, heading back downstairs unaware of the damage she has done. Aimes and I are lost in a world of questions neither of us are brave enough to ask her. We are well aware of what the answers could do to us.

I can feel Aimes staring at me. She is searching for what to say to convince me "that one" was not Lawless. She wants me to believe he would never do something like that. Our past has proven otherwise in the years we have been playing as a couple. We both know it, so we say nothing as we follow Shelia continues down the stairs to finish the morning paperwork.

"Totally going to shank that skank," Aimes says to me, proving once again we think so much alike as the doors shut behind us, keeping the many doubts between us.

Paula is indeed found in the kitchen of the cafeteria. She is a larger woman with perfectly styled hair. Its short cut frames her plump face. The soft, blonde coloring highlights the pink under- tones of her ivory skin. She is wearing what appears to be scrubs in a soft teal color. They further accent her coloring perfectly. She is pretty in a well-manicured soccer mom kind of way with a dash of fifties housewife thrown in for good measure. She greets us with a smile when she finally notices us in her domain. All that is missing here is the freshly baked apple pie on a white painted windowsill.

Up until now, she had been cleaning the many cooking utensils from the morning meal and preparing for the next one. Many plates and their coordinating silverware lay in long rows, ready for their next use. Bulk boxes and bags are waiting on the counters in preparation for planning the rest of the meals for today. I am once again amazed at how easy it all looks. She is the Martha of the end of the world.

"I was wondering when you would find me," Paula croons. Her smile fills her face. It lights her eyes with the warmth of it.

"Sorry," Shelia blushes at the implications of the words saying, "I was a little distracted this morning. We had a little girl time." She whispers the last part like a naughty secret.

I wonder what kind of saintly life this woman must have led before human flesh became a main menu staple to think our conversation on the stairs about boys is "girl time". She is blushing a bright pink with her confession to Paula. Perhaps it's best we never mention to her what Aimes has stashed in her bag for her nightly recreation.

"Well, we all need a little "girl time" here and there, don't we?" Paula asks, smiling at Aimes and me.

I smile back, thinking how very disappointed she would be to discover the truth. Unless everyone in this place was such a saint like Shelia and would agree to our slut-like status. If so, my vote is to haul it out of here quickly before Aimes and I are stoned in the courtyard.

"You two must be what has this place buzzing. Normally it's pretty boring around here. The joys of everyone knowing every- thing about everyone, I guess." Paula smiles with a hint of mis- chief like a gossiping housewife, still laying out the many plates and silverware.

"As awe-inspiring as we are, I don't think we can take all the credit. Majority, sure. I hear we are quite the naughty girls," Aimes nonchalantly replies. She is letting our past conversation color this one, looking to Shelia with a shared smile.

"I too heard something along those lines." Paula still wears her smile of a secret knowledge.

I think "girl time" may have just gotten interesting.

Before I can ask the reason behind her smile, a familiar whistle cuts through the air. It startles both Shelia and Paula, but Aimes and I just groan. We know that sound. It's our shock collar of a calling. We are being summoned. Paula gets to keep her secrets for a little longer.

Aimes returns the whistle, as we are trained to do, with an impressive eye roll. Rhett's tall frame enters through the doorway following the sound and he is missing his normal mischievous smile. That does not bode well for us. Wordlessly holding the door open with his body, he waits for us and like children being caught in the act of doing something wrong, we walk over to him to be told what our punishment will be.

"J.D. wants everyone upstairs. We have been looking for you two for a good while now. Caused a bit of concern," Rhett says with his lowered voice, due to the two women in the room who are pretending to not listen.

Paula is better at it, humming to herself with her chores. Shelia's glances are giving her away as she pretends the paper in her hand is very interesting.

"We weren't aware we had a curfew." Aimes does not hide her unhappiness using her voice and her posture to let the tall man fully understand how little she cares what J.D. wants.

"I know there has been a lot of crap back-and-forth, but it would be best to put on that pretty smile of yours when we go up there. It has not been a fun morning for any of us so far." His voice is almost a growl with the emotion it carries.

I shiver with it. I have forgotten what this man can become, and I wonder what has happened while we were away. Who did Daddy punish now?

"Chapel?" I ask, becoming aware he has been alone with their group all morning while we were able to escape.

"What about him?" Rhett looks at me, answering my question with more than just his tone.

Chapel has continued to stand his ground against J.D. and the rest of them. The only real question left is doing he stand alone or did one of them finally slip rank? Are the rest of them growing weary of these games as we are?

Rhett's tone tells me it may be so as everyone is slowly becoming a target for J.D. with his misplaced rage over the current situation. It does not send me into shivers of delight looking forward to whatever is waiting for us upstairs. Paula is right. What does a girl have to do to get some serious "girl time" around here?

Chapter 28

"I think we should stay," a voice breaks the tension.

Marxx is the first to speak after we have been told why we were all summoned to the room serving as the men's apartment.

J.D. feels he has humored us long enough with his conceding to our idea of coming here. Now he is ready to take his control back. Each man in the room stands a good distance apart. J.D. and Lawless are standing in the center of the room across from Rhett and Marxx. Chapel is sitting to the side on one of the cots still unmade from the night before. The tension in the room can be felt from all angles with no one looking at another. I only have guesses as to what has happened within their happy little men's club while we were away, and I am trying not to smile with my thoughts.

"It's a nice set up. Just from a defensive state alone. There are no outside windows on the bottom floor for Risen to break into. There are only two doors from the bottom floor to enter the stairwell. One has been welded shut. The other bonus is the courtyard, which is always being watched from the floor above. Other than that, we are surrounded by thick walls and many windows making it impossible for anything to go unnoticed," Rhett offers solid reasons to help to point out why J.D. should agree with Marxx.

"Simon already said our help would be welcomed in keeping it secure. We get to keep our weapons and not sit around all day taking orders from them," Marxx says. He knows our leader well and he is pushing the right buttons to get J.D. to join the conversation.

J.D., who until now has been staring blindly at the floor, looks up at what was spoken. Rhett tries to hide his smile as Marxx' words hit home.

"I ain't taking no orders from any Democrat and his sidekicks."

J.D. lets his tone express his thoughts perfectly.

"Won't have to. He said we could do our own thing as long as we agree to not stir up anything," Lawless finally speaks hearing J.D.'s voice.

I wonder if he will roll over next; maybe shake. Play dead would be just as amusing.

Aimes and I sit silently, watching them trying to talk J.D. into the shared opinion of the group. We are as close to the door as possible so we may leave as soon as we can. We know our thoughts have no real value here with this discussion. Nothing we say will hold any sway over the final judgment of what they do.

J.D. did not want us here for that. He just wanted to prove to us, and to them, we will still come when called. Maybe we should be the ones learning to shake. We seem to have roll over down well enough.

"This what you really want?" J.D. asks the room. His tone is soft, almost cautious, as if he is afraid to hear our answer. The exposed weakness takes us all by surprise for a moment, pulling our attention to the man in the center of our storm.

Rhett looks in my direction to see if I am seeing it. If I can see the cracks forming in the man, we all think of as our strength.

There is a sadness about Rhett as he looks at me, an almost pleading in his eyes for my help. He is lost with the many divisions now forming within our group. He is desperately looking for us all to start again and to forget the words and actions that have been done. He wants this new place to be the start of our family bond and laughter again as the cabin was supposed to have been. Our brave and ruthless Rhett is shrouded in doubt and remorse. I do not know how to tell him I don't think I have the maturity to fix us.

"Yeah, it is." Aimes is the only one to speak up and all eyes rest on her as she says, "At least, it's what I want. You can stay or go if you please, but I am staying here."

Rhett closes those sad eyes knowing the damage her words have done.

"And you, Barbie?" J.D. asks. "Where do you stand?"

"Here. I am tired. I want a "home" again," I answer him, letting my voice try to take some of the sting from her words. "Don't you?"

I can feel Aimes' body shift with my soft tone for the man. In her mind, the lines are still drawn, but she was not the one watching Rhett being broken from the weight of it. She does not see Marxx withdrawing further into his shadow with every moment passing. She cannot see the scars Chapel is now wearing as he fights for us. Nor does she see the light fade from Lawless' eyes. She does not see all the steel hearts rusting before us. I do.

J.D. stares at me with his silent resolve. Our eyes meet across the great divide we have created and for a moment I am taken back to days that now seem to be years ago where he was the father I needed and I was the daughter he craved. Just as quickly as those feelings return, I watch them slip away.

"No," J.D. says and now I can hear them slipping away. His voice fills the room with the finality of the word. Like a black casket closing, the hope the men were holding is buried.

One single word, and the room falls back into the darkness. Every man inhales, pulling the armor tight around his soul again.

The small glimpses they had spared me are now a thing of the past as the battle rages on.

I know now no matter what the cost is to them, they will stand by this man. They do not know how to do anything else. The men I once found so brave and strong now seem pathetic to me. The pity I felt for them only moments ago fades at their refusal to stand on their own, allowing J.D. to break them down with his stubbornness. I am just as upset at J.D. for breaking what he is supposed to protect.

"Well then, I guess you five remember where the door is?" I ask, letting my words chill the room with my lack of concern for them now.

I meet each of their eyes as they look at me. Even the ones belonging to the man I once sought to guide me through the dark- ness of my nightmares. Only blank eyes stare back at me from behind their well-constructed walls.

"Not five," Chapel says, with his head down. He stands with a deep inhale of his breath repeating what he has said, "Not five." "Can't say I'm surprised." J.D. attempts to taunt Chapel with his sneer.

"Me either," Chapel lashes back, with just as much disgust for not only J.D., but the others as well. "It must be unnerving to see the girls with more courage than us. It's our job to keep them safe. It's always been our job. Now you've each turned your back on them for this man and a quick lay? Whatever happens next, it's on you. Never forget that." Chapel is staring at Lawless as he opens the door for Aimes and myself. "Come on," he says, never taking his eyes from the men in the room as we exit.

"Peace!" Aimes says, walking past Chapel.

Her voice is deceptively strong. Her brave face is only one layer deep and she rushes out of the room before the layer can be stripped from her. All the anger she was holding like a bonfire inside of her is losing its heat against the truth of what is happening to us as the leaf-covered hills flash back to my mind. We craved the fire and now we are burning from the spark we stirred.

I stand still, leaning against the wall where I have been watching this whole time. J.D. is losing the battle of his blank stare and I watch it unfold on his face like a silent movie. Those cold, steel-colored eyes are swimming in a sea of his own making as he now swims on the edge of his darkest emotions. Each of us is crumbling from his actions and he knows it. The world he has built is turning its back on him, but he is either too weak or too strong to stop it.

"Call a vote," I say to the room, and it is the last life preserver I will throw them.

J.D. reclaims his face with the knowledge of what I have just done. Demanding a vote is only done when making it deadly clear voices are not being heard and J.D. will now have to stand behind the decision it lands on if the men back the decision.

It's a direct insult to his leadership. Because of that, no one has dared called one in some time. Throw in the fact a woman has called one and it is gasoline to the fire of his pride. As much as a part of them as Aimes and I are, we are just as much not. I haven't forgotten that fact. I am just not willing to let the fire win.

I know with this; the divide just grew between us by miles. The look in his eyes confirms it. The shock on the men's faces seals it. Damned if I do….

Aimes and Chapel both stare at me with disbelief. I could have walked out with them, closing the door forever on all of this. I was inches from my freedom, but instead I retied the noose. This dead horse is not only getting heavy, but it is also starting to stink. "We stay." Chapel is the first to start, stealing the room's silence with his vote. He has backed the decision for a vote to be called when he spoke. The wheels on the bus go round and round as it heads my way.

"Stay." Aimes takes up the chant while still staring at me with her disbelief.

"Stay," I say, with a cold voice. I know this is the last chance for our family and I am preparing my heart to close another door of another room. If the vote does not go in our favor, they will be lost to me forever with what I have just done.

"Stay," Rhett answers, keeping his face blank and turned away from J.D.

"Stay." Marxx' deep gravel voice is strong with his decision dand he stares at J.D. with the full force of himself.

"Stay." Lawless is the last to vote after a long pause. His head is down, pulling his shoulders in with the knowledge of what his vote may cost him and what it could have lost him if he chose the other option.

J.D. is silent. Anger rides his body and I am the focus of it, but there is a different flavor to this anger. I know this man well. Every motion he has ever made, I have memorized like a melody out of fear of him. Now these lyrics are singing to me with a new song.

"See you at dinner," I tell him. I keep this new song to myself. It is a private tune to hum another day. A day I know will be here soon.

"I can't believe you did that!" Aimes says to me after the three of us have left the room. "I don't know if I should hi-five your hand or the back of your head!"

"The back of her head," Chapel offers to help her solve her debate. He is always so helpful like that.

"It will be fine," I answer them both, keeping what I saw in J.D.'s face close to me.

"I am thinking we should have let Rhett choose the other name for you instead of Zombie Barbie." Aimes stomps with her walking, still irked with me at what I potentially risked stepping so far over our unspoken line.

"Which one was that?" I ask, with mild curiosity.

"Wonder Bitch. As in, I wonder what the bitch was thinking!" she says with complete honesty.

Oh, that Rhett, always a charmer.

Chapter 29

Aimes and I had offered to help Paula with dinner, but upon discovering the tornado Aimes is in the kitchen, we were politely asked to stop. If polite is Chapel picking Aimes up and placing her on the counter, threatening her with harm if she moves, then yes, it was a very polite request. Aimes' response, not so much.

Chapel surprises all of us with his culinary skills. The man is a Betty Crocker in an apron, making Paula smile her warm smile the whole time with his knowledge and his eagerness to help her. Chapel was made for moments like these. He is a "home and hearth" guy to the bone and he returns her smiles with his own. Soon the two of them have completely forgotten us amid our hidden giggles and whispered comments. We sneak from the room before our laughter gets the best of us.

"Do you think there are really that many types of whisks or were they totally going sexy-top-secret-kitchen-code?" Aimes asks, her eyes dancing with the thought.

"It scares me you are excited about the possibility. Can you even imagine Chapel…," I leave the sentence dangling, unable to form the words to finish it? We are both lost in a mixture of morbid curiosity and avoidance of the idea and our faces exchange the concept with bursts of expressions.

We are lounging on a bench in the courtyard amid the many metal drums being turned into bonfires for light. The many fires give off enough heat to keep the winter winds at bay. The sur- rounded courtyard keeps the fires from being seen and exposing us to anything in the darkness beyond. It is a nice touch. It pushes the darkness away and lets the many people mingling around enjoy the space before the weather keeps so many confined inside. "Hey, I was just asking about their secret sexy code talk. You are the one that went all hardcore porn viewing on us," Aimes says, feigning innocence and twirling a bright pink streak of her hair. "Who's viewing hardcore porn?"

We both jump at the male voice, almost spilling us off the cement bench. I am glad at this moment there is not a raised window around us with the amount of grace we hold.

Dolph is standing behind the man who was sitting at their table this morning. He is close enough to the flames so I can see him, but deep enough in the darkness to keep his face masked with the dancing flame's shadows. The new man is not as shy, standing proudly as he smirks down at our ungraceful ways.

"Sorry. I didn't mean to scare you. At least, not that well." He smiles and I hear Aimes inhale beside me with it. Come into my parlor said the spider to the fly. His smile draws her in with the same welcome mat.

"I'm Richard," he says to us, almost feeling embarrassed and shy by our silent stares. "I believe we met this morning? You're wearing my bra."

I smile, remembering him and send a wave to Dolph standing behind Richard. It is met with the same signature head nod we have seen from him over and over again. I wonder if he ever gets a cramp from repeating that motion so often.

"So where is the porn?" Richard pushes through the stalemate of a conversation attempt, still wearing an amused smile. Richard should have picked a better partner if he had hopes Dolph would help steer this ship.

Richard's voice is soft. Soft in a way of wanting to hear him sing you to sleep at night. Soft in a way you desire to hear him whisper words in the dark of the night against your flesh. His short cut curly hair is the color of sunsets with its warm red and orange glow. His full beard is trimmed close, holding the same coloring as his hair. He wears his smile with ease upon his friendly face as his mirth-filled eyes watch us. They catch the light of the flames, reflecting their warmth back at us. Other than their similar body shape of well-toned workings, he and Dolph have very little in common.

Richard seems warm and inviting where Dolph is shy and cautious. Richard has already spoken more words to us than I believe Dolph has our entire time here. I wonder if Aimes and I are so different or does Dolph have a different side he keeps hidden from those he has not deemed worthy of his trust?

"It's in the kitchen," Aimes says smiling, returning Richard's.

The pixie is ready to play.

"I hope that's not what's for dinner." Richard's smile grows, baiting my friend as he sits on the bench beside her.

He is about to learn why one should not bait Aimes as she continues the verbal match, dropping the pitch of her voice to a soft feminine whisper of intentions. "I hope it is," she says.

"Well," Richard says, leaning in close to her with her invitation, "I guess we will have to go find out. The only real question is will we need utensils or our fingers to eat tonight?"

He lingers there staring into her eyes for a moment with his enjoyment of her expression before returning to Dolph. I think Aimes was just out Aimes'. Dolph is shaking his head with amusement and pats Richard on the shoulder as he passes. I am still wondering what just happened when I hear her whisper in my ear.

"Dibs," she calls, as she follows them with more speed than I have seen her move all day.

Dinner is relatively uneventful as we join Simon's table, much to Shelia's delight. I suppose she is not the only one who grows tired of being the only girl amid a male-centered group. I let the conversations flow around me, keeping myself reserved in my own bitterness of how things once were. It's not only J.D. who is having a hard time accepting the many changes taking place for our group with our bonds slipping away.

With her meal already complete, Kira dances around the table in a game of "Duck, Duck, Goose". Simon is the only "goose" she ever picks, and he chases her each time, resulting in her high- pitched laughter. My sinking mood helps me reach the darkness inside me faster than normal tonight. Doors open on rooms I have tried to keep nailed shut with each laugh circling me with their game. Their hinges creak like a soft moan as memories escape from the cracks.

When laughter of a different pitch joins in with the one around me, I refuse to look up. I'm too afraid of what I may see running around the table. Will Lilly's eyes be joyful or hateful with my failures? Will her gown be white, or crimson soaked, leaving red footprints in her wake? Will she be alone or surrounded by the rest of the Angels I have failed with their damning eyes watching me?

"Won't your boys be missing you?" Dolph's southern drawl startles me when he asks me the question. He nods when I stare at him, not understanding him. His eyes are looking behind me to where I imagine the rest of our group is sitting.

"Didn't have plans to ask them." I resist glancing behind me, and his eyes lock with mine. He is searching my face and try as I might, I slip my mask.

My mortar has been cracked today, leaving my walls vulnerable and weak. He sees it, but just nods. I have never appreciated his avoidance of conversation more than I do right now. It is times like these when I appreciate the advantage of being friends with males. They do not feel the need to ask any in-depth questions to push deeper into your troubles. They don't expect for you to either. My scars. Your scars. There are no "our scars" with men. "You think your group is up for a little fun?" Simon asks us.

I hope he means more than just us for whatever he is thinking with the glint in his eye.

"Define "fun"?" Aimes must be holding the same thoughts with her direct question.

Paranoia is our new perfume. It is like Obsession, but cheaper. "Looked over the list today. We are running low on some of the things needed. Seems your boys could use a little escape and I've seen what you consider as amusing," Simon says, and his smile reaches his eyes as he teases me about the incident with the truck.

"We don't hold much sway with them anymore. You'll have to ask yourself. They don't normally pass up the chance to cause a little mayhem though." I smile back, pretending to not catch on to his meanings.

"Rhett is growing bored," Aimes offers.

"Always a dangerous thought," I say, as we fall into our normal pattern of conversation.

"True story," she begins

"They probably miss their bikes."

"Been a whole, what, two days now?"

"Devastating."

"To be sure."

"We are running low on C's"

"Which C?"

"The most important one."

"I thought they were all important?"

"Not like this one." She pauses in our volley to make eye con- tact trying to hint of which one she is speaking. The eye shift to Richard across from her gives me the best clue.

"Truly devastating," I offer with condolences.

"Is that a yes?" Simon is trying to follow our conversation. The look on his face telling us he has not. He does glance at Richard though, wondering what he has missed.

"It is a "yes" we will ask them. Not a "yes" they will do it," I explain, helping his mental train get back on track. "Hand me the list of what you need."

"We need," he corrects me. "One big happy family now, remember?"

"Of shining happy faces," Aimes adds as she smiles.

I take the list to give the men we have been avoiding all day. She cannot pass up the chance to tease Dolph, who still refuses to join her fan club.

"Hey Dolphers, say porn for me?" she asks him sweetly.

Dolph's face holds confusion for a moment before a slow smile spreads across his lips. He looks to me with those deep colored eyes of his. "Porn," he says, letting the word develop more syllables than it should hold with his southern drawl.

I smile. I did. I smiled.

Aimes and I take our trays to the drop off window, signaling for a very happy Chapel to come with us. At least he was very happy. Now as he falls in behind us, he is closing down the emotions he was allowing himself to show with Paula. We walk to the table before us as if we are preparing for war. Each step is pulling us deeper behind mental shutters to help protect and to help us face the man watching us. J.D.'s face shifts from cautious to amused seeing our path leading us to him.

"Well, well, lookie here, boys. You are playing messenger now, Barbie, or have you just come to your senses finally about where you belong?" J.D. smiles at me, sharpening his stick to poke me where it will hurt the most. The wooden shavings will stay lodged in as burning splinters for days to come.

"...and here that is why I thought we were sitting over there, Hells," Aimes counters his verbal attack. It takes some of the joy from his eyes.

"Simon wants to know if we feel up to a supply run," I say, as I ignore them both.

So much for Aimes not getting involved in our little domestic drama as I had earlier asked her. She is sharpening her own stick ready for the fight. Sometimes I wonder if she really listens to me or just nods to shut me up.

"We, huh?" J.D. asks.

"Yeah. Guess Simon still seems to think we are a part of this group." Aimes yawns, showing her boredom with having to be near them.

Yup, she just nods to shut me up.

"Either you do, or you don't want to get the items." I try to interrupt their verbal match before the blows start going low. "If you don't, then fine. I am sure Dolph, Richard and I can go find them." "We got it," Lawless says, taking the paper from me. He is as shocked as I am with his sudden outburst. We stand staring at each other, unsure of what to say to one another anymore.

"You will need my truck to carry it back. I will meet you in the morning when you're ready to head out," I offer. These are not the words that I want to say to him. These are the only words I can say to him with so many watching us, hoping for a show.

"You will be staying in that truck," J.D. tells me, taking the paper from Lawless before heading out.

"You forgot your tray," Aimes tells him, still not ready to let go. I am thinking of a few nicknames for her at this moment. Chihuahua comes to mind first.

J.D. nods, picking up his tray with a false smile. "Anything for my girls," he says, with a sarcastic bow as the other men follow him with theirs.

Aimes sighs in frustration, heading for the courtyard, which is conveniently in the opposite direction from the path the group takes. I watch as we split into two groups again with a sigh of defeat. Holding a closed fist up to Chapel, I offer to play "Rock, Paper, Scissors'" to figure out which path we will take, but he only laughs, leading us to follow Aimes. Like we really had any other choice?

Chapter 30

Those sitting in the cafeteria did not miss the little play of power. The further whispering of rumors rapidly spreads through the confined space as so many are wondering what this new group holds for their peaceful lifestyle. One table sat watching with vested interest while the scene played out before them. Their ears strained for any piece of the conversation to reach them, but the distance was too great between where they sit and the table that became the center of everyone's attention.

The people were too skilled at keeping their voices and their movements subtle and between only their circle. Fighting the urge as hard as they could, they could only grab moments of eye contact being too worried over being caught staring. When the fragments headed in different directions, each person of the table formed opinions of what had happened.

"Think they will do it?" Dolph asks those at the table around him.

"We'll see. Looks like it's a go," Simon says, but he is watching the larger of the fragments walking away. His hopes lie with them.

"I think it is horrible to set them up like this." Shelia rocks the sleepy Kira in her lap. "They are mean enough to those two without you three adding to it."

"It is not a set-up." Dolph tries to sooth her, trying to ease her concerns over the situation. "We need to see where they sit and not just the girls. All of them. We need to know if we can trust them or not after this morning. It's better this way."

"Well, I don't agree," she hisses, picking up the sleeping child to leave. "Leave me out of it."

"Shelia," Simon calls to her but the only answer is her continued exit from the room.

"Will she be alright?" With a touch of concern for the situation, Richard looks to Simon for advice.

"I'll talk to her. I'll help her understand it. She has grown close to the girls," Simon sighs, sensing the battle ahead for him.

"I'm wanting to grow close to the blonde." Richard smiles a male smile with a hint of a blush.

"You would," Dolph teases his friend with his own half smirk. "What? She's fun." Richard nudges his friend. "She may just be very fun."

"That one will eat you alive and use it for her next comedy skit when bored." Simon laughs.

"No, that is the other one. What's her name?" Dolph asks. "Helena. Why do you say that?" Simon moves his seat to get a better view of the men sitting at the table with him.

"You can see it. In her eyes. That one has ghosts. She's been through it," Dolph says, remembering the way she looked at dinner.

The men grow silent, each remembering their own past events, which have led them here. Shadows cross each face as the joy of the previous male topics flee from them. How quick conversations can turn the tides of emotions.

"Any clue about what is going on with them?" Dolph asks. He looks to Simon since he is the one with the most exposure to the new group.

"At first, I thought it was just them pissed off at Helena for risking her life at the Welcome Center for us," Simon says. He drops his voice to an almost whisper before saying, "Something has happened though to make them this broken. You should have seen them at the Center. Like one mind kind of deal. J.D. just had to do a slight move and they all knew what to do. Now, they seem lost, like he is losing control over them. Maybe the girls don't like Leslie sneaking in on what they think of as theirs. I know there is some tension between the darker one and Helena. Picked up on that when she tried to run him over." Simon cannot help but smile at the memory. It piques the curiosity of the other two sit- ting before him.

"Run him over?" Richard wears a smile with his question. "Yeah, in reverse." Simon lets his laugh finish his sentence.

"Should have heard Leslie scream. Best moment by far."

"Don't think there are too many men in this place left who haven't heard her scream," Dolph counters, not bothering with any hidden meanings with his look.

"That includes you?" Richard smirks, letting the trap Dolph has walked into snap shut.

Dolph shoots them both a look of disbelief with their assumptions and laughter. "Screw you," he says to them, only gaining louder laughter from the two until he smiles with their teasing. "Think they will figure it out?" Dolph asks once their laughter has faded into sly smirks.

"Most likely. You don't get to where they are in life without pulling a few of your own moves on people." Simon is still recovering from his laughter. "Do you care?"

"Nope," Dolph says. "Just want to be prepared and just don't want it coming back to bite us." He stands to start his nightly rounds.

"Ross knows what to do," Simon says, stretching and standing as those at the table are preparing to leave.

"Yeah, just smile!" Richards says, imitating the big smile of Ross' with his sentence.

Each man laughs as they say goodbye for the night. Each has a duty to do before he can escape to a world of secret dreams. A world of their own needs where things are better for them and loved ones are still close to them. A world they can never find again.

There is one among them who knows well the sting of walking alone. This one stands with his mind racing for what tomorrow may bring for everyone under this roof. This would not be his first time watching a group fall apart. He knows the aftermath a fall-out can bring and the weaknesses it can cause when people are pushed to having to act. Dolph heads into the night as his ghosts are whispering into his ear.

Chapter 31

This is bullshit." Rhett's voice vibrates the room with his anger after reading the list.

The men decided to make a trip to the school's weight room after breakfast before heading out to fulfill the obligation they were trapped into taking on last night. They each have their own issues to burn off with the exertion of their workout and the emptiness of the room allows them to talk freely. Knowing what the day holds for them, their moods are darker than the vests they normally wear.

"Yup." J.D. pauses, straining to press the weights he has al- lowed Lawless to place on the bar.

"Why are we doing it then?" Lawless asks, keeping an eye on the man he is spotting.

"We ain't doing it for them," J.D. says, placing the bar back onto its steel holder. "We're doing it for our girls," he says. "We are taking back what is ours. They are getting too close and cozy with the new folk. That includes Chapel. We need to remind them three where their loyalties lie."

Rhett and Lawless stare at J.D., only half curious where this new plot will lead them because they both know they have no choice but to follow along whatever course J.D. places them upon. "Thought that's what you wanted?" Marxx asks. He has continued his presses with disinterest in the conversation. He is not the only one missing the feminine laughter, which was once theirs to enjoy.

J.D. stands with one graceful movement of his anger, making his way to Marxx' bench. He stands staring down at the man, making eye contact before lunging. J.D. presses his full weight down on the already heavily weight-loaded bar and it comes to rest on the throat of Marxx. J.D. never breaks eye contact with the man below him.

Marxx fights to keep the bar from crushing his throat under J.D.'s weight while they stare into each other's eyes. Rhett and Lawless become statues as they have been trained to do, investing no emotion and harvesting no satisfaction from the situation. Anything else could put them both in the center of a storm no one can predict.

"Did you say something to me, Marxx?" J.D. holds constant pressure on his neck, seeing if Marxx will continue speaking against him.

He does.

"You pushed Chapel away. You pushed Hells away. We all knew Aimes would follow her. You did this." Marxx is fighting against the weight and the rage of J.D. and yet the other man's rage is not as hot as his over what has happened by the hands of their leader.

J.D. leans harder against the bar, daring him to speak more. Marxx accepts his dare.

"You pushed Leslie on Law. You knew what it would do to Hells. You're just pissed you didn't break her. You made her stronger. Now you can't control her. She isn't yours anymore, neither of them. You were too much of a dumb ass to stop when you had the chance. She gave you the chance, but you threw it in her face. You've lost them. You've lost," Marxx says. He is almost spitting the words out as the bar and his rage push him to his limits.

J.D. forces the bar down on Marxx' neck, crushing it. He holds the pressure, making the other man fight for every breath as he kicks and struggles to free himself. Marxx fights against J.D., desperately trying to get any inch of space between his throat and the bar. His face is growing redder with each passing moment as air is denied to him. Without warning J.D., releases his hold on Marxx, walking away from the man to sit back on his original bench.

The room is silent. The only sound comes from Marxx as he tries to fill his lungs with the air from which he was deprived. His throat is discolored from where the bar was pressed, but it pales in comparison to the molted shades of his face. Each man in the room is waiting for either an explanation or exclamation from J.D. with a different expression as they wait.

J.D. sits staring at the floor while he rehears Marxx' words over and over again in his mind. "I know," he finally says when his silence makes the room almost suffocating.

J.D.'s voice is so quiet at first the men doubt they heard him. Their brows furrow with the doubt as they look to one another. "I know," he says again, placing his head in his hands to hide from their eyes. "It's why we've got to do this. We've got to prove we can keep them safe again, that they can trust us. We've got to bring them close again. Those girls have been with me since they were teens. You remember, Rhett. You remember how small they were when we first saw them. How shy of us they were? Just little things," he does a small laugh with his memories, remembering the days gone past.

"I remember," Rhett agrees with the man with hopes to encourage him to keep speaking.

"And Lawless," J.D. laughs as he says, "you were just a street punk. Nothing more than brown puppy eyes looking for skirts. Now look at you."

J.D.'s voice grows fainter with his emotions. Emotions he has never dared let them see. Emotions are for women and the weak.

J.D. is anything but weak, at least not in the old world. Everything has changed now. Everything is changing now. The world he knew is like water in his hands. The harder he tries to hold on to it, the more it slips away until his hands are empty, leaving him with less and less to hold in them.

"I don't know how to do this. Life used to be simple. Someone pissed you off, you kicked their teeth in. Now, man now, it's all changed. I've seen the way you've been looking at me. I've seen how you're watching me. Marxx is right. I did this. I took us here," J.D. says, more to himself than to the men in the room. "You remember the cabin? We had good times there. Good times." He smiles remembering. "You remember poor Aimes when she figured out what she was eating? That girl cried so hard over that rabbit. That girl wailed "Thumper" all night long. Now look at her, full of sass and ass. Helena too. She was so broken when we found her. She was so unsure of her own breath, much less taking on these things like she has been. I'm proud of her. Really, I am. She's finally standing on those two feet of hers. That daddy of hers would not stand a chance now against her. I'd pay money to see their showdown. Front row tickets," he chuckles, remembering all the tears she once spilled over the man that caused her soul such grief.

J.D.'s honesty has left those in the room fidgeting and unsure of what to say when J.D. pauses while his memories overtake him. His emotional wounds are bleeding before them. Their silence is the only tourniquet they have to offer him.

"I want them back," he says, finally recovering. "I can't do it on my own. I've done burned the bridge. Set it right on fire and watched it burn. Lawless has, too."

Lawless' head sinks low when he hears his name. Marxx' does not though.

"That's your fault, too," Marxx says with his voice more gravel-filled after their fight. "His dumb ass may have started their fight, but your pride started their war."

J.D. stands, coming off his bench to face Marxx again. His anger is refilling with Marxx' declaration of his actions.

"We'll fix it! We'll make it right," J.D. says, finding the end of his rope with Marxx' constant verbal assault.

Lawless doesn't look up. His fists are clenching to keep a grasp on the many emotions and words he wants to let escape. A part of him is envious of Marxx' bravery.

"Rhett, they listen to you. You make them listen. You reach Chapel first. Bring him back around. That will be our way back in. Get in with him and they will come around when they see it. Hells is smart. She is always watching. If she sees him coming back, then she will too. Like Marxx said, Aimes will then follow," J.D. says, staring at the tall man.

Rhett has been with J.D. the longest, forming a bond of the darkest deeds between them. Now the request put before him is one of tender care. It's a role reversal of the highest degree for him and Rhett doesn't know if he will able to perform the task set before him. The wounds have been dug deep and he is not well known at repairing damage. It has always been his job to cause it. "Yeah," he says, unwilling to voice his doubts. "I can do that.

I'll talk to them."

"So, we do this then." J.D. crumples the list, sacrificing it to his anger the way he yearns to do with Marxx. "We do this bullshit errand run of theirs. We know they are just testing us. Simon and Dolph want to see how well we take orders. We'll swallow their bullshit. Let them think they have pulled one over on us. If it gets our girls back, what of it?" He shrugs, knowing they will silently agree with him. "We will let Hells do her thing. She's proved we can't stop her anyway, but you keep her safe, Law. You stick to her. No matter what she says to you. No matter how deep Aimes tries to hurt you. You stick to her. We have to get through the wall of hers. We have to wear her down. That girl is hiding some pain and it's festering. You break her walls boy and she's yours. Past won't matter. You just be there to catch her when she falls. That's what she really wants. She just doesn't know it."

J.D. is standing before the young man he has helped mold and destroy as Law fights to keep his mask in place. J.D. knows Lawless will have to break through his own wall as well. J.D. has watched the two kids grow together only to fall back apart as their scars become too close to being examined by the other.

Pulling Law's face close to his, he keeps their eye contact saying, "You got to be stronger than her. You're the only one here who is. You take her back to that little world of yours. She will fight you. Every inch of the way, she will fight you. If she lets you take her back there, she will have to relive whatever she is hiding from. You got to get her there." J.D. watches as Lawless blinks past the many emotions stirring within him. "We've already seen it. She is losing herself more each day. When she stood up to me that first day, it wasn't bravery with her. It was the lack of care at the outcome. When she stops caring, she'll stop living. It will only be a matter of time till she does something stupid in this death wish she is walking. I can't lose my girl." J.D. pats the face of the man he has been coaching in the closest sign of compassion he has.

"...and Leslie?" Rhett asks.

"I'll take care of Leslie," J.D. says, slipping back into the skin he normally wears. Stopping in front of Marxx, he asks, "You got it all out of your system now? Because if you ever forget your place outside of this room, I'll leave you with more than just a sore throat to remind you of it. I'll break it. You got me, boy?"

J.D. leaves them and yet they follow behind him without any thought to the action. Marxx' eyes fight to hide their anger as   it simmers in their pools of color. Marxx knows J.D.'s days are numbered, and Helena will be the key to either saving the man or destroying him. Marxx just isn't sure anymore which door he wants her key to unlock, but he is not about to entrust her safety to Lawless; a man who cannot stand up to the man who will destroy them all with his madness. He makes a silent vow to himself to also be keeping an eye on her, because if Hells does fall, Marxx doesn't trust Lawless to be strong enough to catch her.

Chapter 32

Aimes and I are awaiting the boys in the hallway between our new apartments. We haven't seen them all morning and it makes my nerves whisper warnings over what they might be up to. They did not make it to breakfast or either they ate early to avoid us. Neither option is sitting well with my mind.

This will be the first time we have all been together since I forced the vote. My hands almost tremble with the anxiety of having to deal with the fall-out. Knowing also I will be spending the whole morning with Lawless makes other parts of me tremble. I am not proud of either fact.

"You have got to be kidding me," Aimes says, and her voice pulls me from my thoughts.

I follow her shocked face down the hallway, and I feel my jaw drop to match hers.

Rhett walks towards us wearing just a towel and a smile and his smile is larger than the towel. I stare, completely unsure of which is more alarming. If it is the barely there towel on his tall frame, or his wide "I'm sexy and I know it" smile on his face as he stares at us or if it's the combination of it all, but whatever it is, he knows he has our complete attention.

He is watching us as we watch him with no shame about either fact. He runs a hand through his dark, thick hair, flexing a bit more than is needed for such a simple act. Like high school girls, we follow his hand's every motion.

His walk slows to an amused stride with his performance. It stretches each muscle in his well-defined legs. Every female's head turns to watch him pass and he is loving the attention. I can almost hear a theme song to his walk with the amount of time it takes for him to reach us.

"Enjoy that?" I ask him, when he comes close enough to hear me and I can't help but smile at him.

"Did you?" Rhett returns my question, raising one eyebrow to match his very self-satisfied smile when he frames my body with his much taller torso.

"Not as much as they did." I motion to the women lingering in the hall as they pretend to have things to do around us.

"Pity. Let me try again," he says, as he turns abruptly to walk away.

I laugh, catching his arm to keep him from following through with his plan. He flexes under my hand, continuing our game. The problem with Rhett is his games do not have rules or limits. It's always risky to dare Rhett, but I think I have this one. I smile at him, watching his smile widen with my acceptance of his dare. My fingers trail along his arms, dipping into the crevices of his toned muscles. They explore the shallow of his collarbone, before I place both palms flat against his shoulders. He pulls me close, trying to match my dare and he locks his thick arms around my waist. The feel of my body in his arms quickens his breath and I know he is mine to punish now with this flaw of his plan. Luckily for him, I know my limits and what lines I will not cross. I'm not going to tell this him though.

I slide my palms down his chest, watching them with hooded eyes as they trace every curve of him, making a path to that small piece of a towel between us. I match the pace of my breath to his, feeling him growing aroused against me. Tracing the span of his hidden skin underneath the top of the towel, I raise only my eyes to look into his. He is fully erect now, pressing hard against me and I smile. I win.

Rhett leans in close to my face, stopping a breath away from my lips. "Bitch," he says with amusement before letting me go as he kisses my forehead softly.

The hallway comes alive with clapping. The men have finally showed themselves and this is the moment they decided to do it. Now they stand a few feet from Rhett and I, clapping and whistling at our show. Even Aimes joins in with her appreciation.

Rhett bows to the other men with a great show of amusement and his short towel rides up high enough to silence Aimes who is standing behind him. She freezes mid-clap and the look she wears creates another round of laughter from us. For these few moments, the past few days with their drama-laden hours fade away. I can almost hear the jukebox playing around us as if we were back standing in Grit. I only wonder how long it will last.

Their entire group is in some form of undress from their showers. None are as brave as Rhett though with his fraction of a towel. They walk past us into their room, leaving Rhett with us in the hall. It is a buffet for the eyes or one hell of a long dry spell for me. Looking to Aimes, who is wearing the most perfect blush, I am voting on the buffet and thankful Shelia is not around to endure the sights.

"Do I even want to ask where you four have been?" I ask Rhett, who is still wearing his smile with his eyes on Aimes. I almost feel sorry for her with the jests she will now have to endure from him. Almost.

"Dunno, do you?" he returns, starting another game. "Where were you four this morning?" I ask, calling his bluff.

He shrugs and the towel dips a bit lower, as do my eyes. "Testing out the weight room before the run. Not too many ways to burn off steam around here."

"Tell me about it," Aimes says, making her blush deepen upon hearing her voice speak the words she was hoping to keep locked away.

Rhett's smile widens as he sees a better target to play with. "Been awhile since I have- "

"No," Aimes says, cutting him off before he can finish his sentence. Her blush is a full-forced red now knowing where his mind was going to invite her, but too afraid to board the ride.

"If you ever change your mind," he leans his tall, well-formed body against hers, bending over to whisper in her ear, "you don't even have to ask."

Aimes goes stiff with his implications, watching him like the prey she is as he walks to the door.

It is my turn now to clap and he turns to smile at me.

"Win some, you lose some. Rematch?" Rhett asks me, as he closes the door behind him.

"Did you know he had arms like that?" Aimes asks. Her voice is a little more breathy than normal.

"No," I answer, enjoying her torment. "Did you know he had a chest like that?" "No."

"Did you know he had a stomach like that?"

"What are you, Little Horney Riding Hood?" I ask her. "All the better to seduce you with, my dear?"

"No, I want to be the Grandmother. She gets eaten," she says, with pure honesty and we both laugh.

We are still laughing when the men return, fully dressed now and ready for the run. Rhett's eyes sparkle with the hopes he is the target of our hilarity. When Aimes blushes again as he walks by, it is all the proof his male ego needs. They are all wearing   a smile over her blush and it's not the only thing they have in common.

Each man is wearing the dark, black leather vest of G.R.I.T. with its grinning skull. Our laughter dies with the realization of it. They ignore our shock, continuing to make their way down the very crowded hallway. People split to either side of their path, letting them through and we are forced to follow behind them or either be left behind.

The vest has always been a way for them to show the town who they are and how little they care for their opinions. It's a silent message of solidarity, boasting of rank and deeds done in the name of the club. The skull on the vests' back wearing a jagged smile is a grim hint of the personalities and attitudes held within and how they are not afraid to face life, no matter where it may take them. The one silver tear on its cheek serves as a reminder of those who have come and gone. The black eye patch with the 1% in its center reminds the MC it is "an eye for an eye" world of theirs. The double guns behind the skull lets each member know no one stands alone as long as they are standing with their brothers. The black, leather vest is as much of a way to bind them together, as it is a way to keep them apart and that is exactly the point of wearing it today.

"J.D.," Aimes whispers, with a hiss when we reach the shelter of the closed stairwell, "what are you doing?"

"Why, I am walking down the stairs, Sweetheart," he calls back to her, ignoring the real question she has asked him.

"What's up with the vests?" she clarifies, not letting him slip away so easily.

"We can't all look good in just a towel." J.D. still avoids her question and we both know he will not answer us.

"I think we need to see how well the girls look in one." Rhett does answer though, still unwilling to let our game go.

"Looking to lose again?" I bait him, just to see his smile again. "I'll lose to you any day," he says, and I earn my prize.

"What about all night?" I ask.

I watch Lawless miss a step and I smile as he tries to hide it. It feels as good as if I had pushed him with my hands, not my words.

I don't know what Rhett may have said as his answer. J.D. gives the man a look, silencing Rhett and his smile melts from his lips. Aimes looks to me with the curiosity of it. I shrug to her. I refuse to play with their hidden plot lines anymore. If sexually teasing Rhett will help me get through the next few hours, then by the end of the day we both may be in desperate need to visit the weight room.

Ross is waiting for us in the courtyard with his high wattage smile. He leans against my truck with Chapel watching us head their way. Chapel looks to me when he notices the dress code   of the men before me. Aimes and I shrug, letting him know we are not on the "need to know" list about their agendas and our annoyance over the fact.

J.D. tosses something to Chapel, never stopping to talk to the man. "Get dressed," he says over his shoulder without a hint of compassion or anger.

Chapel unfolds the bunched fabric to find his leather vest in his hands. The emotions washing over his face fold over and onto themselves while looking at such a simple piece of clothing. He glances to the men who file past him, each patting him on his shoulder or his chest as they pass before he slips on the matching leather.

I am confused as to what he feels at this moment as the men show him signs of camaraderie or at what point J.D. stripped him of his vest removing the same link. The men who we have drawn our lines against, and circled the wagons from, are now welcoming Chapel home. Something clicks for him with their renewed brotherhood, setting a different tone to his posture. For the first time, I see how much it has cost Chapel to be on the outside of their circle jerk, even if he does not agree with their actions.

"Man down," Aimes says to me with disappointment, as we watch Chapel rejoin the group who mingles around their dark warhorses.

"Maybe. Maybe not." I try to reassure her. The sight of Leslie running toward them removes any hopes I may have tried to hold over what today will bring.

"Where to?" I ask Ross, ignoring the scene in front of us.

"I'll show you," Ross says. His smile may still be bright, but his voice does not match the wattage.

"Something wrong, Ross?" Aimes asks him, noticing the difference in him as well.

"No. Not at all. We're good!" he says to us a little too perky and a little too clipped.

His voice is a little too forced. His smile is a bit too big. Either we are making him very nervous or he is hiding something.

I look to Aimes to gather her ideas on the topic. She makes a face at me, exposing her suspicions. We have both come to a similar conclusion he is hiding something from us. The day just keeps getting better, and with his smile, brighter. When Marxx glances at me over the shoulder of Lawless, I suspect Ross isn't the only one hiding something. Revving my truck's deep engine to hurry the men up, I'm ready to twirl a certain finger with the joy of it all.

Chapter 33

Ross directs us to a strip mall not too far from the high school. Just like most places these days, it sits vacant and abandoned. This place though screams its discernment like a banner of helplessness.

Store windows are covered in thick layers of dirt. The grime shields whatever items the stores may hide within. The parking lot holds random forsaken cars, forming yet another frozen moment of time.

Ruined newspapers and other forms of litter from spilled containers left unchecked lay spread throughout the area by winds. I almost expect to see a tumbleweed roll by with the lack of life surrounding us. Instead, a shopping cart rolls by when a strong gust of winter wind sends its wheels screeching with anger over the movement.

As we watch it roll across the lot, the comedy is not lost on us. Small sounds of our mirth slip from us when it rolls into a parked car. I can't imagine anything is left to be found in this place, much less a whole list of needs to be fulfilled.

Perhaps Ross is having those same concerns. His nervousness has grown with each roaring motorcycle pulling in beside my truck. Motorcycles bare of a redheaded thorn in my side. Did the sun just peek out or did the sudden lift of my mood just make   it seem so?

The men don't seem as surprised as I am over our location. They almost seem to be amused at what is surrounding us as   if it is exactly what they expected to see. Only Marxx looks as annoyed as I feel by what we are seeing. Chapel's eyes go dark and it worries me I may be the only one not catching on to what is happening.

"Well this looks like a big pile of nada," Aimes says to me, more than to Ross reassuring me I am not the only one.

Ross has lost his ability to form words. He just head nods like a dashboard bobble toy with too loose of a spring. His smile is still with us though. Lucky us.

J.D. opens my door, holding out his hand for me to take. He is staring into the empty shopping center as he waits for me. His inability to look at me bares his weakness in this moment. I know he is covering his fear of my refusal for his help with the act of scouting the area ahead of us and I am tempted to slide past him. I am tempted until I see the many faces watching us, waiting to see my reaction. J.D. is attempting to cross the many spider webs of cracks he has escalated between us with this simple gesture. The option to allow him is now up to me, making me the heroine or the villain. Well-played J.D. I lift my arm and reach for him, hoping what is left of our foundation still has the strength to support us both.

"Well, Smiley," J.D. says, still holding on to my hand, more tightly than necessary as I stand beside him, "what's the plan here?"

"The items should be in the stores. I'll stay here with the girls and help keep an eye out. I'm not feeling all that exploratory after the last excursion," Ross says. He seems almost ill with his nerves.

Something Ross has said makes all the men look toward him. Their faces slide to their blank looks and I now know he is hiding something. Something the men have already figured out. Something I should have figured out, but I haven't yet.

J.D. drops my hand, reaching past me into the truck. Grasping a firm hold of Ross, he pulls the man from the truck with such force Ross stumbles as he violently spills forth into the parking lot. Ross falls into the waiting arms of Marxx. He may have kept Ross from falling, but

Marxx does not allow the action to be friendly as Ross is spun around to face J.D.

The men crowd around Ross with their blank faces and stances of male posturing. Ross has seen this before and panic settles over him, making his smile return. I feel myself heading towards their cluster without being aware of the decision. I may not be a fan of Ross, with his toothpaste-commercial-worthy-smile, but I cannot stand by and watch them terrorize such an easy target. Dolph or Simon, yes, maybe even Richard. I would even grab some snacks to watch their show, but not Ross. I hear Aimes falling in step behind me with the same determination, my little, constant Chihuahua.

Rhett smiles at us as we head towards them. He slides through their circle, coming to block us from their game of "Toss the Ross." He stands in front of us, using his body to keep us from going and seeing around him. He stands playfully here with his "look at how harmless I am" smile, but he is ready to stop us if we force him. I have seen them go from this laid-back state to full brawl without a second to spare and something inside me just can't let it happen.

"Move, Rhett." I try to match my voice to his stance.

His smirk tells me I have failed as he says, "Nope." He and I both know I am not a threat to him no matter how many emotions I put into my voice. "They are just having a friendly chat. Nothing will happen to him."

"Nothing will happen to him as long as he does what?" Aimes asks him, letting him know we are both well versed in their games.

Rhett graces us with a true smile as she catches him off guard. "Nothing, Sweetheart. Truly."

"Then move." She places her palms against his chest and pushes him to further to prove the lies of his words.

"Nope," Rhett says, without even a sway from her shove.

We both sigh at him and over the lack of options really left to us. Thumb wrestle?

"If they are just talking and nothing is going to happen to him, then why not? Why won't you let us go over there?" Aimes gestures around him.

I am pretty sure though he knows where "there" is without the help she provides pointing behind him. Then again, maybe not.

"Because quite frankly my dear, I don't give a damn." Rhett's smile is in full bloom. He has fully recovered from being knocked off guard by her first comment and he is ready to play again.

"You totally did not just "Gone With the Wind" me!" Aimes shouts at him with shock and annoyance over his barb.

Rhett and I laugh together at her outrage. I can't help but wonder how long Rhett has been holding on to that little gem. Sometimes life gives us these perfect moments for our one-liners. Life has finally granted Rhett his moment and he is completely enjoying it.

Lawless walks from behind Rhett, patting him on the shoulder and releasing us from being watched. Rhett did his job well because we still have no idea what their anger is over. Marxx is leading Ross into the strip mall with blatant shoves. Every time Ross tries to turn around and protest, the rest of the men file in behind them with laughing jests about his bravery.

Lawless falls back from the group. He is waiting for us to catch up to him, signaling it is now his turn to watch us. Did I mention how the day just keeps getting better and better?

Aimes and I catch up to Lawless with our minds racing over what is going on. Rhett has taken a too invested interest in us today with his flirting smiles. J.D. is actually trying to mend our many shattered fences. Now Lawless, to whom we have been invisible, walks with us through the area. He is wordless and on edge, but he is here. My tongue is pressing tight against my teeth to keep the many words I want to say from flowing out. With how silent Aimes is, I imagine she is chewing hers clean off. I know it's only a matter of time before she gets her stick out. This time, it won't be J.D. she sets her sights on.

Lawless stays with Aimes and I as the men go into the stores to begin gathering the items on the list. He keeps his back to us, using himself as a shield for any threats which may occur. He must be seeing some small detail of this place differently than I am. Unless dust and litter are going to combine forces to take us out, I think we are rather safe. Nonetheless, here we three stands in silent formation. Unfortunately for one of us, Aimes has reached her breaking point. Her glances and the faces she is making speak of her frustrations. I can only shrug with her, unsure of anything more to do about Ross' predicament or ours. The swooning over Lawless has passed for both of us. It should sadden me, but it doesn't. I feel nothing in this moment as I stare at his back. A part of me knows it is a lie. I have a room shoved full of feelings for this man. I have just shut the door, keeping them locked safely away. A heart can only take so many scars before the soul turns its back.

He is doing his best to appear he is not aware of us, but Aimes has found a new game to prove just how very aware he is actually. She will slide her foot to the far side of him, making his head come down to see behind him without having to fully turn to look at us. She can make a noise directly behind him and his shoulders will pull back as his head tilts just enough to take notice of her. When we are walking, she walks away from me to leave a larger space between us than normal. He will automatically adjust his pace to fall into the gap to keep us both in his sight, and as she pulls in, he will readjust his pace to allow her back beside me. She is proving he will not ignore her, and she doesn't have to use words to make him aware of her. Like the men's silent game of stares, she is playing a version of the game just as well as they have over the years. For me, it's just incredibly amusing to watch.

Standing outside the fourth store, Lawless finally grows tired of her game.

"Really?" he asks her, when she is on her third round of "guess which side of you I made the noise" game.

"Really, what?" I can hear her sharpening her stick. I wish I had popcorn.

"Give it a rest," he snaps at her. His voice holds none of the warmth from our playful days.

"Or you'll what? Go tell Daddy I am being naughty?" Her voice is dripping with her sarcastic charm. "Gee Lawless, will you spank me, or just go back to pretending we aren't alive while you sneak off with Leslie?"

She has found the pointy end of her wooden dagger and his head tilts back and forth stretching his neck with the jab.

"It wasn't like that." His voice is flat and fighting to stay neutral while he keeps his back to us.

"Not like what?" Aimes asks him. Her tone hints she already knows his answer.

He says nothing while staring off into the distance. His eyes roll between the details of the shops before us, busy with his thoughts and not what he is seeing.

"Go on Law," Aimes presses, "tell us what it wasn't like?"

I'm not sure where their conversation is going, but the beat of my heart hastens just the same.

"Noooo, of course not. You're just "friends"?" Aimes asks him, daring him to speak.

"We aren't friends," Lawless says bitterly.

"You and her, or you and us?" Aimes asks, as she tilts her head with her cheerful smile beaming at him.

Lawless rolls his eyes to her direction and the heat in those amber pools would singe lesser people. Aimes just smiles wider.

"Come on Lawly, "she whispers to him, "sniff for me."

She has pushed his final button. His body slowly turns dangerously toward her. My mind is racing with how I'm going to come between them and to whose side I am going to stand. Aimes isn't finished yet, nor is she frightened of the man before her.

"No, you're not "just friends" are you Laws? Which explains exactly how she knows about the nice lower tattoo of yours she was giggling over this morning. It explains why Shelia saw her in your bed and why I caught the two of you creeping around last night," Aimes says. She braces herself against the wall behind her dramatically, tilting her head back and starts to mockingly shout, "Ohhh Law. Ooohh Law. Don't stop! Don't stop!"

Lawless flinches as if she has hit him. His anger melts from his posture as shock fills the void left behind.

"Best friends forever now or just until the sheets grow cold?" she asks him so bitterly I can taste her acid.

Aimes has dragged every truth from him forward. I am now face-to-face with the lies I have been telling myself. Lawless stares at me as the shock of it starts to climb into my throat.

My amusement fades as I feel my heart drop. My breath catches as I wait for his answer with our eyes locked. The door from behind which I have tried to keep my emotions for him vibrates my heart. It skips beats with its thundering force.

I held him and Leslie in just speculation up to this point. It might have been there, but without confirmation, I have been able to ignore them. Now as his head tilts back to stare up into the blue sky with her words, my heart breaks with every moment of his silence that passes between us. He can't look at me and I can't be near him.

I turn from them. One step at a time, I leave them behind me where my heart lays, still fighting to beat. He calls for me, shouting my name, but I will not stand there and let him see the damage he has done to me. I will not allow him to see the last piece of me break.

He will not see the last fragment of a world I have been trying to convince myself is still there fall away from me. I stood up to

J.D. to keep us all together and all this time he has been throwing us away behind my back. It's not his cheating which is shredding me. It's the blind betrayal.

Even Aimes' voice calling my name does not turn me around. She knew the pain the truth would hold for me. She was there every moment I fought against it. She knows how the sight of them together strips me. She knows my silent denial is all which has kept my hope whole. Lost in her own bitterness, and the need to wound Lawless, she has wounded me. Something I never thought would happen between us. I hear her shouts of apologies and it does nothing to soothe the ache.

"Helena," Lawless is catching up to me, calling my name to stop me.

I refuse to slow for him. I am fighting to rebuild the walls they have demolished. He grabs for my arm to turn to him, but I pull free with the strength of my anguish. I know his strength well and the fact I was able to so easily escape his hold proves how worried he is to face my reaction.

"It's not what you think," he says to my back. His voice is pleading for me to listen to him.

"It doesn't matter anymore. None of it matters." It's not to him I am giving an answer. I am telling it to myself because what is the point to keep fighting for someone who is no longer fighting for you?

I pull open the door to the store nearest to me, feeling too exposed to feel this weak in the open area. I hold the hope the narrow store will help me collect myself. I did, until I hear him behind me again.

"Talk to me. Please," his voice is fragile with his pleading. "Leave me alone," I tell him, refusing to give in to my pain.

"You know I won't." I feel his fingertips gently touch my hair, carefully coaxing me to turn to him.

"You already did," I answer him, with the full poison I have been storing for him in pretty mental bottles. I feel his touch fade with my words, and he gives me my desire.

The door shuts and the hinges seem to be connected to my knees. I sink down with the closed door under the weight of my pain. Alone, finally, I can allow my grief to escape. It pours forth from every locked door I have kept shut. I relive every moment he and I have spent together through the years; from our laughter to our pain, our first touch, our first kiss, and our whispered shared dreams.

I feel his arms around me from when I was scared and alone. I know his scent from when he would shelter me from the world. The songs he used to sing me to sleep with now haunt me with their melodies. The loss of my Angels devastated my soul. Losing my lighthouse is devouring it.

I am broken all the way down as I kneel here on my knees. My tears leaving wet marks on the dirt-covered floor better than any blood I could spill for him. I know he will be my last failure as I feel my soul retreating into the safety of the darkness. I can't fight to keep what doesn't want to be collected. As I tell myself this, I know it wasn't to them I was throwing the life preserver to that day. It was to me and now I am throwing it away.

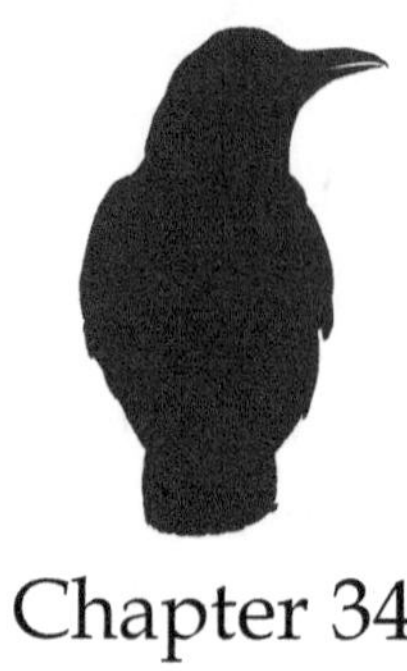

Chapter 34

They are all waiting for me when I leave the store. Their faces show different levels of concerns and I know Aimes has filled everyone in on what has happened. Lawless and Aimes sit together on the ledge of a store window watching my exit. Their faces mirror the others with their sorrow, and I cannot help to bitterly think how wonderful it is for my pain to bring them together like this with my salt-filled ocean of bitterness. Aimes stands as I exit the store, heading towards me with her face covered in her dried tears and fear over the words she let fall like acidic rain. I turn my back to her, turning to face the man we have all turned to at some point in time to lead us when we are in our darkest hour. No one understands the internal darkness better than J.D. "What's left?" I ask him. My voice is rock bottom with emotional weight. I am wasting no energy to fill it with anything less than nothing.

"Just one store left." J.D. stands, placing his arm around me, leading us away from the group and their peering eyes.

He does not leave me stranded as my fire is going out. I have come full circle from needing him, to hating him, to needing him again. He doesn't gloat or acknowledge it as the rest of the group weakly falls in behind us. I have come home to him in my hour of need just like he always knew I would. I am the daughter he never had and all I want right now is my daddy's arms to hide me. The last store is worse than the rest. Its windows are covered in a thick film from being exposed to the elements for so long. No care has been put into this place as trash is piled so high in front of the door J.D. has to kick it away to clear a path for us. He holds the door open as we enter until Lawless walks toward him.

J.D. walks in front of Lawless and Aimes, blocking their en- trance as he lets the door close behind him. I don't want to smile at the act, but I do. The look Chapel gives me for my smile tells me I should be filled with shame, but I am not. J.D. pats my arm as he walks by, further demonstrating his support for me and my smile widens.

"Nice vest," I whisper to Chapel, letting him feel the irony with his judgment of me.

"Should be in the back," Ross' voice fills the store, distracting Chapel and me. "I'll just wait here with Helena."

Yes, because my day has been so wonderful so far. I completely want to finish what is left of the morning alone with Colgate here. I let J.D. see my opinion of his offer with my face. He chuckles, turning to Ross with a wide smile.

"I don't think our girl wants to be alone with you. She can come with us," J.D. tells Ross, who grows suddenly restless with the idea.

"It's a small back room. She'll feel more comfortable out here," Ross tries, almost desperately, to make me understand the need to stay here with him.

I am in no mood for any more drama, and to prove my point, I walk past them all to the back room. I am not a weak, frail girl who needs their protection. One exposed moment over Lawless does not mean I need to be sheltered from a dusty back room. I plan to prove that, not only to Ross, but to everyone else as well. One day I will learn to think before I act. Obviously though, today is not going to be that day.

Two things happen as I walk through the door in front of me. The first is Ross screaming the word "no" and the second is my empty screaming of no words at all. In my moment of pride, I have walked right into a room full of Risen. There are so many in the room they are able to circle me in seconds, blocking the door from being opened again. The sight of me stirs the ones closest to the door quickly. Their excitement spreads throughout the room like a ripple in water, as each ring slowly turns to face me.

They have been deprived from food for so long their faces and bodies are gaunt and deceptively fragile looking. The clothes which once fit perfectly, are now hanging, barely holding on to the many sharp angles of their bodies. The deep-sunken eyes before me become alive with each step closer. The sounds filling the space around me lock my voice with fear. The horrific sight steals my breath. The smell stirs my stomach with terror. Death once again has come for me. I have cheated him from his prize so many times before, and as I look for an exit, I feel his cold hands finally upon me.

Male voices are screaming my name on the other side of the door as they push against it. Their force is only pushing the Risen closer to me with how many of them are in the room. The only weapon I have on me is the hunting knife I have kept this whole time. Suddenly, it does not feel adequate enough for what is creeping closer to me.

I am afraid to move, or reach for it, with the fear it will signal their frenzy. This many in such a short distance will destroy me in moments. If I wait too long to reach for it, there will not be enough time to defend myself with whatever slim chance I may already have to live through this. I know I have to get my back to a wall to help protect me, but with them encircling me, I don't see any way to reach one. That is until I watch the door.

Each shove from the men on the other side pushes the rotting forms a little more off balance. The Risen have not begun the attack yet because their starved minds are taking longer to animate their bodies. They stumble against the force of the door, almost tipping from it as it collides with them. If I can get the men to push hard enough, I may be able to use the resulting moment of confusion to at least reach the wall. The rest, I can figure out once my back is safe. My mind is screaming in panic with the failure rate of my plans so far. I'm taking my self-doubt to a whole new plateau.

"J.D.," I gently call out to him, refusing to scream.

I watch the bodies become still in front of me at the sound of my voice. Their eyes are swaying back and forth, staring at me with their confusion. It's unnerving to be in the middle of so many that are now so focused on me. Their slack faces show their thoughts as they try to gauge my next move.

"Helena?" J.D. calls from the other side in the same soft whisper. The hope in his voice touches a part of me I thought was dead for him.

"I need you to shove the door as hard as you can. It will put them off balance enough I may be able to reach the door," I tell him.

Heads are tilting now as if they can understand what I am saying. Their minds are racing to sort the vocabulary and meanings my words might hold. I feel like a parent trying to spell out a gift in front of a young child with prayers they won't catch on. It won't be a holiday that is ruined if they do. It will be me.

"May?" he chuckles, but it is not out of amusement. He just doesn't want to voice his fears with so many depending on his strength on his side of the door.

"Yes, it may. It may not. Anything is better than standing here waiting to be attacked," I say, giving him my honest truth. It does not comfort either of us.

"On three," he says. He holds as much faith in the plan as I do.

I am in a serious need of new cheerleaders.

"On three," I return, cementing our plan. "One."

My hand reaches for the blade. A room full of eyes follows the motion, pulling their faces into sneers.

"Two."

I brace, ready to run. Growls erupt around me with my sudden movement.

"Three."

I run as the door swings open. I run straight into the rows in front of me. They reach for me, welcoming me to them. Death is cheering in my ears with my suicide as fingers grab me, pulling me to them. As the first few mouths come close to me, I fear he may finally earn his prize.

A female's bone-sharp fingers clamp down on my arm. She is leaning into me with pure hunger over the flesh of my neck. I can feel her wet saliva dripping on me. The chill of it removes any self-confidence, rooting me to the floor. The smell of her triggers my fear. The smell of my fear triggers their excitement. I scream exciting them even more.

Their voices rise with mine. I feel her teeth touch my neck and I scream for him. I scream for the only man I have ever screamed for in my life. His name is torn from me with my fears, forgetting all that has happened between us. Like I may never see him again, I scream for Lawless.

Lawless answers me, pushing hard against the door with his own heartbreaking fear overhearing my scream. He would always come for me; he told me that once. What feels like years ago, he told me he would never leave me. He is here now. My lighthouse in the storm, even as we both know, he cannot reach me.

The hunger of their desperation finally reaches all of the Risen around me. The teeth of the woman slide across my flesh as she is pushed by the rows behind her. Her tumbling knocks her into the one beside her, who slips, releasing their hold of me. It creates a small pocket of space between them. It will bring me deeper into their formation of death, but closer to the door. I turn into the space, pivoting from her to pull my neck further away and using her own disadvantages to free me. My arm slips away from her as I push backwards into that small space with their howls of rage surrounding me. As I walk through the valley of the shadow of death, I fear this evil.

The continued pushing against the door gains it more of a swing with each shove. I time my movement with the swing that is knocking those around me off-step. Seeing their first meal in so long escaping from them, the other half of the room is now rushing forward. It only causes more chaos in the room with the movements tilting them back and forth. The small room seems to grow by miles with my backwards crawling through the enfolding tunnel of bodies and all of the motions and sounds around me.

I collide with the wall and sink down. I pull my knees to my chest in an attempt to make myself as small as possible. My hands tremble, barely able to hold the knife before me, as I wait for the Risen to find their hidden meal. They do.

I see them crawling towards me, using the same space I escaped through. For such frail looking creatures, they crawl with the speed of a toddler on crack and I laugh with my mental thought as my panic takes me. This is the moment where I know I have finally lost my mind, so it does not surprise me to hear Ashley in my ear.

"Scoot over," she tells me.

Her voice sends shivers through a deep part of me I have kept locked away. The world slows around me as I watch Death racing for me, and I hear what I allowed Death to take from me whispering in my ear.

"I can't," I answer her, looking into her blue, blue eyes.

She is sitting on the floor beside me, holding her knees to her small body just as I am. Her soft pink pajama shirt is shredded and torn with wounds oozing dark fluids in the spaces of the missing cotton. Her arms are a series of lacerations that suck the fabric into the missing gaps of the flesh around them. She wears my sins upon her body like a beauty queen wears a sash and her crown is the perfect blonde shade of her hair that separated us and my parent's love.

"You can. You have to." She is staring at me without any emotion. I am looking at her with enough emotion for us both.

"I don't want to." The truth of my words cuts me and frees me at the same time.

"You have to. They need you." Her voice is so gentle. So gentle with me, considering what I allowed to happen to her.

"You needed me," I say to her, watching the Risen grab at my legs with numbing calmness.

"Yes, I did." Her own truth cuts me even deeper than my own. "Scoot over, now."

I feel a soft touch on my arm with her final words. I turn my head to see Marxx reaching for me with his fear and desperation racing over his face as Lawless is straining to hold the door open with his body. Marxx is stretching as far as he can to reach me, but surrounded in my own fears, I had not seen or heard him screaming my name. I only need to scoot over for him to grab me and help me escape the room to safety. I look for Ashley, but I know before I turn, she is gone. She does not need me now. They do, just as she had said.

I scoot across the wall, kicking at the face of the man with my already battle worn boots who's trying to bite me. With each kick reducing his face further into ruins, his blood coats the leather with his thick fluid. Marxx' hand grasps my arm tightly, almost painfully, in his desperation to reach me.

Marxx is pulling me up the wall so I can wedge past him and Lawless to exit through the doorframe. Inch by inch I slide along the wall kicking and shoving their bodies from me as Marxx' grip demands I keep moving. Their hunger for my death animates them to such a level of activity that one moment of lost aware- ness will cost me my life. I am almost out when Death demands its pound of flesh with his own desperation. He refuses to let me completely escape from him.

The same female who had come so close to my neck, has found Marxx' extended arm. I notice her too late, but he saw her. He just refused to let me go. He watches her bite into his arm he is using to pull me from the room. We scream together as she pulls back, tearing the flesh of his arm with her teeth.

Blood soaks her chin, running down her neck with her mouthful of him. Her eyes close as she chews, showing her enjoyment of it as more of his blood slithers down her body. His blood washes her clothes the way his flesh washes her face in ecstasy.

He never lets me go as his wound is dripping heavily onto the floor. He tries pulling me from the room when the shock of what has happened locks my knees. My name is being shouted by many voices, yet all I can see is the female in front of me, as we stand face-to-face.

I cannot let her live. My fear is rolling into anger as she chews with those closed eyes of hers. They open, seeing me standing   in front of her. They are now bright and fully awake, and I am grateful she will see what I am about to do.

I kick her knee, smiling as I hear the bones snap, tumbling her down in front of me. Her head looks up at me with her anger riding her features. It pulls her lips that are ruby red from Marxx' blood back to expose yellow-tinted teeth. Lifting my knife, I smile at her one last time. The blade slips in with no more resistance than thick cardboard with my rage. I watch as her eyes go back to a glazed state as life finally leaves her rotting body.

Bracing against the wall, I kick her face from my blade, shoving her back into the arms of her brethren who are still fighting to reach me. The sound of my blade dislodging from her thin flesh brings me a deep-rooted joy. It should fill me with horror, but that was before. Horrors are hard to find anymore with Truth doing so much evil on her own.

"Are you happy now?" Lawless asks, still fighting against the door with his strength.

He grabs me, roughly pulling me through the door before I can debate the answer, letting it slam shut behind him when he moves.

The noises its closure causes could be the soundtrack of hell itself with the many demonic fists pounding against the wood.

Marxx is on the floor with the rest of the men rushing to him. Except for Ross. Ross is standing with Aimes in the far corner, both of them safe from it all. He and Aimes refuse to look at the man bleeding in the middle of the room. If it is weakness or guilt, I don't know. Either way, they both make me angry at their sought-out seclusion from what is happening.

Chapel and Rhett are trying to stop the bleeding with the many shirts they have pulled from the hangers around them. Their hands are covered with blood and it continues to seep through despite their best efforts. Their love for the man before them escalates their fears, rushing their movements as his blood coats them, staining them with the warm, red proof of Marxx' loyalty to us.

I walk to Aimes, grabbing her overly large purse. She flinches as I search within it for what we need with mental clarity from some depth

I am not aware of having. I pull a pastel-pink wrapped square from inside the purse before tossing the large bag back at her. I refuse to acknowledge her in any other fashion. I don't have the time to ease her fears or anxieties. For once, the room does not revolve around our pixie.

The paper refuses to cooperate with my shaking hands. I whim- per with my frustrations and my need to help Marxx, the man who has risked his own life for mine. Lawless takes the package from my hands, leaving me still frozen with the movement of holding it. My mind wants to shut down, too much has happened in too short of a time, but I fight against it. There is still too much to do.

Lawless takes it, silently opening it for me as he leads us back to Marxx and the many crimson-soaked pieces of fabric piling up around him. God told his people to paint their doors with the blood of a lamb and they would be spared. We are painting the floors with ours and have been spared nothing.

J.D. laughs when he sees what Lawless has in his hands. "God damn, Helena. Your sweet ass may just be worth it to keep saving," he says with misplaced mirth.

J.D. takes the maxi pad and pushes it firmly onto the gaping section of Marxx' arm. He holds it there as Rhett rips more shirts into long pieces of fabric to tie around the arm. The adhesive backing clings to the fabric, keeping it situated over the wound. The bleeding is finally contained and Lawless and Rhett help him stand. Marxx is weak from blood loss and I know if he dies, it will be another grave to add to my collection.

"We need to go, now." Ross keeps staring at the back door.

The knob is slowly starting to turn with their frenzy dying down. The Risen have switched back to their hunting mode. No one argues with him or with the cold dread the motion of the rotating knob stirs in us as we watch it moving.

"Go. Go. Go," J.D. whispers, shoving us out the store door. "Whoa," Ross says, as he exits the building. He stops short when he sees the new crowd forming outside the store.

What was once empty and desolate is now filled with many broken shapes that are mingling around one another like a dinner party in hell. With their new guests spilling out of the store, they turn to see us with as much eagerness as any host would. They are not interested in inviting us to dinner though. We are the dinner.

"How many rounds you have?" J.D. whispers to the men around me.

"Full clip," Lawless answers, shifting Marxx' weight so he can give his gun to Chapel.

"Same," Rhett says, but he is not handing his off. He will have to be the one to defend them with Lawless now unarmed and Marxx floating in and out of consciousness from his pain.

Ross says nothing. Somehow, I am not surprised. Maybe we can blind them with his super white teeth and buy us time to run. It seems to be a legit plan in my mind. I miss my mind.

"Get him out of here," J.D. tells Rhett and Lawless, speaking of Marxx. "Get his bike loaded in the back of that truck. Take Blondie with you. She's useless to me here."

They do not question him. Nor does Aimes as she follows them out, searching for another way back to our vehicles. The path we used to come in is now blocked before us with various Risen staring at us. J.D. hands me the gun strapped to the top of his boot with a grin. He means for me to stay with Chapel and him to keep the exit safe. A part of me wants to be flattered, but I am mostly just tired and ready to go "home".

"Try not to get up close and personal with them this time, okay, Barbie? We need to keep some space between us and them to buy our crew some time," he tells me, still wearing his misplaced grin. I nod as my vocabulary is failing me. I force what energy I have left into this moment. Marxx may die for me. The least I can do is try to stay awake for him, buying Rhett and Lawless time to get him to safety. Seems simple enough after the morning we have had.

The horde in front of us is watching our slightest of movements, trying to gain a clue to our intentions. Many of them were not aware enough to notice the few of us who had escaped from them moments ago. The maxi pad is collecting the blood, keeping its intoxicating scent locked away. If we play this right, we may not need to shoot at all, but when has life ever been so gracious?

Something slams against the store window next to Chapel. He fires the first shot, hitting a Risen directly and it crumples to the ground. J.D. and I turn to look at him with disbelief and he follows the motion, turning to look at the window that startled him. Encouraged with their loss of food, the Risen from the back room have figured out the doorknob, allowing them to escape into the store's center. They are now pounding on the glass, trying to break through it to reach us. I am grateful we are no longer standing in front of the swinging door with the new skill set the Risen have learned. It's frightening how they can adapt so well.

Monsters are not supposed to be smart. They have an unbalanced playing field already.

"I think I got their attention." Chapel watches as the group outside stares at their fallen friend before looking back at us with the realization of the cause of it.

"I think you have," J.D. says without emotion. "We are going to walk backwards, real slow like. Try not to shoot anymore unless we have to. Never was really good in math, but I count more before us than our clips can hold."

Ross stays behind us like the winner he is while we walk backwards. The Risen on both sides of the glass are mimicking each step we take. The ones outside are watching us and the store group, trying to form the missing link for the anger. Should the outside group also be lured into a frenzy, we will lead them right to the very people we are trying to protect. As J.D.'s math problem pointed out, we cannot stand against this many.

"You know the way out?" Chapel asks Ross. His gun sweeps the space before him, keeping track of the space between him and the creatures following us.

"Yeah. Take a right," Ross calls out each turn for us to take in our backwards escape.

We never take more distance than what is already between us to avoid agitating them. As long as they can see us, they seem   to be content in stalking us, plotting our deaths with their ever-watching eyes. This plan will not help us escape though. I wonder if J.D. is starting to see the folly of choosing a motorcycle as his apocalyptic vehicle.

J.D. abandons his backwards walk beside me. It stirs growls and other noises from the Risen in front of us as their eyes focus on his sudden change of movement. His kicking over the many standing trash bins we pass, to scatter the mess in front of us, brings their beasts forward. Anger and hunger drag snarling faces into action with J.D.'s noise and movements. They are close to their frenzy.

"Man, what are you doing?" Ross asks, with the panic of seeing their reactions.

"My job," J.D. answers, as if it should be plain for anyone to see other than someone like Ross. "Run if you want."

"Do and I'll shoot you," Chapel tells Ross, knowing the sight of him running away will be the final push needed to trigger them. Ross actually has the nerve to look to me for protection. Sorry, all I want is a nap and a warm blanket. A hot bath would be nice with bubbles foaming thick with their perfume. Too much to hope for?

The value of his life on my to-do list must have shown on my face. He does not run. He is not smiling either. Bonus.

Chapel has figured out what J.D. is doing. He too begins to kick objects of the various littered items in front of us. I am a tad disappointed I have, yet again, failed to grasp what is going on. Instead I stand, keeping my aim locked on the closest Risen, trying to look very intimidating. I giggle with the many faces I make at them in my pursuit of intimidation.

"Shit," Chapel says, staring at me.

I must have finally found a scary face.

"Yup," J.D. answers him, his voice still empty of emotions, but I know he is agreeing with my face. "Girly, I need you to stay focused just a little bit longer."

"I need a nap," I tell them, thinking it explains everything. Little do I know, it really does.

"I know, Girly. Just stay with me a bit longer then we will get you that nap," J.D. tells me.

J.D. leans over the pile of trash he has somehow made into a thick line in front of us. I am not sure how I missed him doing that. The Risen seem to have snuck up on us a lot faster than I remembered them moving. My head clears with the awareness of the missing time.

"Focus," Chapel whispers to me. Reaching around me, he takes the gun from my hand. He feels so warm behind me. I had not realized how cold I had become. "When he lights that, we will run. Stay with me, Hells."

I don't understand why they keep telling me to "stay with them". I have no desire to stay here. I am cold, tired and having a hard time focusing. Not to mention, we have already discovered Aimes' driving skills with a stick. They need me, I hear Ashley's voice tell me again. I don't think this is what she had in mind.

The fire is instant and bright. The Risen pause, being unsure of what this is before them and what it may do to them. They search the catalog of their broken minds to find the clues they need to piece this new puzzle together.

J.D. runs to me, turning me around as Chapel drags me for- ward. My feet will not keep up with him with how heavy they feel. Screams of hell's anger start behind us at the sight of our escape through the bright fire. My feet are fine now, light as a feather.

Lawless and Rhett have wasted no time as they waited for us. The motorcycles are running, vibrating the area in noise with their throaty engines. Even my truck sits with her engine purring with broken pieces of what is left of the makeshift ramp they had used to load Marxx' bike in the long bed scattered around her. Aimes is sitting in the cab of the truck, keeping pressure on Marxx' arm. J.D. stops me from climbing into the driver's seat. He turns to Ross with the full weight of his cold, steel-colored stare. "Get them back. Safely. No more games," he tells Ross, pushing me further down the bench so Ross can drive. J.D.'s words punctuate the possible risk of severity with Ross' failure to do so. For once, Ross does not smile. He does not argue. He climbs silently behind the steering wheel, tossing the bag with the list and its items onto the floor in front of Aimes.

"Keep her awake," J.D. barks his final command to Ross before slamming the truck's door shut.

The men ride out of the parking lot as the first of the burning corpses comes around the store's corner. Its whole body is in flames, but it keeps coming towards us as the flames climb up its body. It has no need of the organs the fire is melting or any knowledge of the pain the fire causes to them.

One by one, the parking lot fills with the walking torches. Their flesh is melting and bubbling from the heat of the licking flames. Some make it further than others before they fall to the ground with the damage the fire is doing to the muscles of their bodies. The sight is horrific with the amount of the still moving, burning bodies filling the parking lot. The imagery of their crawling forms, roasting from the fire, trying to reach us, grants me new nightmares. Like the smell of smoke on my clothes, the smell of their burning flesh will always linger in my mind.

"Stop looking," Marxx whispers, weak from his wound to Aimes and myself with the shock of what we have seen on our faces.

Ross pulls out onto the street and puts it all behind us. I only wish it would stay there. I know when I close my eyes tonight it will be back. It is always so much worse in my dreams.

"Did you know what was in that room?" Marxx asks Ross, with his eyes clamped closed. "Is that why the store had the most build up blocking the door? You stored them in there?"

I am not sure the implication of his words to Ross. I stay silent, as does Ross.

"You're a dead man. They will kill you for this." Marxx' voice is deeper than normal.

I shiver with it.

He places his hand on my leg, trying to reassure me, "You did good."

Looking at his grey face, I do not feel as if I "did good". I feel as if I have led another to slaughter. Seems I have run out of lambs and have now moved on to black sheep. I'm a busy girl.

He smiles at me saying, "Just a flesh wound. My ex used to do way worse."

"Was she a biter, too?" Aimes asks him, trying to bring a laugh back into the situation.

Marxx chuckles and it is enough. It is enough to let us know he will make it "home." I am just unsure of what will happen once we get there.

Chapter 35

The courtyard is clear of the many mingling people it normally holds. Even the numerous metal barrels used to provide the area with warmth are unlit. There are no signs of life and if it were not for how completely unrealistic it would be, I would think the place to be deserted.

With how much the sight sets me at unease, it seems to confirm something for the men. Their faces hold their anger as they pull in beside us, scanning the area for signs of something I don't see. Chapel seems to be the only one who is as confused as I am.

J.D. swings open the driver door, once again forcing Ross from the truck. He skips, staggering as his feet try to steady him. J.D. kicks the man to the ground, watching him fall on the hard cement. With uplifted arms, Ross tries to protect himself from the blows J.D. is landing upon him. When he is satisfied Ross is too broken to escape, J.D. stops his torment. With a look of boredom, he walks slowly around the man crippled and bleeding before him.

"Get him on his knees," J.D. commands and it's Lawless who rushes to do carry it out.

"What are you doing?" Chapel asks them, lost in his confusion and outrage.

Someone must pay for the spilled blood of their brother. Chapel is just unsure why it is Ross.

"You ain't figured it out?" J.D. asks him. "Let me know the moment you do."

I watch as J.D. pulls his soul's coldness to the surface of his face. He is reaching deep into the darkest parts of himself for what he is about to do. Even as he forces himself to reach for it, he will love every minute of it.

J.D. turns to the building's high walls as Lawless and Rhett hold Ross between them. Ross is bleeding from the face with the many kicks from J.D. and his breathing is labored hinting at the damage done to his ribs. J.D. chambers his gun and points it at Ross, waiting for any movement towards us.

"I know you are watching up there," J.D. shouts. It echoes off the high walls and repeats back to us as if the building is mocking him. "Bet you didn't think to see us again, did ya now?"

The courtyard vibrates with his anger and still no acknowledgment comes from the building. J.D. turns to walk behind Ross and points the gun to the back of his skull. Ross starts to make sobbing sounds between trying to form words, begging for his life. He is suddenly "very sorry" for something.

"Helena?" Chapel leans into the truck door looking at me.

His eyes are pleading with me to do something to stop what is about to happen. At what point did I become the champion for J.D.'s targets? Someone seriously failed to give me the memo.

"No," Marxx' deep gravel comes from beside me. His eyes are closed, and he seems paler than he was moments ago. "You two still don't get it, do you? They knew. They knew what would happen. Ross did his job for them. Now he has to pay for us."

There was almost a sound when it all comes together for me. The pointless items on the list for us to get, how nervous Ross was this morning, how he did not want to leave the parking lot, and how he had refused to go into the back of the store but tried to keep me with him to send them in alone. It was never about our finding the items on the list. It was about the men finding the dead in the store and to see what would happen when they did.

Marxx laughs a tired laugh, seeing it finally make sense for me. "J.D. won't kill him. It's not Ross he wants," he says.

"What does he want?" Aimes asks. She is her own shade of grey with her small voice weaker than normal.

"For you three to come home," Marxx tells us, as his fight is fading from him with the pain. "He wants you to see what they really are. We aren't the only monsters, Helena. We are just honest about being ones."

Right now, Marxx looks furthest from any monster I have ever dreamed. He is pale and fading in front of me. His face is contorting from the pain in his arm. The pain my own pride has caused him. He had risked his life to save me from not only me or the Risen, but also from the people I thought were our new friends. He could have let me go to save himself, but he didn't. He held on to me through the pain and the terror.

Monsters do not do that. Monsters let you fall while watching the pain the fall causes. I wonder if they are watching us now.

"You best plead to your pals, Ross. Not to me. I ain't your pal."

J.D. smiles his soul-damning smile to the kneeling man before him. "You would have let us die in there. That was your job, right? Lead us to them? Take notes about what happened to report back to your pals here? Pals who sure don't seem to give a shit about you now."

Ross is incoherent as he fights against the many words pouring out from him with his fear.

"He almost cost us our own today. How's that make you boys feel?" J.D. steps back, letting his words settle over the two men supporting Ross.

He puts his gun back into its holster, signaling it is Lawless' and Rhett's turn to do as they will. He has given his blessing to do what they want with Ross. A priest's blessing can save your soul for heaven. J.D.'s can torment it to hell.

Lawless drops the arm he is holding, letting Ross droop from the sudden lack of support. He reaches into the top of his boot, pulling the hidden pistol from its hiding place. I should have known Lawless would never be completely unarmed. He makes a great show of undoing the gun, checking it for ammo before looking down at Ross.

Every one of us knows he is aware of exactly how many rounds each of his guns are holding at all times. Every one of us, but those who are watching behind the wire patterned safety glass and Ross does not. He chambers the gun, letting the metal sound echo off the high walls around us. Every metallic snap brings Ross that much closer to panic.

Lawless kneels down to look Ross straight in his face. "Tell me, how can we all work this out now?" he asks him, repeating what Ross had said at the Welcome Center.

Lawless makes a simple nod of his head and Rhett understands the meaning completely. I wish he had not. My eyes can't look away and my soul doesn't want to watch.

Rhett grabs Ross, pulling his head back with the leverage of his brown, shaggy hair. He forces Ross' mouth open by applying pressure to his cheeks, threatening to break his teeth if he does not cooperate. The pain from the pressure forces Ross to submit, finally opening his mouth for him.

Lawless shoves his gun barrel into the opening, forcing Ross' mouth to open wider or risk similar damage. He stands, pulling Ross' head up with the force of the barrel. Rhett is stepping to the side, away from J.D. and Chapel who are watching, and waiting to see how far Lawless will go with this.

"Scream," Lawless' voice holds no more emotion than commenting on the weather. It gives his words so much more of a chill. "I want to hear you scream. I want your screams to comfort me tonight as hers will haunt me."

Ross looks confused by the request. He shakes his head not understanding, rattling his teeth against the metal of the gun.

"Scream!" Lawless yells into his face. His rage is exploding finally under the release of its restraints. He shoves the gun further down Ross' throat, tilting his head back further with the action. Screams and tears fall from Ross when he finally submits. Each scream is louder than his last. Each tear falls faster than his first. The courtyard fills until the sound is one long echo of terror. I am dancing on a tightrope with my emotions and the knowledge of the fact another may die from my actions. I should really come with a warning label.

Marxx said J.D. would not kill Ross. He never mentioned Lawless wouldn't. It's the small words you have to be aware of in their secret life. A simple switch of a name and all promises are wiped away.

A noise from the archway behind us pulls my attention to the mirror on the truck's door. Shelia is running towards them, her face a visible testament to how their actions are affecting her. Like a spider in its web waiting for the prey to become trapped,

J.D. is still and watching her run towards them. He had fun playing with Ross, now he has a better subject to use to taunt the people in the high school. Their Queen is now his.

One moment he is relaxed and watching her, but as she grows even with him, he lunges and holds her in a backwards styled hug. He picks her up off the ground, spinning her in two full rotations as she screams, beating against his arms with her tiny fists. It encourages him, his laughter a strange sound to be mixing with Ross' mumbling pleading and Shelia's screams.

He drops her, letting her fall to the courtyard's hard cement floor, dizzy from the spinning. Kneeling over her fallen body now shaking with her silent sobs, he runs his hands over her shoulders and down her back. He lets his face show the male enjoyment of her skin under his hands. His long, unfulfilled hunger is showing before us.

"Where is your Simon now?" J.D. whispers into her ear, as his eyes scan the upper windows for any movement. "Now we can have us a party, boys!"

J.D. pushes her forward, making her fall to her hands and knees and the forced position hints at his intentions. At least I hope it is a hint. Of all the sins J.D. can claim, never has one been rape. He has always told the other men of the club only the weak force themselves where they are not wanted. A real man doesn't have to sink to such levels to strike fear. Fear is something to be flavored and drawn out. It should be the least expected, not the most expected of what a man can do. With this new dare for those inside the school, I wonder how much wiggle room he has left himself to carry out his bluff.

Lawless made Ross scream for what felt like hours condensed into minutes with no response from inside. Shelia's first real scream and the doors open with such force their hinges fight to keep them from hitting the stone walls. It makes J.D. smile his wide grin, pulling Shelia up and close to him.

"There he is. Smile for him. Let him see that pretty face of yours," J.D. says, holding her as she fights against him. He lets her sway with her efforts. It puts on a better show for the others to see her so distressed and held tightly against his body.

Marxx is right, the ones he is holding now are not his targets. Shelia never was. Ross never was. What he wants is standing a few feet from him now. He wants their grief, their anger, their fear with not knowing what will happen next. He wants them to beg for his mercy as he feels they should have from day one.

"Enough," Simon says. "Just let her go."

"Just let her go, he says. Just like that he asks? Oh brother, I don't think so. You and me, we going to have us a little chat first," J.D. tells Simon, pausing to inhale the scent of Shelia's neck. Feeling him so close to her makes her fight harder to be free.

Simon's panic is flooding his senses.

"We can talk about whatever you want, after you let her go," Simon says, stepping away from the door. He lifts the rifle on his side in a peace gesture, placing it on the cement next to him and with his hands raised he says, "You want me? You just let her go and I'll come to you. A simple switch."

"That's real sweet of you, but you ain't really my type." J.D. smiles. His hand cups Shelia's inner thigh. It has its desired effect. Simon rushes forward, even as Richard grabs him, tackling him to the ground. Richard is speaking in his ear, trying to reassure him, to calm him, but the words are not reaching him.

J.D. knows how to play this game well. He knows which pressure points will spring forth reactions. Everyone is a book to J.D., and he read Simon's chapters a long time ago.

"What do you want?" Richard shouts across the courtyard. "You want to talk? Talk!"

J.D. pauses, his mind reassessing this new target. Shelia's abuse will not bring the same anger from this new man before him now. To keep the pressure going, he has to find a new method of torment. He must find a new weakness to exploit.

"You know, I find it real funny no one has begged for Ross yet. Do you find that funny too, Hun?" he asks Shelia. He is testing these new waters rocking underneath him. Ever seen a man die? It's a messy business. At this short range here, his head will explode. It will spray Smiley's bits all over this area. That kind of stain, it will last and last. Always here to remind you and yours how you let us kill him."

He turns Shelia so she is fully facing Lawless and Ross.

"Now keep your eyes open. You don't want to miss this." J.D. whispers to her. It works.

"No!" She screams and Lawless eases his finger from the trig- ger. "Don't do this. It wasn't his fault. They told him to. Don't do this!"

She is begging Lawless, not J.D., but Law's eyes hold no mercy for either of them as he stares at her. She whimpers with his coldness.

"You want to see what they told him to do? Keep your eyes open. Let me show you what they told him to do." J.D. looks to Chapel, tilting his head towards us in the truck.

The Jedi mind trick works and Chapel understands exactly what he wants. Perhaps if I had a nice, shiny leather vest, I too could figure out what is going on around me. If Santa is still alive, it is totally going on my list this year.

Chapel helps me from the tall truck. My legs are jelly underneath me, and I have to brace against its bed for support. Next, he reaches for Marxx, who is pale and panting from the wound on his arm. He too is bracing against the truck, but for worse reasons than mine. Aimes slides out on her own, standing to the other side of Marxx. I am not sure what this display is supposed to accomplish until I look at the three of us. Evil genius, our J.D.

Aimes is covered in Marxx' blood. Her shirt is as covered from keeping pressure on his wound, making it hard to tell if she is wounded as well. Marxx is worse. His normal rich ivory skin tone is now a pale ashen grey. The wound has left a trail of blood from his arm, to his chest and down one side of his leg from the amount of time it took to treat it and now its new seepage. The pad has been pushed to its limits. It's painting a bright shade of red upon him where it sits and from what is spilling around it.

Aimes is not the only one bathed in Marxx' wound. The act of the bite, and his refusal to let go has me just as covered where he held onto me. Together, we must paint a pretty picture of our morning. No amount of coffee will make this less depressing.

Shelia stares at us, her knees growing weak from what she sees. "I told them not to do it. I told them it wasn't right," she says, and her knees finally give out from under her.

J.D. lets her go. She is in a new prison now. Her prison no longer needs his arms to keep her secure because she is trapped with the sight of us. Trapped in the conclusions her mind is forming over what she is seeing.

"Do you know what they did? What they wanted to happen? They wanted them dead. Your boys wanted us dead. Led us right into a room of trapped Risen while they sat here waiting to see what happens from behind the comfort of these high, safe walls. How many of us were meant to make it back?" J.D. whispers his tormenting words to her.

Every word he says hits its intended destination. She is a protector. She has spent these past many months keeping everyone safe under this roof. Now the very men with whom she has formed a family attempted to jeopardize it all.

"They said they wanted to see if you would get the list. If you would do what we needed versus what you wanted to do. That's what they told me. I thought it was wrong to trick you, to test you at all. It wasn't supposed to be this." Her words are a soft whispering of regrets.

J.D. has applied the correct pressure again. Richard may not care as much as Simon about her screams, but the look Shelia is now sending him makes a ruin of his face. The anger and the hate she sends their way makes even Dolph look away from her with shame.

"It wasn't supposed to be this way." Simon tries to reason with her from across the space between them. "The girls were sup- posed to stay here. They were never supposed to go."

"So, you just planned to murder the men?" she screams back. "Murder is murder. You sent Ross to do your dirty work because you were too afraid of them. Too afraid to just trust them and try to work out your differences and your egos. Is this how we solve our problems now? If you don't like someone, are they your next target?"

"Shelia, come on. Look at them, they can handle a couple of those things. It was just supposed to prove a point. See if they would go through with the list versus rebelling again. We needed to know if we could trust them to stick by us when it gets rough or if they would revert back to "theirs first" mentality," Richard pleads for her to understand. His eyes though keep floating behind her to Aimes who seems smaller than normal with her blood-soaked clothes and despair-filled face.

In one moment of glory, J.D. has reversed the roles. Now their girl sits on our side where before his girls sat on theirs. He must keep the pressure going to keep this play in action. To let up for one second may cost him his finale.

"He is right," J.D. says. "We could have handled it, but he knows what Hells is like. It was her that saved your boys after all and look how they repay her. They try to kill her. If Helena had not risked her life at that Center, your boy may not have come home to you. How much more trust does a man need?"

J.D.'s words sink into her, lapping her conscience. You can see it on her face. I would clap with his performance, but my hands are busy holding me up.

"Now, we have us some wounded here, Shelia. My people need your help. Marxx might die over there while your boys are keeping us out here. You going to let that happen?" J.D. asks her.

He does not ask for her help for himself. That would be too easy to refuse. To refuse a wounded group, that is not in her nature.

"I'll tell you what, I'll make my boy there release Smiley. A show of good faith," J.D. says, shrugging. "I can still control this. I can make it all go away, but you, now you got to get us back in there so I can get them help. You okay with that?" he asks her.

J.D. is removing her fear of him by showing her how desperate he is to help his people. He is making her their savior and their mediator with one request. A role her heart loves to play and cannot pass up.

"Paula will be in the kitchen. We don't even need to go past them or have their permission." She smiles with triumph as she pulls a key and its pretty blue ribbon from around her neck. "I can get you in," she says.

Seriously, all together now, standing ovation for the man.

J.D. looks to Lawless with his silent command. The first kink in his plan is happening. He didn't count on Lawless' rage or his disobedience.

Lawless stares at Ross with eyes filling with anger over being forced to let him go. There is no more mocking or taunting from him. I watch his hand holding the gun still embedded in Ross' mouth tremble. The tremble spreads through his body and I hear his sharp inhale. Lawless is no longer daring. He is about to take the dare.

In two steps, J.D. reaches him. He is whispering in Law's ear words, which do not reach anyone else. J.D. will not take the gun from him. If he wants this, J.D. will allow him to take it. J.D. plans to make sure it's what he really wants though before ruining his well-played performance.

Father figure and adopted son stand locked in a whispered debate. Ross' eyes swing from one to the other with the exchange going on above him. His face gives us a better understanding with its many expressions as to the state of the debate.

Rhett stands there watching as well. His face is missing the smile it has worn for most of the morning with the turn of events the day has taken for us. I know with the look in Rhett's eyes Ross may be safe today, but tomorrow is another story. Once again, the small word change will be the death of Ross.

I missed Lawless releasing Ross from his hold while I was watching Rhett. Lawless is squatting, covering his head with his hands as he tries to collect himself. His gun is still grasped in his hand as if he is still rethinking his decision. A part of me wants to go to him and tell him everything will be all right. Another part of me wants to take the gun from him myself and shoot them both and still another part of me is just waiting on the nap I was promised. Not sure yet which side will win.

"No hard feelings, right?" J.D. says to Ross, pushing him to- wards the men across from us with whom Ross conspired to set this plan in motion.

Rhett watches Ross walk by with his one timid step at a time. Every muscle shows how much Ross wants to run, but pride will not let him. Rhett is not the only one who is watching him.

Lawless watches the man's back with such anger I am not sure how Ross does not twitch with it. Lawless' anger strips Rhett of his calm exterior until they both are sharing the same rage over having to let Ross go, watching him retreat to the other side of the courtyard.

I have never pretended to know what the men did behind closed doors or what they do when not around me. Not to say I hold any illusions to the type of men they can be; I just prefer to not admit it. Now as I watch Rhett and Lawless, I know how well sheltered Lawless has kept me from this part of him. The same hands he has used many nights to heal my soul, inflame my desires and fill the air with music have done so much more. From Rhett I have always expected such things, but not Lawless with his gentle eyes and charming smile.

I had hoped I had my fill of truth for one day from Lawless. Now as I watch him and Rhett, another truth he gifts me and each one is becoming more of a curse. The most obvious truth is how much danger

Marie F. Crow

Ross is still in as both men look to him again. His days are numbered, and the timer started long ago.

Chapter 36

It seems Paula is not only the master of end of the world dishes, but also of last-ditch efforts of medical survival. When your friends and family start to eat you, there are not a whole lot of emergency rooms left open. She and Shelia have brought us to what once served as the sports medicine area for the gym. Now it serves as a makeshift triage to help those who call this school home. Its many doctor-office style benches are still covered in the thin noisy paper waiting for use. We are not going to disappoint it. "How bad is it?" Shelia is hovering over Marxx like a mother with a wounded child. She even holds his other hand, either in the attempt to give him comfort or to find it for herself. Marxx has gone past caring to refuse her smothering as Paula cleans and tends to his wound.

"It's pretty deep. A lot of muscle damage," Paula tells her. Her voice has lost that playfulness.

I guess stitching up a human's bite on another human's arm kills the mood for "girl time".

"Is he going to turn?" Aimes' voice is small and nervous from risking her question.

I had forgotten about her with my own issues. She is being cradled in Rhett's thick arms and their size difference resembles more of a father and daughter than two adults. I am annoyed with how they treat her. I am mostly annoyed that no one is holding me, but I am not going to admit it.

"Turn to what?" Paula is half listening to us around her as she concentrates on repairing the damage to Marxx' arm.

"He's been bit," Aimes continues her whimpering.

Hurrah for Captain Obvious with her pink streaks of perception. "I can see that," Paula answers with the same tone I am holding mentally for their conversation.

"So, is he going to turn into one of them?" Aimes' question sets the room at unease. Even Marxx now opens one of his eyes to gauge Paula's response.

"If a raccoon bites you, do you turn into a raccoon? You've watched too much television girl," Paula clips her response with frustration.

Have I mentioned how much I like Paula? No? I like Paula. "It doesn't work that way?" Marxx' nerves make his voice weaker than its normal deep gravel.

Paula gives him a reassuring smile, stopping her stitching long enough to look at him, saying, "No, it doesn't work that way."

"How do you know?" J.D. asks.

J.D. has been silent this whole time in his normal "watch and see" fashion and to give Shelia room to recover from their encounter. His concern for Marxx keeps him from being too close, unwilling to risk showing his emotions for the man.

"I just do." Paula is back to being annoyed now. Apparently, only Marxx gets a free pass to talk to her.

"That's not good enough," Rhett replies.

He is watching every inch of the thread pulled through Marxx' wound. Each stitch is serving as another memory for him in his own locked chamber. It's a chamber different than mine and it unsettles me with his fascination. As much as I feel I know the man, it's moments like these when I see a different light in those eyes, reminding me how very little I do actually know.

"Didn't think it was going to be," she answers.

Her deep sigh tells us there is a story to be told. Our stilled breathing lets her know we are waiting.

"I used to be a nurse at a drug clinic," she starts, still focusing on Marxx' arm to give her courage to speak. "I had a little girl of my own. I wanted to help change the world for the better for her. So, I went into the research of vaccines. I thought I was helping to stop the spread of illnesses. So noble," her voice is bitter.

She is focusing on Marxx' arm like it's a raft in a storm. He winces with the needle now more than before. Something about the words she has said tries to spark a fuse of a memory. It sputters, but goes out before the flame can catch. At least for me, Chapel though seems to be remembering something with how he stares at her.

"Years of research went into this new vaccine. It was supposed to be the wonder and cure all of the many different strands of the flu, but also many other winter aliments in one dose. Think of it, the common cold, strep throat and pneumonia being nothing more than another mention in history books. It was supposed to be amazing, groundbreaking even. It was. It has broken all sorts of new ground," she says with a pause. "It was fully tested on all levels. Some levels I was not even cleared for but made to document the passage. No one had any clue to what was about to happen. We were offered the option of having one dose for our own private use. I wanted my little girl to have it. I wanted her to be healthy just like every mother does. To avoid the many illness- es winter seems to bring with it. How could we have known?" she asks us, but I think she is still mostly talking to herself and Marxx' arm.

Her voice has fallen in its pitch with each word as a new emotion comes forth from her. It almost sounds like shame, but I can't imagine why. All eyes are on her now with her weakness so exposed. We all stare at her with confusion over where her story is taking us. All of us, that is, but Chapel.

He is not confused. He is torn between anger and grief. That spark keeps sputtering for me, but it has caught fire for Chapel.

"It was the children first. All of them: one by one. We thought maybe it was because they received most of the vaccines, but we will never know. There was not enough time for testing. The results varied depending on how it was administered. The shot had the fastest onset, doing the most damage to them. The inhalant still had the same effect, just a few days slower and a longer time of degradation of their minds once the fever took hold. Once again, not enough time for the research." Paula's voice is neutral now. She might as well have been giving a lesson of studies with the lack of feeling she has for what she is telling us.

"Not feeling well, fever and then death. Then they become what they are now?" Chapel asks. He has put the pieces together and he is calling her out with them.

"Not exactly, but yes those are the basics of it," Paula replies.

She does not flinch from his anger. She has faced her own anger over this and survived it. Chapel's does not frighten her.

"The shots put the children into a feeling of unease within minutes. Their bodies are telling them something is not right, but their inexperience makes them think they are just ill. Nothing really stands out as being wrong, so it is ignored. Within hours, the vaccine takes hold of the host. The antibodies react, causing a high-grade fever as the body attempts to fight them off. This somehow feeds the vaccine, allowing what we thought of as the weakened virus to mutate. This new mutation attacks the brain. It shuts down all normal life supporting activity allowing the host to appear dead. They aren't. They never really die. The vaccine literally becomes alive. It becomes the host," Paula tries to explain.

Her words leave more questions than answers. They cause more panic than comfort, but she is not finished yet.

Paula pulls the stitches slower now as she further explains, "They no longer need their organs to sustain them the way we do. They can go months without food or water. Their bodies in essence die, but the vaccine turns the brain into a self-sufficient machine, only functioning at the level it needs to for its survival. They still have their basic logic and function. They can still hold on to some piece of their personalities. Some can even have memories and can recognize people from their past. There is no cookie cutter mutation. It seems to all depend on who they were in life as to what they will become. Leaders are still leaders. Followers are still followers."

The image of another school comes to my mind. A memory of a room full of tiny bodies matching up into smaller groups flashes before me. It was not a game of "Follow the Leader". It was not a game at all. They really were following clues and commands from another as their socializing had taught them to do, but why had so many transformed at the school to begin with?

"Why wasn't it pulled? Why did they release it if they knew?" Chapel's voice shakes with his emotions. He is remembering his two small children who might have been saved.

"It was too late by the time we were aware," Paula says, looking at Chapel like a drowning sinner. "It was fully tested and ready for use. Something fatal happened when it was mass-produced. Something we didn't have the time to correct. All we could do was alert the proper people about a possible reaction. Schools all over the country pulled students into localized locations to wait and see after the shots were given. They were told to be prepared for reactions ranging from illness to extreme rage. How do you tell people to watch their kids go through what was really going to happen? How do you warn people of what they were going to become?" She is looking to us as if we could offer her any answers.

We have none. We have not had any for a long time.

"Slowly reports started coming in of whole school's being wiped out. Elementary seemed to be the first to report symptoms. The shots were part of a school government health wellness program. Parents were asked by the school nurses to keep their kids in school "under the weather" because there was nothing really wrong with them. We have been told as parents to expect certain off behaviors after shots. It didn't raise any parental alarms. The fever would hit after the shots. School nurses did the best they could, but they were not prepared for this. Whole schools were transformed and disappeared from the grid before we could offer any help. It's why I am here at this school. This is the school I was sent to," Paula says. She is silent with her afterthought.

I do not need to wonder what it may have been like. I was there.

I wish I could forget.

"If it was just the kids, then why the others, too?" Shelia asks. I guess this is the first time Paula has shared the story. "Because not only the kids received the vaccines. Every medical

professional, adults, the elderly as is the normal routine." She is watching me as she talks now. She has finished with Marxx' arm as best one can do in this facility. I almost squirm under her gaze wondering what it is she is seeing.

"There should be a set number of them then? If we just wait it out, we can make it through this?" Shelia asks with hope radiating through her voice.

"Did I forget to mention the military was also signed up for the first round? Which means the whole government, as we know it, also was going to be included. So yes, if we find a few groups of people willing to go out and fight who knows how many of the transformed roaming around out there, it could happen. That is, if those groups do not become food, chicken out, die of basic injuries, run out of supplies or just stop giving a shit," Paula explains. Her cold tone pours icy water all over the hope Shelia held.

All we need is a little pixie dust, and flamethrowers. It could happen. I am not volunteering, but it could happen.

"How do you feel Helena?" Paula asks me.

I feel as if I have been caught doing something naughty with the way her eyes are watching me.

"Like I need a flamethrower," is what I hear come from me. It is not what I told my mouth to say. My confusion must show on my face, making her come over to where I am standing.

Why does every medical person have one of those tiny flash- lights with the retina burning light? And why do they never warn you before waving it in front of your face?

"Let's lay you down," she tells me, as I am helped onto my own crinkly paper bench.

With how disobedient my mouth is being, I simply nod. I want to tell her about how cold I am. How I keep missing pieces of time and facts. How tired I am. How I should not be feeling this much confusion and this agitated. How I never meant for Marxx to get hurt. How very sorry I am for everything, but I don't trust my voice, so I say nothing.

"She didn't get bit." Lawless comes into my view. He holds himself apart from me, but close enough I can see his distress.

"Shock." J.D. comes over and pushes a stray piece of hair from my face. "She seems to be coming out of it though. Not so bad now. She's tough, aren't you, Barbie?" he asks me.

"You promised me a nap." I close my eyes to refuse the scene before me. His sudden tenderness will undo me.

"You go right ahead," Paula tells me.

The blanket is warm. It lulls me to the sleep I have been fighting against this whole time. I give in to my tired body and escape the pain. I let myself be a girl and I let them be the men I need. When I wake up, who knows who we will be?

"What was her name?" I ask Paula before I finally slip into the comforting arms of sleep.

"Emily. Who were yours?" She is tucking the blanket around me, sealing in its heat.

"Lilly. Ashley. Conroy."

I let their names escape from me like a whispered prayer. I let their images from behind my closed eyes from happy memories long gone. I let my tears fall like a river of regrets from which I now bathe.

Chapter 37

How does it feel?" I shyly ask Marxx.

I am cautiously approaching the subject of his arm. My guilt still consumes me long after the need for it. He and I have been making a normal routine of our morning coffee. Some mornings we talk to each other. Other mornings we just enjoy the sunrise in silence. It's our way of daring the dawn with the fact we are both still here. Even with all that has been thrown our way, and with what is still waiting for us, we are defiantly still here. I wonder if there are other people somewhere gazing at the same sunrise who are also daring the sun with their continued existence.

"Worth it," Marxx tells me. He doesn't really answer my question, but his wink does.

His voice is strong again with its deep gravel pitch. Just to see him slowly healing, regaining pieces of himself, makes the dawns easier for me. As bright as his smile is, my guilt still worries at my conscience.

"I don't know about that," I say. My voice colors with the hues of my remorse while I stare at the breaking sky.

I feel the knuckles of his hand float along my cheek. I pull my eyes from the various shades gracing the light blue sky. His smile is so unlike Rhett's mischievous charm or even J.D.'s bold grin. Marxx' smile is filled with a gentle touch as soft as his fingers now on my flesh. These past few mornings have shown me a side of him I have never noticed before as he slowly pulls further away from the cold, dark shadow from which he has been living within.

"I do. I just wish you would see it again. I miss your smile, Hells," he whispers such tender words, and I feel nothing with them.

"You and Aimes better?" he asks me, pulling back some with my blatant numbness.

He already knows exactly how she and I are doing. Not a day goes by without every one of them asking me with hopes of a change in my answer. I won't budge and they won't yield.

"Haven't seen her," I answer him, swinging my eyes back to the window.

There will be no change today. Since recovering from either true shock, or just the shock of that morning, Aimes and I have been tiptoeing around each other. I have finally moved into my own room, unable to take the tension building between us with all the unsaid words. From what I have seen of her, she is receiving plenty of comfort over our fallout. It does nothing to entice me to "make nice" or to forgive her for what has befallen us.

"She needs you, Helena. She is not strong like you. It was always your strength that strengthened her. I don't know what all was said. I really don't need to. I know her and Lawless are now ghosts with it. Don't push them away when they are needing you," he implores me.

I have started to notice a trend. The men only use my full name when they want me to do something. It's almost the same way a parent will call a child's full name when they are out of line. Apparently, I have been out of line a lot lately.

"There are questions in your eyes," he continues, using my silence as encouragement. "Questions you need to ask so you can finally nail this coffin shut. You won't be able to get past it until you hear it all. You can't forgive what you don't know."

"Maybe I don't want to know. I get the idea. I don't need the graphic novel of it." I hope my honesty will end this path of counseling he has decided to travel down today. I am starting to prefer our silent mornings.

"Don't you?" His eyes meet mine with that simple question of damnation. I cannot hold his stare, and it gives him his answer. Yes, a part of me wants to ask every detail. The truth of why he felt the need to do it. Truth has been so tormenting as of late though, I am too afraid to touch her barbed answers. I may be unable to deny it happened, but I can still hide from the details.

Once truth is invited in, there will be no more hiding. There will be no more white lies to help me sleep at night.

"What do you know?" I ask Marxx, thinking baby steps will be better than a full ambush.

"It's not my story to tell," Marxx says, stalling as his eyes glance around the room. He is the one staring at the sky now. Look Marxx, pretty blue lights.

"…but it did happen?" I ease into the sentence with as much grace as a child asking if Santa is real.

"Did what exactly happen?" He is going to make me fight for this.

So much for his whole "I need to know" advice he was pushing down my throat moments ago. I let my silence carry the conversation as I brace for him to answer me.

"Yeah, it happened. That's all I am telling you. You need to get your answers from Lawless. You two need this conversation. Not you and me," he says, sealing his statement as the sun reaches past the many bright shades of the sky.

"Was Leslie with anyone else?" I ask, refusing to let him get away so easily. I am pushing my luck. It is one of my many talents it seems as of late.

"She tried," Marxx replies, and his tone lets me know he was one of her "tries".

He slips from our conversation with the same gentle kiss on my head as he does every morning since our first morning as the room starts to fill with other voices. Life is stirring in the hall- ways. Residents are starting to fill the tables of the cafeteria with the start of their day.

Their timing saves him from my growing bravery or maybe it saves me.

He leaves me with my thoughts and the stares of strangers. The sheep, as J.D. calls them, have noticed the change again in our group. It causes more of their soft whispers and hidden stares when I pass them. It's not just the alteration to our group that has them scared.

Shelia is now just as shy with hers as I am with mine. Together, our groups have tried to reform a thousand times, a thousand different ways, trying to figure out how the puzzle pieces can work. The ends do not match as well. The corners are too sharp to connect it all. Yet, we keep trying. Like a three-year-old with a peg game and a hammer, we keep trying.

I would be content to sit here all morning in my little corner, watching the many go about their mornings as I avoid mine. I have almost gotten used to the taste of basic black coffee now as it provides the perfect diversion to my morning's start.

Sip. Watch. Sip. Return a shy smile. Repeat. How simple life could be? Not my life, but how simple it could be. My life just keeps rolling ahead like a roller coaster built by a sadist. Why, is that another hill I hear us climbing? Yes Sir, yes Sir, three times more.

Aimes glides through the double doors with Rhett and J.D. on either side of her. Her eyes are focused straight ahead, but theirs are not. They find me right away with one scan of the room.

Both men share a simple sign of greeting with me. It's slight and goes unnoticed by the female they appear to be escorting like guards through the room. My bitterness creeps up my throat, leaving a sour taste in my mouth while I watch them.

Part of me wonders how she and I have fallen so far from where we once were. Another part of me is cherishing this. It gives me a new pool of which to swim. Unlike the uncharted river that was pulling me under before, this water is warm and feeds me.

Not to say there are not moments when I turn to share a laugh with her, forgetting she will not be there. Sometimes, when the night is at its darkest, I crave her laughter to chase away my loneliness. To admit any of this out loud, would be more truths I would have to share. The truth of them surrounding her, while I sit alone, is enough sharing for one morning. The truth of Lawless is waiting. Screw Truth, she's a fickle woman and I have enough drama already.

"Miss them yet?" Simon's voice clenches my stomach. I had not heard him approach with how deep I have sunk into my dark thoughts. Apparently, life thinks I don't have enough drama.

"Miss Shelia yet?" I return his question, still staring at the random bodies around us. I will not give him my eyes.

"Every day," Simon replies, not afraid of my bite or bark.

His words should have held regret, but they are hollow. His voice is not empty. It just comes deep from behind a shelter he will not let me see. Simon and I no longer hold enough trust for the other to allow our true emotions to show. He is standing nervously with two trays of food by my table. I hope he is not planning what his body language is trying to ask for permission. "Paula says you have not eaten breakfast in a few days," he awkwardly hovers as he says these words as if he is expecting I will help him.

"I'm not a big breakfast person," I tell him, swirling the remaining coffee like a hint. See, it is the food I am refusing, not you. I smile at him, trying to convince him.

"Or lunch," he says with his continue stare at me.

"Gee, so much going on, who has time for lunch these days? Things to kill, people to avoid, shit to stir. It gets really exhausting sometimes," I say with wide eyes. Look, I'm a sweet little girl. Don't you see my smile?

"Or dinner," he continues.

I guess I am not very convincing. I ask, "Would you believe me if I said I was on a diet?" I widen my smile at him, even as he drops a tray in front of me. "Guess not?"

"We don't have to talk," he says, dropping his tray as well. Simon takes the seat that once held a tender smile for me. There are no smiles before me now.

I sense another plot stirring. For men to believe females are so conniving, I seem to keep falling more and more into the center of male drama proving the theory is wrong. I can't help wondering what sharp bend my roller coaster is about to take now. I wonder, but I am not going to ask. I plan to ride this denial thing until the end.

Simon and I don't talk. We sit in silence, rolling the food around our plates more than we are attempting to eat it. His eyes lock on mine for moments as if he wants to say something, but he never does. Which is fine with me. I have had enough conversation and pep talks for one morning. Feeling the eyes of Rhett and J.D. on my back, even if it were painted purple and teal, there is not enough pep in this whole building to inspire any unneeded male conversation today.

Chapter 38

I saw you and Simon this morning," Shelia tells me, but her voice is more of a question.

"He was worried about my nutritional habits," I tell her. It's not a complete lie.

"I'm just glad you two are talking again. If you can forgive him, then maybe the others can too," she says and she smiles to herself with the thought, as Simon's plot comes to light.

"…and you? How are you two doing?" I ask, focusing on the many piles of towels and other assorted piles of laundry before us. I am not sure how the keeping of all the laundry has fallen to Shelia and me, but here we are, folding towel after towel and sheet after sheet. It's a great job demotion from Zombie Barbie to Laundry Barbie in my desperate attempt to hide from those who I used to seek. This one has a better severance package though. "He is still rooming with Dolph and Richard," Shelia says, with the forced pep I have been avoiding. "I am sure it is one giant male sleepover for them."

She still has the strength to hold the positive spin her people cherish her over. I can see how much it hurts her though with the look of her eyes. So much for the Risen keeping marriages together after all.

"It sounds to me like you miss him. It is okay to forgive him," I tell her, and she turns to look at me with doubt. "You don't owe me anything, Shelia. Marxx is healing. I'm fine. The rest of them are just waiting for an apology to ease their hurt male egos. I wouldn't leave them in a room with Ross anytime soon, but then, that was probably true before all of this anyway." I smile at her, trying to make a joke of the situation.

"It just still seems wrong what they did," Shelia says, returning to the never-ending pile of laundry. "I don't know what kind of apology would ever make up for it or for what might have happened." Her voice is whisper thin with shame. "Look at what has happened between you and Aimes?"

I shrug at the mention of her name. "That actually has nothing to do with them."

"What does it have to do with then?" She is testing me with her question. She has been hinting at asking this for days, but has never held the courage until now.

"Just something she said," I offer her curiosity.

"You have to talk about it," she tells me while placing her hand over mine with her gentle words.

"So, I keep getting told," I mutter to a very uncooperative sheet. I know I have run into a brick wall, blocking any escape from her. She will not let me evade her now. My suffering is a red cloak to a bull for her. She can't take her eyes off of it and she is rushing forward to discover it. She stares at me, waiting for me to begin like a child waiting for a bedtime story, and as every parent has thought at least once in their life, I wonder how much I can just bluff to make her leave me alone.

"I wasn't ready to learn the truth about Lawless and Leslie. I really didn't want to learn it in a moment of my best friend's bitterness," I rush my explanation. I omit my real anger is not over the cheating, but the betrayal. I held some illusions over their past lifestyle, but Lawless' enjoyment of female attention was never one of them.

"All of this is because of that? That seems silly to fight over. Even I knew about them," she retorts.

I say nothing because the contempt in her voice is making me regret not running through the brick wall for dear life.

"Just have her do an apology and appease your ego," she says, turning my words back onto me. Someone has been learning from

J.D. a little more than I have been aware.

"It's not that simple." I shrug from her contempt as I start to pile the folded artwork of ragged sheets and bleached towels.

"Why?" One simple word from her and I am left drowning without answers.

I don't know why I can't simply make the first move, or why   I can't let it go. The sin is with Lawless, not Aimes, but I am clinging to my bitterness for them both like shining armor of righteousness.

"It's how they treat her," Shelia whispers.

She is determined to clean more than just the piles of laundry today. I am glad the bottle of bleach is out of her reach for my still open wounds.

"They have left you to figure it out all on your own," she says, shrugging to ease the ache. "They huddle around her, keeping her safe. Even Lawless is still in their clique. Only you seem to be on the outside now."

"The men talk to me," I answer her, trying to defend them for some reason. Maybe I am just pouting.

"Alone yes, but when have more than just one of them sat with you? Or acknowledged you in front of her? They don't want to upset her, but you they don't seem to care if they do. It's like they think you are doing fine on your own. Are you?" She asks me, and I am really wishing there were more towels to focus on.

"I'm fine," I say, walking right into the classic trap.

It's what every female says when they are not. She knows it and I might as well be wearing the red cloak again with how her eyes focus on me. This is about to get ruthless.

"Sure. You eat alone. You sleep alone. You spend all day alone. Sounds perfectly fine to me," she says.

I think she has found the bleach. At the very least, she found the lemon juice.

"I'm not alone right now." I look at her, trying to smile. Down, Toro. Down.

"I'm not Aimes. Never will be. I'm not Rhett. I'm not Chapel. I'm not Marxx. I'm not Lawless. I'm not even J.D.," she says, ripping off more of the scab I have been using to heal their dis- appearance with each name she calls. "I appreciate all the help these past few days, really I do. I do enjoy our friendship. It has not been easy on either of us to get through this."

She is going for the salt now, and I brace for it.

"...but?" I ask, letting her know I am waiting for it. Sprinkle me, Sister.

"...but Paula and I cannot replace them. It's obvious you have lost one family already. Why are you so desperate to lose another?"

Her words rip the scab raw. How little she knows and yet how directly her words hit.

"Helena, they need you," Shelia tells me this, but I hear another voice saying it, "but you need them, too. Talk to them."

My face must have shown her my fear. I don't want to admit to her how afraid I am over the thought of approaching them.

"Look, if it goes wrong, then Paula and I are still right here. At least you can say you tried. It might at least give you some closure," she says, with her sugar sweet smile and it's just as damaging.

I never understood this fascination with closure. I do not under- stand why people want to hear words that will only hurt them, or the need to say words that will only hurt others. What door can be closed in peace when so much more is piled upon the situation propping it open?

I have always preferred before to just let it go. I let the hurt dampen and dry, so it can be buried somewhere deep inside, al- lowing me to forget about it. It allows me to walk away, but also, to keep on walking.

I stay in silence, allowing her to think I am considering all the words of wisdom she has spoken to me. Her smile is telling of how proud she is to have been such a pivotal piece to solving my dilemmas. It makes a much easier time of restocking the towels in the locker rooms with her this way. Besides, who am I to pop such a fragile bubble when she is so happy? That's me: always a giver. How am I rewarded? By coming face-to-face with those I was trying to avoid all morning. The sound of their laughter snakes up my spine almost in a chill. It fills me with a cold dread of having to walk through the room.

I can already picture their aloof manner while watching me like wolves. Their eyes will follow my every step while their voices continue to talk over my appearance, only further punctuating how little I now mean to them. They will huddle around her to protect her fragile senses from my evil presence. I start my silent retreat from the swinging door to the weight room with hopes I can slip away unnoticed. Hopeful until I feel Shelia's hands on my shoulders. "Good luck," she whispers into my ear, and shoves me through the swinging door.

My entrance is anything but graceful. To say I crashed through the door would be praise to how I stumble and trip into the room. It's not an entrance one can recover from with any dignity. An amazing comical one-liner, maybe, but guess what I am all out of as the room falls silent around me.

"Boots giving you trouble again, Barbie?"

I hear J.D. ask me, and I look to him without meaning to.

He smiles at me from his weight bench luck has placed nearest to me. His tank top is shaded from his workout, even with his calm voice proving he is not being pushed to his limits. They do not work out for the exertion of it. It's just a spot to help fill the new boredom of this life.

I am grateful for J.D. speaking first. With that simple greeting, he has explained the rules. I am welcomed around him as far as he is concerned which means they will follow his example and welcome me as well. If he had ignored me, it would have been a different declaration. The tension in the room reduces with the grin he is giving me at my amazing entrance. I mockingly bow for him, hiding the fact my voice is locked with my fear standing here and I'm rewarded with his laughter.

They are all here. Our once little happy family is spread out on the various weight machines and I stand frozen like an outsider who just walked into the wrong room. Right about now, I am picturing a few things I would like to shove Shelia from as payback. Tall things. Really, really, tall things.

"Towels?" I offer like a perky hotel staff. "Shelia and I were just restocking the locker rooms." Even to me, my explanation sounds lame.

Of course, it would be Marxx who holds his hand up in the air, waiting for one. Marxx, the one who is the furthest in the room from me. Marxx, who to get to, I will have to walk right past them all with their watching eyes. Hold on folks, we are about to climb another hill with this never-ending roller coaster of mine.

I walk past each machine with a different person pretending to not notice me. Even Aimes, with Lawless spotting her, continues in her presses. The sight of them, with their newly healed bond, gives me the fire to walk firmer with each of my steps. The sight of them together now coats my words with venom. Like poisoned apples waiting in a tree, I only need the right wind for them to fall. Marxx pats a spot on the bench beside him where he has been pressing weights with his legs. His arm may be wounded, but he refuses to be left behind in the male bonding.

"Don't be so hateful," he tells me, hiding the words behind the towel he is using to clean his face. "What did you expect them to do?"

"Oh, I am not surprised," I reply. The wind blows and apples fall, and they start to roll. I won't stop them.

"Don't," Chapel whispers to me from the bench beside us. "Don't worry, Chap. I was just leaving. I would hate to make anyone feel uncomfortable. Why then all of you big strong men may have to stop and rush to coddle the little girl. That would just ruin your workouts." I let my voice carry, coating it with southern sugary sweetness.

"Helena," Marxx says to me, grabbing my arm to pull my attention to him.

"Let me guess, I am out of line?" I ask them both, tilting my head with my question and my building tantrum.

I am fighting to keep the pain from my voice with their constant rushing to her side. I hold on to my anger instead, ignoring Chapel's look of imploring. Chapel, who is once again finding himself in the middle of it all, stares at me with eyes wide open with his emotions. The still does not simmer my rage.

J.D. stands, watching over the room of his naughty children with my sudden outburst. He nods for me to come to him when our eyes meet. Sitting like a pouting kid in the back row, I pretend to not see him. Not that I think it will really save me from detention. Aimes has turned her back to me, leaning into Lawless who watches me behind his blank mask. I have no choice now but to be pulled into the principal's office with her reaction.

"Hells, walk with me," J.D. barks.

He turns to leave the room, not waiting to see if I stand to follow him. He knows I will. Besides, I need an exit from this room that will leave me a spot of dignity. If it is anything like my entrance, it will be a small spot.

Marxx drops his hand from my arm with a great sigh of defeat. There is no anger to feed me the courage to walk back between all of them. Watching, who was once my best friend in the arms of who used to be my only strength, has poured ice water all over any fire my anger might have fueled. The sight only proves to me how far I have fallen from their graces.

No one stands to voice any outrage over this new bond. No one comes to me with the comfort of a hug or a kind word. There are just blank faces to watch me walk past and Rhett's smirk. Rhett knows I have one spark left somewhere inside me. He winks and I let it flare.

"Your roots are showing, Amelia. You should try red this time. It would give you one more thing you and Leslie can have in common," I say as I pass her. No, I am not sorry. It felt good.

J.D. is waiting for me in the hall. His frown shows he heard my last words.

"Feel better?" he asks me.

I shrug, leaning against the wall and waiting for the lecture. "You're better than this," he tells me. I wait for his Pro-Aimes chat. Someone should be making tee shirts for them to wear. "That was rather weak."

It takes me a moment to fully hear what he said to me. When I do, I open my eyes to see him smiling. His eyes are vibrant with his mirth.

"From someone who just about runs over a man for flirting, that roots comment was a letdown." He smirks, seeing my con- fusion. "What? Did you think I was going to give you a talking to? Convince you to go in there? Hug it out?" He smiles, almost leering with the thought. "That's not my Barbie."

"Yes, sorta. It seems to be the popular line of thought."

I wait for the violent mood swing, the instant icy stare, the things which signal he was just setting me up to make his threat that much more severe.

"When have I ever given a shit about being popular?"

He is right. The Christmas card list never was really long for J.D.

"Barbie, look here, I am about as sick as you are over this. They walk around on eggshells with her. Chapel about loses his mind if she so much as sniffles. Law blames himself, letting that guilt smother his logic. Rhett and Marxx are just about willing to do anything to make her shut up," he says.

I roll my eyes at the mention of the word "anything", not needing to repeat it to let him know what I think of her actions.

It ain't reached that yet," he chuckles. "She's not you, Hells. You have to be the only girl I have ever met who could make me drop my bike and have me laughing about it. You have taken all of this with a giant middle finger to them. They don't know you like I know you though. If I held my arms out right now, you'd fight me on it. You'd fight me even if I forced them around you, but deep down, you want it. You want someone to save you. You just don't want to want it," J.D. says.

His voice drops, and for a few moments of silence between us, he proves how right he is. J.D. holds his arms out to me in this dark, silent hallway. All I need to do is take two steps to him and I will have the comfort I need. His arms are the only father to have ever held me, giving me comfort.

I will have a warm chest to hide against and strong arms to hide my pain. I could listen to his heartbeat, with its solid rhythm, chasing away my doubts. I could drown in his very male scent to ease down the girl in me. None of it happens. I stay leaning against the wall staring at him. I still remember the gulf between us.

"A man won't go where he is not needed, Hells. You want them back? Show them you need them," he says, standing there, still holding out his arms to me waiting with my silent war of my will. Ashley told me I had to live for them. I had to keep fighting because they needed me. Now as I lean here, staring at the invitation before me, my heart beats a different truth. It terrifies me. They don't need me. I need them.

I go to him, those two steps feeling like miles, until I find myself resting against his chest. His arms wrap around me and he holds me close. His head rests on the top of mine as he holds me, allowing me to nestle against him with my need for human contact.

"You're not weak, Helena. Allowing someone to see behind those high walls of yours doesn't make you weak. We all need to be reminded where home is now and again. It doesn't make you weak. You remember that. Only the lonely are weak, Barbie. It takes the strong to keep fighting for what is theirs," he whispers this into the top of my hair as he holds me before adding with classic J.D., "But let's not repeat the bike stunt, okay?"

I say nothing as I feel him smile into my hair. I have no idea how to tell J.D. if what he is saying is true, then I am the weakest person he knows at this moment. I don't want to fight anymore. I don't want to fight them or him or the Risen. If I could close my eyes and let it all slip away, I would. I'd let it all go just as easily as I let my Angels fall from my hands.

Chapter 39

Over breakfast earlier in the morning, Simon had asked me to sit at his table for dinner. The idea of eating with him was only a tad bit less depressing than eating another meal alone. That tad bit was the only reason I had accepted. Now as I am sitting here with Simon, Dolph, Richard and Ross across from me, I am rethinking the exact measurement of a "tad".

"We need to fix this. The lines are being drawn more between us every day," Richard says.

The men have been debating the current status of the groups since I sat down. I listen to what Richard is saying. Literally, I am just listening. If they want conversation from me, they will have to talk about something I have a care about. After all they have done, fixing their male drama is not one of those things.

I look behind me to where J.D. sits with the rest on either side of him. They are seated along one side of a long table directly behind ours in their dark leather vests. With each group of men sitting in this style, they appear to be matched up for a standoff.

All it needs is for one group to start snapping their fingers or to start dancing to be any more comical. Who's bad?

"You seem to be the only one willing to work on this," Simon says, and I have to smile at that idea. "You told Shelia all that is needed is some form of apology. What kind of apology?"

"Want me to put together a list?" I ask them. I am met with eye rolls and sighs, except for Dolph. He smiles at my boldness.

"Is there anything, at all, you can think of?" Richard asks me. He is almost pleading with me to help them. I wonder what those naughty boys behind me have been doing.

"The only thing they understand is revenge for things like this. A fruit basket isn't going to do it," I answer them honestly.

They sit staring at me, waiting for me to give them a better example.

"You hurt their own. They want yours to hurt. Whatever it is they are doing to have you here begging for my help, they won't stop it until one of you gets bloody," I answer them more honestly, watching the male light bulbs go off one by one. It's so pretty.

"…and if we agree to this, will they stop this bullshit?" Dolph asks me, with his southern drawl coating his doubts of my words. "I don't know what "bullshit" they are doing, but normally, yes.

It stops it," I say with a shrug.

I watch their faces shadow with different emotions until they each nod in agreement. Everything from fear to resignation flash- es before me. It also is very pretty to watch.

"Fine, tell them one hour in the gym. Their three against our three. We will keep it low key so as to not alarm the other residents. The deal is whatever happens settles it and it stays in the gym," Simon says, gathering up the trays. He does not look as confident as his voice sounds.

"Just three?" I am looking to Ross who has been sitting silent the whole meal.

"Just three. They will kill him if given the chance. I am not into murder." Simon hears the trap shut as soon as the words leave his mouth.

I heard myself ask it before I actually asked it, and I still couldn't stop it. From my mouth tumbles, "Since when?"

I turn from them to once again play messenger. Last time though, I had others with me. Now, I walk to their table alone as they watch me. It makes me miss their blank faces.

"I find it amusing they keep sending you to deliver their messages," Rhett says to me, when I come to stand across from him. "I always meant to talk to you about your idea of comedy," I reply. I place my hands behind my back to hide how hard I am shaking from his direct attention.

"I find it funny you keep doing it, too," he says, skipping over my comment. Rhett is staring right into me. He is a predator, and he can smell my fear. "Want to know what else I find funny?" he asks. His voice holds no warmth for me. It is a deathtrap of an ambush just waiting for me to step closer.

"Not really," my honest answer brings a smile to his lips. It is not his playful smile though. He is enjoying that he won this round. I liked our other game better.

"What do they want, Barbie?" J.D. raises his voice, trying to save me from anymore of Rhett's attention.

I watch Rhett physically retreat upon hearing our leader's voice, but his eyes never leave me. Like an animal in a zoo that has been caged too long, he watches me waiting for another chance to attack. I try to hide my shiver with a roll of my shoulders as if I am simply working out a chink in my neck. His smirk grows, calling my bluff.

"They want you to meet them in the gym in one hour," I answer

J.D. and my answer bring me further into all of their attention. "Your three against theirs. They want it done secretly so it will not draw a crowd. Whatever happens, happens and it's then done between you and them. It stays in the gym." I continue keeping my eyes only for J.D.

"What, like Vegas?" Rhett asks, and finally I see his normal smile.

My hands slow their constant vibration by just a fraction.

"Except this is going to be a lot better than Vegas." Lawless' voice dances with his smile. My hands speed back up when I hear him. "What of Ross?" he asks, just as Simon had hinted, he would. "Just Simon, Richard, and Dolph," I answer his question, but I still keep my eyes on J.D.

"Figures," Marxx voices the same disappointment the whole table is feeling.

"…and you?" Lawless looks to me. "Which side are you going to be on tonight?"

I stare at him, this man I have been locked in an emotional war with for what feels like years and I wonder if I am ever going to understand him. "I will be on whichever side of my bed tonight I am on when it happens. This is your fight. Not mine. I stopped fighting a long time ago."

"I know."

I hear him tell me as I am leaving the room. His voice is dangerously deep, and it makes me want to add a few extra steps to my retreat. J.D.'s words dance through my mind, and I cannot believe what I am about to do.

"Give me something to fight for, Law," I tell him, letting him hear the full weight of my desire in my voice.

I mentally hi-five myself, but I do not turn back to glance behind me. Baby steps here people. Baby steps.

I find myself unable to sleep with so many of my thoughts chasing it away. A stronger person would just admit to being nervous about what is happening two floors below me. With just the dark- ness and me in the room, I do not have to be strong. The darkness, with its coal-black coldness shields me. It steals my whispered secrets, smothering them within itself. Like a documented diary of my regrets and yearnings, any sleepless, crying nights it keeps private between us. The darkness has become my lullaby and eventually it sings me to sleep despite my nerves.

The air smells sweet from spring's blooming flowers. Ahead of me, I can hear their laughter. My Angels are playing within the tall walls of the green hedge maze in front of me. My legs tangle in the chiffon of a dress I have no memory of owning as I run towards their sounds. My heart soars to hear them so close to me. With every corner I turn, I swear I will find them. When I don't, their laughter becomes higher pitches of their amusement as they call my name.

Turning the last corner of the maze, I find them. They are sitting with their backs to me on a white cement bench in a gazebo. Lilly is still laughing, and I smile with her giggles.

"What are you doing here?" I ask them, encouraging the sound of their voices.

Ashley is swaying her feet and she says, "Waiting."

"Waiting for what?" I smile with my question, climbing the wooden steps to where they are sitting.

"For her," Ashley says.

She turns her head to look behind me and I too turn to look. Margaret, with her blood-painted face limps from where I have just entered the clearing. Behind her is her army of damned children.

Their clothes are soiled and dripping from the blood they have spilt. The blood that belonged to them and the others they had murdered. I know the sounds coming from their throats and my stomach drops when I hear it. The smell of their decay is over-powering the flowers as it fills the clearing around me.

"Why are you afraid, Helena?" Lilly asks me.

When I feel her tiny hand take mine, I look down at her. My heart is ripped from my chest by the sight. Lilly is one of them with her once beautiful blue eyes hazy as she stares at me. Turning to see Conroy and Ashley, they too are staring at me with eyes of the Risen.

I don't fight as Lilly's teeth tear into my wrist, drinking from the torn veins. I don't scream as Conroy takes my throat in his mouth, pulling the tendons with his baby-sharp teeth. I let them take me. Watching Ashley as the children from the school cover me, I know she finally has her revenge.

I wake suddenly from a dream I am happy to escape when I feel my cot sinking lower behind me. I freeze, waiting for my senses to give me a hint at what is happening in my already heightened panic.

"Your knife is on the floor. Not the best place to keep it if you were to need it," his voice only stirs more panic inside me when I hear him speak. "I'd appreciate it if you would let me know now if you have any stolen guns hidden under that pillow though."

I roll onto my back to stare at Lawless sitting on my cot. In the darkness, I can only see his shape, but I would know his voice in the darkest of nights. He sits silently beside me, giving me his back and letting the darkness hide him. Each silent moment is stealing more of my breath being so close to him.

"You were calling out in your sleep and we need to talk," his voice finally comes with an explanation for his arrival.

I startle hearing him after the room having been silent for so long. I can see his head turn to me with its outline in the dark- ness. I feel his fingers trace my face with soft patterns. My body betrays me after being starved from his touch for so long. I can hear my breathing quicken with his gentle touch.

"I miss you, too," he tells me, answering my body's response to him. His lips touch my forehead, hesitantly placing a kiss.

"I'll give you whatever you want, Helena. You just have to let me know what it is," Lawless whispers against my flesh.

I shiver from the hidden meaning of his words. He leans in closer with my body's invitation. His mouth trails hotly against my neck, quickening his own breath with the taste of me on his tongue.

"For you not to stick your dick in other people," I whisper, answering his question and pouring cold reality upon his body's lustrous hopes.

I feel him retreat from me with such force it makes the cot shake. His entrance may have been silent, but his retreat is not.

Every step he is taking from me echoes in the room with his anger. His slamming of the door vibrates the room with it.

I take another bite from my poisoned apple, listening to his fading footsteps retreating back to the room he now shares with Aimes. The bitter juices coat my tongue and throat. It burns me with its wickedness and my loneliness is the resulting effect it has. I lay in the darkness, listening to their muffled voices rise and fall like the tides. There is no moon giving their waves strength. It's the force of their emotions carrying their voices forward before lulling them again.

I know from the pitch in her voice she is trying to talk him down from whatever crest he is reaching. I listen to her voice seep through the wall separating our rooms and wonder what honeyed words she is feeding him. Is she convincing him of my wicked ways? Is she baiting him with her fragile sense of self, snuggling up to him for comfort? Is he offering her what he was so ready to offer me just moments ago? The only real question is do I have the strength to discover any of these answers?

Right now, no, I do not. So, I let sleep take me again with the taste of my poison still on my tongue, sweeter than candy, and as deadly as arsenic while my Angels plot my death and their revenge.

Chapter 40

I watch the dawn from my window instead of the table across from Marxx as I normally would. I do not feel like listening to any more pep talks, or lectures, about how I should be doing things with the images from my dreams still clinging to my heart. Nor do I have any interest in eating another meal watching the many happy groups around me. Instead, I sit on my window's edge watching life flow below me. I am woman: watch me pout.

I heard when each of my former family members went past my room. I listened to their words, and happy voices, and it filled me with only more emptiness. I know one day I will be strong again. It's just not today. Today I want nothing more than to hide from all the many requests and stares. I want to hide from my many memories that stalk me, waiting for me to close my eyes. Not that any of it is going to happen. It's just what I want.

I hear the door open behind me, and in the window's reflection, I see Aimes leaning against its frame. If this is any hint as to what the rest of the day is going to be like, I am just going back to bed now. I will tie a sheet into a white flag and hang it from my doorway.

"Anything else you want to say to me?" Aimes asks me and her voice is itching for a fight. I am tempted to give her one.

"Nope," I hoarsely say. Tempted, but I am not willing.

"I don't believe you." She stands her ground, edging up to her anger.

"I figured that out by how you are half hiding in the hallway," I say to her reflection, staring into her eyes.

I call her bluff, removing her bravado. It steals the courage for her to continue in her halfhearted attempt of a fight. I feel like Rhett with the smile I give her.

We stare at each other's reflection in the window. Its thick glass dulls the colors, casting us both in a grey wash of shades. Nothing seems to be as vivid as it once was between us.

"Is this your new plan? Are you just going to hide out like a spoiled brat?" she asks me. Her bravery is growing again with my ignoring her.

"The victim role seems to be taken already. I wonder, are you even alone out there right now? No constant bodyguard of the men you used to hate so much? It really is amazing how fast you flip your opinions these days," I tell her. I watch her shrink with each of my words. If I had a screen-printed tee shirt right now it would read "Bring It".

"That's not fair." She crosses her arms, cradling herself under my direct attention. "You turned your back on me. What was I supposed to do?" she asks me.

"That is what everyone so loves to point out to me. What were you supposed to do? You, who just had to push that extra little bit for your own satisfaction. You, who is always so protected and sheltered from the world. You, who always seem to land on your feet while the rest of us fall to our knees. Yes, what were you supposed to do?" My question lets my anger finally find a release. "How about not question loyalties when you so easily walk away from them? How about not sleep with the only man that has ever meant anything to your friend? How about, just once, stand on your own and not need someone else to hold you up?" I watch her cringe from each of my questions. It brings me no joy, or remorse. "I didn't. We aren't, Hells. You should know that." Her voice is as broken as she looks.

"Tell me, Amelia, did you sleep alone last night? Have you slept alone any night since this all started? Do you feel safe in his arms? Does his body next to yours in the morning give you the strength to keep going? Do you feel any guilt at all over being so wrapped up in their support?" I stare at her, waiting for any answer she gives me. "You might not be fucking him, but you have taken my place just the same. You can paint it any way you want, with whatever brush you desire. Tell yourself whatever you need to. You know the truth, and exactly what the truth is. At least Leslie was honest in what she was doing. You think by wrapping it up in female frailty forgives it. It doesn't. It makes it worse. Now get out."

She pauses for a moment before closing the door and tells me, "I talked to him, Hells. I gave him a chance to explain things. You should, too. He misses you."

She closes the door on my many replies I am biting back. I know every word I have already given her she will share with them as it is. Soon, my room will fill with men and their stares telling me how I have once again been naughty. It presents me with two choices. I can sit here hiding, waiting for them to find me, or I can go out there daring them to find me. I never was one to make life easy for people. If they want me, they will have to find me. Mostly, I do not want to be waiting here for Rhett. I do not like our new games.

Chapter 41

The library, with its many shelves of thick, faded books, proves to be the perfect hiding spot from my world. There is no alcohol, no strippers or any over eager women waiting here. They won't bother to come.

There are only a few others in the room with me. With their refusal to address anyone, I gather they too are seeking some level of escape from their own private hells. I find the ability to become invisible frees a great weight from my shoulders as I escape into a fantasyland of print and paper.

The smell of the old books creates a soothing perfume around me like a hot bath at the end of a long day. The many dust particles dance around my chair in the sun's rays, casting an illusion of magic when I turn the pages. I devour the books, letting the stories create new images for my mind to replay tonight. I cling to each character, as if I am forming new friends with the stories, they tell me. From romance to horror, I find a new person to fill the many empty holes in my soul within the hardbound novels around me. Ashley would have loved it in here.

"They want you in the gym."

I startle from the whisper of a voice in front of me. Aimes is standing there watching me. The next time I am forced to do laundry, I am sewing bells on her stuff. Loud bells.

"They who?"

I return my attention to the novel with my dismissal of her.

Unfortunately, it is not that easy.

"Who else would want you to come to the gym?"

I don't think she meant for her question to form the way her words do.

"I guess you're right. It is a short list these days of those who want to be around me."

I mean mine.

"I don't want to fight anymore." Her voice is still a whisper, but not because of the social rules of where we are.

"Then you should just stay silent," I tell her, closing the novel in my hands. "This is where you run away."

"I can't," her whisper skips with her breath, sinking in her emotions. "He said if I don't come back with you, then not to come back."

I already know who would give her such an order, but I ask anyway to make her say it. "Who told you that?"

"Lawless," she tells me, and my face holds shock with the name she gives me. "He wants you to see it. I think he has some idea that it will reach you in some way."

"What will?"

My curiosity is one of my many downfalls. I would list them all, but my self-esteem is already on a downward spiral as it is.

"The fight. They didn't go through with-it last night. Not sure what happened, but they are doing it now. The only thing every- one seems to agree to is you need to be there. So here I am." She holds her hands out in a grand sweep of presenting herself.

My lack of amusement takes some of the glow from her smile.

"We don't have to talk on the way, but if we don't get back soon, they will send Rhett next. He hasn't been a lot of fun and games as of late. Well, he has been a lot of games, just not any of them fun," she says.

Her words are eerily similar to another's from only a day ago. I try to tell myself it's not me, it's them, but who am I kidding? I am just a ray of sunshine as of late.

I take her up on her offer of not talking as we walk to the gym. A few times, she does try to engage me in conversation. It does not go well for her, and after a few well-landed verbal blows, she finally relents to silence between us. My mind still fills with what I want to say though. My tongue wants to scald her, but my soul is tired of these mud-slinging games. So, I too, relent to the silence between us.

She pauses in front of the gym door. I can't see her face, but I know she is working the courage to say something to me. Something she is worried about how I will react to when I hear it. "You should know, they will be watching you. Rhett is worried you are turning against them. I told them you aren't. You just don't care about the politics of it. You never have. You have always been strong enough to do your own thing. You may be the only one of us that is," she says with a shaky breath.

She pauses before turning to me. Her blue eyes, so much like the many other pairs who were once in my life swim before me. Her eyes are pleading with me to help her, asking me to not let her fall. Pity for her, I am not wearing my cape and tights today. "I know you hate me," she continues, "I know you think I have turned them against you. I haven't. They talk about you all the time. They just don't know how to talk to you anymore. None of us do. You always were the heart of us, the one who took care of us. Give them your heart again, Hells. They need it." Seriously people, no cape today.

She does not wait for any answer from me. She knows I am not going to give her one. Instead, we walk into the gym together to watch the best of "when male egos attack live". She, the one who was sent to summon, and me the one they summoned with no other options between us.

The atmosphere of the gym is thick with testosterone. Normally, a girl would enjoy the sights before her, but not under these circumstances. Our delay has not stalled their fun. J.D. sits on "our" side of the gym holding a bag of ice across his nose with Paula over seeing his care. Rhett is resting beside him with a few marks of his own on his face, but his smile speaks a different story than his bruises.

With both of them being shirtless, I can see the marks along their chests and sides. I am not sure what the rules of combat were, but there seems to have been very few. The amount of shading covering both their bodies makes me wince.

Shelia is the attending nurse to "their" side. Simon also has a bag of ice across his eyes. Even with his natural dark coloring, I can see the bruises already shading along his skin. She fusses over each one, allowing him no male pride with his injuries.

Richard is lying on his back and clutching his wrapped ribs. His breathing is unsteady, causing grimaces of pain in time with each of his inhales. Most of his bruising is on his lower torso with only a few to his face. I am not familiar with their fighting styles, but looking at their injuries, I know whom from "our side" they were matched against.

Kidney shots are Rhett's favorite, second only to the ribs. He prefers to leave long-term damage, not just bruises, to remind you of him. J.D. is a straight brawler. Wherever he can land a punch, he will. Looking from one side to the other, I cannot determine a winner.

That's my girl mind at work though. Their male minds see it differently. Both sides have returned and received blows in the insanity of appeasing their male egos. There does not have to be a winner.

"He's watching you," I hear Aimes' little whisper in my ear. Lawless and Dolph are standing in the center of the room staring at me. White tape is around them in a large square on the floor, dictating the boundaries of the makeshift boxing ring for today's main event. From their hands to their wrists, white fabric and tape is bound tightly to protect them.

Law is standing, facing me, and giving me his full attention as he waits for me to see him. Dolph stands to the side in his typical style of keeping everything in sight. He glances from Lawless to me. His face may be unreadable, but I still feel his unease with the way his eyes continue to look down before finding us. They are both rather calm considering what is about to happen. It only further proves their insanity.

Chapel comes to stand between the two men, telling them the agreed upon rules. Aimes and I are too far back to hear him but looking at the damage already done to the others, I cannot imagine there are many to list.

Lawless is staring into Dolph with seething anger. His anger makes this seem more personal for him than it was for the other two sets. Chapel keeps pushing Lawless back as he is talking, only to have him creep up again to him and Dolph. Dolph takes the threat in stride, watching the other man with enough caution to let Lawless know there will be no backing down.

Chapel is having a hard time keeping the two men apart before the fight starts. I can see them exchanging whispered words to provoke the other further. Rhett and Simon have come to either side of the white tape, hoping their presence will calm their counterparts.

Lawless and Dolph are not even aware of anything around them anymore, much less, the men standing beside them who are shouting to talk to them. Their eyes are focusing only on the other with how consumed they have both become with their anger. It is frightening to watch, and the real match has not yet even started.

"You have to choose a side. It will settle Lawless some," Marxx' voice startles me when he sneaks up behind me.

As he pulls me to "their" side of the room, I am mentally counting the many bells I am going to sew on their clothing as I follow him. Elves will be envious when I am through with them. Marxx positions himself between Aimes and me as if he is expecting our own brawl to begin at any moment. If they had Jell-O, I am sure it would be encouraged.

I glance again to the "ring" in the middle of the room as I follow behind Marxx. Rhett and Simon have had to step in to help Chapel separate Lawless and Dolph. There seems to be more vocal commotion now they have been pulled apart then when they were standing toe-to-toe.

Rhett is whispering in Law's ear, but he is not listening to the words. Lawless' eyes are on me, following me, as I walk to "our" side. The weight of their anger makes me stumble under his gaze. Never have I seen such rage from him. Never do I want to see it again and I lower my head to hide my weakness with not being able to face him.

I grab Marxx' hand when we reach "our" side of the gym. I can feel his shock travel through his body at my touch. I can't look at him. My head is too heavy to lift with my fears of what is about to happen. I can't do this alone. They cannot ask me to stand here and watch Lawless do this without someone to help me.

My hand trembles in his with my fears. The tension in our arms slackens as he comes to me. I feel him slide against my back, cradling me in his arms.

"I'm here," Marxx' deep voice whispers into my ear. "I'm here, Hells."

I give in. All the strength I have been hiding behind, I let it fade in this moment. I let Marxx hold me, pulling me close to him. I let his arms support me and his voice soothe me.

I don't want to fight them anymore. I want to hide from this before me. I want to hide from what I have left behind me. I want to fall to the floor in my sorrow and fill the room with my tears, but not yet. I cannot yet. I pull Marxx' arms tight around me, using them as seams to hold me together. I am still taking baby steps.

"You have to watch. If he can take the blows, you can at least watch," Marxx tells me.

"I didn't ask him to take any blows," I reply, and my voice is haunted with the guilt of the thought.

"You don't have to ask him. You haven't figured that out yet?

Now get ready," Marxx whispers.

I feel the pressure of his arms increase with his words, and I know the fight is about to start.

I did not see it start. I heard it. I hear the sickening sound skin makes as it is connected against repeatedly. I hear the sounds of pain from those connections from both of them. I look up to see them being separated by Simon, Rhett and Chapel. Each is fighting off their captor with the agreement to keep space between the two of them. Already blood is flowing from both of their faces from lacerations. Now they circle one another, collecting their breath before they attack again.

"Were the other two fights this brutal?" I whisper to the man behind me.

"No," Is the only word he gives to me, bringing my fear back to the surface.

"When does it end?" I ask with weak words, afraid of each answer I am seeking.

"When one steps over the tape," he says, causing my stomach to clench with the realization of how far this could go.

"Did Rhett or J.D. step over the tape?" I am afraid of his answer.

"No," he says, offering me the same word and it doubles my fear.

Law cannot step over the tape. He must be the one to finish it, following the lead of the two who have gone before him. To do anything less, will cost him more than just the fight. Unfortunately, Dolph is in the same situation.

He cannot step over the tape either. It will mean everyone from his side fell to ours. It will allow a sore spot that will forever taunt their pride. It will be the ultimate declaration, declaring which side has the better protectors. Something no male wants to have proven against them by falling to another. As Lawless lands the first blow with this new round of attacks, I see no way for this to end.

The men are panting, and bleeding, as they are pulled apart again. Both are spitting blood from the wounds in their mouths. My tears are flowing as freely as the many cuts upon their faces. Dolph is just as relentless as Law is with his attacks and my body aches with each blow landed. Neither is showing any sign of yielding with their hate still so abundant. With their eyes, even now, they glare at each other around the men holding them apart. They will not succumb to the other, but they may to another.

"I can stop this," I whisper aloud with the shock of my own realization of the logic.

"I was wondering how much longer it would take you," Marxx tells me.

His arms drop from around me. I am without his arms as my shield to protect me now, but I have truth as my lance. For once, finally, truth is on my side.

Lawless' eyes swing to me with my movement from the side of the room. He was not intentionally looking for me. It was his senses, preparing him for any possible attack, which was signaled by my movement. The heat simmers in his honey-toned eyes seeing me walk towards him. His body relaxes a moment with the loss of his anger. It pulls Rhett's eyes to me with how well attuned the men are to each other's every subtle change. They are both waiting to see what I will do. Hell, so am I.

The world stalls in this moment. The colors leak away around me. The noise of their shouting is sinking below me. The fire I have let fade inside me quickens with what I am preparing myself to do.

Aimes told me I have to give them my heart. Marxx told me I have to choose a side. It will settle him. Lawless is not fighting for himself. He is fighting for me. Give me something to fight for, I told him. He is. Now I have to stop it, because he will not. He wanted me to see this. He wanted me to see he is still holding hope for us. I see it. I just wish I had not been so slow to see it. I really do sometimes need my own vest to help with these things. The men relax some with the fact a girl is so close to them as I come to the white tape. I never slow in my path to Lawless. I do not give him the chance to reject me, melting the courage from me I am counting on to carry me through this.

Rhett still holds onto him, unsure of what either of us will do after so long apart and with so much under our bridge. Law's eyes still hold the rage I saw in them at the start of this and my knees grow weak with my new fear of him. It turns my spine into water. My courage fails me in these few spaces left between us, but it is close enough.

Pushing Rhett aside, Lawless fills the steps I could not take to him. He grasps my head between his hands, forcing his lips down upon mine. He kisses me with all the anger he is feeling. The anger he feels for Dolph, from my words and from my actions. His anger is hot, and it scalds me, bringing me to life underneath him. He is rough, forcing his tongue between my lips, and I swallow down all of his rage. I let him bruise my lips the way he let Dolph bruise his body. The feel of his roughness pulls sounds from the depths of me and they feed him encouragements.

He pushes the kiss further and harder. I can taste his blood like warm copper, coating my mouth. I pull from him, separating our lips to see him, but he is not looking at me. His eyes are locked on someone behind us, glowing with an unspoken message in them. "Enough," I whisper to him, with him still holding me tightly, "you've won."

He looks to me with those very simple words. "You've won," I tell him again, and he has.

Chapter 42

Paula makes the rounds of stitching cuts and inspecting the many lumps and bruises between the six men. Every mark is suddenly very funny to them. They are laughing, congratulating the ones with the best bruise or the deepest cut like they were marks of honor while sharing "war stories" of past fights and the better marks they left on their bodies than the ones they are wearing now.

Dolph and Lawless are less willing to fully give into the bonding. They are still sending cautious glances to one another between their stories and the laughter. Rhett, either consciously or subconsciously, keeps placing himself between them as he tries to block their view of the other.

I look to Aimes to see if she is noticing it as well. She nods, telling me she is as curious as I am. Rhett's job has always been to block J.D. from danger. Now, he is mirroring another man's movements and we wonder what it could mean for Lawless. I prefer to think, with Rhett's love for fighting, he's just hoping to catch a piece of the action should they erupt. When Rhett smiles at Dolph, Aimes and I both look to each other with a nod and an eye roll.

Slowly, we all filter out from the gym amid this new male reconciliation. Their male-high is not as peaked with so many watching us when we reach the third floor. Their enthusiasm is reined in with the many looks of shock and confusion from the other res- idents around us. Their laughter is contagious though and soon the whole place enjoys the mood swing of the leading men of our lives.

For once, the two sides do not retreat to their rooms to hide behind closed doors. They sit in the common area enjoying the company around them. Slowly, the other male residents blend in among them, sharing their own stories and laughter. Those who live here are quick to put the pieces together. The first one to shout, "I love you man!" I plan to shoot myself.

Shelia and I stand together watching the melding of our families. She is wearing the same smile of pride she wore when she opened these doors to us what seems so long ago. She and I know though, there is still a long road ahead of us. There are still many things to settle, not only within our own family, but between theirs as well. The tension between Dolph and Lawless is still lingering like a magnetic pull. Their collision could shatter this fragile truce we are holding. If Ross is added, it could explode.

My mood shifts when I see Leslie slink into the room. Her jeans are painted on, sliding perfectly into her knee-high black boots and her walk shows she knows it. The blue tank top she wears allows for no hidden surprises of her body. Her hair is pulled up high, letting the red waves frame her face, drawing the colors of her eyes deeper into their natural shade. If I did not hate her so much, she might make me question my sexual morality. Might.

Aimes comes to stand beside me when Leslie slinks in. We are watching Leslie pretending to not notice that she has our attention. We know she is aware of our eyes. No woman naturally flips her hair as many times as she has unless trying to prove a point.

"Watch this," Aimes says to me.

I turn to see her smiling with mischief with her hidden knowledge of what is about to happen. Aimes and I may not be on firm ice, but nothing brings women together, despite their differences, like the hate for another woman. Especially if that woman is in shoes better than yours.

I watch as Leslie walks behind the couch where the main alphas from our families are sitting. Her fingertips trail along each broad shoulder as she passes behind them. Like a Siren, she leaves them silent in her wake. Flashing a smile at us standing here watching her, she stops behind Lawless, running her hands over his black hair in its close-cropped mohawk. Her body is bent over, allowing her to taste the flesh of his ear, his neck and the hollow of his shoulder. He shivers with her playful action, causing a smile to spread across his lips.

"Yup, this has been super fun to watch. What do you suggest for the encore?" My voice is as sour as the bile I taste watching them. "Shall we hold the camera for them?" I ask. "A little night vision to help set the mood?"

"That is not supposed to happen," Aimes says. She sounds shocked at the show before us.

"Why? Afraid of losing your spot now?" I let the bile burn my question. My attitude is not improving as Leslie's hands disappear from my view.

"They always refuse her. It's like a group game for them. See how long until the skank catches on, we aren't talking to her kind of deal." She ignores my taunt while watching the rules being broken saying, "If she even tries to touch them, they dodge her, still keeping her on ignore mode. I don't understand."

I smile at the pain of his betrayal in her voice. "What isn't there to understand? Perky boobs. Tight ass. Possible end of the world. It is really simple math. Oh, and being easy kind of helps solve the whole what is x and y debate," I tell her.

"No, Helena, you don't understand." Aimes turns to me, placing her back to the couch, telling me, "He loves you. I mean really loves you. Romeo and Juliet deal."

"Remind me again, who gets the poison and who gets the dagger? Just for the sake of staying true to the story. Would hate to mix that little detail up when I kill him," I ask. I smile at her, letting her know how much I trust her opinion of what is happening.

"Actually, Romeo kills himself. Well, Juliet does, too," Shelia says.

I had forgotten Shelia was standing beside me.

She smiles and says to me, "So, just wait and let him kill himself. That is, if you truly want to stay true to the story."

"Here comes the head Montague now," Aimes nudges me, bringing my attention forward again.

J.D.'s powerful body strides over to us where we have been watching their little brouhaha. His face is showing the same feelings we are having over their encore. Lawless has pulled her down closer to him, enjoying the view her low-cut top provides him, listening to the Siren sing her words. Too bad it's me who is drowning with her song and not him.

"You going to just stand here and watch this?" J.D. looks to me with his question, surprised with my lack of reaction.

I stare at him with complete disinterest in his words. "Did you just bite your thumb at us, Sir?"

The female giggling over what I have asked only adds to his confusion. I guess the story was not mandatory reading for everyone after all. Maybe it just wasn't for him.

"I'm getting too old for this shit," he mutters to himself as he joins our picket line watching the show. "I'm gonna have to spell this out for you, aren't I? I think you know exactly what he is doing."

"Trying to catch a serious case of skank?" Aimes asks him. "You should probably warn him, with the whole zombie apocalypse thing going on, there is a shortage of cream for that."

"No, he is testing me. He stepped into the ring today. Now he wants to see if I will, too," I answer them both.

J.D. says nothing but looks at me with a sense of pride having figured it out.

"Please," I roll my eyes with J.D.'s look, saying, "Lawless is a lot of things I have discovered as of late, but deep is not one of them. Ever."

All three of them stare at me now. I am not sure what they are expecting from me.

"What? You want me to walk over there, take her by the hair, and slam her face against the coffee table? How about a metal chair to the back in a classic wrestling style?" I ask them, at a loss over what they are expecting from me.

"That would be totally amazing!" Aimes' excitement of my idea raises the pitch of her voice and widens her eyes. "Can you tag me in?" she asks, spreading J.D.'s smile wider.

"Old Hells would," J.D. says, daring me with his grin of approval.

"The old Hells also caused a lot of people to get hurt and worse. I was thinking I might need a little self-improvement," I reply, refusing to take the bait.

"I totally get the improve-thy-self-stint, but could you do that after you totally smash her face in? Too much to ask?" Aimes asks, dropping to her knees in front of me.

Aimes holds complete hope in my possible answer with steepled fingers of begging.

"I am not smashing her face in," I reply, and she launches her next question before I can take a breath.

"Can you bludgeon it a little bit?" "No.

"Not even a smidge?" "No."

"How about if you just trip her, and let her face fall into the table, all accidental-like?"

"Okay."

"Really?"

"No."

"Buzz kill."

"Sorry."

Aimes and I fall into our old pattern of rapid conversation with- out meaning to. We both smile at each other as our verbal volley comes to an end. Falling back into our old habits so easily is reaffirming our bond may be bent, but it is not broken.

"Never thought I would miss hearing that," J.D. chuckles. "What are you going to do, Hells?"

The idea of smashing her smiling face against the wooden table does fill me with warm fuzzies. A few loose teeth in the smile she is spreading for Lawless would do my soul good. Truth is, with its pointy fangs, she is not the one who owes me any loyalty. The whole "last man on earth" threat could very well soon be true. I don't blame her for trying for Lawless. I blame him for forgetting where home is. As J.D. told me, sometimes you just have to be reminded.

Aimes nudges Shelia saying, "She has a plan. I smell the smoke." I always thought the first step was the hardest. It is not. It is the second step. When your brain finally wakes up to what you are about to do, that's when the fear gets real. The third is not much fun either. That's when everyone notices you are taking steps.

The third might also be the hardest because it's when your friend wants to shout encouragement.

"Hey y'all watch this!" Aimes shouts from behind me, in a form of a war cry.

They do.

The men scatter with my path toward them. Rhett actually has the sense of humor to pull the same wooden table Aimes held hopes for from the couch with his departure wearing a smile. Even Simon encourages Richard and Dolph to give me space. His smile is one Ross would envy. My female outburst must have become legendary with the speed in which they are moving.

Lawless stands as I draw close to him. He doesn't move with the rest of them but plants his feet in a dare to come to him. His hands are resting inside the slanted leather vest's pockets, causing his arms to fold at the elbows with his silent refusal to help me. It gives Leslie the idea he is providing her with extra security with his arms spread wide from the vest's effect. She attempts to lean against his back, but he steps forward, putting space between her and himself. He will not choose sides. It's up to me now.

His eyes are heavy with the unsaid words hanging between us. It tints them a darker brown than their normal warm shade. He is trying to wear his mask, but the edges keep slipping, showing me moments of pleading with his need to end this between us. He is walking a wire with his dare to me and it's cutting him deeper than he thought it would.

"What do you want from me?" he asks as I draw near, and his voice is hoarse with the tension between us.

Leslie knows she is about to lose this battle with his yearning for peace. She slips her arms around him in the space left between his arms and the vest, hinting at her own answer to his question. His head rolls up with her contact, closing his eyes with frustration. "Let go," he says to the ceiling, but he is telling it to her.

His voice is at a dangerous level of anger.

I watch her arms slide slowly from his waist and my own mask slips as he looks back to me. I don't hide my smile. He stands still, waiting for me to give him my answer, not moved by my amusement of his refusal of her.

My body moves with the boldness I thought I had lost. My hands glide along the soft leather to wrap around his neck, cradling his head down to me. I stare into his eyes that are swaying rapidly back and forth trying to gain some clue about my thoughts. I know this man. I know every feature of his body, and I know how to use mine to make his respond.

Rising up to diminish the space between us, I tilt my head, pulling his closer to me. My lips are a mere moment from his and I stand here holding us in this position as we stare at each other.

Our bodies are sealed together, letting him feel the beat of my heart and the heat of my core. He is fighting his urge to hold me, so afraid of what I may say to him with our many biting words haunting us.

"I'll tell you everything," I whisper against his lips, bringing back the memory of his promise to me last night. "Just give me a little more time."

My words are private and meant only for us. This moment draws my pain visibly to the surface. I feel my cheeks grow wet with it. I give to him what he needs from me the most, my heart and my pain.

He nods, forcing his own tears back with the tight squeezing of his eyes. I seal my promise to him with a gentle sweep of my lips on his. Anything more will undo us both at this moment, stripping us of the war we are fighting internally.

"I need you," I whisper against those same lips as they now tremble. I whisper words I have never had the conviction to say to him before, "I love you."

His arms enfold me, pulling me tighter against him. He is trembling in our embrace, wrapping his whole body around mine.

"I'll give you all the time you need. Just don't lose me," he whispers into my neck.

"How could I?" I whisperingly ask him. "You promised to always come find me."

Lawless does a short, amused little laugh against my skin before saying, "It would help if you'd stopped hiding."

I answer him with the press of my body harder against his. It allows me to see over his shoulder to the woman standing behind us. I let my eyes hold the same glow, of the same unspoken message Lawless had given Dolph only hours ago.

He claimed me with his strength. I claimed him with my heart. For never was there a story of more woe than this of Juliet and her Romeo.

Chapter 43

If we thought with the many happy endings of yesterday things would magically revert back to the way they were long ago, we were naïve. Yes, Aimes and I are talking, and even share a laugh with her flair for verbiage. Yes, Lawless and I can now sit beside one another without a phantom of dread between us. There may be laughter again in our family. There may be more smiles than haunted stares. There is still the high voltage of tension should certain wires be crossed as well.

Slowly the wounds J.D. has caused us are healing into faint scars. Scars we will hold to forever remind us of our words, our tears and our pain of having been torn apart. The scars will remind us we belong together. They will remind us so we may know, no matter where we may be, our home is found within each other.

"We need a Christmas tree," Aimes offers to our breakfast conversation. She is almost pouting with her realization.

"Who is this "we" shit?" Rhett asks over a mouthful of his morning toast.

The men laugh over his brashness, earning them disapproving looks from Aimes. "Come on, there are little kids here. There should still be some type of Christmas."

"Think Santa got the vaccine?" Lawless looks to Rhett with his question. They both smile with the joke and the chance to annoy Aimes.

"Nah, just the elves. They're freaky little things to begin with, who then ate the fat bastard," Rhett answers him. They are re- fusing to take her suggestion seriously with their routine sense of dark humor.

Lawless is rubbing his foot against mine with a private flirtation. It's his new game to see how much contact I can handle from him, and for how long I can keep quiet about it. So far, he has won every round with his stone face, refusing to admit what he is doing to me under tables or in corners holding me against him. "Fine, Hells and I will get one. We don't need your help," Aimes tells the table through their smirking laughter.

"Who is this "we" shit?" I ask her, mimicking Rhett's opinion.

My question brings our family fully into laughter. Even the pixie has to laugh with my mocking of her.

"If you girls want a tree, we will get you a tree," J.D. tells us, finalizing the deal among the many groans from the men.

"Marxx, check with Paula and see if she has something that can support it. The rest of you, layer up. It's going to be cold and I don't just mean from Barbie," J.D. tells us as the meal is winding down, casting me a wink.

I give him back a look to convey my thoughts.

A chorus of "Yes, Dad" is his answer to the command, earning us all a glare from which we scatter.

"I can help with a damn tree," Marxx grumbles with his contempt.

Marxx is having issues with his new non-active role. The man we trusted with our security is now resigned to rest as we wait for his arm to heal. He is not waiting patiently or happily.

"Don't worry Marxzy, the boys here will be all out of stamina when we return, and you will be my knight in shining armor, saving the day with your tree prowess," Aimes tells him, patting his shoulder.

Marxx smiles at her while shaking his head.

"I think I liked it better when you were silent and pouting," he tells her, but his smile hints at a different answer.

"Any time you want to test my stamina, Little Girl, you just let me know," Rhett leans down to say in her ear, turning to be on the other side of her to avoid her playful shove from his words.

"What are we going to put on this tree?" I ask her, attempting to stop Aimes' and Rhett's game of tag.

We watch their game with a mixture of looks. They are racing up and down the stairwell around us, using us as obstacles to protect them from being tagged. Have I mentioned how much I hate morning people?

"I guess we are going to have to do another run to find decorations. I know there are things we are starting to run low on, anyway," Chapel suggests. He has no joy in his voice with the idea. Who can blame him with how well the last one went?

"If we do, it is just us," J.D. says, leaving no room for argument. "I thought everything was all punched out between you and them?" Aimes missed his implication as she dodges Rhett. I am tempted to trip her. I am not proud of it, but I am. "It is," he tells her.

J.D.'s eyes fill in his missing words. It's not the other men who are being left behind. It's her and I.

"Oh." She got it that time and Rhett gets her too as she starts to run again.

Just one little trip?

Lawless wraps his arms around me, walking tandem with me to my room. "You okay with that?"

"Yeah, I am," I tell him, and I am.

"Just promise me you'll be careful?" I ask him. "And you won't grow used to leaving me behind."

His playful smile graces me before he pulls his lips together in a tighter grin. "I can do that," he says.

"Which part?" I ask him, turning in his arms to fully see him. "All of the above," he says, pulling his body from mine, leaving me feeling cold without his arms around me.

Lawless kisses me gently and then pulls the door shut between us. He does his double knock pattern on the other side before walking away. It's his private message letting me know he is giving me the space I have asked for, but he is still here should I need him. We both know I will always need him. Smug bastard. The high school's lost and found has been very helpful with supplying the needs of clothing with the changing weather. Years of coats and other articles were stashed deep inside an unused office space. The coat I have chosen for myself was one of the most basic of color. The pattern upon it though, not so much. Its many white slashes over the dark blue are not a pattern I would have picked for myself before. Now though, warmth is warmth. Add in as many contrasting, horizontal and vertical slashes you want if it keeps me warm. The lack of mirrors also helps.

Aimes pops her head into my room. Knocking was never a huge skill set of hers before, why start now?

"Come on, Tweedle Dee," she says. Her excitement has her bouncing in place.

I smile. "Right behind you, Tweedle Dumb."

"Yeah," she pauses, watching me finishing my layering, "that didn't go as well as I planned there."

"It never does," I tell her, forcing the doors to stay shut that are rattling in my mind. "I can't believe you want a tree. Really, a Christmas tree, Aimes?"

"Not you, too," she groans. "Everything is on a constant downward spiral. Can we just try to have this one thing? It's not like I am asking us to go caroling."

"Yet." I smile at her.

"Well we could go room to room-" Her mind is already wandering.

"No." I cut off her thoughts before she has us all dressed as Frosty or other random classic winter characters, traipsing down the hall to melodies in mismatched pitches, which were not enjoyable before, much less now.

Outside snow has started to fall, sending winter's greetings swirling around us. It kisses our cheeks and eyelashes with its many hellos as we exit the high school's gate. Aimes runs in circles trying to catch the first of the season's flakes on her tongue. She is lost in her child-like wonder and it carries the rest of us along in her joy.

"What's the big deal about this tree?" Rhett asks, watching her twirl.

She shrugs, which for her means an in-depth conversation of past trauma. The only time she is silent is when she is avoiding speaking of her parents. I am not ashamed to say that sometimes I would ask about her mom just for a moment's peace. Completely, not ashamed.

"It was the only time we all got along. I can remember every tree, because it was the only time, they stopped fighting," Aimes answers him.

Her parallelism is not unnoticed. It's our first morning without poison and sarcasm as weapons used in conversations. We are not fragmenting into smaller clusters, but together as a whole in this moment. Her somber mood has a blanket effect on ours, leaving only the sound of the snow underfoot. The dark entrance of the forest surrounding one wing of the school does not help to bring any positive changes to the conversation, either.

A dark forest, possible Risen lurking, no immediate exit, this is a great plan Aimes. Merry Christmas to one and to all.

Rhett and Lawless take the lead into the darkness as expected. Aimes makes a great show of twirling the axes we were loaned, trying to comically prove she is ready for whatever is ahead when they passed by us. Her show is not half as amusing as the sudden appearance of Chapel's hand taking the axe from her without a word spared.

"So much rudeness," she tells me with a mocking pout. "Why does she get to keep her axe?" She turns to ask Chapel, still wearing her pout.

"She's the one who always finds the damn things." We can't argue with his logic, as unsettling as it is.

"Then maybe she should go first." Rhett tosses me a teasing smile over his shoulder.

I know, as brave as they both are, how unsettling that dark ring of trees must be for them. Humor makes everything less scary, even in the dark.

"I can if you are too scared, Rhett," I taunt him with my smile. "She does smell better than you," Lawless says, upping the dare to his partner in crime.

"Maybe that's it. All this time we thought it was noise that attracted them. Maybe it's just a girly scent that's luring them to her." Rhett smiles at me, ending the game.

We both know if the Devil himself is waiting for us, Rhett would still be the first one to go in. Rhett will not hide behind his excuses. He would forge his way through his deepest fears if it means keeping one of us from harm.

"If that were true, Ross would be one dead puppy by now," J.D. stirs their anger.

It is an easy emotion to wrap around, and like a shield, they use it to draw their bravery. Great pep talk, Coach.

"He is," Lawless says.

His anger is thicker than our winter coats. It gives him just as much warmth with its inner fire.

The dark forest swallows us with its paths and ice-heavy trees. The branches sparkle with their frozen limbs hanging around us. The dusting of the snow falls more evenly now without the wind to stir it around us. The forest has a feel of another world with her white, winter dress. With the many sparkling jewels that adorn her, she is beautiful in her cold- ness. I wonder if this is how Alice felt the first time she stepped into Wonderland with its dark, enticing beauty. Will we meet the White Queen or the Red Queen or just a rabbit to annoyingly remind us of how precious time is?

"What is it exactly we are looking for?" J.D. asks our Christmas Champion. His mood is on a rapid decent as the temperature mimics it.

"I'll know when I see it." Aimes does not let his gruff mood deter her still wrapped in her seasonal joy with her many thoughts of seasons past.

"See it soon. We are only going so deep," Rhett tells her.

J.D. is creeping along as cautiously as the rest of the men. Their eyes are always scanning the spaces between the hidden trees. Every noise pulls their attention, setting them tense with the curiosity of the source.

"You guys act like we are in the middle of a horror movie. It's just a forest," Aimes dramatically announces after watching them spook and twitch with the many noises around us.

"With snow...," I return, and she latches to the verbal space I left hanging.

"....and trees."

"....and deer."

"....and birds."

"....and two annoying women."

Rhett sneaks into our volley, ending it with the laughter of the men.

"You know, in the movies, it's always in the forest where people die the most." Lawless raises an eyebrow at Aimes trying to frighten her.

"Yeah, but we aren't camping, Mr. Brightside," she tells him, not amused with his teasing but she does glance behind her a lot more now.

"Yeah," Lawless starts again, undeterred by her refusal or the frozen log in his path, "what was the one all about a wrong turn?"

"Look, we are not going all Donner, party of six, today okay?" Aimes asks, and I watch as the light comes to Rhett's face.

"Spare us the innuendos, Rhett," I tell him as he laughs. "Then spare my toes and find a tree already." Rhett is still chuckling to himself.

With my luck, he is storing that missed one-liner I deprived him of for later. Oh, happy days.

"That one!" Aimes startles us all with her excitement.

She is going to get shot one day doing that. Literally, I will shoot her.

"Of course, it is," Lawless sighs, as we all turn to the tree she has picked out.

The tree has a light dusting of snow on it giving its green limbs an emerald shade. It's thick with its many full branches spared from the ice. The round base gives no clues to the size of the trunk. It's a monster of a tree if trees were cast as such. Luckily, we already have enough monsters in the world sparing us from such a threat, but I am not the one who has to cut it down, either. Chapel slides, rather ungracefully, under the large tree with his stolen axe. His vocabulary is four-letter-word tinted with his effort to find the base through the thick sharp needles of the tree's limbs fighting against him. We can't help but silently laugh listening to his many expletives, which are so unlike him. Not everyone is in the holiday spirit it seems.

Rhett nudges Lawless, pointing to the other side of the tree. They exchange a smile mothers of adolescent boys would cringe with the fear over wondering what they are going to do next. They position themselves across from each other on either side of the tree still wearing Mischief's trademark smile.

"Now," Rhett says, and they both begin to shake the tree be- tween them.

It scatters the fresh snow on the limbs around the tree's base, cascading it down where the white waves plummet onto Chapel. "Funny," Is the only response they receive from our Preacher's son with only his lower legs in our view.

It's enough and it sends the two clowns into hysterics.

Cutting the tree down was a three-man effort. How much of it is from having to battle the thick trunk with a hand axe or their lack of trust for being the center of a mischievous joke goes unsaid. Finally hearing the snapping of the trunk's surrender, Rhett and Chapel guide the forest's monster to the ground. The forest echoes from its fallen comrade, sending the birds scattering through the skies with their farewell.

Aimes claps again with her excitement and childlike joy. She tackles Lawless in a hug as he stands, causing him to laugh with her appreciation and return her hug. She begins to clean off the forest floor from his back and arms as I watch them in their friendship.

"Let's not cue that rerun," J.D. says beside me.

My face must have shown my feelings and I fight to regain its placidity, ignoring his private message.

"Man was in the forest," Aimes says, as they look down upon the giant tree.

"You can call me-," Rhett begins, but she cuts his sentence short.

"I am so not calling you anything," she tells him, trying to keep a stern face amid his teasing.

"Not even wolf?" Rhett lowers his voice with sexual tension, hinting his knowledge of a not-so-long-ago conversation.

Her cheeks flush with her memories of that morning. Rhett wins again.

He looks to me in his victory over her. We exchange smiles of our own and I know his mind is now remembering a different game he played. A game he lost.

"Any time," I tell him. "You don't even have to ask."

I taunt him with his own words. The color of his eyes deep- ens with his excitement at the memory. I am watching his face become one of a pure hunters with his racing thoughts of our rematch. His smile grows in proportion to Lawless' shrinking.

"Seriously, not again," J.D. mutters to me under his breath. "We're all still too fresh for this little show of yours."

"I'm not showing anything." I force my smile to stay frozen, sliding my words out between locked teeth.

"Really? Seems to me you are showing him you don't forgive them yet," J.D. tells me, turning his body to appear as if he is scanning the area to cover our conversation. "You were a daisy until she hugged him."

J.D.'s words steal the smile from my lips and pulls my face to him. It's all the confirmation he needs to the power and truth of his words.

"Get over it," he tells me, walking to the rest of the group to help them figure out how we are going to carry our kill back to the high school.

The very last thing you want to tell a woman is to "get over it." The phrase is the exact opposite of what a woman will do when told to do so. Now, I am willing to sit in this funk all day just to prove to J.D. I will not simply "get over it." I am completely secure in the fact I will be the Grinch who stole "over it" in the middle of their Whoville celebration. Unless, I have to paint myself green. Then all bets are off.

Chapter 44

It's the flash of her white nightgown I see first above her bare, ivory feet when she goes by me. The delicate white eyelets of its lace float above the white snow as she runs, keeping pace with me. The trees shield her, keeping her in a peek-a-boo pattern. I can almost hear her giggles as I watch her golden hair trailing behind her.

I am not surprised my mind would bring Lilly forward now. If innocence has a mascot, it would be her. The only thing that made this season bearable for me was she with her loving heart. In the past, this season would always bring the best of humanity from mankind. Those who were already blessed with such depths, only added to its heights of peace and goodwill.

There was not a heart Lilly could not melt with her smile. Years of frost would loosen from any soul she touched with her laughter. This season was her playground and she has come back to play.

She runs beside our group, keeping a line of trees between us in the winter cold. Sometimes she runs ahead of me to see what the men are doing with their heavy evergreen burden. Sometimes she keeps pace with me, running from thick tree trunk to tree trunk, keeping hidden from my full view. Other times, she waits behind, only to have to run to catch up with   us. She runs beside me now just as silently as she stalks me in my mind at night.

There is a clearing ahead and I know I will finally see her fully with the parting of the trees. My heart elates with it. My mind shivers with the dread over what she may show me.

Just as I had anticipated, she darts forward into the clearing, keeping her back to me. My soul pines with the need to see her smile. My mind is screaming, afraid I will.

Her long blonde hair is thick with her unkempt curls. The hem of her nightgown is tarnished from its natural white with the mud and snow it has collected. Like a phantom of winter chilling my mind with fear, she stands so still ahead of me and the world has grown silent with her appearance.

J.D. grabs my shoulder, halting me roughly. I cringe under his fingers grasping me so tightly.

"Shhhhhh," he whispers into my ear.

My confusion turns me towards him, and what I see only con- fuses me more.

His eyes scan the area ahead. He silently takes a position ahead of me, blocking her from my sight. His body is tense with what he is seeing. I don't see the danger. All I see is Lilly, standing so still, so silent and so alone before J.D. and me.

It can't be possible, but I am going to ask him anyway. "You see her?"

He turns only his eyes to me, keeping my body behind his. "Shhhh. Yes, I see her," he whispers.

"…but she's dead," I whisper to him.

Images of my broken flower flood my mind the way her blood poured from her wounds, hotly, painfully and rapidly.

"Yes, that's normally how it happens."

He is as confused over my confusion over a situation we have encountered so many times already. He does not understand this time it is different. It is Lilly. It has to be Lilly.

J.D. stares into the clearing ahead of us with caution. He whistles the men's whistle of warning to gain their attention without startling the apparition beside them. Like statues, they still, mid- step, looking for the danger J.D. has signaled. The tree is forgotten in a gentle heap of a motion when Chapel, Lawless and Rhett stare at what has formed beside them. They were lost in their conversation of laughter and teasing, swept along with Aimes in her joy. They never noticed the girl until J.D. had stopped them. Melting backwards to us, in an attempt to keep the frozen girl's back to them, Aimes and I are pushed behind them as they form a half circle around us. I want to tell them it is okay. She just wants to see the tree. She always loved the tree when it was decorated.

They don't have to fear her. It's just Lilly, my gentle Lilly. "What are you doing?" I hiss at Lawless, as he pulls his gun

from his waistband.

"She's right. If there are more of them this close to the high school, then the shot may trigger them to head this way," J.D. says while reaching over to push Lawless' gun down.

"Too late." Chapel is staring at another spot in the forest.

Many weaving shapes blend and contrast with the sunlight and trees. There is no denying what is slowly flowing our way.

"Plan?" Rhett asks anyone.

His eyes are trying to monitor the shape before us and the many shapes beside us.

"If we get far enough away from their sight, they will go back to their "resting stage." It may keep them far enough away from the high school. We can take out the one in front of us and slip away. The others are too far away to really rush us," Lawless offers.

His plan makes sense, except for the part about Lilly. Why do we need to hurt her?

"Why? She will just go away," I tell him, trying to get him to understand.

"Hells, since when do they just "go away"?" His response chills me.

"Always. They always just go away."

All of their eyes swing to me. Most of the eyes hold confusion, but two pairs are holding much more. They see what I am seeing. Chapel and J.D. capture my gaze with understanding and melting sadness.

Chapel pulls me through the line of men to his chest.

"Don't look," he tells me, securing me tightly against him so I have to obey him.

How can I "not look"? When have I ever been the one to "not look"?

I place my face flat against his winter-soaked coat. This allows me to see from the safety of his arms. I am a small child hiding from the opening of the closet at night. Part of me is curious to see what is about to happen. Another part of me is filling with sadness, knowing what is about to happen.

Chapel had the sense to remove the axe from my hand before holding me to him. He hands it now to Rhett, the only man he deems dark enough to do what has to be done. How little Chapel knows of my sins. The sin who is now standing before us, waiting for me to repent for my wicked, wicked ways. The sin who slowly turn towards me with her desire of a confrontation in my daily denial of them.

I want to yell at her to run. I want her to escape what is about to happen to her. I want me to escape what is about to happen to her. I have seen her laid low once already. I have seen her die a thousand times when I close my eyes. We should not have to go through this horror again, but we do.

The little girl turns slowly, clearing a path of fresh snow, dragging her feet with her motion. Her little toes do not feel the razor-sharp pain from the cold. She can't feel anything anymore. I stare at those tiny fragile feet unwilling to see her face. The sight of her white nightgown is enough. Even as I fight against seeing her, I look up anyway. When have I ever been the one to not look?

Reluctantly, I visually take in inch-by-inch of the white doll standing there, watching us. The front of her gown is not the virgin white I had seen running past me. Many shades blend together from the dark, dried browns to soft yellows of its wear upon her. Her fingertips are damaged and caked from the overly rough use of their tender flesh. Her face is pockmarked with missing flesh in irregular patterns from horrors we will never know. It's covered with the rage only the Risen can hold at the sight of their prey. Faded brown eyes hop from each person before her as she gauges which one to attack first. Rhett takes the debate from her with his sharp axe and smirking face.

"It's not her," I whisper into Chapel's coat.

"It's not her," I whisper again to myself with each wet, thick sound Rhett fells upon her.

"It never is," Chapel whispers into my hair.

I know at this moment; I am not the only one haunted with the sounds of delicate laughter and the scent of baby shampoo.

"Let's go." I hear J.D.'s voice fills the now very silent space around us as other sounds stop. "You got her?" I know he's asking Chapel about me without having to peek from my shelter.

Chapel's sliding of me under his arm to cradle me, still in his protection as we begin to walk answers J.D. He doesn't tell me to not look. At this point, we both know his words will be hollow advice.

She lies on her back with the many brutal cuts to her torso gaping up to the sky. Her once white nightgown is embedded into each slash and it slowly pulls the dark blood into the material, staining it with his assault. Her face is a ruin of blows to her skull, leaking blood and thicker materials to the ground around her. Only her eyes stay intact, and for a moment, they are the crystal blue of warm oceans peering out at me amid so much destruction before my mind can switch them back to their true color. The red snow is seeping into the white snow crystals as her blood creeps, expanding its circle with its escape. Her body is truly broken now from Rhett's massacre.

This is not my Lilly. My flower is withering, pressed between the yellowing pages of my memories. She sleeps with so many other angels lost to this cold world. The angels who have turned their vision from those of us still remaining here in this hell. Just as I had mine, I leave this broken blonde child behind as she spills her life onto the white floor surrounding her.

Is someone missing her the way I am missing mine? Does someone screams her name into the darkness of night with the fear of what has happened to her? For her sake, I hope not. I hope they are now finally all at rest, together.

I dared to ask my Wonderland a question and it answered me in the most horror-filled answer pulled from its darkest secrets. It brought forth its White Queen to me. Now, as we follow the red dotted trail of her blood dripping from the axe that took her head, her army searches for us. Silently, we escape with our stolen winter prize among her army's vocal fury.

"It's a poor sort of memory that only works backwards," said the White Queen to Alice. If she only knew how correct she was.

Chapter 45

Dear Lord, what has happened?" a female's voice calls out to us.

Paula rushes to us, skipping around the many red teardrops Rhett leaves behind in his wake.

"The tree fought back," Rhett answers her with his "prove me wrong" smile.

We know it means he does not want to talk about it. She doesn't. "Are you hurt?" Paula rubs her hands over him, looking for the

wound she cannot see.

I guess she has not caught on that, unless it is self-inflicted, the axe in his hand is a glaring oversight.

"He's fine," Chapel offers, trying to save Rhett some dignity.

His annoyance with her is amusing. Do I sense a little jealousy there, Chappy?

"Did you find something to put this in? And where?" J.D. asks her.

"Marxx is waiting for you upstairs," Paula tells him, motioning with her head to the stairs. Her voice is icy, sensing Chapel's disapproval.

"Why is it always upstairs?" Rhett sighs, adjusting the weight of the tree in his hand.

"Not you," J.D. remarks and motions for Rhett to hand his side to Chapel.

"He's right. You can't go up there looking like a Christmas version of Macbeth," I tell him, "and no, I will not help you wash out the spots."

Rhett performs a mocking pout over my words, but laughs just the same, saying, "Stars, hide your fires. Let not light see my black and deep desires."

He kisses the top of my head, the way the men have found the habit to do. Unlike the rest of the men, his hand slides down my back, cupping me in his hug providing further weight to his quote. One never knows with Rhett how much of his personality is games and how often they are not. This is no exception, but it stirs something inside me just the same. I watch his back retreat to the showers of the gym with many thoughts swirling in my mind. "Somehow, I find it very fitting that he can quote Macbeth,"

Aimes whispers in my ear.

She overheard our exchange, and with a sly smile, she joins me as we watch him leave. He turns, feeling the weight of our stares and flashes us both an amused smirk before rounding a corner.

"Somehow, I find it very strange you knew it was Macbeth." I point out my amusement of her literary sense.

"You always fill me with such great confidence," she says. Her words might be formed to be biting, but the tilt of her head as she watches Rhett turn the corner takes any heat from them.

"It's a gift."

We both almost sigh when he fades from view.

"You ready to get this upstairs?" Lawless' voice shreds the images of my imagination, as if they were smoke. They slip away in wisps of unspoken desires.

"Three flights of stairs, sharp bends and cussing galore? What is not to look forward to?" Aimes asks as she leans into the heavy metal doors, propping them open with her body to help the men with their haul.

That is exactly what followed, a lot of cussing, a lot of stairs and a lot of sharp turns requiring many attempts of reverse to shimmy the tree up the stairs. Aimes shouts her helpful advice at each bend until finally the glares reduce her to silence. True to Aimes' earlier words, once the three are able to get it through those final metal doors, they drop it. Chapel, J.D. and Lawless collapse on the couches near the door with their refusal to help in any more of Aimes' holiday planning.

"I said if you wanted a tree, I would get you a tree. There is your damn tree," J.D. pants around his words. "The rest is on you."

"Merry Christmas," Chapel echoes his agreement to being done. "Well, this went well I see," Marxx' deep voice arches the panting men's eyebrows with their answer for him.

Paula had said he was waiting for us and here he is. Marxx is holding a tree stand that has seen better days. I think it may have seen better centuries with the amount of rust and misshapen pieces in his hand.

"We found it in storage," Dolph answers the doubts, which must have been showing upon my face.

He steps over the large tree where the men had dropped it. It blocks the entrance to the room and Dolph stares at the tree stand with disbelief and mild amusement. When reinforcements arrive to further the tree escapades, Richard and Simon share the same look as Dolph.

"What did you do, pick the biggest one out there?" Richard is eyeing the heap of an evergreen on the floor with as much faith in the tree stand as I hold.

Lawless and Chapel both point at Aimes simultaneously, and her face expands with the shock of being outed so bluntly.

"It looked smaller outside," she tries to defend her tree selection among the many annoyed stares.

"They always do. That's why I don't go naked in the forest," Rhett says, letting us know he is back and as charming as ever.

"And eyehook…," Aimes recovers the conversation for us all with an exaggerated eye roll aimed at him.

Paula and Shelia join Aimes and myself from our safe vantage point to watch the comedy show. The tree may be down, but it has far from lost its fight. Each struggle draws more words from the men's mouths until they are just one giant, long string of amusements for those of us watching. How many men does it take to screw a tree into a tree stand? Don't know. Ask me again in an hour.

Chapter 46

You still see them, don't you?" Chapel's eyes pierce my soul as he watches my face for a reaction to his question.

I give him nothing. My eyes lock on the tree now centered in the middle of the third floor's common area. The couches have been positioned to either side of the massive evergreen, allowing a view to be shared by all with the hopes of lifting spirits with its sight. Nothing quite says Christmas like the many shared curse words and explosive tempers that decorating can bring.

"I sometimes think I can hear Kay. You know, right before I wake up, I think I hear her laughter or footsteps around me. When I open my eyes, she is never there," Chapel almost whispers to me.

His eyes are now staring at the tree also. It has become a navigation beacon for us both to guide us through the conversation. I just hope it's large enough to guide us back home after we travel the depths of where he is leading us.

"Back at the cabin," he continues, "I used to lie there just keeping my eyes closed. I was too afraid to open them. Too afraid she may actually be there and hoping she would be at the same time. Now, I just wake up as fast as I can to make her go away."

Chapel sighs with a weight lifted off of his shoulders. The family man has been hiding the fact he wants the memory of his daughter to go away and it has been soul-searing. I should comfort him. I know I have the words to apply the balm to his wounds, but my mouth is locked, keeping my secrets safe.

"I swear sometimes, just sometimes when I am alone, I can smell Trina's perfume. She always had this one brand she would wear. I can't remember the name of it, but the smell. That smell I can," he sighs with the memory.

"Like her baby shampoo," I hear the words escape from their confinement of my mouth, shocking us both.

"Yeah, like her baby shampoo," is all he says.

It is all he has to say. I have confirmed exactly what he is asking me. He does not need my details. He just wanted to know he is not alone in his torment.

I can feel his eyes staring at me, but still I keep watch on the tree like a sailor with the North Star. I can feel the seas churning underneath me. Waves threaten to topple my fragile ship with their power. If I take my eyes from the tree, all will be lost.

"Looks kind of bare," I say, with an attempt to pull his eyes back to the monster of the holidays standing before us and away from me.

"I'm not telling them." Chapel does a half laugh remembering how much joy the tree has brought the men already. The sound of it brings the mood to a different level.

"Let's get Aimes too." I smile with the thought of throwing her under the bus, or in this case, a Harley.

"You two work all of your shit out?"

My eyebrow rises hearing his slip of vocabulary. Someone has been with the boys a little too much.

"Minute by minute," I tell him. It is the best answer I have for our situation.

"You and Law?"

The mood has dropped again along with the volume of his voice. "Second by second."

Even as my soul aches for his comfort, my heart is still too sore to fully trust Lawless' smile. One moment, I want to run into his arms and beg him to return to how things were between us. The next, I want to steal Chapel's gun again and make him beg me. It really is a fifty-fifty style of moments for me. My outbursts are legendary people. Legendary.

"You and Rhett?" He stares at me again, and I stare back at him, confused by his question.

How many people have issues with me?

"I didn't know Rhett and I had problems to work out?"

It may have been a statement, but it sounds way more unsettling as a question.

Chapel says nothing. He just stares at me with his soul-searching eyes waiting on me to find my own conclusion. The son of a Preacher has learned a few tricks from his part-time father. It always amazes me how we all do. His eyes hold me grounded in his question while my mind races with it. He will not help me confess my sins, but he will wait until I do.

"You mean our flirting?" I almost whisper the question, hoping I am on the right track.

He still offers me nothing but his eyes.

"It's nothing. Just harmless fun," I say, and my eyes swing back to the tree with hopes to avoid his stare.

Where is that divider to slide between the sinner and the priest when I need it?

"Is that what you think?" Chapel stands, stretching his tight shoulders from the weight of handling the tree today.

He glances one more time down at me with those confessing eyes before he walks away, leaving me feeling judged. The Pope could take lessons from him. That is, if the Pope is still alive. I wonder if God protects his flock when the Devil comes to play, or do they get a pat on the back and a going away hand basket like the rest of us?

His question leaves me spinning with thoughts and doubts. Rhett is harmless with his flirting. There is not a lot to combine harmless and Rhett together in, but this, I feel safe saying. The only feelings he has ever held for me is those of mild amusement for the ability to go toe-to-toe with him in his games. I am a child in his very dark, grown-up world, but the world has changed now. Has it changed other things as well?

"You're gonna get wrinkles if you keep frowning like that and there ain't no Mary Kay out here baby," Aimes says and startles me from my thoughts with her very ungraceful body flop onto the couch beside me.

"Ding-dong, zombie calling."

"That's Avon. Don't mess with my branding here, woman." "Why? Because you are worth it?"

"Seriously, some rudeness simmering in your sauce." "American by birth. Rebel by choice."

"Okay, I don't even know where you are pulling from now, but you are starting to scare me."

"Between love and madness, lies Obsession." "Really, white flag."

"Outwit. Outplay. Outlast."

 "I will seriously hit you."

"Let your fingers do the walking."

"You win. I bow to your knowledge. I am not worthy." "I'm loving it."

Aimes and I both stare at the other, waiting for the next round. When it doesn't come, our laughter does. It fills the common area with its familiar sound, causing others to smile. I am not thinking about ghosts right now. Right now, I am just enjoying this minute. "Have your feelings changed for anyone since all of this start- ed?" I ask her as our laughter settles to giggles and then silence.

"Danger, Will Robinson, danger," Aimes mockingly calls out. Her body position changes with the implications of my question. "Okay, how about this, have you noticed any changes with

anyone you never thought of before?"

Ever notice how a tree can look exactly like the North Star when it is not decorated? No?

"Oh yes, well, when phrased like that, it is much more comfort- able to be asked," Aimes says.

Aimes has found the tree also very interesting. Maybe we should just keep one here year-round, for conversation's sake.

"You are not going to answer me, are you?" I finally ask her after a long pause of tree watching.

"That is a big negative, good buddy." She smiles at me with her refusal. She asks me, "Why are you asking, anyway?"

"Something Chapel said to me about Rhett has me thinking," I say. My answer snaps her head forward again. Her sudden panic tells me the little pixie knows something.

"Have you talked to Lawless, yet?" she asks me. Her voice is solid, but it holds a moment of worry. "I mean really talked to him?"

"About what?" I watch her the way Chapel was watching me. I search for any hidden facial twitch to give me clues.

"About your amazing slogan skills that totally rock the Casbah. What do you think about?" she asks me.

Her frustration over the situation shows in her voice, and it is my turn to answer her with silence.

"You have to talk to him," she says when my silence grows too long. "Hells, you have to talk to someone. I know something horrible happened. You would never have left those kids behind otherwise."

Oh, Christmas tree, oh Christmas tree, how I stare at you so dedicatedly.

"I am not saying you have to take him back," she tells me. "You don't have to go back to Lawless Land if you don't want to, but at least talk to him. He was the only one who could ever reach you. Not saying I am not awesome or anything, but you two had this thing. You need that thing, Hells. You need it now more than ever. You tried to talk them out of killing one of those dead things today."

Aimes' words pull a topic from me I am not ready to debate yet. My words keep escaping like water through my fingers. I cannot hold on to them.

"They are not dead. She said they are not dead," I whisper.

I feel my chest flutter with the panic of the voiced truth, like a hummingbird with its fast wings has taken home in it. It claws me internally, bringing hot tears to my face with the pain.

"Helena?" Aimes is torn between pity and fear watching me break.

I am supposed to be the strong one, the one of icy, cold steel and I sit now before her losing it with one sentence.

"Don't. Just don't," I tell her as much as I tell myself.

I leave her sitting on the couch still staggering from my reaction. Everyone has their kryptonite. Mine just happens to be the ghosts of the little children who stalk me with their blue eyes and the crimson coloring of my sins.

My room is shielded from the sun and it seems colder today than normal. I hug myself, trying to hide my weakness.

"Whose arms are you craving right now?" Lawless' voice drifts in from behind me.

Silence is a wonderful thing when unsure of the truth. I employ it now, watching him walk from behind me into my room. He sits on the cot before me, waiting for my answer. He is wearing his mask and that never bodes well for our conversations.

"Let me guess, you want to talk?" I ask.

It's an easy guess with the theme so far of my afternoon.

He shrugs with his whole body. One of his shoulders goes up countering the height of the other. His hands flip over to show me his palms. His lips frown for a moment with it before he returns to his placid calm.

"Yeah, I do," he says.

"I don't," I tell him, turning from him, to leave from where I thought I would be safe from so many questions.

He is instantly in front of me, shutting the door and blocking me from my escape.

"You always do this. You always run. I'm tired, Helena. I can't keep up with your running anymore," Lawless tells me. He is leaning against the door with his back, securing it in place and securing me in the room.

I guess we are going to talk. Yippe! Skippie!

"I didn't ask you to." My arms cross in front of me, preparing for the battle ahead. I am armed with sarcasm and deep glaring stares.

Unfortunately, I do not think either of those will frighten him anymore. Where is Chapel's gun when I need it?

Lawless laughs. It is a laugh of ironic pain, not amusement with what I have said.

"You're right," he says. "You would never ask for my help. I am just supposed to give it, and if I don't, how quickly you can hate, Hells."

I stare at him, not giving him an inch of reaction with my silence. He said he wanted to talk, not me.

"You push me away just as hard as you pull me close. I don't know which way to turn, or what to say to you anymore. Every time I think I am getting close; you shove me away. At least, with Leslie I knew where she stood," he tells me with a smirk, and I feel the poison sneaking onto my tongue.

"Stand? That is impressive. I didn't know she had that mode. I figured she just laid down for you and that is why you so enjoyed her."

We are not going to talk. We are going to fight. There is no stopping our storm now.

"Alright, yes, forgive me, but I did. I enjoyed it. I enjoyed every moment of it. I enjoyed her wanting me. I enjoyed her flirting with me. The way she wasn't ashamed to let others see us together. She wants me," Lawless stresses the words which would hurt me the most.

He closes some of the gap between us with his anger. His voice sounds like thunder in this small room.

"….and the sex?" I ask, attempting to stop some of his forward progression towards me.

The winds begin to pick up around us with my question. We are going graphic novel.

"It was great. She couldn't get enough. The way she screamed under me; it was perfect." His voice clashes with the grin upon his face. I can feel the rain falling from his words.

"You're lying." I hear my voice crack, stripping me of my courage to fight this fight.

Venom fills his words as his anger takes him.

"No, I'm not. I could walk out of this room right now and find her. I could take her right where she stands. No questions asked. Not with you. Never with you. I could never suggest such a thing with you. No one gets a piece of Helena Hawthorn's heart until she needs them and wants them," he says to me.

His words become more agitated with each sentence. He is standing toe-to-toe with me now. His eyes are burning with his anger as he stares down at me.

He rides his anger, saying, "...and then, when you are done, you are just gone. You fade away back behind this stonewall of yours. Keeping everyone out. Shoving everyone away. Keeping me out. Even though I know all of this, I stay. Knowing how each time would end between us. Knowing when the sun comes up, you will be gone. When people are around us, you'll be cold again. All of this I know, and I still can't walk away from you."

He does his ironic laugh again. This time it mixes more with his self-disgust over his actions rather than disgust over me. I watch him walk past me with his head heavy from his thoughts. He puts his back to me, trying to control his anger.

"When you let me in though, Helena, when you let me see behind that wall of yours, I feel like I'm whole. When I used to hold you at night, I was whole. Your smile would bring me peace. Your laughter used to heal me from all the shit I've done. All the shit I have to do. My whole life was for those moments. Nothing in-between mattered. Just those moments for me when you would stare at me like I was some hero. Our moments were everything to me. I've tried to find it with others. I've tried hard, so tired from your games. It was never there with them. They were just faces. Just guilt when I had to look at you afterward."

He sits back on the cot, silent for a moment and I am not sure if we are in the eye of our storm or if it has blown over.

"When you pulled that stunt at the Welcome Center, watching you in the middle of all of those things again, do you have any idea what that was like? I get it. You couldn't just stand there and watch them be attacked. I get it, but they wouldn't let me go to you. I had to stand by and watch as those things came for you. If you were killed, and worse, I would have had to watch." He casts those amber eyes on me and asks, "Did you ever think of me? For one moment, did you think what would happen to me if you didn't survive? Were those strangers so much more important to you than me?"

He is begging me for an answer to help him understand me, to understand us. I never saw it in that way. I never thought of my actions as wounding him or filling him with so many doubts of my feelings for him. In my efforts to save others, I have damned him.

"Leslie was never supposed to go this far. I was just enjoying her attention. I knew it would upset you. I never meant for it to do this to us." His guilt is covering him, shrinking him down with the weight of it.

"It wasn't just her. We are not here just because of her," I tell him.

He turns his head with my words; his eyes focus on something further into the room, and away from me.

"No, I guess not." Law's eyes are staring at something only he can see. "I was so mad at Chapel for being the one to stand up against him. It should have been me. To see J.D.'s hands on you like that made me want to tear him apart. I wanted to, but I didn't.

I let him hurt you. I let him say those things to you. Not Chapel though. He stood right beside you, and I hate him for it. Not as much as I hate myself for being so weak."

He pauses, trying to collect himself. His foot begins to bounce with his anger.

"Then Rhett. Rhett who has been with J.D. the longest was right beside you. Laughing with you the way we used to. The way he looks at you now. The way you look at him." His whole body now vibrates from the force of his foot. "He actually asked me if I would mind. Like I wouldn't mind. Now Marxx. Shit Marxx, the coldest bastard we have sits each morning with you. Just the two of you sitting at a table, in your own little world each morning, while I am still on the outside, waiting. I'm still waiting for you to want me again. Each glare from those eyes of yours cuts me deeper than I thought I could be cut. Your words, shit, Hells, you know how to hurt me."

He stares at the ground with his body shaking from his emotions. He is pulling down each brick for me to finally, really, see him. His mortar is loosening with each secret he has kept from me he is spilling forth.

"…and I started it all. I wanted to stop it so many times, but it was so far from my grasp. We just kept slipping further away with my anger, your anger and my guilt until I didn't know how to get us back. So, I stopped trying. I just let it all fall apart. I let it all fall down around me. I let us go, Hells. Even as you stood there trying to hide the pain from me, I let it all go. When you stood there begging me with your eyes to help you with J.D., I just threw it all away. I used Leslie as much as she used me. Each time I was with her, I lost more of myself. I lost more of us. I knew each time she screamed my name it was not who I wanted to hear it from."

I listen to him, biting my tongue to keep myself still as I wait for him to start again.

He looks at me to weigh my reaction to his confessions, saying, "I thought if I lost enough, it wouldn't hurt anymore to watch you slip away. It wouldn't hurt so much to see you with the other group. It would stop hurting to have to watch you sitting with Dolph, right across from me, giving him your smile. I'm just lost now though, and it still hurts, Hells."

He is crumbling before me. He hides his face in his hands with his shame. Lawless is no longer vibrating but rocking back and forth from his confessions.

"Say something damn it. Anything. If you have something to say, say it to me now. I don't want to lose you to some bullshit. I've lost so much, I can't lose you, too," he says, breaking with his guilt.

He is forcing himself to stay in this moment. He is fighting to stay lost in his weakness before me. Even as my body trembles with the urge to avoid this, I will not run. We are so far from the path we came here on and I don't know if I can retrace enough of our steps to fix us. I take the first step just the same.

"I hated you the moment she touched you. The moment you let her touch you and made me watch. I tried so hard to deny you were sleeping with her; that you were able to just walk away so easily from me when here I was trying my best to keep us all together. You were my security. My strength. You held my heart and you just let me go. You didn't just let me go. You watched me fall. You let me fall for your amusement. It should never have been Chapel beside me, you're right. It should have been you. It should have been your arms I cried in at night. Your arms that hid me when I didn't want to do it anymore. It never was. You stood there with your blank face, watching me break and you did nothing to stop it with your fear of upsetting J.D.," I tell him, giving him what he had asked me to do.

He says nothing, keeping his head buried in his hands and I can't stop the words now they have been let loose.

"You chose Leslie over me. You chose J.D. over me. You chose Aimes over me. You asked me, did I ever stop to think of you. Did I ever wonder about what would happen to you? No, I didn't. I thought no matter what was to happen, you would always be there with me. Always. You proved me all wrong though, didn't you? You proved me wrong each day with your smiles to her, your whispered words to her and her touching you. You proved me wrong by drawing this line between us. What a big funny joke I was for you and J.D. to enjoy?"

It's not just my mouth now let free, but my body, as I stride forward with my anger. I stare at him, asking him, "Did J.D. give you a big pat on the back when you finished each time? Atta Boy Law, way to bang a ho! Do you want a round of applause for feeling gross for sticking your dick in her? A big hug reassuring you it's only for you who she screams? She is just as big of a slut as you are, and martyr really isn't your color."

He nods his head with each word I shout at him, accepting my rage.

"I'm not stupid. I knew about all those other times. White roses, just because? Right. You really wonder why I run? Why I have never fully let you in? I'm tired of your running, too. Don't blame me for the doubts you have caused," I say, hissing my rage. I want to be angry. I want to scar him with poison-tipped words.

I want to see him hurt, but I can't. My pain is too great from our separation. My anger died long ago. It is just empty pain now inside me with the memories of us. We have both scarred each other and been scarred by the other enough as it is.

"You stopped fighting. You walked away. When I needed you the most, you stood right there and watched me fall. Now you want me to just walk right back into your arms after you left me all alone?" I ask him.

He looks up to me from behind his hands to let me see him. His face is wet from his tears and they trace patterns along the dark, amber coloring of his skin. I have never seen him so broken. It doesn't bring me the joy I hoped it would hold for me. He has always been so full of life, but now as he hangs with defeat, it speaks more to me than any words he has said.

"It shouldn't always be a fight. I shouldn't have to always fight for you. Everything is falling down around us, Helena, but here I am still fighting for you to let me in, but I never left you," he whispers the words, so weary from the truth of them. "I am here, every night, right beside you. I watch over you when you sleep. I whisper in your ear with your nightmares, telling you that you are safe. Just sleep baby, you are safe." His voice breaks with the words, and my heart skips as the words spark a memory.

I thought the sound of him at night beside me was a dream. I thought it was nothing more than my own loneliness conjuring the feel of his arms when the demons came to play in my dreams. He was here. Through all my bitter words, and poisoned acts, he was here. My lighthouse was here to guide me to the dawn.

"Every day I ask Chapel about you," he confesses. "I ask him to keep you safe when I can't. I watch you slowly give up on everything, but I am always standing right beside you if you need me. You were burning every bridge, but I never left you. I am still here. Hanging on.

Even as you burn me. Even as you cut me. I am still here. Just as I promised you."

"Then why do I feel so alone, Larance?"

The sound of his real name on my lips brings him to me instantly. He wraps me in the security blanket I have ached so desperately from with its loss.

His lips tenderly touch mine, and he whispers to me, "Because that is how you want it. It's how you've always wanted it. Let me love you, Helena. Please, love me."

With his words, I no longer want to throw stones. This fragile glass house of ours cannot handle any more blasts. Its walls are coated with so much of our mudslinging already and I can barely see the heart of it.

I only want to calm this hurricane we have become. I want to calm the storm that howls around us with so many of these doubts and fears of ours. He refuses to look away from me, and I pray he sees just how much I need him now, even if I cannot say the words.

We are both children forgotten. His embraces cannot make up for the ones I was denied so long ago, the missed embraces that laid these first bricks of mine, but I am going to let him try. I am going to let us try.

Our kisses start out gentle and shy. We each wait for the other's refusal or rejection. We test each other's boundaries until there is none to be found, and finding none, passions are sparked as our bodies remember the feel of us. The gentle touch of his lips builds into the caress of his tongue before it penetrates my mouth with his eagerness.

His mouth tastes the flesh of my neck before it travels lower, exploring the spaces exposed by his fingers with the removal of my clothes. The small buttons of my shirt overcome his desires with their defiance at his hunger-driven clumsiness. My fingers, which had been doing their own exploration of his body, take over the act for him. His eyes devour every inch I expose until I lie bare for them.

The pause he takes to visually roam my body inflames me with the need for his touch, flushing my skin with my desires. He smiles a very male smile, expressing his enjoyment of my situation as he traces the curves of my sides with his palms. I arch for him with the feeling of his warm hands on me. He moans a male sound of appreciation with the sight before rewarding me with his mouth again.

Circle upon circle, motion after motion, his mouth and tongue return to their previous task. He licks and samples with different speeds and urgency upon my breasts, my neck, and my shoulders. My leg is wrapped around him and he cups my thigh, bracing it, allowing our hips to mock the motions of our future acts.

My arms have been clinging to him, pulling him to me with a refusal for any space between us. My hand caresses the back of him, trailing a path to his shoulders and to his neck before repeating it again. My other hand guides the back of his head along the path he is taking with his mouth, providing the clues to the spots of where I want to feel him the most. My voice is a soft combi- nation of moaning and pleading with his hot, wet torture of me.

I am lost in the heights of the sensations he is driving me to when I feel his voice against my neck.

"No more running, Helena," he tells me. His hot breath whispers along my flesh, "You are either all in, or I am all out."

My heart races, not from his actions, but from his ultimatum. All this time I have blamed him for pulling away, but it was me who was pushing him away. I was so lost in my failures before, and now worse with their deaths still haunting me, I have become disgusted with myself. I have encased myself in a prison of bitterness and it has turned my actions and words into acid pouring over him and those around me with my self-hatred.

Now my Lawless, my lighthouse, stands before me trying to find me one more time. He is offering me everything, his heart, his body and his soul. All I have to do is accept him, completely, and I do. I take what is mine. I take it fully.

Chapter 47

"The tree is still bare." Aimes is pouting, staring at the evergreen with its defiant height mocking the ceiling of the third floor. "It is all naked and depressing," she says, with pursed lips.

We are lounging in a common area of our making after dinner. Spare furniture from unused teacher's lounges has been brought up to accommodate the many more people who now mingle with winter's chill keeping everyone inside. Somehow, our little group remains aloof even as we interact with those around us. The leather vests, still a staple of their wardrobe, turned this corner into ours even with our absence. It has the same effect on those who live here now as it did for those who used to live in our town. If given the chance, I am sure J.D. would paint their grinning skull on the wall above us to finalize their space.

The vest is not the only thing they have reclaimed from our past. The men have fallen back into their ranking system as they sit around the table. J.D. sits at the head, silently watching our banter while the rest of them ascend down on either of his sides with their held position. Routines are slowly forming again with the drama easing around us. If we loot a jukebox, we may just be at Grit again.

"Sweetheart, nothing naked is depressing." Rhett begins to tug on his shirt with a smile. "Here, let me show you."

"What is it with you and your hate for keeping your clothes on?" Aimes' voice may hold disapproval, but her face does not.

I can feel Lawless' arms tighten around me automatically with his doubts still open to me after yesterday. I slide deeper into his embrace, trying to settle them. It's a little thing, but it's enough. My mind still sometimes revolts with my efforts to embrace him again. I find myself biting my tongue to keep my words at bay. Baby steps, such tiny, painful baby steps I am still taking.

"She is right. If we are going to do this, we need to finish it." Chapel twirls his cross ring with his nervousness.

The many gems set around the cross' framework catch the overhead lights and glow with the reflections. The center gem sparkles with many different shades as he twists it with his habit. The ring is as much as part of Chapel as the vest has become.

"Seriously, how does this "we" shit keep coming up?" Rhett's flirtatious nature melts to annoyance with his question.

"Getting weak in your old age, Rhett? You ready to retire that bike?" Lawless taunts him.

His words hold mirth, but just like J.D., they also hold so much more. How much has our little Prince learned?

"Anything you can do brother…." Rhett lets it hang between them with his dangerous smile coloring the words.

"That means you can take your shirt off, too." I relax in Lawless' arms, bringing him back to me.

He kisses the top of my head, but I can feel his tension still making his body taunt. He will not take his eyes off Rhett with the tension now between them from their hidden innuendos.

Rhett breaks his stare first. He cuts his eyes sideways, inhaling his anger with the act. Lawless has won this round and it shocks me when Rhett caves so easily. I look to J.D. with my questions on my face, but he only gives me those empty, cold eyes, warning me to stay silent. It seems it's more than just Lawless' changes I have missed with my departure.

"What does it mean to "retire your bike"?" Aimes apparently missed the whole stare-fest to be stirring the pot so nonchalantly. "When you can't ride any longer." J.D. is the one to answer her, refusing to let the stalemate between Rhett and Lawless start again.

"What happens when you can't ride any longer?" I ask. I am afraid the answer to my question may be exactly what I think it is. "You're out." J.D.'s voice holds his normal cord of finality. He is looking to the man across the table from him and fighting to stay disconnected.

Marxx sits at the base of the table avoiding our stares. Paula has warned, with the extent of his injury, he may never fully regain the grip in his hand. It's the very thing could keep Marxx from ever riding again and regaining his place next to J.D. I wonder, with reality now looming before him, if he still thinks it was worth it.

"If we are going to do it, then we should do it now. There seems to be more of them as of late than before. The darkness will help cover us," Marxx says. He ignores my stare, but I know he feels it.

"It will help cover them as well."

I know that Siren's voice. I pull from Lawless' embrace, replacing my missing bricks with Leslie behind us. He tightens his arms around me, feeling me retreat from him. It does not comfort me. It feels like I am smothering. He lets me go, dropping his arms to his sides and it is my turn to avoid their stares.

"…and?" Lawless asks her. His tone is dangerously flat with her.

"And it is not safe," she tells him, exasperated with his response. "Good thing no one invited you." Lawless signals for me to move so he can stand.

The rest of the men at the table stand with his head nod for them. Even J.D. obeys Law's silent command with a smirk of trouble on his lips. They file out of our area in a single-file line, still in the formation of rank and silent with their solidarity. Their body language parts the space before them as they near the other residents. Men nod hellos as they pass, trying to gain their attention with the yearning for acceptance and any chance of acknowledgments. The club is back in its power even in this small community with the respect and fear they inspire.

Aimes leans into Leslie as she strolls past her to join our group and whispers in a mockingly compassionate tone, "Sorry, Skankerbell, you must be all out of whore dust."

I wonder how long I will continue to give this woman power over me with her past and if I can become like her to give Lawless what he needs for his future. What happens if I can't?

"It is only a matter of time," Leslie says to me, echoing my thoughts now that it is just, she and I left.

"…until you catch on that you are not wanted anymore?" I ask her, with a bittersweet smile. "But don't worry, I'll clap to keep you alive. After all, I do believe you are a skank."

I give her wide eyes of innocence before turning my back to her. Aimes and I clap, loudly, as we walk through the heavy doors, we shout together.

"Clap! Clap if you believe. Clap!" We shout together with our exit.

The men are already preparing to head out into the bitter cold when we catch up to them. They are pulling on the many layers of winter barriers to help reduce the wind chill from the bikes. The sun has not yet fully set, giving the day some warmth, but when it does the temperature will drop with it. The risk of this run is not just the Risen, but Mother Nature as well.

I don't speak with Lawless as I help him slip into his gear. His eyes survey my face in our silence, waiting for me to speak. He is afraid I will run again. I am afraid I will not.

"Be careful," I tell him, when I finally find my voice. "You won't have your zombie bait to find them for you this time."

"I plan on using Chapel." His lips curve with his joke and I wonder how much of a joke it is after our conversation. "I'm kid- ding. It is a simple in-and-out. There is one of those giant super stores back up the road a bit. I doubt the decorating items have been ransacked. Tinsel isn't high on the survival guides."

"Nothing is ever simple." I press my head to his chest before I zip the winter jacket. The small device makes our parting feel final once I pulled it closed.

"Hey," he pulls my face to his so I may not only see him, but also see his words, "I'll be fine. We will be back before you even notice us gone. Don't worry so much. Keep the bed warm for me?" he asks with teasing hopes, bending his body to look into my eyes. Pressing my body against his, I kiss his smirking lips, pulling him deeper into his passion. My tongue explores his mouth, savoring the taste of it before I pull away. His face shows his amusement and enjoyment of my boldness. Let him hope.

One last parting touch and he slips from me, leading them into the courtyard. He never looks back to say goodbye. I did not really expect him to. He has switched to a different man now from the one he just was. He is no longer my Lawless. He is theirs.

Chapel pats my back as he walks past me. He is still sheltering me, lending me his strength as my heart races watching them leave me behind with my many imaginary scenarios of the run. I feel Aimes' hand in mine as the same fears root her to this spot beside me.

The roar of their bikes fills the night with their departure. My warhorse, with Marxx behind her wheel, answers their battle cry with her heavy engine, leading them into their charge. I watch the four grinning skulls fade from my view, feeling my stomach drop when the courtyard gate swings shut behind them.

Sometimes falling in love feels a lot like fear. The heart races with the thought of it. Hands shake with the worry from it. Sometimes, it is even just as life changing when it is upon you.

"I'm going back up. You coming?" Aimes' voice is timid, and her eyes are still glued to the last spot they held for us.

"In a minute."

I know if we both go up together it will be our undoing. Separate, we can force our emotions down, not having to watch them on the face of the other.

"Yeah. Okay," she whispers, heading to the stairway.

I watch her reflection glance back at the gate with every other step she is taking until she is behind her own closed door.

"So just like that?"

Dolph's voice brings my eyes to his direction. He is leaning against the hall with his normal half turn. I meet his eyes in the thick glass mirroring us.

"Just like what?" I ask, watching his face run through many emotions as he carefully chooses his next words before looking back at me.

"After all he has done. Just like that?"

His southern drawl is tighter than normal. His body more twisted from me, keeping him only half invested in the conversation, but those eyes, his eyes watch me so deeply.

"It isn't that simple," I tell his reflection, too scared to face him with his accusations of my weakness and Lawless' actions.

He nods, pulling his bottom lip between his teeth. "Yeah," he tells me, "I guess nothing ever is."

He returns to me the very words I had just told the man whose loyalty Dolph is questioning. We stare at one another's reflection with his words between us before he pulls himself from the wall. I watch him walk away from me the way Aimes watched the gate. He glances back at me one final time before the heavy metal doors close behind him, leaving me alone with his words still echoing in my mind.

I stand alone in the dark hallway, staring out the window at the one black motorcycle they have left behind. Its handlebars are turned, pointing the front of the bike severely, giving it an almost broken look as it stands alone in the courtyard where so many were once placed beside it. Its headlight is ominously watching me from its side of the glass, trying to whisper to me as snow begins to cover it with a soft, white blanket. Like an apparition dissolving from my view, it slowly begins to fade with its black frame obscured by the swirling snow. For reasons unknown, it fills me with dread, sending cold shivers into my soul.

"Please be careful," I whisper to no one, and yet, to everyone at the same time. All I can do now is wait and pray. I can pray.

Chapter 48

Aimes and I sit in our corner like bad little children as we wait patiently for their return. By patiently, I mean feet tapping, window glancing, deep sighing, heart racing and pausing with every sound we hear hopeful it's them. Maybe we are not so, patient after all.

Silence hangs between us. My mouth is dry from my fears and anxiety. I doubt I could form any words right now, much less hold any meaningful conversation. Simon and Richard sit with us as we float in our river of worry. Its current is taking us faster and deeper into horrors we have imagined awaiting them.

"I'm sure they are fine," Richard tells us.

It is his voice, but it is Ross' smile. Neither brings me any com- fort, and looking to Aimes, she is not rejoicing either.

"Knowing them, they have most likely found a deserted bar along the way and have stopped in to see what is left," Richard continues with his oh-so-helpful parade.

"Rhett is probably playing spin the bottle with the Risen." Simon joins in Richard's debate to try to lighten the mood.

"When necrophilia goes both ways?" Aimes is slowly lured out of her silence by their discussion.

"Does it really count as "cold packing" if they are still moving?" Simon shocks me with his knowledge of such topics and his knowledge of Rhett's topics.

The shock brings laughter from Aimes and myself. Simon, always appearing so squeaky clean, holds a hidden dark twist to him. Richard also chuckles with embarrassment over enjoying the joke.

"Dead is dead, right?" Aimes is still giggling with a naughty hilarity.

Paula's words slither into my mind, stealing the laughter from me. "They never really die," she told us. "They never really die." "Shhh," Aimes stands hearing a sound I yet do not. "I think they are back."

The whole floor pauses in activity, as one by one they turn to face the courtyard below us. The roaring becomes louder, and smiles spread throughout, as headlights gleam in the darkness. Conversations grow louder as a welcome home to our antiheroes. I watch from my upstairs window as the courtyard gate swings open admitting their return, but something is wrong. Something is terribly wrong.

Aimes and I run down the flights of stairs with our hearts pumping fear through our bodies with what we both saw from our window. The number was wrong. A single white headlight is missing. Someone did not return with the others. Someone was left behind.

Of all the imagined horrors I have brought forth in my mind, none were as horrible as this. Truth is again daring me to come explore her devious depths. She wants me to come see whom she has stolen from me now. How much of my heart is she about to shred with her evilness?

Truth so hates to be ignored, and we have done just that again. Safe behind these thick walls, we have forgotten how dangerous she can be. So caught up in our pettiness, we lost sight of the real danger lurking all around. Now she is here to remind us of it with the loss of the one who is not here to be with us.

Aimes stops me, holding me to her, to keep me from going out- side once we reach the bottom floor. My truck is blocking them, and I cannot see who is here or not here. Panic builds with my frustration of not knowing the answer. The world seems to have stopped as we wait for

Truth to reveal herself to us and then she does. I will never ignore her again.

Their shapes form from the darkness that encloses the space before us. I recognize each one as they come into the hallway. The one I do not recognize steals my breath and the strength of my body to support me.

I fall wordlessly to the ground, dragging Aimes with me in my defeat. She wraps herself around me rocking us both. Unable to yet breathe, my tears cascade freely from me. My lungs release their pressure from the shock and my first inhale drags a moan from me like a banshee on a high hill. I scream for him as they stand around me, their own grief tearing them apart with mine. My lighthouse is gone. The one black bike that is missing, it is his. "How?" Is all that I can form once my grief is spent. It's such a small fragile word and it can only bring me more pain.

My body is numb and yet, I still rock, fallen on the floor. My eyes see nothing. My hands feel nothing as they shake, sending their refusal to believe it through my arms. My arms that will never hold him to me again.

J.D. leans against the blackened window. He stares at the ceiling with sightless eyes remembering what has happened.

"We were overrun," he begins, and has to stop just as abruptly, with the grief that the memory brings. He breathes in shallow breaths and holds them, trying to get control of himself. "The damn things. They snuck up on us. They were waiting in the   lot. Had the bikes all surrounded. No way to get past them. They watched us ride in on them so they just waited for us to have to ride out."

I know where my small fragile word is taking me and yet, I still have to hear it. I have to know. Truth so hates to be ignored.

"He ran right out there. Never said a word. Just did it. He just ran right out there," he whimpers.

J.D.'s voice breaks as he breaks. His body slides down the wall, unable to support the weight of his grief with what his mind is showing him; the death of the only man he thought of as a son.

"You just left him?" Aimes asks. Her breathing is short and shallow, hyperventilating from her pain.

She does not understand yet. She does not see what is on their faces. Their faces so wet with their grief. Their shoulders are silently shaking on their kneeling bodies all around us in the dark. I do. I understand. Truth so hates to be ignored.

"There was nothing to leave. They left us nothing to leave," J.D. shatters with his words.

Truth is finally with us. Her gown is the color of the blackest of mourning. It's a shade so dark with evil she glistens in it. She dances around us with her presence, spreading her pain like a haunting melody. This melody she is singing will scar us with its words forever.

Lawless will not be coming back to me. So much time I wasted while she waited. So much I left unsaid with my anger. So many things I have done for which I will never be able to apologize, and my moaning starts again with the truth of it.

Truth waited for this night like a bride planning her wedding. Each detail was undertaken with great care. Every moment planned for her perfect night. She and I are wed now with his loss. She will walk with me until the end of my days. Until death do us part. Amen.

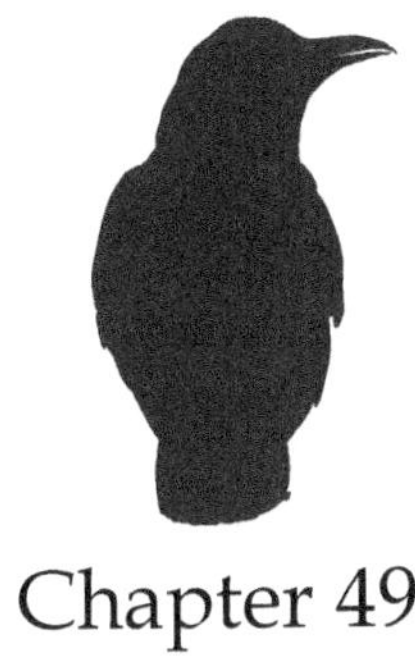

Chapter 49

I dreamt of them that night. Lawless, with his effortless laugh, is chasing Lilly and Conroy around a park on a summer day. The sky above us is a crystal blue with the whitest clouds I have ever seen. A soft, warm breeze caresses my face, chasing away the many tears I have cried. The birds sing their songs of happiness, filling the air with their joy. I watch them play a game of tag that only they understand in the midst of so many other children surrounding them.

Ashley swings beside me. She floats higher and higher as her legs pump and her body sways with the swing. She smiles down at me at the crest of the swing's path, and while I watch her descend, everything changes.

The soft white clouds roll together, forming a grey mass above me. The breeze turns cold with the lack of the summer sun to warm it. I search for them, and by their laughter, I find them still enjoying their game. They run among the many children who turn to stare at them as they go by with faces void of any childhood emotion. Their blank faces are so contrasting with the scene Lawless provides chasing Lilly and Conroy around them that something unsettles my heart.

I stand, confused by the silence the children mold into with their passing. I look to Ashley who is still swinging, still smiling down at me, trying to gather any sense of what is happening. The rhythmic creaking sound of the metal hinges of the swing adds to the unease of the situation.

The colors are fading to shades of greys and contouring blacks. I call to Lawless, trying to get him to see what I am seeing. He waves to me, and Lilly copies it, before tagging him and running away to be chased by him and Conroy. They both wear their coordinating blue pajamas, hers with the dancing bears and his with the cowboys on horses. The soft blue is the only color left around us and it separates them so much more from the watching statues gathered around.

The children stand in waves, synchronized with the creaking of Ashley's swing. Each moan from the metal bringing more of them to their feet and still Lawless does not take notice of them. The children watch the game, silently with hungry, jealous eyes. They are stalking every movement of their prey.

I scream for Lawless, but no sound comes from me. My feet are rooted to the ground, and no matter how hard I pull, or how loud I try to scream, I am stuck motionless and mute. The only sound is the creaking of Ashley's swing and the laughter of those I have lost. I am unable to stop what is about to happen as Margaret comes to stand beside me with her perfect pigtails and their white ribbons of childhood innocence.

The small children have become walking nightmares. Their once pretty and delicate clothing is now many stains of bright reds among the muted shades around them. Soft baby faces melt into grimaces of unnatural rage, exposing dark mouths no longer lined with the pinks of gums and the whites of teeth, but drip- ping black crimsons from unspeakable sins. With the style of a barbaric "Ring Around The Rosie", they encircle Lawless and the two children who are still laughing with their game.

They are frozen around them, snarling and waiting as I attempt to scream. My throat burns with the force of it, but still no sound comes forth from my desperation. I buckle from the strain of it, pleading for them to hear me, but they do not. The ring of children turns to me, smiling with their motives and my body shakes with the horror as their eyes glaze from their once bright colors to dull interpretations.

All at once, they launch at their victims, pulling them down and shredding into them among screams filling the air. Tiny hands pull chunks of flesh, sending it into the air with their destruction. They coat themselves in the murders and all there is to see is red. So much dripping red.

I become weightless with their death, swaying with each breath I take. I feel Margaret's hand grab mine, tugging on me for my attention. Disbelievingly, I look to the red-haired girl beside me with her white ribbon-tied pigtails. She is smiling at me in her blue dress with its white flowers and denim jacket.

"We appear dead, but we aren't. We never really died, until you." Margaret's voice is as sweet as the Serpent's was to Eve and her words are just as damning as her dress slowly starts to become discolored with the blood from the death, I gave her.

"…but we are. We are dead, and it is also because of you," Ashley says in response. She too is slowly becoming the destroyed doll I let her become with her ruined face and torn body.

Ashley is still swinging behind me and her words rain down on me like acid. The metal screeching of the hinges does not cover the wet sounds of the murders taking place or the wet blood, dripping from her as she swings.

I can't look away from the little girl whose hand I am holding. She begins to hum a song. A song of pastel hallways and beady black eyes as she swings our hands in time with Ashley's swing, still clutched together.

"… and everywhere that Helena goes, her lambs are sure to die," Margaret sings and I scream.

I scream, tearing the flesh from my throat with my spare hand as grief rapes my senses.

"Helena! Helena! Breathe. Breathe for me!" I can hear Rhett's voice. It pulls me from this nightmare with the rough shaking of my body. "Helena!"

My lungs burn when my eyes open to see him above me. They force air into them, expanding the pain to cover my whole body as they expand. I cry out with the many images of my dream still so vivid to me, and Rhett cradles me in his arms.

He melts his body to mine, encompassing me in his strength and scent. He holds me and we both cry together, hidden in this dark room with our shared sorrows over what we have lost. I cry with it until my body grows weak, lulling me back to sleep, even as I try to fight against it.

Rhett pulls me tighter into him, wrapping his arms firmer around me with his desire to protect me.

"I'll be right here. Right here," he whispers to me. His voice is thick with his grief and suffering, and it pulls me deeper into mine. "Sleep, Sweetheart. Sleep, and escape." He rocks me gently in his arms, and I feel myself slipping under again.

I want to tell him he is wrong. I cannot escape from what I have done. I want to beg him to keep me awake so I do not have to see them again. But I don't, and the park looms before me again with its blue skies and its emerald green grass.

Chapter 50

She screamed for him most of the night. The rest, she just screamed. Every time I got her calmed down, she would just start back up again."

Rhett's voice eases me into the dawn I am blinking to fight against. I know by the muffled tone he is outside my room and attempting to whisper to someone who waits with him. He has been with me all night. His presence was curled around me when the demons came to play, and they played their dark games well. The scene might have changed, but it was always the same.

Lawless and my Angels stolen, massacred by child-like demons in front of me while I was unable to stop it. Their bodies were torn and mutilated with the children's anger as I tore the flesh from my body myself. Sometimes Ashley would be an added sin, or an added sinner, as she and Margaret stood there damning me for my past.

I feel no more rested from my night's sleep than a marathon runner feels after a race. My body aches with it, unable to move from the tight ball I have become. I can feel where my nails have raked my real flesh. It's as sore and raw feeling as the rest of me. I don't want to move. I just want to stay here forever, unwilling to face the first day without Lawless.

For brief moments, I am convinced I can smell him on the cot we shared. Small pockets of his scent will wrap around me so quickly, and fade just as rapidly, leaving me feeling betrayed with their departure. A shirt of his still lies on the floor where he left it. It's a coiled snake with its dark hissing of what I have lost, what I had only hours ago and what I took for granted. I told him I never thought of him because I thought he would always be here. He would always be with me. I was wrong and now all I can do is think of him.

Rhett has come to kneel in front of me, blocking the view of the snake and its hissing. I am aware of him, but I do not see him. I feel his touch gently pushing my hair from my face, but it does not move me. I am finally drowning from this new world and I hope my last breath is soon.

"You need to eat," he pleads.

His voice is whisper-soft with his concern. Even as I hear him, he does not reach me. He sighs, sliding down to the cold, tiled floor to sit with his back to me. We both stare at the crumpled discarded cotton shirt on the floor, afraid of it with the memories it holds.

"He was a good kid. Real good. A little cocky with that ego of his when it came to the girls, but a good kid. How the girls loved his attention. That smirk of his could drop panties for miles," Rhett chuckles with his memories. "Not just white cotton either, he had everything from G-strings to silk. Until he met you. One look and done. You put up a good fight. Had him chasing his own tail like a whipped puppy. That boy would go out with us, brawl all night or whatever we had to do, then return to the bar to stare all moon-eyed at you. Funniest shit I had ever seen."

"Why are you telling me this?" My voice is harsh and gravel-filled, interrupting his memory lane.

"One of us needs to talk." He shrugs as if it is nothing more than a discussion over what to have for breakfast, not the burial of my soul.

"I don't want to talk." I stare at the grey shirt and I can see Lawless in it.

"Then you will listen."

I wonder if Rhett is seeing him, too. "I don't want to listen."

He wore it just two days ago. I am the one that took it off of him. "I knew he was going to do it. I saw it on his face. The way he handed his bag to Marxx, I knew. It's my job to keep him safe. It was supposed to be me. To stand by him, you know, when it gets real. That is my job," Rhett says.

I do not want to listen, but Rhett ignores my request. I don't want the details. I have seen him die plenty in my dreams from last night to fill me with enough wet, red details but I listen. He kept watch over me, now I keep watch for him.

"The little punk knew I wouldn't let him go. He clocked me right in the face. Sent me down for just a second to distract them all. Then, just like what J.D. said, he ran out there. Just ran right the fuck out there. Never looked back."

Rhett holds his head between his bent knees as the memories take him. He is shielding his eyes as if he could hide from what he is seeing. I know he can't. You cannot hide from your own demons. They are yours and you own them as much as they own you.

"They were on him so quickly. Soon as he ran out, they ran after him. Hell followed him. Hell followed him all the way down. There was nothing I could do. I promise you, there was nothing we could have done," he is almost pleading for some forgiveness. I have no words of comfort to give him. I am selfish in my own mourning and I do not have the energy to carry another. I hold my words behind my locked jaw, gifting him with only my silence. "I'll sit here as long as you need. I won't let anyone near you until you are ready. As long as it takes, Helena," he tells me this, as another man told me something so similar only days ago.

"Why?" At the sound of my voice, he twists around to see me. "Why what?" His voice is soft with concern again as he stares at me. I must be having a very bad hair day.

"Why are you doing this? Before all of this, you never said a word to me. I was taught to steer clear of you, for my own good. Guilt that bad?"

I did not mean for the words to come out this rough, but they have. He flinches from their implications, and for a second, I feel my own guilt before a cold numbing wave washes over me again. "Part of it," he says, returning to staring at the wall ahead of us. "When you first came to us, you were what, fifteen? Sixteen? Just a kid. Kids don't last long in our world. Shit, grown adults don't always last long in our world. We aren't about people pleasing. You come in. You earn your spot and you keep earning it. It doesn't ever stop. It breaks people down.

J.D. breaks people down." He smirks his twisted smile of enjoyment. "The things we do. Tears some of them right up. Only a real few really make it inside. Where it counts. Where the trust is earned."

He stalls with a chuckle before continuing.

"Like Law. You wouldn't believe the bets that boy had against him. We put him through so much just to watch and laugh at him. He did it all though. Not saying he didn't bitch about it, but he did it. No matter what you needed. No matter how mad he was with someone. If he was needed, he did it."

Rhett sighs, rubbing his face with his hands. I guess I am not the only one whose memories ride them now.

"Now seven years later, here we are," he breathes deep before starting again. "Still here. Still together. Still fighting. Fighting things, a little differently than I thought we would ever be, but still fighting. I've watched you grow up. Maybe your life should have been more proms and parties than bar fights and stitches, but you stuck with it. You've earned your spot, Helena, and you keep earning it. You're a pretty girl. Smart. Stubborn, a little too stubborn. Before all this, with their social norms on age, would I have enjoyed our games?"

He pauses, letting the question float between us while he debates it.

"Yeah, probably." He shrugs, unashamed in his lack of care for society. "It's all changed now. Who knows what the rules are? If there are even rules. I sit here not out of guilt, but because I care about you.

Plus, you have this soft little moan you make in your sleep that does it for me."

I can see the smile on his face without him having to look at me. "Perv," I say, nudging him with my knee, and even as I try to fight the smile, I lose.

"Takes one to know one, Sweetheart." He does turn to me now wearing the smile of his that lures so many women to their doom. "You ready to go down and get some food?"

"No," I tell him, feeling myself fading again as my smile leaves me. "…but you're going to anyway."

His smile has left us now, too. He understands me so well. "…but I'm going to anyway."

A little too well.

Chapter 51

I walk to the gallows would have been easier than walking to the cafeteria. Eerily, with the many sad faces around me, it feels the same. Rhett parts the crowd, which has grown the way well-wishers do at the most inappropriate times. Marxx walks behind me, keeping them from overtaking me with their sad eyes and the need to touch me, giving me false comfort as they gain their own. It is hard for them to think of someone they saw as being so formidable lost to us. It brings their own fears of their fates too close to their surface. If one of us can fall, then what chances do they have?

Every step we take holds a visual ghost for me. The phantoms are the strongest in the suffocating stairwell where so many moments were shared. Fate is strangling me with dawn upon us. The sun reaches every dark corner, forbidding me to hide from her.

"Just keep one foot in front of the other," Marxx encourages me, as the distance grows between Rhett and myself with each failing step of mine.

Rhett has gotten too far ahead. The darkness of my mind with its black grief slams into me with the fact Lawless should be between he and I. It clenches everything in my body with the force of a fist colliding with a wall.

"I can't breathe," I whisper.

Marxx wraps his arms around me, helping me to sit upon hearing my words.

He holds my back against his chest, rocking me with his body, telling me, "Yes, you can."

I shake my head as panic sets in with the sensation.

Rhett backtracks, running to where Marxx and I sit. He catches my head in his hands, steadying it so I am forced to look at him. "You can do this. Just look at me. Breathe with me," Rhett is chanting, and I fight the dark shadow holding me a prisoner to hear him.

Together Rhett and I focus on filling our lungs with patterned inhales and exhales and nothing else. Slowly the pain subsides as the panic leaves me. My numbness penetrates the space it once filled, and I feel weaker with its cold blanket around me.

"That one wasn't so bad." Marxx helps me stand when my sagging body disobeys me.

"That one?" I ask him.

I feel as if I am walking on quicksand. Each step could be my last should it suck me below forever.

"You'll have more. Each time a little less till there are no more." Marxx' hands rest on my waist and guide me down the stairs behind Rhett once again.

I want to ask him what it is he is talking about, but with the numbness chilling me and Rhett unable to look at me as he collects himself, I lack the energy to care. Besides, every time I ask a question the answers just get worse. Perhaps I should save some answers for later, before I am so far into them, I have none to spare. When the noise from the cafeteria hits me, I have a lot less than just answers. I have lost all my bravery to continue.

At what point is it okay for me to go running off screaming, regretting my decision to do this? The answer? Five minutes. Now, six minutes passed, I am fully regretting not running off screaming back up the stairs. I have a good idea of what I would scream, too.

Breakfast is painfully silent as we all feel his loss. There are muffled condolences as people go by. Each time I begin to breathe normally, someone leans in to remind me of what I cannot forget. It's a vicious cycle of my endless regrets, brought on by those who only mean well with their soft touches and silent nods. That is normally how bad things happen. People always mean well. When Rhett has reached his breaking point, his glares keep even the sincerest at bay.

"We should hold a funeral," Aimes says as she is making her idea of art again on her plate.

I have no clue as to what it may have started out. I have no clue what it is ending up as either.

With no one agreeing with her, she pouts harder, taking her emotions out on the artwork.

"We should do something. It's Larance," she whispers his name like a Catholic at Mass, holding it sacred upon her lips.

"We will." Of course, the Preacher's son would volunteer, as the rest of the men sit stone-faced and sour with their grief.

"Tonight. Around the fire. He would like that." Aimes' masterpiece of oatmeal, and something thicker, is clumping from her abuse.

"He's dead. He doesn't care what we do now. He's gone." J.D.'s anger is startling among such levels of silence.

I almost welcome his rage. It feels more real than the sad faces and long stares of the sheep.

"It's not for him. It's for us." Chapel attempts to calm the beast beside him. It only propels J.D.'s rage deeper.

"You want to do something? You want to ease that suffering of yours? You want to paint the facts of what happened to him all pretty-like? Then get off your padded assess and get out and kill them things instead of holding up here like cowards. He died a man. The rest of us, we are just gonna die. There is your pretty little fact," J.D. says. His voice carries through the cafeteria with the depths of his anger.

The families closest to us huddle their children to them with protective arms. Some begin to whisper as the fears they have been thinking all morning long are now in vocal form floating around them. Soon, the room becomes alive with the whispered hissing of fear and the many different reactions it causes around us.

"You want to light a nice pretty fire? Gather all around it? Share your precious little memories? Tell yourself his death was worth it?

That he lived a long and full life? That these sheep are worth more than our man?" J.D. is staring into the souls of the men around the table. He sneers as he says, "Then you go right ahead. Go right ahead. Don't be looking for me to be standing out there. I know the real truth. This whole place just got a whole hell of a lot weaker without him. We keep getting messed up and they keep sittin' safe and pretty behind these walls. We are done."

J.D. stands, staring at the many frightened faces around us. They clutch their children tight to them, trying to protect them from his anger. Tiny wide eyes peer around shoulders with an innocent curiosity.

"Yeah, you hear me," he shouts to those staring at him. "All   of you do. We are done. You want your supplies? Then you take your candy asses out there. You want your high fences all safe so you can sleep at night? Pick one of your fat bastards to go out there. And tell me," J.D. pauses with the heat of his anger to chuckle with his thought, "tell me how when food is in such a high demand, so many of you are so fucking fat? I got your weight loss plan right here. We gonna gather all of you up, tie you together and say run. You run for your lives for a day or two. Dangle you fat bastards out there for those things while we stroll around watching it all."

He laughs now, fully lost in his mental image of the event. One of us should stop him. By one of us, I mean one of the men. I am enjoying the show. My own small laugh joins with his. Yes, I'm a bad person. I'm becoming okay with it.

"Oh man, I would sell tickets to that shit. Watching your upper crust, with your still pressed linens at the end of the world, running for your over-priced lives. It would be golden," J.D. says.

He turns to me, taking my laugh as an endorsing agreement. "What is it you say, Hells? The cherry? The cherry would be to see how many of you sheep would actually run or just stand there cryin' and pissin' on yourselves. Yeah, that would be the cherry." The laughter dies from him as suddenly as it came over him now as he looks to us. His steel eyes burn with the pits of his rage. "So, if you want to throw a little going away party, you go right ahead. But me, I know our man died for nothing. These sheep, they don't even care. They will kill us all off before they lift a finger for themselves."

"He died for us. He died so we could make it home. Don't tarnish that." Chapel stands, staring at our leader and trying to edge him down.

"Yeah man, I guess he did. I guess he did." J.D.'s agreement is more unsettling than his rage.

I know there are more hidden thoughts in his mind to that statement than he is expressing. The way his eyes roam the room only proves it. The Devil may walk the earth outside, but he may have his match waiting for him inside.

"Whatever you are thinking, don't." Chapel is also watching the stillness slide over J.D.

Predators do that before it goes graphic. The prey must be located and watched for weakness. There is a lot of pretty, pretty prey around us for J.D to pick from.

It is not the sheep that his need to destroy something lands on first. It was so fast and sudden the room erupted with the shock of it. Even our men, so well attuned to the shifts around them, missed the clues reminding them why we should always fear J.D.

J.D. swings, fully connecting his fist with Chapel's face, knocking him to his knees. His head bounces off the table as Chapel succumbs to the force, so unprepared for it and the damage it does. Blood already pools between his cupped fingers holding his face.

Our leader hauls Chapel up and onto the table by the vest they love so much, pinning him to the table on his back. J.D. tugs on the vest as if he is looking for something that he can't find before securing Chapel to the table. This time, he uses Chapel's throat to press him to the table and leans in, keeping his words between those closest to him.

"I don't see a rank on this vest of yours. There is just your name, son. You ain't earned the right to talk to me. I give it to you. Which means you sure as hell don't have the right to tell me what I should or shouldn't do. You ain't nothing more than a chair warmer around my table. You got me, son?" J.D.'s voice is viper deadly. One wrong move and he will strike with poison so deadly it will cripple Chapel.

"Yeah, I got you. Want to call a vote?" Chapel's question is acid to the other man's poison with his bleeding nose still spilling forth.

"There ain't nothing to vote on, son. Unless you want me to call it on your place by my side?" J.D.'s threat hangs heavy in the air. "I'm just a seat warmer, remember? I'm not by your side."

Chapel shoves J.D. off him, tired of the threats, he does not flinch under the steel eyes upon him the way so many do.

Rhett steps between the two when Dolph and Richard arrive. Their added presence will only intensify J.D.'s needs to force Chapel into submission. That is the one thing Chapel will never do again, and as he stands toe-to-toe with J.D., we all know it.

"If you two want to play touch-my-ego, we need to go else- where," Rhett tells both men as he watches the area around him. Dolph and Richard have noticed the room's anxiety and it is not hard for them to figure out the source. It's a visual tennis match with the residents watching the two groups from their sidelines.

Make it three groups as Ross and Leslie stroll in.

It is a piñata of a morning, as I get beat from all angles. Tie a rope around my neck and hang me in a tree. Let's just call this done already.

Ross is showering Leslie with his support as the woman sags with her movements. Her sobs are evident with the amount of shoulder motion she portrays. Ross' smile is nowhere to be found with his mouth moving so rapidly to smother her in comforting words. Ironically, watching them, my smile is firmly in place. Funny the things we find amusing when we feel we have nothing left to lose.

"You have got to be kidding me. Skankerbell is totally not trying to sponge. Shiv her, Rhett. Shiv her!" Aimes demands as our ever-darling pixie once again shares with us her true feelings about the situation.

"Don't tempt me," Rhett mutters, watching the two who have seated themselves across from our table. "I already promised Law that coward would die for what he did. I am about ready to cash in that chip."

I remember a day not too long ago where Lawless and Rhett both stood staring down Ross with a mutual understanding between them. Ross has been very careful with his presence. I guess some- one is feeling braver now. I guess also he forgot their vests are not black because of their grief. They are black because of the grief they cause others. I think he is about to be reminded of the fact.

"We can do that," J.D. agrees with Rhett, patting the man's shoulder as he slides by in their table's direction. "We can do that really well."

"Not here," Rhett stops him with the sound of regret in his voice. "We can't. Not here. Not with what I have planned for him. Not now. I will make it perfect."

"We are going to make a lot of things perfect real soon," J.D. says.

We watch him walk away, leaving his statement hanging in the air like a cloud of poison. It will choke someone, somewhere, soon. It will not be a quick death. It's going to be bloody. The casualties will be numerous.

Chapter 52

You really going to this thing?" J.D. brushes my dark hair as he watches my reflection in the square bathroom mirror of the restroom.

It's longer now than I normally wear it. Something with its new length encourages the men to touch it and play with it in an unconscious fashion. It freaks me out a little. The fact J.D. is standing behind me brushing it, freaks me out a lot.

I shrug, not having a real answer for him. I do feel a little silly going to this bonfire. I also know how painful it will be to hear, and share, in the memories passed along tonight. The bonfire farewell is not a new event for me. This is how G.R.I.T. says goodbye to their lost brothers.

A funeral demands a certain level of decorum. It's a respect being paid not only for their passing, but also for their family's grief. Depending on the rank of the brother, the trail of motor- cycles can extend for miles to show the family a sign of support and to let the community know the level of respect he held in their world. Aimes and I have often rode surrounded by so many somber men repressing their grief. Men do not handle such emotions well. That's the purpose of the bonfire.

It's a true farewell for them. Hours will be spent swapping stories of the deceased, which can only be shared in their circle. The stories they share would have wives, or girlfriends, livid, ruining their memories of the man.

Drinks will be passed. Stories will be swapped. Memories will be shared. It is their way of saying goodbye. Not with their tears and sobbing, but with their laughter and the camaraderie of their club.

"Why aren't you going?" I ask, watching him become still at my words.

"I have things to do."

I shiver under the intensity of his eyes. I watch their shade melt from blue to the steel, ice coloring of his mood swing.

"Are you asking for my help?"

His eyes have never left mine. They don't know either.

"Tell me, Hells, why don't you want pay back? Convince me they don't need to pay for this," he says. His voice is neutral, its deadliest tone.

"It wasn't their fault." I say these words out loud, but my heart beats a different pattern with my thoughts.

A part of me I am not proud of does agree with J.D. It's our men who have sat in the cold night's air watching the perimeter while the others slept in warm beds. It's our men who have helped hunt and supply food while so many just show up for meals. It's Marxx who might be permanently disabled with the extent of tissue damage done from their testing of us. Now we have lost Lawless. How many more scars do we obtain while the rest remain untouched?

"Don't say that. Not you, too," he growls with his grief.

J.D. throws the brush he was just using in my hair against a far stall door with his disappointment in me churning into rage. It shatters, filling the room with the loud noise of its destruction.

I wasn't really done with it, but I am not sure now is the time to point it out to him.

"Out of all of them, I thought you would be the one to agree with me. You have always seen things better than the rest. You always know what has to be done. You may not like it, but you and I, we get things done," he tells me.

His face is one of pleading to understand him, to help him. J.D. is one minute from falling to his knees asking for my support. It scares me more than any fit of rage, or threat, he has ever said to me. His hands wrap around my shoulders with a strength making me afraid I will hear the cracking of my bones under them.

"We can do this. You and I, we can right this. We can take over this place, as we should have when we first walked in here. Instead, we take orders from a bunch of sheep. Simon, that man would jump at his own shadow if Dolph wasn't there to stroke him off. This is what we take orders from? Us? Rhett wanted to kill them all when we first got here. You know that? Slice them right up in their sleep. I should have let him. We might still be whole now if I had let him. We can make them pay for it all. No more games or trying to play nice with them. We can't get him back. We can never have my boy back. But we can get them back for it."

J.D. folds over with the pain of his words, bringing him to the ground beside me.

"They took my boy. They took my boy, Hells. I watched them take my boy," J.D. whispers, rocking with his mental destruction from his grief.

His eyes are seeing something far away. He is somewhere so deep within his pain to a place I cannot go with him. I sit on the cold tiles beside him and do the only thing I can. I hold his hand while he cries. We do not acknowledge it. We just sit in the silence of the room around us, and support one another, until we are strong enough to stand again.

His body maybe warm, sitting beside me, but his mind has escaped from the room around us and his eyes are cold with wherever he is. The room echoes with the words he keeps repeating in his pain. Each time he says them, my heart sinks a little lower.

"My boy. They took my boy," he says over and over again, tearing us each a little more every time he does.

We sit for hours on the cold floor together. I almost startle when he turns to me with how accustomed I had become to his behavior. He stares at me as if he does not recognize me before kissing my forehead and standing.

"You're a good girl, Helena. Don't let anyone tell you otherwise. Ever."

His voice trails behind him as he leaves me sitting there, still confused and startled by his random actions.

The walk alone to the bonfire refills my numbness. My eyes see what is ahead of me, but my brain does not admit to the images. It blocks the many sad faces around me and the still bare evergreen tree, which mocks my mood.

My numbness shields the sighs of Leslie sitting in what is our corner with many people surrounding her, giving her comfort. It keeps the view of Ross, who now wears his smile, from my fragile state. If only it could remove the sounds as well. Maybe if I clap loud enough? Nope, they are still there, but Leslie isn't as weepy anymore as I exit the door. Small bonus.

The winter wind bites my face with its dark hello as I step into the courtyard. It sucks the air from my lungs with its kiss as I make my way to the little family I have acquired, standing around one of the barrels. The fire casts sparks and shadows into the air around them. Their faces glow with the warmth-giving light. It is beautiful to watch.

"You're late," Aimes tells me with a hug and smile.

I embrace her back, letting our past finally bury itself. This is what he would have wanted. It's what I want.

"J.D. isn't coming, "Marxx says.

Marxx is not asking me. He is accepting the fact by admitting it out loud. I know he sees this as an insult, and as much as I want to explain what happened three floors up, I remain silent. J.D.'s grief is not mine to share.

A bottle is passed to me and I take a deep drink before I look to see what it is. The fire in the barrel is not the only source of heat as the liquid slips past my tongue. My throat and stomachache as the liquid slides down them, bringing coughs and rapid motions of my spare hand. Male laughter builds around me as my body burns from their betrayal.

"I wanted to warn you, but they thought this would be more amusing to watch." Aimes takes the bottle of dark liquid from me. "Somewhere these clowns found whiskey and scotch. Neither was enough to make a full bottle, so what did Rhett-stein decide to do? Mix them. Clap for, Rhett. He is very proud of himself."

Rhett reaches for the bottle, and in a salute to his brilliance, he takes a long drink. He mockingly shudders at me when he finishes.

His eyes glow with his amusement when he says, "Got to love it when a plan comes together. Want another?"

He points the bottle at me with a smile. My rejection only adds to their mirth. The fire in my belly only adds to my resolve to never take a bottle from Rhett again.

"Law would drink it. He could out drink us all." With that, Marxx has started the bonfire. "He would never admit to the hangover the next day."

"Do you remember that one St. Patrick's? The next day we had a charity ride. The boy kept calling for a break to hide the fact he was losing his guts in the bushes," Rhett laughs with the memory. "Getting sick on the tot-banger that day though, that was priceless," Marxx adds to the story and the laughter from the men. "Do I even want to ask?" Aimes caustically voices her concern over Lawless' past.

I know the story, so I just smile.

"No. No you don't," I tell her, and with the admittance of knowing the story, the men form a complete uproar of laughter.

"I miss his music. He always had that beat up black guitar with him." Aimes shifts the mood with her memory.

"He made up some twisted songs." Chapel smiles and we are back on track. "Singing about drunken hookers and addicts with his face all serious. I don't know how he kept serious with it as the rest of us were losing it all around him."

We all laugh with the memory of his antics. The way he would walk around Grit strumming that black guitar of his while strolling from table-to-table, making up lyrics using those he came across as the subjects. Each lyric would become more ridiculous than the last with his twisted sense of humor. There was not a topic he wouldn't twist into a song for his amusement.

"I didn't think he'd survive his mom's death," Marxx pulls from a different pool now. "Even when she had him arrested for de- fending her from his old man, he was still there for her. He took a lot of blows that were meant for her. He was always there for her." "That's how he was," Rhett's sentence pulls a cord too recent in my heart. "If he cared for you, he was there. No questions. No judgments. Just how he was."

The turn of the memories requires the men to pass the dark bottle around as each mentally is reliving their own version of it. "He was loyal. Never asking whys or how's. He did what he had to do. Then he buried it." Rhett stares at the crackling fire, seeing something other than what is before him. "He did shit no one should ever have to do. He did it for the club. He did it for J.D."

The men grunt their approval of Rhett's words. The fire has become a safe beacon for their eyes, and they watch it, trying to not drown with their memories. The bottle makes another round. "That damn bike of his. I wanted to kick his ass when he showed up with that V-Rod." Rhett brings the mood back around again, with another long draw from the bottle.

I am not helping them carry this large man up the three flights of stairs when his concoction kicks his ass.

"…. until he left your ass behind on it," Chapel taunts Rhett with his smile.

"No, then I wanted to kick his ass twice," Rhett's answer revitalizes their laughter.

"You would have to catch me first, Old Man."

The voice freezes us faster than winter's deep kiss. My heart climbs into my throat when I hear it. The feel of his arms sliding around me unhinges my knees, making him catch me, pulling me close to him. I feel his lips on my temple, and as if he pushed a button, scalding tears escape.

"You have to catch me to kick my ass," Lawless says with a smile at the stunned faces standing around the barrel. "Y'all look like you've seen a ghost."

"This is so much better than a Ouija board," Aimes whispers, before springing into him with ear shattering squeals.

Laughter fills the courtyard now, his laughter, my tears and Aimes' squeals of joy vibrate the walls around us. This is not one of my haunting ghosts that demand to walk beside me. This is not a judging memory to shred me with its presence. Lawless stands beside us with his warm eyes watching me, battle worn and tired. Only Aimes is secure enough in her emotions to fully embrace him as the rest stare wide-eyed and slacked faced at someone we had thought forever gone from us.

Truth howls in the winter winds that whip around us with the disappointment of her failure, and I know she is plotting to make us pay for this victory over her.

I'll pay it. I'll give her my soul. My lighthouse has found me.

Chapter 53

"Pass me the bottle, would you?" Lawless asks, holding his hand out to Rhett.

Lawless still takes all of this calmly as if it is everyday someone walks back from the grave to visit their own memorial. I guess, giving everything, we have seen, it sort of is.

Aimes is huddled under one of his arms, her tears freezing like crystals on her cheeks with the openness of her emotions. Lawless knows I am not as brave with my emotions and he's giving me the space I need to collect myself from the shock. A task at which I am failing with my breath still caught in my lungs and my eyes still too large as I stare at him.

"How the fuck...," is all Rhett says, as he hands the bottle across the fire.

The statement is repeated in the men's faces around us.

"I told you. You have to catch me to kick my ass." Lawless drinks deeply from the bottle, keeping his eyes on the man across from him. His eyes shine with laughter at their perplexed looks.

Chapel steps closer to him, the first of the three, wrapping him in a giant hug mixed with many hard, echoing pats on each other's back. Aimes has to escape from their bonding before her small frame is broken between them. She switches to my side, holding my hand, as we watch the men rebuild their bonds.

Marxx walks over next, shaking his head with a smile upon his face and he embraces Lawless for a little longer than their "guy code" would normally allow.

"You are one tough son of a bitch and just as dumb," Marxx says with a voice more gravel-filled than moments ago as a new emotion stirs inside him.

Marxx roughly rubs Lawless' head, shaking him with his joy of seeing him again. The three men now stand laughing together and patting their backs. Chapel and Marxx are lost in their amusement and pride of the one who they thought they had lost. Rhett stands alone still watching them. His face is locked tight from any escape of emotion. His eyes roam from one man to the

other watching, but not joining.

"I saw you. I saw what was left of you. I saw what they did to you. I've seen it each time I close my eyes." Rhett's voice brings stillness to those around him.

It is icy, and frost ridden, with his confusion. Anger treads lightly on the tips of his words.

"It wasn't me," Lawless drinks the dark liquid as memories form for him. "It was one of those damn parking lot dogs who always seem to be lurking around. It was huge. The type of dog, that if a bunch of people who eat other people weren't screaming behind me, I would have been afraid of. Fido wasn't so scary after the stuff we've seen."

Lawless pauses. Each word seems to lower his head as he seeks the answers for Rhett's confusion.

"The damn thing ran right at me when it saw me," he says when he speaks again, "being so used to strangers for its survival. I kicked it. Kicked it hard enough to break something. They fell upon it. It never had a chance the way they tore into it. They spread it wide. I just wanted it out of my way. I never meant…."

He pauses again, taking a deep breath and exhaling it. His breath floats around him as the temperature drops, anticipating the ending of his tale.

"I've seen it every time I close my eyes, too." Lawless takes another long drink from the bottle to dull the guilt he is feeling. "That wreck a bit back along the road, I jimmied the trunk of one of those cars. It wasn't the warmest bed I have ever had, but I figured all the dead from the wreck still in their cars would cover my tracks from those things. It was still another full day's walk this morning. These boots were made for a lot of things, walking isn't one of them." He smiles, encouraging Rhett to relax.

Rhett and I both have yet to come to terms with him being here now. We are locked tight behind our wall of emotional safety. We had just begun to accept his death, to fully embrace the fact of it and the pain that goes along with that. Now he is here, and our minds do not sync with our hearts. One is screaming how impossible it is, while the other beats in celebration. Our wires are crossing, refusing to connect the two and it's a recipe for a bomb that could destroy more than the building around us.

Lawless turns to me slowly, with timid steps, not risking the chance of my spooking with his sudden movements. His cold hands slide along my neck and into my hair, pulling my forehead to his. He stares into my eyes, trying to reach behind the wall he has so declared as a source of his suffering.

"I told you I would always come for you," he says, staring into my green eyes.

With his whisper, my wall is broken. The bricks are tumbling down around us, and he catches me in his embrace with his arms and with his lips.

I cling to him in our kiss. It deepens with the need to comfort one another. He feeds me the reassurance that he is really here. I feed him the relief of making it home. Winter sends her tears at our reunion as snow begins to drift around us. She blesses us with her cold sprinkling of frozen water, sealing our souls together again.

Rhett's sharp catcall of a whistle cuts through her approval as the men around us give their own with clapping and jeering. It makes Lawless kiss me deeper as he fights the forming smile on his lips. Still, all the noise they make, it is not enough to cover the sound of the first shot fired. Nor is it enough to cover the screams following it.

Chapter 54

Screams shred the celebration with many sets of razor-sharp talons. Windows flash, white bright, accompanying each shot that cracks like a drum inside the walls of the third floor. J.D.'s words roll back through my mind as I listen to the soundtrack of horror from above. The men are already running into the high school, preparing clips and loading chambers without a second thought of what may be occurring above us. Lawless slips from my arms, sliding down them until we can no longer hold to the other with his exit. I should have listened to the wind. I might have heard Truth's plotting if I had.

"This is going to be bad, isn't it?" Aimes stands beside me as we watch the men in our lives once again run into danger.

The screams seem worse now being alone in the dark with them radiating all around us with an illusion of their source. We both know pure terror is waiting for us inside, but our protectors, and our family, are in there also. Damned if we do….

The first body lays twisted, and distorted, in the hallway we enter. I cover Aimes' mouth to stifle her screams, still unsure of what to expect deeper in. Unseeing eyes stare at us as we tiptoe past the body, but even in death, he seems to watch us.

I expect his body to twitch towards us at any moment with how his eyes seem to follow us. The blood is already thick and discoloring around his fallen form. The broken neck gives the body a more visually disturbing allure than normal as his head rests at the wrong angle. I know this image is now stored with so many other sources of nightmares for me.

The heavy metal doors are propped open by something we cannot yet see. Everything inside me clues me in to the fact it won't be something I want to see and yet I creep closer anyway. "Sometimes I give myself very good advice, but I seldom follow it," said Alice when in Wonderland. There is nothing to wonder about in this land and I seldom follow any advice.

Legs are stuck between one of the doors keeping it open. A fragile ankle is twisted the wrong way in broken stilettos. Her toes point with rebellion in the opposite direction of her other leg. The heavy door has slammed against her legs, lacerating them. Her blood mingles around her in separate thick, cooling pools with her twisted legs blocking their joining.

Aimes shudders, hiding behind me. The many constant screams only adding to the climate of the room. I push against the other door and feel it rub against something before opening. The sharp metal edge of the door's bottom has serrated the flesh on the woman's face. Blood oozes, but does not flow, from where the flesh once sat. It gives her face an evil mask of dark crimson as it coats her, slipping into her once pretty features. The cause of her death still protrudes from her blood-soaked chest. It is J.D.'s hunting knife.

Shouting now melds with the screams from above and it fills us with a false energy to run up the steps. There are more bodies waiting to shock us with their tortured deaths as we climb. I pull on Aimes, keeping her close to me, as we avoid deep pools of dripping crimson as it slides down the stairs and the outspread limbs of the dead waiting to trip us. We focus our eyes on the space above the steps, praying to save our minds from what lies all around.

Sometimes it works. Sometimes you can't help but see. When have I ever been one not to look?

We rush through the final set of doors, hoping to leave one nightmare behind us, but we have only stepped into a much more horrific version of it. Bodies lay dropped like used dolls around the common area. The walls are bathed in the brutality of their murders, dripping with the evidence of it. So many sightless eyes stare in random directions and they all seem to find their way   to the double doors behind us as if positioned to do so. It is as if

J.D. wanted whoever enters this hall to be seen by the dead and judged for not being here to save them.

The mammoth evergreen now wears a cloak that Red Riding Hood would envy. Like the decorations it has been waiting for, its branches are heavy with the gore shimmering in the moonlight. It's now alight with red-rimmed remnants of those who once sat around it and it sparkles more than any tinsel, we could have applied to it with their death coating it.

It even has a topper now, as in some strange act of karma, a real doll has been thrown into the branches. It rests there with a smiling face and its arms spread wide for the one who used to own it to save it. It too wears the red baptismal of their deaths. I know the owner of this doll. My mouth grows dry as I remember the little girl dancing it across this same floor with Simon watching her.

We step over the many dead residents as their faces match with memories and their damning eyes stare coldly at us while we try to make our way to the shouting. Aimes is whimpering from the sights around us as her panic flutters in her chest. She slips on a pool of thick substance, falling into it as it applies a thick covering to her body. I pull her to my shoulder as she vocally releases the buildup of her terror when seeing the cold film on her body. Her scream is ear shattering just as Ashley's had been.

I pull her with me as I walk backwards through the hall. I keep her head down, sparing her the chest full of new materials to feed our nightmares. I don't let her see the red smears from the falling bodies that are resting against the walls. I hide the handprints on the floor as a few tried to drag their bleeding bodies to safety. Most of all, I save her from the children who are now mingling with the other dead.

The many broken, porcelain dolls who lay limp and shattered around us. Red flowers bloom underneath their bodies with petals that reach long and wide. Their winter pajamas once in soft shades of childhood innocence are now turning dark shades of corruption with what has been done to them.

I recognize one of them and even as I had expected to find her here, my stomach clenches with her death. Sweet, laughing Kira stares up at the ceiling from her deathbed. J.D. did not shoot her. No, that would have been too easy for such a perfect victim for his rage. Her head lies unevenly with the damage from her crushed skull supporting it incorrectly. Dark fragments and long streaks of thick substances have been splattered around her broken head from the viciousness of the assault.

Her fingers are disjointed and bent at strange angles from her desperate attempts to fight against the large man for her life. The long tee shirt is crumpled, raised upon her legs she had used to kick at him, exposing too much of such an innocent. She never stood a chance and yet she fought. Everything about her utterly still form says she fought against her death. It makes it so much more tragic than the rest.

I spare Aimes from this even as I absorb it all. The blood running together in thick dark rivers between the grout of the tiles, the bodies spread wide across the spaces who seem to watch us as we creep past and the heavy scent of the slaughter is waiting with sharp teeth to tear into my sanity when I sleep, but I do my best to spare my best friend from it all. The way I failed to do   it for others who had counted on me to do just this same exact thing for them.

A door opens to our left, startling us both. A man waves us over through the small crack the opening provides for him. His eyes are wide with the horrors he has witnessed tonight.

"They got him cornered down there. You'll be safe in here," he says, and his voice is barely a whisper with his fears.

"Go," I tell Aimes as I push her to the door. "Don't open this door until one of us comes for you."

My words bring her to a level of awareness she has tried from which to hide. Her face is no longer fear-filled. It is sadness she wears now, furrowing her soft features.

"I can't just sit by," I tell her as an apology for leaving her here. "I know. You always were the strong one."

She hugs me as the screams start again. This time I know the voice who holds it. J.D. has found Shelia.

Chapter 55

Lawless, Chapel and Rhett stand with pointed guns at J.D. He is holding his own long handgun to Shelia's temple. His black vest shines under the moon's light with the many layers of his victims dripping from it. His handshakes with confusion and fear at the sight of Lawless standing in front of him. The gun in his hand trembles against Shelia, unsettling her more with its vibration.

Ross leans against the wall, bent over from a wound to his stomach staining his clothing. Richard is pressing his hands against it to slow the blood flow with a frozen face of wrath. Dolph stands, blocking his friend with his body. His eyes dart from J.D. to the men who are trying to defuse the situation, as Simon kneels before them, keeping his eyes level with Shelia.

"They had to pay. You understand, don't you, boy? They had to pay for what they did to you." J.D.'s voice is high-pitched with his pleading. "I couldn't just let it slide. Not for you. Not for my boy." Lawless remains mute as he watches J.D. His mask, like those around him, is firmly in place, giving no hints to his thoughts or emotions. Their fingers are resting firmly on their cold, metal triggers defiantly showing the only clues to their mindset. No matter which road J.D. takes us down now, someone is going to die.

Marxx sidesteps, blocking me from any crossfire which may occur. He places his hand on my arm, begging me to remain silent. It won't be me who fixes this tonight. Another nightmare is about to be made for someone, if not for all of us.

"I raised you like you were my own. All those times it was unsafe for you, it was my house you came to. I taught you how to shoot that thing. I taught you how to ride. I taught you how to be a man. I raised you. You were mine and they took you from me. They took my boy. My boy who was worth more than all of their lives combined. My boy," J.D. shouts to us and it echoes down the long hall.

J.D. continues to talk to the Lawless from his past. He's either unaware or doesn't understand Lawless is here with us now. He is pleading with his ghost of Lawless to understand and forgive him for his actions. Our once powerful leader is now crushed from the weight of this world. He is shattered with the loss of the only child he was ever able to claim as his. His son, the man he thought he watched die for him, Lawless.

"I am going to make them pay. I will make this place pour red for you, for my boy. You'll rest at peace then. Won't you? You'll rest knowing I made them pay for you. Don't stare at me like that, son. I'll make them pay. You'll see. I'll make them pay," J.D. pleads for Lawless to comfort him.

J.D. is motionless with just his hand trembling as he stares at us. Those once cold eyes are streaming with his loss. The lips, which once spoke threats like compliments, shake as words break before forming on them. I feel myself move to him as Marxx snaps me back to his chest. I plead with J.D. with my eyes to stop this, to see who is before him. My heart is breaking the way he broke so many in his life.

J.D. looks to the ghost he believes is here to torment him. He says, "She's a good girl. Don't let anyone tell you otherwise. She deserves so much more than we could ever give her, son. But I can give you this. I can give you peace like I never could her."

J.D.'s eyes leave Lawless and it is the signal that ignites the room. The gunfire is ear splitting with its reverberation in such a small space.

J.D.'s body jerks with each round that lands, the resulting blowout sprays the space red behind him.

Shelia's body falls forward, limp and devoid of the life J.D. has stolen from her. I hear my screams tear through my body with the same burning fire as the bullets tearing through J.D. and I fall in time with him as our legs give out from under us with Simon echoing my misery.

J.D. watches me as we fall, the gun slipping from his hand, he now reaches for me in his death. Only Marxx' weight keeps me from crawling to him as he pins me with his body to the cold tiles of the floor. Tiles that are as cold and unfeeling as the faces of the men who have stolen the only father to ever hold me.

J.D. stares at me as he fights for his breath. Red bubbles form at his mouth in a soft foam. The color matches the life spilling from him, soaking the tiles with his final judgment for the crimes he has committed. His crimes have colored the hall with the same shade of red as his blood now covers the floor.

Lawless walks to the dying man he once thought of as the father he never had. A father who supported him when his father had hurt him. A father who had taught him how to stand up for him- self when his father had beat him down. Their bond was ironclad with the many private moments they had built between them. Their eyes lock one final time as they exchange the knowledge of what is about to happen.

"My boy. So proud of my boy," J.D. tells him, as Lawless puts the final bullet into J.D.'s head.

All of this time, we had been fighting to keep this place safe from the monsters outside wishing to harm us. We believed they lurked with glazed eyes waiting for us in the dark around every corner. Now as I hear Truth laughing again, I realize, the monster was with us all along.

It is not the Risen who have destroyed this safe haven, but J.D. The guilt and betrayal flow through me. It turns my body into a pain-racked casing of torment, and even as I hate him for what he has done, I weep for the man I have come to love and depend on. "Do you know what today is?" The soft whispering sound of

Aimes' voice draws the attention of everyone. "It's Christmas."

She falls like a marionette with its strings cut, exposing a red flower blooming on her chest.

"No, no, no, no!" Rhett screams, with each inch that she falls.

He runs to her, pulling her limp body to him, rocking her in his arms as her eyes close against the world.

J.D. fired twice when he was shot. The first shot found its target, hitting Shelia, as his goal was set. His second shot went unknown with his death and found another target just as precious. Now that target lies in Rhett's arms as he screams his frustration into her blonde hair with the full force of his lungs. In a sick joke, the Fates gave us back Lawless, but want now to take our pixie. Chapel is screaming for help, as he presses against Aimes' wound with Rhett still rocking her.

The world slows for me as the sun rises on this Christmas morning. There are no sleepy-eyed children creeping from warm beds to see if Santa has come. No cookies and milk to be inspected for its consumption. There are no brightly wrapped packages for them to open, just the red, red blood of so many spilled. There is no naughty or nice list, just the list of the living and the dead. A list causing the voices from the halls to lift up, not in songs of the season, but in screams of their misery.

Dawn does not wait today any more than it has any other morning since the first day the dawn watched it all start. It comes with the same blinding cruelty, disguised under soft pastel shades marking another day we must live through. It always comes; forcing us to accept another morning is here with no degree of tragedy to spare us from the bright beams of the sun.

This is our dawning. This is our new world, and this is the lesson it teaches us each day. A world filled with monsters walking and waiting for us in dual forms. With every strike of the second hand, Death dances with Truth in a courtship of suffering only they can inspire.

They are reminding us of their power over us, as another dies under the hands of one who refuses to accept it. Even as those hands fight to keep the life-giving blood inside, it spills out from the body that once contained it. Its red refusal is a final sacrifice to the many demons that now rule the earth where God and his angels once stood watch. Our nightmares now walk among us and we are all wide-awake.

Epilogue

A gate rattles against its metal clasp with fingers searching to understand the cause of the barrier blocking its entrance to the music it hears floating in the air. Translucent eyes follow the length of the metal wiring looking for a clue to its operation. Its fingers slide along the diamond shapes looking for a gap, or a break in its pattern, to reach through.

The gate gives its secrets away under the examination, unable to keep them hidden forever and the hand slides between the two metal poles finding a new pattern. It feels along the two poles with its mind racing to put the puzzle together. This piece rocks against pressure applied to it, sliding along the other metal pole and a faint memory comes forward.

Before long, the eyes find the logic, which has been escaping it. Pulling upon this new piece lifts it up, freeing it from where it was held. The barrier still does not move for it and it voices sounds of frustration over the failure as it tries again to solve the puzzle.

The barrier does shift now, whereas before it was a constant force blocking it. The eyes watch as different focal points of pressure affect the movement of the barrier. Gripping the metal tightly, it pulls it sideways instead of pressing upon it and is rewarded with the sound of movement.

Growing more confident with the newly discovered logic, it walks down the length of the barrier, pulling the metal shapes with it, watching with grinning satisfaction as the barrier moves with moans of its betrayal. The music that drew it here is no longer blocked. The barrier is removed, and it smiles with the victory, as screaming pitches of a melody lure it into a newly discovered area.

It is not alone. Others join it just like it. Others who have followed with the same curiosity as to what they are hearing. Others who are hungry and have run out of prey to feed them. The new area fills with their many forms, as they creep silently into the darkness before them with one shared purpose, death.

About the Author

Marie F Crow weaves her stories around the human element of the horror verses the 'monsters' themselves. She believes that the real horror of life does not come from the expected, but from the unexpected responses of the human nature and what depths of trauma a person must survive in certain situations. She began writing The Risen series when feeling that the popular genre was slipping too deep into the realm of pure 'slasher' and forgetting what the horror of zombies can mean for a story.

Now, with her children's series launched, Marie hopes to use her favorite 'monster' as a teaching tool to inspire children to understand that not everything that looks scary, is scary. With Abigail and Her Pet Zombie series, Marie hopes to further spread her love for all things "that go bump in the night" with small children showing them that it's okay to be different and to embrace those same differences in those around them.

Social Media Links
Facebook: @MarieFCrow.Author
Instagram: @authormariefcrow
Twitter: @MarieFCrow

Additional titles by Marie F Crow:

The Risen Series
Dawning
Margaret
Remnants
Courage
Defiance

The Siren Series
Crown of the Betrayal
Crown of Remorse

The Great Hexpectation Series
The Little Lies

The Abigail and her Pet Zombie Illustrated Series
Abigail and her Pet Zombie
Zoo Day
Spring
Summer
Halloween

The Abigail and her Pet Zombie Chapter Book Series
Abigail and her Pet Zombie

About the Publisher

www.kingstonpublishing.com

Kingston Publishing offers an affordable way for you to turn your dream into a reality. We offer every service you will ever need to take an idea and publish a story. We are here to help authors make it in the industry. We've been hurt by publishers in the past and we want to provide a positive experience that will keep you coming back to us.

Whether you want a traditional publisher who offers all the amenities a publishing company should or an author who prefers to self-publish, but needs additional help - we are here for you.

Now Accepting Manuscripts!

Please send query letter and manuscript to:

submissions@kingstonpublishing.com

Visit our website at www.kingstonpublishing.com